GW00647265

MIDNIGHT DAYS

WHITE NIGHTS: BOOK 2

ANNA ZAIRES

CHARMAINE PAULS

GREY EAGLE
PUBLICATIONS

Copyright © 2021 Anna Zaires and Charmaine Pauls
All rights reserved.

Published by Grey Eagle Publications
www.greyeaglepublications.com

Cover by Coverluv
www.coverluv.com

Photography from Regina Wamba
www.reginawamba.com

ISBN: 978-1-64366-260-2
Print ISBN: 978-1-64366-261-9

KATE

The full impact of the last twelve hours only hits me when Alex Volkov's private plane comes in for landing over St. Petersburg, Russia. I sit up in the double bed where I've been sleeping and look out the round window that's next to the bed. The sky is a magnificent thin, winter blue. Far below, a city is mapped out on the ground. Judging from the increased pressure in my ears, we're dropping in altitude.

I check my watch. It's seven in the morning in New York City. That makes it two o'clock in the afternoon in St. Petersburg.

The side next to me is undisturbed, the sheets unruffled and the pillow undented. There's no sign of Alex. When he ordered me to bed, he was in the middle of a hushed, intense discussion with the guards who boarded the plane with us. The usual guys, Igor, Leonid, Dimitri, and Yuri, were there, as well as a few new faces. Has he been working all night?

A knock falls on the door, startling me from my thoughts.

"Kate?" a gruff voice calls from the other side. "We're landing shortly."

Igor.

I have a good mind to tell him to go to hell, but it's not his fault I'm locked in here. Taking my anger out on the guard won't help.

He knocks again. "Did you hear me? You have to take a seat and buckle up."

I rub my eyes in an effort to clear the lingering grogginess. "Give me a few minutes to get dressed."

"You have ten."

I suspect Alex slipped something into the juice he insisted I drink with my dinner. My sleep was almost comatose. Under normal circumstances, I would've been too apprehensive to drift off after the events of last night.

Last night.

A shiver creeps over me at the memory.

After someone delivered my hospital access card to Alex's house, he had our bags packed in a hurry. Despite my protests, he bundled me into his plane and took me away from my home, my job, my mom, and my friends. For *several months* maybe. He delivered the blow with reserved regret but unstoppable determination, telling me in no uncertain terms that I no longer have a choice.

It's nothing short of a kidnapping.

Yet that's not the most troubling thought at the forefront of my mind. It's the knowledge that someone wants Alex dead. After the failed assassination attempt in New York, his life is still at risk. I thought—I hoped—that whoever shot Igor gave up when they didn't succeed, but the card delivery indicates otherwise. Whoever is after Alex is going to try again and is willing to do whatever it takes, including using me to get to Alex.

Not only am I a liability to him now, but my life might also be in danger—and Alex refuses to go to the police. He thinks they can't help, and maybe he's right. Other than my card going missing for a few hours, we don't have any evidence of foul play. Also, there's the possibility of corruption. I didn't consider that before, but it's not uncommon, especially where the Russian mafia is concerned. Alex's business dealings aren't exactly clean.

What a freaking mess.

Throwing the covers aside, I swing my legs over the edge of the bed. Without the warmth of the soft blanket, goosebumps run over my arms. I'm naked. I vaguely remember Alex undressing me and asking if I wanted a sip of water. After that, everything is a blank.

I look around for clothes and spot an overnight bag at the bottom of a closet alcove. I've never seen a plane like this. The cabin even has a vanity and en-suite bathroom.

After finishing my shift at the ER last night, I didn't

have time to shower. Everything happened in a whirl-wind of action. So now I have a quick shower and dress in the clothes Marusya, Alex's housekeeper, packed for me. They're not my own clothes—which would've meant my standard casual wear of comfortable jeans, a sweater, and Uggs—but the new ones Alex bought for me. The off-white slacks and matching cashmere sweater are more formal than my usual style, as are the similarly colored high-heeled boots.

I'm brushing out my hair when the door opens. Alex stands in the frame, still dressed in the black pants and shirt from yesterday. Stubble darkens his jaw, and his hair is messy, the short strands standing in every direction as if he's dragged his fingers through them several times. Despite those signs hinting at a sleepless night, his gaze is alert, as is his stance. His tall, powerful frame crowds the space, trapping me like a rabbit in a cage.

Bravely, I maintain our eye contact. I'm not angry at him for trying to keep us safe. What upsets me is how he's going about it. He took away all of my choices and dragged me onto this plane. His single-minded resolve is nothing if not scary. Only I'm not going to give him the satisfaction of knowing he intimidates me. I normally pride myself on being a self-assured woman, but Alex is in a different league from anyone I've known. Just how different, I'm still discovering.

The cold blue of his eyes matches the color outside the cabin window, yet appreciation warms those frosty blues as he takes me in from top to bottom. "Sleep well?"

My wounded pride makes me immune to the unspoken compliment. I can't help getting in a jab. "Why bother to ask when you already know the answer? What did you give me?"

A smile drifts onto his face, as if he finds my sarcasm amusing, but the strain doesn't leave his features. "Just something to help you relax. You worked a long shift and needed your rest."

I put the brush away. "How considerate. I suppose I need my strength for whatever lies ahead."

He doesn't acknowledge the not-so-subtle hint. Offering me his hand, he says, "Come. We're about to land."

Ignoring his proffered hand, I squeeze past him into the main cabin. The plane dips, making me lose my balance. When Alex grips my elbow to steady me, I yank my arm away and use the backs of the seats as support.

"Katerina," he says behind me, his voice carrying a hint of a warning. "I don't want you to fall and injure yourself."

"I can walk, thank you very much," I say without looking at him.

The guards sit up front, leaving empty a set of plush leather couches with a foldable table between them. I plop down next to the window, trying not to look at Alex as he folds away the tray table.

Reaching over me, he grabs the seatbelt and secures the clip.

"I could've done that," I say, finally meeting his gaze.

"Yes." He settles next to me, fastening his own seatbelt. "But I like to take care of you."

I grip the armrests of my seat, digging my nails into the leather to prevent myself from doing something disgustingly violent, like slapping him. "Does said care involve kidnapping and drugging? Because that's what this is."

His smile stretches, the gesture patient even as displeasure sparks in his eyes. "In time, you'll come to understand that I'm acting in your best interest."

"My best interest?" I whisper-cry, keeping my voice down so the guards won't hear. They know Alex is kidnapping me and they won't lift a finger to help. They don't need to witness my humiliating, helpless anger. "You're doing this against my will. Explain to me how forcing me to leave my job and home is in my best interest. Forcing me to abandon my *mom*." My voice cracks. "She's *sick*. You know she has no one but me."

"Your mother is in good hands." He cups my hand where I'm clenching the armrest, his big palm warm and dry on my chilled skin. "I don't expect you to fully understand my world. Nor do I want you to. It's much too ugly for someone as pure and beautiful as you." His eyes tighten, that spark of displeasure bleeding into something darker. "Just know that disobedience isn't an option, not where your safety is concerned. You can throw your little rebellion if it makes you feel better, but it's not going to change anything. Is that clear?"

I glare at him as painful emotions churn in my chest. He's just told me in not so many words that I no longer have a say in my life, that he's taking away my freedom and right to make decisions. How does he expect me to react? With gratitude? I'm angry and hurt. Most of all, I feel betrayed.

Tears prick at the backs of my eyes. Before he can see that weakness, I turn my face away.

Only he doesn't allow me the reprieve of the limited privacy. Even though he doesn't force me to look at him, the words he whispers over the shell of my ear won't let me off the hook. "I asked you a question, Katerina."

Taking a breath, I find a semblance of calm and force my voice not to quiver with the tears I'm desperately trying to hold back. "Yes."

"Yes, what?" he asks, brushing his lips over my temple.

I lean away from the touch. "You've made yourself crystal clear."

This time, he lets me escape. Not that I have anywhere to run or hide. There's no place to lick my wounds where the many eyes on the plane won't see. All I can do is pull into myself.

Unseeingly, I look out the window. This is not the future I envisioned when I told him I was falling in love with him. I've read articles about women who were seduced and lured to foreign lands with love, pretty promises, and luxuries, only to find themselves prisoners of the very men who were supposed to save them. The ones lucky enough to escape got to tell their stories.

You're such an idiot, Kate. You should've known.

Yes, I should've. I should've learned from those women's press interviews and recognized the signs. I knew from the start that Alex might be dangerous, but I never thought this would be my fate, not for one minute.

I have no one but myself to blame for the mess I'm in. Will I be one of the fortunate few who gets to tell her story? Or will I disappear like thousands of others, slipping through the cracks of a Russian city?

Alex's voice penetrates the fog of my tumultuous thoughts. "Hungry?"

"No, thanks."

It's not as if I'll be able to eat. Not that it matters. He'll probably threaten to hand-feed me if I don't eat everything on my plate, just like he did last night.

"It's past lunchtime in Russia, and you haven't had breakfast," he says. "I'll make sure a meal is waiting when we arrive."

I don't reply. What's the point? He's made it clear my opinion doesn't matter.

After a while, he releases my hand to check something on his phone, and I breathe easier. The anger and worry don't diminish, but I don't have a vent for those emotions. I have no choice but to bottle them up inside.

The buildings grow in size until gray, drab blocks dominate the view through my window. A control tower and runway become visible. Alex braces me with an arm around my shoulders even though the landing is smooth. The minute the plane touches down, he's on his feet, barking out orders in Russian.

The men don their jackets and weapons. Alex leans an arm on the overhead baggage compartment above the window, scanning our surroundings with singular attention as the plane taxies to a hangar on the outskirts of the airport.

Leonid, who's examining a computer screen, says, "No interference detected."

Alex doesn't take his eyes off the window. "Keep the satellite surveillance active."

A convoy of black cars with tinted windows is parked on the tarmac. Men in dark suits with automatic rifles are stationed around the area in a circle. The blatant display of firepower makes my mouth go dry.

It looks like a war zone or a drug deal about to go down.

When the plane comes to a standstill, Igor appears with an off-white coat that he hands to Alex. Alex says something to him in Russian as he accepts the coat, at which Igor hurries to open the door.

"What did you say to him?" I ask, anxious to know what's going on.

Alex holds the coat open in silent instruction for

me. "I told him to make sure it's safe before we go outside."

Stomach knotting with worry, I look at the armed men through the window as he helps me into the coat. "Why wouldn't it be safe? Who are those men?"

"Don't worry," he says, turning me to face him. "They work for me." He adjusts the lapels of the coat before buttoning it up. "Checking things out is just a precaution. I prefer to take nothing for granted."

"What does that mean?" I try to read his expression, but he's good at keeping a poker face. "That they'll betray you?"

He takes a scarf from the overhead compartment and winds it around my neck. "Unlikely, but a man like me shouldn't take chances. Now stop concerning yourself with these matters. I have everything under control."

Igor sticks his head around the door. "All clear. We're good to move."

"Come," Alex says, making his way to the front.

"Alex," I call after him.

He stops to look at me.

"You need to lay all the cards on the table. This is my life too."

There's no amusement or patience in his smile any longer. "I already told you that I'll protect you. You'll have to learn to trust me."

Yeah, sure. Treating me like a prisoner has destroyed our trust, and keeping me in the dark won't help repair what he's damaged. I want to say as much, but he's already taking a hat with a wool lining from a coat closet next to the door. He waits until I've caught up with him and hands me the hat. When I've pulled it over my ears, he gives me a pair of leather gloves the same color as my boots.

I watch him from under my eyelashes as I pull on the gloves. His stance is rigid. I've never seen him so tense, not even when Igor was being treated for the gunshot wound.

His stress rubs off on me. Whatever he's expecting isn't good, and his refusal to explain only makes my anxiety worse.

A gush of frosty air hits me in the face when he ushers me outside. The winter feels different here than in New York City. This cold penetrates the wool layers of my expensive clothes all the way to my bones.

Alex throws an arm around my shoulders, sheltering me against his side as he leads me to one of the cars. It's as if nothing is wrong between us. I try to break free, but he tightens his hold.

A man standing at attention next to the car opens the passenger-side door in the back. Alex helps me inside and takes the seat next to me. I scoot all the way to the window, leaving space between us. With how I feel about his actions, I'd rather be exposed to the subzero temperature than huddle against him.

We wait inside the chilly interior of the car while the men carry the luggage from the plane and load it into the trunks. It looks like Marusya indeed packed for several months. When the last suitcase has been loaded, Igor shifts into the front passenger seat of our car while Yuri takes the wheel.

The engine starts up. As the car rolls forward smoothly, the finality of the situation sinks in, followed by a wave of nauseating fear.

We're here.

There's no turning back.

The car picks up speed, transporting me to an unknown future.

2

KATE

he drive passes in silence. I stare at the scenery through the tinted window, taking in the apartment blocks that eventually make way for statelier buildings. We follow a broad river for several miles before crossing a bridge. The signposts are in Russian. I have no idea where we're heading, and the uncertainty adds to my fear.

As if reading my mind, Alex says, "We're going to Krestovsky Island."

I have no desire to look at him, but the sound of his voice pulls my gaze to him in a reflexive reaction.

"I realize this is all new and strange to you," he continues. "If you want to know anything, you only have to ask."

One question runs on repeat through my mind. "How long before you'll let me go home?"

The tall buildings throw shadows over the road that intersperse with the bright winter afternoon sun. They play over his face as we speed along, making the laugh lines etched from his nose to his mouth appear deeper.

"Katyusha," he says after a tense beat. "I'm trying to be patient, but don't push me. Not on this."

"Fine." I shrug. "Why don't you just tell me what you want me to say? It'll make the road forward considerably smoother for both of us."

He clenches his jaw. "This doesn't have to be hard on you."

"Are you for real?" I twist in my seat, facing him squarely. "What did you expect? That I'd be excited about this trip?"

"You could be." He lays his arm on the backrest behind me and rubs a finger over the curve of my shoulder. "Think of this unforeseen getaway as a vacation."

I shift to the edge of my seat, escaping his touch. "This is *not* a vacation, and I'm not in the habit of lying to myself."

He lowers his arm to his side. "Your attitude is only making it worse."

My attitude? What about his? My nails dig into my palms. "What I think and feel doesn't matter, right? So why do you even care if it's new, strange, or scary for me?"

His eyes crinkle in the corners. "That's not true, kiska, and you know that. If you want a reminder that I care about you, you don't have to search very hard. The fact that we're here spells it out in bold letters, don't you think? Now stop being difficult. You're looking for a fight to appease your anger, and it's not going to happen."

I grit my teeth in powerless fury and angry frustration. This isn't about picking a fight, but there's no winning this argument with him. There's no way of making him see the situation from my point of view.

When he reaches for my hand, I wrap my arms around my body. Rejecting him hurts me, especially when I fear more for his life than for my own, but I don't know if I can forgive him for what he's done, not when he doesn't show a stitch of remorse.

He drops his hand, letting it rest on the seat between us, close enough for his knuckles to brush against my thigh. "We're going to a house I own on the island. It's one of the best neighborhoods in St. Petersburg."

I want to ask if that's supposed to make me happy, but I bite my tongue. Things are bad enough, and further conflict won't help. We're talking in circles. A sudden spell of exhaustion washes over me. These bizarre circumstances are emotionally draining. I'm too tired even to think.

Leaning back, I sink deeper into my seat, escaping my thoughts by focusing on the sights through the window. We cross over another bridge and continue to drive along the river. My jaw drops as I take in the mansions set on generous, snow-covered gardens facing the river. The deeper we drive into the island, the more luxurious the properties become.

These aren't houses. They're palaces, and their gardens are parks.

One property is so big it takes up the whole block. A green metal roof, maybe oxidized copper, is visible through treetops from behind a high wall. The driver pulls up to eight-foot-high iron gates that swing open as we approach. The garden we pass through is a winter landscape dotted with naked trees. Right in the middle of it stands an imposing four-story sandstone palace with a turret on each corner and decorative balcony rails in front of the windows.

The tires crunch over the gravel driveway that has been cleared of snow. The car slows to a stop in front of the dwelling. Two cars from our convoy are already parked outside, the men carrying our luggage into the house.

I turn to look through the back window. Another two cars are entering behind us. Movement in the garden catches my eye. Men dressed in white combat pants, matching snow jackets, beanies, and yellow-tinted anti-glare sunglasses walk along the perimeter of the wall that surrounds the grounds. They're armed with automatic rifles and knives strapped to their thighs. They're so well camouflaged, blending into the white scenery and the stark, charcoal lines of the winter trees, that I didn't notice them until they moved. There must be at least two dozen of them. I stop counting at twenty.

When I turn back in my seat, Alex is studying me. Yuri and Igor get out. Igor heads toward the back of the mansion while Yuri gets Alex's door. Freezing cold air barrels into the car, but Alex doesn't make a move to get out.

"Ask me," he says.

I blink. "Ask you what?"

He lifts his gaze to the landscape beyond my window. "About the men."

I requested that he lay his cards on the table, and I'm not going to waste an opportunity to gain a better understanding of my situation. "What are they? Soldiers? Guards?"

"They're here for our protection."

Another vague answer. So much for hoping he was finally going to give me something. "Right." I look through my window. "I suppose a job title doesn't apply then."

"I don't tag them with a label like soldier or guard."

"Or mafia," I say under my breath.

"Look at me." When I obey reluctantly, he continues. "They're well trained and they're loyal. That's what matters."

If he says so. "How many of them are here?"

"Thirty, give or take a few. The rest are training at a base camp on the outskirts of the city. I want my men to keep in shape and up to date with their weapons."

"Thirty?" I exclaim. "How many are there in total?"

"I have two hundred men in this particular line of work in my employ at any given moment. They rotate between here and my offices, taking turns with patrolling, training, and resting."

Shivering from the cold that has invaded the car, I glance up at the façade of the house. The building is huge, big enough to house twenty people. "Do they all stay here?"

He takes my gloved hands and rubs them between his, warming them through the butter-soft leather. "They live in the barracks at the back of the property."

I gape at him. "You have a barracks?"

"It used to be a barn—storage space for foliage and a stable for horses. I had it converted into a dormitory for the men." He takes my arm. "Come. You're cold. We'll talk more in the house. I just wanted to put your mind at ease about the presence of the men before we went inside."

Not having a choice, I follow him to the front door, but I refuse his arm when he offers it for assistance. My heart is still aching too much.

A tall, blond woman, whom I judge to be in her fifties, greets us at the door. Once she's closed it behind us, she offers Alex a bright smile and launches into rapid-fire Russian.

He holds up a hand. "English, please. We don't want Katerina to feel excluded."

The woman's smile is much more reserved as she acknowledges me. "Your girlfriend doesn't speak Russian?"

"Not yet," Alex says, removing his coat. "Katyusha, this is Lena, my housekeeper." He opens an entryway closet and hangs his coat on a hanger. "She'll take care of all your needs."

Politeness compels me to say, "Pleased to meet you."

In turn, she gives me a cool once-over when Alex's back is turned.

Since I'm rooted to the spot, overcome with the grandeur surrounding me, Alex takes charge of unwinding my scarf and unbuttoning my coat. Coming somewhat to my senses, I push off my coat, remove the hat, and comb my fingers through my hair.

While Lena busies herself with putting my clothes in the closet, I look around the foyer. The opulence is overwhelming. Downton Abbey has nothing on this place. The high, domed ceiling looks like the pictures I've seen of Michelangelo's painting on the Sistine Chapel ceiling, except this one depicts a czar and his court. A double staircase with a golden balustrade runs from both ends of the foyer to meet on the landing. Expensive-looking rugs cover the marble floors, and a red carpet runner decorates the stairs. Chandeliers throw soft yellow light over moss-green walls adorned with Russian baroque art. I'm not a connoisseur, but I've picked up bits and pieces in conversations with Ricky, an artist who's dating my best friend, Joanne— enough to know that if these paintings are originals, which I suspect they are, they must be priceless.

The housekeeper disappears down a hallway, her sneakers not making a sound on the floor.

"You look like you're miles away," Alex says. "What are you thinking?"

I wave a hand around the space. "This is very impressive."

"This palace belonged to a czar. Later, during the Communist era, it was used to house military officers. When capitalism was reinstated, one of the first oligarchs bought the property and restored it to its former glory. It came back onto the market after the death of its owner, which is when I acquired it." His voice holds a note of pride.

I wander to the foot of the staircase, staring up at the patterns on the pressed ceiling. "This is very different from the style of your house in New York City."

"To be honest," he says, his footsteps falling behind me, "I prefer the minimalism and simplicity of the house in New York, but this one has the best location in the city."

I turn to face him. "And location is important?"

He shrugs. "I prefer Krestovsky to the city. Would you like a tour of the house? If you'd rather rest, I can show you around later."

In spite of my turmoil, I can't help but be curious. Besides, if this is where I'm staying for the foreseeable future, I'd better get acquainted with my surroundings.

"I'd like to see it," I say.

Leading the way up the stairs, Alex shoots me a smile from over his shoulder. "Then I shall oblige."

As I follow him through corridors and up and down stairs, my astonishment grows. Every room is luxuriously decorated with its own theme, the furnishings fit for a king. Apart from ten bedrooms, each with an en-suite lounge and bathroom, we visit formal and informal lounges, reading rooms, a library, a study, and an indoor heated pool with a skylight. Next to the pool, a gym overlooks the garden. A sauna is nestled into the corner. Working out seems to be on Alex's list of priorities. Like in his New York home, there's every imaginable piece of equipment one would expect to find in a gym.

We finish our tour in a modernly renovated kitchen with stainless steel shelves, where a man is chopping vegetables on an island counter.

"This is my cook, Timofey," Alex says. "Tima, this is Miss Morrell. She hasn't had lunch yet. Since it's only breakfast time in New York, prepare a light meal and have Lena take it up to the room."

Timofey salutes. "Yes, sir. One light meal coming up."

"His skill compares to that of a Michelin star chef," Alex says. "You're in for a treat."

Timofey clicks his tongue. "Michelin? Those stars mean nothing. Me?" He pulls away the collar of his shirt and points his knife at a tattoo of a star on the curve of his shoulder. "I earned this."

Alex chuckles. "Don't mind Tima. He can be overdramatic."

I take an immediate liking to the cook. "It's a pleasure to meet you, Timofey. I look forward to trying your food."

"The pleasure is all mine, Miss Morell."

"Please," I say, "call me Kate."

"Only if you'll call me Tima." He swings the knife,

splitting a carrot down the middle. "You want something special? You ask Tima. I'll cook you anything you want."

His enthusiasm makes me smile. "I appreciate that."

Putting a hand on my lower back, Alex moves me along.

"Do all of your staff members speak English?" I ask, sidestepping his touch.

He steers me into a pantry the size of my studio apartment back in New York. "I insist that they take lessons. It's good to have language skills. But I can't take credit for teaching Tima to speak English. He was a chef in a high-end restaurant before he came to work for me. Speaking English was compulsory, not only for training, but also for conversing with the clientele."

Fragrances of dill and tarragon infiltrate my nose. Bunches of garlic and dried herbs hang on strings from a beam running along the ceiling. "Aren't chefs normally bound to the kitchen?"

"In those kinds of restaurants, chefs are often called to the table to be paid a compliment. It's the highest honor a diner can bestow on a chef. It will reflect negatively on the restaurant owner if a chef isn't able to thank an important English-speaking customer in his own language."

"That's a bit harsh." I duck to pass underneath a bouquet of parsley hanging upside-down from the beam. "Does that mean top-end Russian chefs are required to be polyglots like you?"

He acknowledges the unintended compliment with a crooked smile. "Most people can manage in English."

I look around the well-stocked space. The shelves are filled with jars of preserved fruit, pickled vegetables, and honey. A cured ham, partially covered with a linen cloth, stands on a chopping block. Baskets filled with fresh fruit and vegetables hang on hooks from the walls. A bigger one on the floor overflows with bread rolls.

"You don't risk a food shortage here," I say.

"Tima cooks for the men who live in the barracks." He crosses his hands behind his back. "In their line of work, they have high caloric demands."

I nod like feeding an army of men is a normal household occurrence. "I see."

He stands aside, letting me exit ahead of him. "Let's finish our tour. I have to take care of business, and you need to rest."

We go down the hallway and through a dining room with a table that can seat twenty people. Until now, I hadn't truly comprehended how wealthy Alex is. His house in New York is on the upper end of the scale, but it's a lot humbler than this palace in St. Petersburg. It seems he has a full-time housekeeper in every house he owns, and there are two hundred men on his security payroll. I don't even want to know how many people his various businesses employ. Not to mention he smuggled me into Russia on his *private plane* with no passport or visa. Who can do that?

Who is the man I fell for in New York City? He's so

much more powerful than I could've imagined, and it frightens me. I'm completely at his mercy. We're on his home territory, and he has all the control. It would be difficult, if not impossible, for a woman with no resources, no passport, no phone or money, and very limited knowledge of Russian to escape from such a powerful man.

At the top of the first-floor landing, he pauses. "You're very quiet."

"It's a lot to take in." And I don't just mean this house or palace or whatever you call it.

His expression softens. "You need a little time to adapt, I understand."

It'll take a lot more than time, but I swallow my retort as he opens a carved wooden door and guides me into a spacious bedroom with a big window that overlooks the front garden. A four-poster bed stands in the middle of the floor. The burgundy velvet bed curtains tied back with golden cords look like something from a medieval scene.

His voice drops an octave, the deep timbre sending a shiver down my spine. "This is where we sleep."

At *we*, my heart trips over a beat. Does he think our relationship will continue unchanged when he's made me his prisoner? I don't even know how I'm going to explain my disappearance to my mom or to my supervisor, June.

Below in the garden, the men in their white camouflage combat gear scout the property. The gigantic iron gates are closed. From this level, I can make out the spikes on top of the wall that make scaling over it impossible. A surveillance camera is fixed every few yards. Like creepy robots, they turn their heads constantly, scanning the surroundings with electronic eyes. There must be a control room somewhere.

It's like being locked up in a prison. I have no way of communicating with the outside world. Yet if I don't inform my mom and my employer about my impromptu trip, they'll be worried sick. They may even report me missing. With how meticulous Alex is in everything he does, he must've already thought up a plan to explain my absence, but I don't want to disappear without giving my mom some kind of explanation.

Whatever I tell her, I can't admit the truth. I won't put that burden on her shoulders. Besides, if she learns what Alex has done, she'll want to leave the clinic where she's being treated for rheumatoid arthritis. It's a ridiculously expensive program that Alex is paying for, and she'll refuse to benefit from the charity of a man who's kidnapped her daughter. This is her only chance at a better quality of life, and I don't want to ruin it for her. She's been in pain for so long, and she deserves this more than anyone I know.

I hate asking Alex for anything, but I don't have a choice.

Schooling my features, I turn away from the disconcerting sight of the unbreachable fortress wall. "Alex?"

He frowns. "You look tired. Did I wear you out with the tour after our long flight?"

"Where's my handbag?"

A shutter drops in front of his eyes. "You don't need it for now."

Renewed anger heats my blood, indignation burning like a flame in the pit of my stomach. For the sake of my mom, I swallow it down and say evenly, "I need my phone." The man facing me is dangerous. Ruthless. I remind myself of that fact as I carefully choose my words. "I can't just vanish without an explanation. I have to call the hospital and my mom. She'll worry if I disappear. You have to let me speak to them."

His easy agreement as he says, "Sure," and takes his phone from his pocket surprises me. Unlocking the screen with his thumb print, he hands me the device. "I was planning on letting you call later."

I take it gingerly, glancing at him from under my lashes as I type in my mom's number. Instead of giving me privacy, he eavesdrops unabashedly.

"Put it on speaker," he instructs, ignoring the cutting look I give him.

Not wanting him to snatch the phone away, I do as he says.

The call connects, and the ringtone sounds.

My mom answers with an uncertain, "Hello?"

"Hi, Mom." It's a battle to keep my voice normal. "It's Kate."

"Katie!" She sounds upbeat. "This is a surprise. I didn't recognize this number."

"I'm calling from Alex's phone."

I briefly meet his eyes. His intense gaze is unnerving.

"Aren't you at work?" Worry filters into her tone. "Is something wrong?"

"No." I force a smile onto my face, hoping she'll hear it in my voice. "Don't worry, nothing is wrong." Flinching, I brace myself for the lie. "Quite the contrary, in fact. We've taken an impromptu vacation." I've never lied to my mom, and I hate both myself and Alex for starting now. "A trip to Russia."

"Russia?" she exclaims. "Where in Russia?"

"St. Petersburg," I say brightly, trying to sound like an excited tourist. "Alex has a house here."

He holds up a finger and shakes his head, indicating I shouldn't say more.

"What about your job?" Mom asks.

I imagine the confusion on her face. "I really needed this vacation."

Her voice softens. "Yes, honey. You're right. You've been working too hard."

"If you need me..." I swallow, biting back an uninvited bout of tears. "I didn't activate roaming on my phone." I give Alex an inquiring look.

He nods.

"You can reach me on this number," I continue.

"All right," she says slowly. "But why doesn't Alex activate the roaming for you?"

The lies are piling up, drawing tighter around me in a web. Flustered, I look at Alex, who faces me stoically.

My brain shuts down, unable to come up with a plausible explanation.

"You don't want calls from work," Alex whispers.

"I-I don't want the hospital to bother me on our break," I say.

"Oh." My mom pauses. "That makes sense, but it doesn't sound like you, honey. You're normally so dedicated to your job, you even go in on your off weekends when they ask."

I tuck a strand of hair behind my ear. "That's exactly why I don't want them to be able to call me. I'm taking a long, much-needed vacation with Alex to recharge, and I don't want work problems in the back of my mind."

"That certainly is a wise attitude." Mom sounds considerably more at ease. "I'm glad Alex has such a positive influence on you. I've been nagging you for years to take a proper vacation."

"Enough about me." Turning my back on Alex, I face the window. "How are you?"

"Wonderful. I'm already so much better, and with the new diet, I'm losing weight."

"That's great," I say, my chest warming with gratitude. All the more reason for keeping up the charade. If the treatment is working, I can't take this opportunity away from her. "I'm so happy to hear that."

Alex lays a hand on my shoulder, tightening his fingers lightly. In the reflection of the glass, I see him extending his other hand, asking for the phone.

"Listen," I say, holding back a fresh surge of tears, "I

have to go. Promise you'll call me if you need anything, or if you don't feel well."

"Don't worry about me. I'm having the time of my life. Just enjoy your vacation with that generous and amazing man of yours. You deserve it."

Taking a deep breath, I let it out slowly. "I love you."

"Love you too, honey. Say hi to Alex for me."

I cling to the phone, unable to end the call.

Turning me toward him, Alex takes the phone gently and pushes on the red button. His gaze isn't entirely without sympathy when he asks, "Who's next? Your supervisor?"

Unable to speak with the tears clogging up my throat, I nod.

He swipes a thumb over the screen and selects a number. It doesn't surprise me that he has June's contact info programmed into his phone. When it rings, he gives me the phone.

"June Wallers," my supervisor answers. It's clear from her brusque but not unfriendly tone that she's busy and tired.

My guilt doubles. "Hi, June. It's Kate."

"Kate? Please tell me you're making your shift at ten. Rose is sick and Lettie is stuck in some mountain resort where the roads are snowed over. It's chaos here today."

Biting my lip, I drag in another long breath. "I'm so sorry. I have a family emergency. I'm afraid I have to take a leave of absence. I don't have a choice."

"Wow." A beat of silence follows. "I hope it's nothing too serious?"

"I can't—" Checking myself, I say, "I'd prefer not to discuss it. All I can say is that it's a private matter."

"If it were anyone else, I would have doubts, but you're one of our best and most serious nurses. For all the times you sacrificed your days off to stand in when we were short-staffed, I can only say take as much time as you need."

"Thank you." Her understanding makes me feel even worse. Glancing at Alex, I say, "I'll email HR and deal with the necessary paperwork."

He nods, giving his silent agreement.

"Good luck, Kate. I hope you sort out your emergency soon. I'll tell the girls you say hi."

"Thanks," I mumble.

Alex takes the phone and ends the call. "I'm sorry, but you can't be on the phone for too long. This number is secure, but I'm—"

"Not taking any chances," I say hollowly.

"Exactly. Eat something and rest. I'll check on you again later."

"Wait," I say when he turns for the door. "I need to call Joanne. I agreed to meet her for lunch today."

His tone is uncompromising. "Two calls are enough for today."

I take a step forward. "I can't just not show up. She'll worry."

He unlocks the screen and types something. A moment later, the phone pings.

"What did you do?" I ask. "What did you say to her?"

Turning the phone toward me, he shows me the screen. I read his text message and Joanne's reply. He told her the same thing I said to my mom, that we took a spur-of-the-moment vacation and that she can reach me on his phone. He said I'm tired from the flight and sleeping, but that I'll call her soon. She replied with several gasping emojis, telling him to have fun and to take good care of me.

"Happy?" he asks.

I can only look at him.

"I'll see you later, Katyusha."

When he bends down to kiss me, I turn my face to the side. My feelings are too raw to accept his advances. When he created this imbalance of power, he pushed an obstacle between us. I can't just give in. My self-respect won't let me.

He straightens with a tight smile. "If you need anything, let Lena know. I'll be home tonight, my love."

Not sparing me another glance, he walks through the door.

It takes me a good moment to come to my senses. Belatedly, I grab a decorative cushion from the loveseat and throw it at the door he closed behind him. It hits the wood with an ungratifyingly soft thump. It's an immature and pointless display, a sadly ineffective outlet for my cooped-up, frustrated anger. When the door reopens, I'm ready to hurl another cushion at him, but it's Lena who enters with a tray.

She walks over to the lounge area by the fireplace

and leaves the tray on the coffee table. "Tima prepared French toast and a fruit salad. There's tea and honey." Straightening, she asks in a formal tone, "Would you like anything else?"

"No, thank you," I say, still battling to get my temper under control.

Nodding, she briskly leaves the room.

Movement outside draws my attention to the window. Yuri walks to the car we arrived in and opens the door. Alex exits the house, followed by Leonid and Igor. The four of them get into the car. Dimitri gets into a second car with some of the men who escorted us from the airport. Three cars pull out ahead of their convoy. The five cars roll down the driveway and through the open gates.

When the entourage is gone, I seize the opportunity. I approach the door and feel the handle. The heavy door swings open without a squeak. I stick my head around the frame. The corridor is empty. Somewhere, a grandfather clock strikes four times.

Tiptoeing into the corridor, I move quietly but swiftly. The study is one floor down. Thankfully, I don't see anyone as I climb down the stairs. My heart beats in my throat, but I make it to the study without running into the housekeeper or a guard. I close the door behind me and let out a shaky breath. My pulse jumps with relief at the sight of the landline phone on the desk.

I hurry across the floor and grab the receiver from the hook even though I have no idea whom I'm going to call. The American embassy? And say what? I don't know, but I want to test the limits of my imprisonment. I want to know the telephone number of the embassy just in case.

My hesitation only lasts a second. My best bet is to call Joanne and ask her to look up the number for me. I'll say I lost my bank card. The lie bothers me even before it's left my mouth, but I don't think about it as I punch in her number.

Before I'm done, a voice sounds in my ear, saying something unintelligible in Russian. Giving a start, I almost drop the phone.

"Hello?" I say in a hushed tone.

The man on the other end of the line switches from Russian to English. "Good evening, Miss Morrell. What can I do for you?"

Swallowing, I ask, "Who are you?"

His Russian accent is heavy. "I'm Mr. Volkov's telephone operator. All calls from the house go through a central system."

Alex has a landline operator? Hiding my shock, I try to say in a normal voice, "I need to make a call home. Can you please connect me?"

"Sorry, ma'am," he says without missing a beat. "I'm only allowed to connect you to Mr. Volkov. Would you like me to dial him for you?"

"No," I say quickly, dejection setting in.

"All right, then. Good evening, Miss Morrell."

Stunned, I hang up without returning the greeting. I guess that answers the question about my limitations.

How far is Alex willing to go? Why not just lock me in while he's at it?

Wait. He wouldn't. Would he?

When I leave the study, I'm no longer discreet about wandering through the house. I stride decisively to the front door. Once there, I take a deep breath. I don't really want to go outside into a garden from which I can't escape. I just *need* to know.

Gripping the doorknob, I turn it. It slips in my sweaty palm. I wipe my hands on my thighs and try again.

It's locked.

I can't believe it. Why I expected otherwise, I don't know, but being locked in only adds to the claustrophobia closing in on me. Running from door to door, I try each one, but the verdict is the same. They're all locked.

A baffled Tima stares at me as I storm into the kitchen and sprint for the back door. I yank on the handle, pushing with all my might, but the heavy door doesn't budge.

"Kate," he says, his tone apologetic. "Don't wear yourself out like this. It's no use, my poor little rabbit. You know it."

Leaning with my back against the door, I slide to the floor, finally admitting defeat. There's no sugar-coating this truth.

I'm Alex's prisoner.

"Come on," Tima says, discarding the spoon he was stirring something in a pot with and pulling me up by my arm. "Let's get you back to your room." He lowers his voice. "You don't want Lena to see you like this. You can't show weakness if you want to survive, am I right?"

I take a closer look at his face. His skin is marred with pockmarks and his nose is knobby. The light is his gray eyes is friendly.

"Tima, you have to help me."

"I am helping you," he says, guiding me to the door.

"You have to let me out."

He clicks his tongue. "Now, that won't be helping you, little rabbit. That'll be sending both of us straight to a shallow grave."

3

ALEX

The security team jumps to attention when I enter the basement of my office building in the tech district of St. Petersburg.

"Anything?" I ask, loosening my tie as I walk down the aisle that separates the state-of-the-art workstations.

Igor and Leonid tail me, their weapons within easy reach, while Dimitri guards the door. With the measures I put in place, we're safer here than anywhere, but there's a weakness in the system I can never overlook—humanity. Human beings are fickle, and human nature is always an unreliable and inconstant variable in the equation.

Like I explained to my pretty, angry kitten on more than one occasion, I'm not taking anything for granted. That's the only reason I'm not six feet under.

The head of my security team, Pyotr Nelsky, waits at the wall-mounted monitors in the front of the room, standing in a military pose with his arms plastered to his sides.

"Nothing, sir," he says when I reach him, an undercurrent of fear in his tone.

I slide my gaze toward the flatscreens on the wall, which reflect the status of every workstation. The results of the data each employee is compiling are summarized in code. "Did you get the hospital security tapes?"

"Yes, sir. We're going through them as we speak."

Going over to one of the monitors, I press the button to wake up the screen. A mosaic of black-and-white photos is puzzled together. These makeshift mugshots are freeze-frames taken from the video feed, singling out the patients who frequented Coney Island Hospital's ER yesterday.

At best, the images are blurry. In some of them, only the backs of the patients' heads are visible.

Frustration eats at my gut. "What's the operation status?"

"We're in the process of trying to identify all the patients and visitors who were present in the building yesterday," Nelsky says to my back.

I turn to face him. "How long?"

"It may take us a couple of days." His Adam's apple bobs as he swallows. "We pulled the records of the patients who signed in. The staff aren't a problem since they clock in and out for work. It will be harder to trace the visitors and service providers, especially considering that there are camera blind spots."

"What are you saying?" I ask, drumming my fingers on his desk.

He fixes his gaze on a spot over my shoulder, not looking me directly in the eyes. "It will be impossible to draw up a list of everyone who moved through the building in the span of twelve hours."

The news infuriates me, not that I expected otherwise. Still, it's worth a shot. "What about Ms. Morrell?"

He stumbles over his feet in his eagerness to boot up the second of the five monitors on his desk. "I already put together a visual file for you."

He presses a button, pulling up a kaleidoscope of faces, some with Katerina in the picture and others without. Many of the faces are hardly discernible. Others are partially or fully hidden from the cameras.

"Patient list?" I ask, my irritation growing.

"Here, sir." Grabbing a printout from his desk, he offers it to me. "As you'll see, there are a lot of Russian names, but seeing that the hospital is situated in an Eastern European neighborhood, nothing out of the ordinary jumps out."

I scan over the names printed on the paper. The list is long. "Pull whatever records you can find on every one of them. Use my government contacts to speed things up."

"We're already working on it, sir."

"Good." I shove the paper back into his hands. "Report to me on the hour, and let me know the minute anything comes up."

The paper trembles in his hand. "Yes, sir."

I make my way to the door with long strides. My employees busy themselves as I pass, not daring to meet my eyes. I suppose I have somewhat of a reputation. People fear me, including the ones who feed their families on the generous salaries I pay. Good. In my world, you don't get very far with kindness. No one is complaining, though. They'll search long and wide to find better fringe benefits or working conditions.

The kind of work they do requires the room in which they spend eight hours a day to be underground. The walls, ceiling, and floor are fortified. No radio waves or infrared beams can penetrate the structure. That means the industrial intelligence I keep in this room is safe from unwanted eyes and ears, but it also makes the room blast-proof. A sophisticated system carefully monitors and purifies the air. The lights are bright without being harsh on the eyes, and the temperature never varies from a comfortable twenty-three degrees Celsius. Wallpaper depicting a mountain landscape covers the gray concrete bricks, and trees planted in pots provide greenery. A fountain in the corner creates the tranquil sound of a waterfall. It empties into a pond populated with koi fish. Apparently, the fish have a calming effect on the human psyche. As per the advice of the interior designer who specializes in Zen environments, the air purifier releases minute organic notes of bergamot and citrus into the air. The fragrances are supposedly uplifting and revitalizing. Yeah, there are worse bunkers to work in.

The metal door shuts behind me with a soft click. Dimitri straightens from where he leans on the wall. Leonid watches me from under hooded eyes.

"What?" I snap. "If you have something to say, say it."

Leonid's chest expands with a breath. "It's unlikely we'll uncover anything via this route. You've seen the quality of those tapes. A lot of people walk in and out of that hospital on a daily basis. Anyone could've snatched Kate's access card."

Spearing my hands through my hair, I practice the control I've mastered through the years to get a handle on my anger. I've come to the same conclusion, but I don't have anything else to go on. "What do you fucking suggest we do?"

Igor gives me a worried look.

Silence.

That's what I thought. No one has any better ideas. If only I knew who dared to threaten her. If only I knew why.

"I need answers," I say through clenched teeth, shoving my hands into my pockets as I circle the space. "Who? Why?"

"Maybe a competitor," Igor offers. "Someone who wanted to send a message."

It's not a new suggestion. We'd already considered this possibility after Igor got shot. Where my business is concerned, there's no shortage of competitors. Power is both a valuable and dangerous commodity in Russia. As the saying goes, the highest trees catch the most wind. Getting to the top takes hard work and dirty fighting, but the real war only starts when you reach that level. Once you're in the number one spot, you're a target for every man beneath you on the ladder. You have to fight twice as hard to stay at the top than to get there.

Threatening a woman who has nothing to do with my business just to send me a message is a low blow, but it's not uncommon. Women make men weak. Enemies have exploited that weakness since the beginning of time.

"For now, we wait," Dimitri says, always the pragmatic one. "It looks like we don't have much of a choice. Whoever took Kate's card wanted your attention. Now that he has it, he'll make known what he wants sooner or later."

Twisting the cord of the hospital badge in my pocket around my fist, I caress the name printed on the laminated card with my thumb. I've traced the letters so many times with my gaze that when I close my eyes, I see them behind my eyelids. "I'll be damned if I sit on my ass and sip tea while some *ublyudok* threatens Katerina."

"We'll get the motherfucker." Igor's upper lip curls. "Only a coward hides behind a woman's skirt."

I nod grimly. I won't rest until I put that cockroach in his grave.

"What do you want us to do?" Leonid asks.

"For now? Keep your ears on the ground. Ask around. See if we unknowingly stepped on any toes or if there are any changes in the power hierarchy we're not aware of."

"Yes, boss," Leonid says. "I'll talk to some guys in the city I know."

"Go with him," I tell Dimitri. "Igor, you stay with me."

Dimitri nods, already following Leonid to the exit.

When they're gone, I consider my options. I still hope we'll get lucky with the hospital tapes, but since we haven't found anything after ten of my best men and women have gone through every second of the security feed frame by frame, the chances that we'll pick up something are slim.

"Fuck." I kick the chair next to the door, nearly sending it flying. Frustration eats at me like acid.

"What do you want to do?" Igor asks. "It's dark. Shall we go back to the house?"

I'm eager to be with Katerina, but she could do with a little space to get over her anger. In time, she'll see this is the only way. For now, at least she's safe.

Somewhat calmed by the thought, I say, "I'm going to spend a few hours in the office." I may as well catch up on some work while I'm here. There are new contracts to sign off on and some investment opportunities I'd like to suss out.

Making my way to the elevator, I take my phone from my pocket to check if there's a message from Lena. There's still nothing, just like ten minutes ago when I checked. Before the door opens and I lose my signal in the elevator, I type a quick message and send it to Lena.

A reply comes a second later. Katerina is napping and all is well at home. Reassured, I pocket the phone, enter the elevator with Igor, and press the button for the top floor.

My executive assistant, Grigori, is a young man who reminds me of myself at his age. His desk stands in the foyer of the top floor where Igor and I emerge. Grigori always dresses formally and fashionably. Today, he's wearing a navy suit cut to the latest Italian fashion, paired with a red cravat. Very European.

Rising to his feet, he bows his head. "Mr. Volkov. Igor. I didn't expect you."

"I didn't plan on coming in," I say as I cross the floor. "Messages?"

"In your agenda, sir. I filtered the unimportant ones. The urgent ones, I emailed to you."

"Good. Anything new?"

Grigori is my eyes and ears when I'm not around. Whenever something happens, like when someone isn't happy with the way I do things, he lets me know.

"Nothing new, sir. Would you like me to order tea or dinner?"

"No, thank you. We're not staying that long. On second thought, bring a bottle of vodka and a chilled glass."

He acknowledges the instruction with another bow.

Igor takes out his phone and makes himself

comfortable in the visitor's lounge area in the back while I push open the door of my corner office.

The furnishings consist of a glass desktop suspended on metal cables from the ceiling, a chair in which I've spent more hours than in my bed, and several monitors locked away behind a fireproof metal shutter that covers the entire wall facing the desk. A simple lounge area with a sofa and coffee table is set up against the window for meetings. A door on the side leads to an en-suite bathroom. One of my favorite paintings, a piece by David Hockney, hangs on the wall to the left of my desk. Other than that, there are no knickknacks or photos. Nothing to hint at an attachment. As the situation with Katerina has so effectively demonstrated, flaunting your weaknesses only gives your enemies ammunition to use against you.

While I make myself comfortable behind my desk, Grigori enters with a tray on which a bottle of premium vodka and a glass are sitting. He keeps the alcohol and the glass cold at exactly the right temperature. Once a month, a technician verifies that the bar fridge is set at two degrees Celsius—the optimal temperature for drinking vodka, not a degree more or less.

Grigori places the tray on the corner of the desk, uncaps the bottle, and pours a double shot while I unlock the fireproof shutter with my thumbprint on the electronic device attached to my desk. When the shutter lifts, Grigori gets the laptop I keep there for when I'm in the office and carries it to my desk.

"Shall I leave the bottle, sir?"

"No, thank you," I say, opening the laptop and booting it up.

He picks up the tray. "I'll be here until eight if you need me."

I acknowledge him with a nod before he leaves.

For the next hour, I try to lose myself in work. I've always enjoyed the challenges of running a business empire. The hard work and long hours ground me. Having a knack for figures, I enjoy playing the stock market and investing in high-risk projects. The financial part of the business is the most rewarding, especially when the money rolls in.

At six, a light dusting of snow starts to fall. I was going to give it another hour, but my mind isn't on work. Shutting the laptop with a sigh, I scrub a hand over my face. I haven't slept in twenty-four hours. It would be wise to get some rest, but the agitation and gnawing worry won't let me. The vodka hasn't taken off the edge as I hoped it would.

Pushing to my feet, I shove my hands in my pockets and stare at the lights of St. Petersburg shining through a veil of snow. Dinner isn't until seven. The thought of a warm house, a long shower, and Tima's food is inviting, but not as much as the idea of seeing my kiska, of touching her—when she lets me again—and reassuring myself that she's here and safe. It's that last notion that makes me decide against heading straight home. I should give her another hour like I promised myself. She'll come around.

Igor stands when I exit the office.

Grigori lifts his head. "Good night, sir." For a moment, his formal mask slips as he says to my guard by way of greeting, "Igor."

Well, hell. I would've never guessed. Who knew Grigori had a soft spot for my bodyguard?

If Igor picks up on anything, he doesn't show it.

At the reception area downstairs, Igor gets our coats where the clerk had checked them into the coat room. The clerk is gathering his satchel and umbrella, heading out for the day. The night guard is already there to take his place.

Yuri sits on a sofa near the exit, reading a book. After we go through the security scanners, he shuts the book and gets up to open the door.

Once we're seated in the car and the engine is idling for the heater to run warm, Yuri asks, "Home, Mr. Volkov?"

Rubbing a thumb over my lip, I consider my answer as I look through the window. It takes me a second to make up my mind. "To the graveyard. The Orthodox one on the hill."

Igor shoots me a look from the front passenger seat, but he doesn't ask questions.

I've only been there once in recent years, not long ago. In fact, it was right before I left for New York City.

The traffic is heavy. We make it around the city and to the hilly part in just under an hour.

"Wait here," I tell Yuri, getting out of the car and unfolding my umbrella.

Igor exits, pulling a beanie over his shaved head. He follows a few steps behind as I make my way to the graveyard entrance. The pedestrian gate is locked. A sign on the driveway gates says the graveyard closes at six. An iron chain dangles from one gate, the attached metal lock hanging open.

Igor pulls out his gun as I slip through the opening between the gates. I know what he's thinking, because I'm thinking the same thing. Maybe some kids broke in to vandalize the graves and paint the walls with graffiti. Street gangs steal the fresh flowers and sell them on the sidewalks. The graveyard is also a popular place for drug dealing. The police are clamping down on the unlawful nocturnal activities, but cleaning the city of criminal elements is like trying to get rid of a cockroach infestation.

The graveyard is well lit. Spray lights cast a yellow glow over the family tombs in the back and the humbler tombstones near the gate.

Our shoes crunch on the gravel road as Igor and I make our way along the simple crosses and marble slabs. Keeping vigilant, I check in the dark corners of the shadows and prick up my ears. Below, the river flows strongly. The gush of the water reaches all the way up here. Except for the river and the noise from the traffic on the nearby highway, nothing else makes a sound.

When we get to a sheltered corner under a big tree in the back, we stop. Sadly, the yard seems to be empty of thieves and drug dealers tonight. I need a fight to vent my frustration and anger, and I was looking forward to one.

Igor hangs back on the road while I take the path to the double gravestone. The angel guarding it is a work of art. She kneels on the steps, one arm resting gently over the tops of the graves. The hem of her long dress drags on the grass. It's so well-crafted that the marble is almost see-through where the fabric gathers in soft folds around her hips. To have given her no grief in such a setting would've been a lie, and a lie would've distorted the beauty of the artist's work. She wears the signs of suffering and pain that I can't show the world. What I've locked in my heart, she displays in the quiet of the graveyard, her only audience the ghosts. She's perfect, down to the broken wing and the teardrop that runs down her cheek. The sculpture in the garden of my New York home is a copy of her. I had it made so I could look at it because the pain wouldn't let me come here.

While the artist was at work with the original, I visited his workshop every day. I oversaw the project in its finest detail. I knew once she was brought here, I wouldn't see her again. And I didn't for many years. Yet before I left for New York, something compelled me to visit. I'm not superstitious. I don't believe in premonitions. However, that day, as I stood on the same spot I'm standing on now, I knew in my gut something was going to happen in New York City. And it did. Someone tried to kill me, but Igor took the bullet.

Maybe that gut feeling was my parents trying to warn me.

I stare at the names engraved in marble.

Viktor Volkov.

Anastasia Volkova.

A shrill chirp cuts through the air. The leaves above me rustle as a bird lifts into the sky with a loud flapping of wings.

I turn. Igor is searching the area, his gun pointed in front of him. When a black cat saunters from behind the tree and crosses the road, he lowers his arms and blows out a long breath.

Shaking the snow from my umbrella, I say, "Let's go."

Since it wasn't my plan to come here, I didn't bring flowers. Just like it wasn't my plan to drag Katerina across the ocean and lock her up in my house. But it is what it is now.

I'll come back with roses.

My kiska will adapt.

She has to, because I won't let her refuse my advances for long. She's mine. We both know it. The world knows it. I'm carrying the proof in my pocket in the form of her access card.

Movement near the gates makes me stop in my tracks. A bent figure trudges over the snow-covered lawn. Igor draws his gun again, but I stop him with a hand on his arm. I recognize the drab black garb and thin gray hair that's plaited down the woman's back, sticking out from underneath a wooly hat.

I saw her here on my last visit. She's the grave keeper who lives in a small house inside the cemetery, not far from the gate. She asked my name and whose grave I was looking for, claiming to know every grave in the yard by name and date. The woman is as old as some of the graves themselves, practically part of the so-called furniture here. I didn't need her directions. Even though I hadn't been to the graveyard since my parents' funeral twenty-one years ago, I remembered exactly where to find them. But to appease her, I played her game. I gave her the names, and she pointed out the high spot with the weeping angel.

"Why have you never visited?" she asked in her croaky voice.

Not wanting to spew some bullshit, I didn't answer.

Now, she looks up at the sound of our footsteps, not seeming the least bit alarmed at our presence.

"Ah," she says, looking me up and down. "It's you."

I take in her worn shoes, shabby coat, and the holes in her mittens. "What are you doing out in the snow?"

"Came to lock up," she says, motioning at the gate. "We close at six. You should come back during the day."

"I'll do that." Taking my wallet from my pocket, I empty it of the stash of cash I always have on me and place the bills on her palm. "Go inside before you catch your death in this cold."

Looking from her hand to my face, she gives me a toothless grin. "May the dead protect you and God bless you, sir."

"Go in," I say. "We'll lock the gate."

Her grin stretches. "That's my job. I've been doing it for fifty years. Never missed a day of locking up in my life."

Igor holds the gate for me.

"God bless you," she says again, waving the money in the air as I walk through the gates.

Yuri gets out from behind the wheel to open my door.

"You know she's going to blow that money on booze," Igor says on our way to the car. "She reeks of cheap spirits."

"You'd rather I buy her a cup of soup at the soup kitchen?" I hand my umbrella to Yuri and shift into the back of the car. "She's eighty years old. Cut her some slack."

"Soup would've been better," Igor says, a rare reprimand.

I let it slide, not only because I owe him my life, but also because he's right. "Tomorrow, place a standing order for a meal delivery at the caterer we use for our office functions."

His mouth tightens, but he doesn't argue, seeing that he stupidly brought the task upon himself. I would laugh at the expression on his face if it weren't for a foreboding—that pesky premonition I don't believe in —that slithers down my spine.

The hair on my nape stands on end. My scalp prickles. Like the last time I visited my parents' graves, I have a feeling that something is about to go down. Something ugly. Maybe it's my imagination that my parents are trying to warn me, but I can't ignore my gut feeling. That feeling saved my life. It left me with an uneasiness, a strange awareness of doom, and when that sniper took a shot at me, I was alert enough to sense it, able to escape in the split second when my sixth sense told me to move.

The notion worming its way into my gut now is the same, yet different. This time, the hunch is far worse. This time, I don't fear for my life, but for the life of the only woman I've ever cared about.

4

NEAR DETSKIY SEVERNY BEACH, ST.
PETERSBURG

*T*he club is pulsing with music and sweaty bodies. Naked waitresses strut around on spiky heels, offering drinks and blowjobs or other services in the back rooms. Officially, prostitution is illegal, but the club belongs to Vladimir Stefanov, one of the wealthiest men in Russia, and for the right price, the authorities turn a blind eye.

Tonight, Vladimir barely spares the women's perfectly proportioned bodies a glance. Pushing through the throng of people on the dance floor, he makes his way to the private room reserved for VIPs.

Under the jacket and waistcoat that stretch over his stomach, he's sweating. He's been on edge ever since word reached him two hours ago that Alex Volkov arrived in the city. Oleg Pavlov, like the coward he is, has already fled St. Petersburg with his family, jumping on a private plane to go hide in the States. If he thinks Vladimir believes his excuse of taking his wife and kids to warmer weather, he insults Vladimir's intelligence. Oleg is weak. Running with his tail between his legs is proof of that.

Vladimir has always known that Oleg could become a problem. It would take little pressure to make Oleg talk. He's certain Oleg is holding on to some of the evidence, just like Vladimir is. Vladimir has kept photos as insurance in case he has to blackmail Oleg with them one day, and Oleg likely has something similar. There's no telling what will happen if that evidence comes to light.

The situation Vladimir now finds himself in is a clusterfuck of epic proportions. He never should've trusted Oleg to deal with Alex Volkov. Things would've gone smoother if Vladimir had gotten his hands dirty from the start. But he wanted to keep a back door open by pinning the assassination of Volkov on Oleg if the shit hit the fan. Problem is, you can't trust any-fucking-body but yourself with your dirty work.

His bodyguards, having circled the room, shove the clubbers aside to create a path. A young woman who gets a rough push on the shoulder stumbles. She trips over her feet and goes down face first. A man dressed in a well-tailored suit crashes into his date, causing her to spill her cocktail down the front of her glittery dress.

No one says a word. No one dares. The clubbers stand aside, leaving the way to the lounge clear for Vladimir.

A bouncer wearing a microphone and a holstered

handgun opens the door to the VIP room. Ivan Besov—Bes—is already there, reclining in a chaise lounge with one arm in a sling and a coffee cup in his free hand. A fucking coffee cup. After fucking up, he dares to sit there and drink coffee like he owns the place? The sight of that alone makes Vladimir want to break the assassin's fingers and let them mend crookedly so he can never hold a cup or pull a trigger again.

Two of Vladimir's guards enter the room ahead of him. Bes puts the cup on the table and gets to his feet, knowing what needs to follow. Once he's been patted down for weapons and none have been found, Vladimir steps inside. The bouncer stationed outside closes the door. His men stand at attention in each corner of the room. If Bes takes offense to the open display of distrust, he hides it well.

"Sit," Vladimir says, motioning at the seat Bes has already warmed.

Bes acknowledges the order with a humorless smile. "Why am I here?"

Vladimir walks to a liquor tray and selects his favorite brand of vodka. A waitress could've served the drinks, but he needs the distraction. If Bes notices how nervous he is, he'll lose face. It's important—paramount—that he's feared.

After pouring two glasses, Vladimir carries one to Bes and offers it to him like a generous host.

"No, thanks," the assassin says without accepting the drink. "Alcohol isn't advisable for a man who needs steady hands."

To be served a drink by none other than Vladimir Stefanov is an honor. Refusing it is an insult. Vladimir will take great pleasure in making Bes suffer for that slap in the face. Soon.

Tipping his chin toward the sling, Vladimir asks, "How's the wrist?"

"Almost healed." The assassin stares up at him with unblinking, emotionless eyes. "The cast comes off in two days."

Vladimir downs the liquor as he considers his reply. A guard rushes over to take his empty glass.

"Will you be able to handle a gun?" Vladimir asks.

Bes's gaze narrows minutely. "I'll hit the target, if that's what you're asking."

Vladimir downs the liquor in the second glass, stretches out his arm, and drops the glass. "That's what you said when Oleg paid you to take out Volkov."

The guard who hurries to Vladimir's side catches the glass just before it hits the floor.

The line of Bes's jaw turns hard, but his regard remains expressionless. "As I told Oleg, Volkov moved. One second more, and I would've had him."

Vladimir rolls onto the balls of his feet. "Unfortunately, one second is all it takes to blow a plan to pieces."

A muscle ticks in Bes's temple. "Mistakes happen in my business, but I've never failed to finish a job. I don't intend to start now."

"Mistakes." Vladimir utters a soft laugh as he

crosses the floor, coming to stand in front of the glass wall that forms one side of a Perspex pool.

The turquoise water is lit. The filter pump causes a gentle current, the movement throwing soft waves of light over the walls.

"Once, maybe, it's a mistake," Vladimir says, studying the way the water distorts the figure of the woman who walks over the stage to the edge of the pool. "But twice?"

"Slipping and fracturing my wrist was an unfortunate mishap," Bes says. "If not, you would've had Katherine Morrell by now."

The woman looks straight at Vladimir. From behind the wall of water, he can't make out her face, but she knows for whom she's performing. She stretches out her arms in front of her and dives gracefully. Her naked body comes into focus as she glides through the water and swirls like a ribbon, making a stunning live portrait in the Perspex frame.

"The truth is, Bes," Vladimir says, focusing on the way her nipples contract into hard points from the cold water, "I'm growing tired of excuses."

The dancer bends a knee and jumps elegantly with pointed toes. Her poise is regal. With eyes the color of the water and lips naturally red, like ripe cherries, her delicate face is classically beautiful.

"There won't be another mistake," Bes says in a flat tone.

"Yet you made one."

For that, the assassin deserves a bullet in the head.

The thought alone makes Vladimir's hands tremble with violence. The urge to grab a gun is so strong he has to curl his fingers into fists to prevent himself from acting on it. He'd like nothing more than to crack Bes's skull and paint the walls with his blood, but he can't get rid of him yet. He has bigger plans for the assassin.

"What are you talking about?" Bes asks.

Vladimir allows the woman's graceful movements to calm him. Natasha is an accomplished but retired ballerina. She's one of Russia's treasures. She's too old for the stage now, but her ass is still firm, her tits pert. People flock to the club to see her show. Vladimir's personal favorite is the one where she performs with the water snakes.

"You made a grave mistake by delivering Katherine Morrell's key card to Volkov," Vladimir says.

"That was intentional. I've got him worried," Bes says, meeting Vladimir's gaze in the reflection of the glass. "Worried men make mistakes."

The naked male dancer dives into the water. His strong body is lithe and well defined, his cock thick and long. He scoops up the woman, lifting her in a choreographed dance.

Vladimir follows the dancers' underwater ballet, moving his head to the side and up as they surface for air. "He also ran home to protect his lover, and we both know he's as good as untouchable here."

"An opportunity will come. It always does," Bes continues in a bored tone.

The arrogance makes Vladimir shiver with fury.

Controlling it is difficult. He focuses on the couple diving to the bottom. The man presses the woman against the wall, flush against Vladimir's body. Only the glass separates them as the man spreads her legs and shoves into her from behind.

Not even the highlight of the performance is enough to abate Vladimir's anger. Natasha's breasts push flat against the glass. She snakes her arms around the man's neck and locks her legs around his ass, pulling her supple body into an artistic C-shape as the man pummels her splayed pussy for Vladimir's visual entertainment. A tongue of heat licks through Vladimir's stomach and stirs his cock, but with the nagging worry in the back of his mind, the spark of arousal doesn't catch.

"This is what you're going to do," Vladimir says, not taking his eyes off the show. "From now on, you're following *my* orders."

The woman throws back her head. A bubble escapes from her lips, floating to the surface.

"What about Oleg?" Bes asks.

"Oleg had his chance."

The male dancer meets Vladimir's gaze through the water, a wordless request for permission to end the show. Vladimir shakes his head.

"What do you want me to do?" Bes asks in his infuriatingly disinterested voice.

Vladimir clenches his teeth. The woman opens her eyes. She draws a line with her palm across her throat, indicating she's out of air and needs to surface.

"I have reason to believe Oleg is in possession of certain evidence," Vladimir says. "You're going to get it for me."

The woman starts to struggle. The man's face pulls into a mask of concentration as he pumps his hips faster to finish the performance.

"How am I supposed to do that?" Bes asks.

Turning to him, Vladimir says, "The instructions are encrypted on a flash drive."

A guard jumps forward, handing Bes the plastic casing with the drive.

"I'll let you figure out a way," Vladimir says with a cold smile. "Your file states you have a high IQ. I'm sure you'll get creative. You do this, and I'll turn a blind eye to your mistakes."

Thumping sounds rattle the glass behind Vladimir.

Bes weighs the casing in his palm. Wisely, he doesn't turn down the deal. "By when do you need this evidence?"

Vladimir turns back to the show. He's just in time to see the life wash out of the woman's eyes. At long last, the male comes, pulling out so Vladimir can see the jets of ejaculate he shoots into the water. "The sooner, the better."

Kicking with his feet, the man swims up to the surface, his heavy cock drifting flaccidly between his legs. Finally, Vladimir grows hard. Maybe he'll order the male dancer to his upstairs room tonight.

"Fine," Bes says. "But that doubles my price."

Natasha's body drifts like a four-pointed star in the

water, her long blond hair billowing around her face. She makes a peaceful picture.

For the first time in weeks, Vladimir breathes easily again. All he needed was to take back the control. Facing Bes, he says, "Get the evidence and finish Volkov, and you'll get your money."

The assassin stands.

"If Oleg finds out what's going on, if he so much as catches a whiff of it, you're dead," Vladimir says. "Is that clear?"

Bes's gaze drifts over Vladimir's shoulder toward the pool. "Crystal."

"Good," Vladimir says, feeling much better.

5

KATE

*O*pening my eyes, I blink in momentary confusion. My emotionally drained mind wants to sink back into the relief of oblivious sleep, but something harping at the back of it urges me to wake up. Slowly, I surface to full consciousness.

I'm lying on a bed under a soft blanket. It's so dark I can't see my hand in front of my face, but I don't need my eyesight to know this isn't Alex's bed in New York City. This isn't the house I moved into with him. Then the cobwebs lift, and I remember. That little something in the back of my mind crystalizes into clarity as the memories flood back.

I sit up and stretch out an arm to feel my way. Velvet brushes against my fingertips. The bed curtains. Scrunching the fabric in my hand, I pull it aside. Light penetrates the inky darkness. A nightstand lamp throws a soft glow over the room. Someone must've closed the bed curtains after I'd fallen into an exhausted sleep. Lena, maybe. I find the idea of her being in the room while I was napping disconcerting.

Despite the comfortable temperature in the room, I shiver a little as I get up. The time on my watch says it's seven o'clock. I napped for two hours. My wrung-out body and mind needed the rest. I'd been working long shifts at the hospital for two weeks straight. Physically, I'm still playing catch-up, and the mini breakdown I had at discovering I'm locked in didn't help.

Pricking up my ears, I listen for sounds. The house is quiet. Eerily so. Rubbing my hands over my arms, I head to the dressing room and find a warm cardigan that I pull on over my sweater. I catch sight of myself in the full-length mirror. My slacks are wrinkled from sleeping in them. My hair is disheveled, the waves untamed. I smooth down my hair with my palms and don't bother to find shoes. I pad on my sock-clad feet to the window and pull the drapes open a crack. Whoever closed the bed curtains must've also closed these.

The powerful spray lights don't leave a single corner of the garden in the shadows. As earlier, men patrol the perimeter of the wall and stand guard at the gates.

Taking a moment to go over everything that's happened since last night, I consider my options. Now that I'm calmer, I can think clearer.

I'm locked in the house. Tima and Lena won't help me. I don't have access to a phone. Whatever liberties I'm allowed from now on will happen at the sole discretion of Alex, which means it's in my best interest to appease him. Somehow, I'll have to win back his trust. Seeing that he's broken *my* trust, that will be very hard for me to do. But how am I supposed to sit here and do nothing while Alex is out there risking his life? How am I supposed to bear the thought that something might happen to him while my hands are tied?

Lost in my troubled deliberations, I go downstairs to see if Alex has come home. A guard stands next to the front door.

"Good evening," I say.

He acknowledges me with a nod.

"Do you know if Alex—"

The door opens before I can finish my sentence, and Igor walks through it, dusting snowflakes from the shoulders of his coat.

He stops when he notices me.

"Igor," I say, part in greeting and part in relief.

I look over his shoulder, trying to see if Alex is with him, but he cuts off my view by closing the door, presumably to keep the cold from coming in.

"Where's Alex?" I ask.

"He'll be in shortly," he says, moving around me.

I take a step to the side, blocking his way. "Where is he?"

A beat lapses. "Getting an update from the men at the barracks."

Testing my boundaries, I ask, "May I please use your phone?"

His large frame sags with the sigh he blows out. "You know I can't do that."

"That's what I thought."

At least he has the decency to look guilty. "You can't call home. It's for your safety." Averting his eyes, he walks away.

"Miss Morrell?" a female voice says.

I spin on my heel.

Lena stands at the foot of the stairs. "Dinner is served in the dining room. Mr. Volkov will join you as soon as he can. He said you shouldn't wait." She drags her gaze over me, pausing on my socked feet. "Normally, Mr. Volkov dresses for dinner."

"Do you know where he's been?"

She waves a hand toward the corridor. "The dining room is this way."

"Alex showed me already."

She gives a cool smile. "In that case, you won't get lost." Without another word, she disappears down the hallway.

Clenching my hands into fists, I turn back to the guard at the door. If I was hoping for an explanation from him, I'm in for another disappointment. He's facing straight ahead, ignoring my presence as if I don't exist.

Not having anywhere else to go, I walk to the dining room. The table is set with a dozen dishes. None of the intricate pastries or colorful salads are familiar, but they're all beautifully presented with garnishes of radishes and tomatoes artfully carved to resemble roses.

My stomach grumbles, reminding me I didn't touch the French toast and fruit Tima had prepared earlier.

Tima enters with a steaming platter. Giving me a bright smile, he says, "I hope you rested well. Please, have a seat. You must be hungry." He places the platter in the center of the other dishes and pulls out a chair next to the head of the table where a place is set. "Here. Come. Make yourself comfortable."

A whiff of garlic and parsley reaches my nose. I want to decline out of spitefulness, but I'm starving. Grudgingly taking the seat and letting him adjust the chair, I say, "There's enough food here for an army."

He chuckles. "There *is* an army, in case you haven't noticed."

I scoff. "How could I have missed that?"

"I made you some comfort food." He motions at the dish from which the aromas are wafting. "Pasta with artichoke. It's an Italian recipe." Taking a serving spoon and fork, he scoops up a generous helping and places it on my plate. "There. Eat up before it gets cold. Then you can try the cold dishes and salads. Those are all local recipes. Delicious."

"Thank you," I say with reluctant gratitude.

Tima pours water into my glass before leaving the room.

The grandfather clock strikes once. The beat echoes in the quiet room. Half past seven. For a moment, I sit motionless, taking in the silence and how unreal this feels. A soft tick-tock follows as the clock continues to count off the seconds. It's a strangely depressing sound and a very awkward situation, sitting alone at a table made for twenty people. I do need to eat, though.

Twisting the hair-thin pasta around my fork, I bring a bite to my mouth. Flavors of garlic, parsley, and olive oil blend with the taste of the artichoke hearts. The combination is delicious, instantly igniting my appetite. Tima was right. This is comfort food and exactly what I need.

I devour the portion on my plate and contemplate going for seconds, but I'm curious about the other dishes on the table. Just as I'm digging the serving spoon into a salad of potato and what looks like dill pickles, Alex walks into the room.

I still as I meet his gaze. He wears a white button-up shirt and dark pants. His jaw is free of stubble, his lightly tanned skin perfectly smooth. The dark brown color of his hair forms a striking contrast to the icy blue of his eyes. His regard is vigilant and observant as his gaze slides from my face to my empty plate.

His smile is reserved. "My apologies for being late."

"This is your house. You can do as you please."

Taking the seat at the head of the table, he says, "I thought it best to give you a little time to cool down."

I'm far from having cooled down, especially after discovering just how much of my freedom he's taken away. It seems stealing my choices wasn't enough. When he takes my hand and lifts it to his lips, I try to free myself, but he tightens his grip and presses a kiss on my knuckles. The moment he lets go, I pull my hand away.

The set of his mouth turns strained. "It looks like time didn't do the trick."

Ignoring him, I finish serving myself a helping of the salad.

"What do you need, Katerina?" he asks, a bite to his tone. "How much time is it going to take?"

I pick up my fork. "How about giving me the truth?" For example, where has he been all afternoon?

He watches me with unwavering attention. "I gave you the truth. Someone stole your card, and I *will* find out who. Until then, I'm keeping you where it's safe." His tone hardens with resolve. "Here."

I clench my fingers around the fork. "As your prisoner."

His voice remains level, but the minute tightening of his eyes betrays his impatience. "As someone I'm doing my damnedest to protect. That's not going to change until I catch the perpetrator, so get used to the way things are. Asking my staff for a phone and trying to call home isn't going to work."

Stabbing a piece of potato with my fork, I glare at him. It's good to know his telephone operator and guards report back to him. At least I know who's on my side. No one, it seems.

A sensual aroma of cardamom and spices drifts to me as he reaches over the table and loads some of the pasta onto his plate. He showered. The smell stirs memories of happier times. I push them away, not wanting to remember him as a kind and skillful lover. The Alex who's serving me small portions of every dish on the table isn't the man who shared starters and kisses with me in Romanoff's. He's the man who brought me to Russia and locked me up in his house.

"Try the *oliv'ye*," he says, serving us wine. "It's my personal favorite."

My appetite for the food is gone. I take a big gulp of the red wine while he watches me with hooded eyes as he brings a forkful of pasta to his mouth.

After chewing, he says, "Don't be obstinate, Katyusha. It's not going to help. The sooner you accept the situation, the easier this will be for you."

I've already come to the same conclusion, but having my choices taken away isn't something I'll easily accept. Carefully, I ask, "Have you considered that you may be overreacting a bit?"

"Not where you're concerned."

"You're locking me in and denying me the use of a phone. What am I going to do? Run away in a strange city where I can't speak the language or call the police? I'm not stupid or naïve."

"I'm not taking any chances."

The jab hurts. He doesn't trust me either. "You could've protected me just as well in New York."

"You're wrong." He pulls the salt closer and adds a generous amount to his food. "I can't protect you if you're on the street or in a hospital with thousands of people passing you on a daily basis."

I lean back in my chair, digesting that information.

What about him and the thousands of people who pass him on the streets? What if someone shoots at him again? What if, this time, the sniper doesn't miss?

"Katyusha?" He takes my hand and rubs a thumb over my knuckles. "Are you unwell? You're very pale. Didn't you rest enough?"

The fear is crippling. "How long is this going to take? To track down the person who wants you dead?"

"I'm doing everything in my power to find the son of a bitch."

I swallow. "Do you at least have an idea of who it could be?"

"A business rival, maybe." His brow furrows as he lets go of my hand to draw his fingers through his hair. "I don't have any concrete leads for now."

"In other words, we could be here for months."

His jaw bunches. "As long as it takes."

The words rush from my lips. "Don't go out there. If you have a telephone operator, you must have a security chief or someone who can find out who's trying to kill you."

"Hey." He leans over and grips my shoulder. "Slow down. I know how to take care of myself. Don't worry about this. That's my job."

Easier said than done. I care about him. My feelings aren't going to vanish just because he brought me against my will to Russia. I've fallen for him, and now it's too late to protect my heart. If anything should happen to him—

I give a start when he pushes to his feet. The man

staring down at me is wearing an expression that says he owns me. The heat in the cool blue of his eyes is the kind that can cut through iron. I imagine the blue flame of a welder melting steel as he rounds the corner of the table without moving his gaze from mine. His expression sharpens with intent. It should be a warning, but the magnitude of the power he exudes hypnotizes me, keeping me frozen in my seat.

He pulls my chair back as if the weight is nothing. Locking his fingers around my waist, he drags me to my feet. I'm a puppet in his hands, overwhelmed with fear, worry, and the notion of being trapped in a dark, endless tunnel. I don't see a way out, not for the foreseeable future and not when he lifts me swiftly onto the table.

My heart is beating a mile a minute as I stare up at his face. The harsh lines are drawn in lust. It's been too long. Too long for us, at least. We're used to making love at least a couple of times a day. His hands on my waist feel right, but my mind can't make peace with the new imbalance of power between us.

He lowers me gently, cushioning my head with one broad hand and going for the button of my slacks with the other. His gaze holds me prisoner, radiating pretty promises of safety and warmth as he pops the button through the buttonhole. My body heats instantly, his effect on me devastatingly powerful. The zipper of my slacks makes a scratchy sound as he pulls it down. His actions are slow and meticulous, his attention focused on my face.

71

I gasp when he slips a hand inside my underwear and over my folds. The mere brush of the pad of his finger over my clit makes my body bow. If he slips that finger inside me now, I'll be lost, and the victorious look on his face says he knows it.

If this were any other day, I wouldn't hesitate to take the pleasure he offers. I would give him everything he wants and all I'm capable of. When he took me in the bed and again in the shower the day before yesterday, we were on equal footing, or so I thought. Did I ever have a say in our relationship, or was it just a sweet illusion?

The thought hurts, adding to the growing mountain of torment in my chest. If I've been blind and naïve, I only have myself to blame.

Gently, he parts my folds, finding the wetness that's proof of my arousal.

"Katyusha," he says in a rough voice, his features tight with desire as he plants one hand next to my face.

When he lowers his head to move in for the kill, it takes every ounce of my willpower to say, "No."

He freezes above me. Inside my panties, his fingers curl into a fist. I don't have to look at him to know his control is hanging by a thread.

Gripping his wrist, I pull his hand from my underwear. Tears burn in my chest as I whisper, "I'm sorry. I can't."

6

ALEX

*T*orn between disbelief and confusion, I stare at Katerina's face. Her beautiful features are drawn into a mask of regret and something else, something that looks a lot like disappointment. She holds my gaze with her large hazel eyes as I pull my arm from her grip and bring my hand to her mouth.

"You want me." I trace the closed seam of her lips with the finger I had in her pants mere seconds ago. "Here's the proof. Do you want me to part those pretty lips and make you taste it?"

She turns her face to the side.

Splaying my fingers over her delicate jaw, I bring her gaze back to mine. My voice is thick with the desire and frustration I try to suppress. "*You want me.*"

And if I don't get inside her soon, I'm going to blow up in more than a physical way. The distance she's placing between us is driving me insane.

"Not like this," she says, slamming her palms on my shoulders and shoving me off her.

I straighten with reluctance, unwillingly creating even more distance. The gap between us feels like a vacuum, as if all the air is being sucked out of the room.

Not meeting my eyes, she sits up and fastens her slacks.

I'm like a pressure cooker, the mounting steam threatening to shoot the lid through the roof. "Katerina."

She looks at me again.

"Is this how you punish me? By withholding sex?" I home in on the heaving of her breasts under her sweater. "It's a very effective method, I have to admit, but I wouldn't advise you to go down that road. We both know this isn't a game you're going to win."

"A game?" Her tone sharpens. "You think this is a game?"

On the contrary, this is serious. Just how serious, I'm not sure she fully comprehends. Nor do I wish to enlighten her. What's the point of tormenting her with the knowledge that if she's captured, my enemies will most likely torture her in the most despicable ways to draw me out of my stronghold?

"I don't want it to be like this," she says. "But you made your choice when you took away mine."

I don't like the way this conversation is going, not one bit. If she's hinting at wanting to leave me, she can get that ridiculous idea out of her pretty little head.

It's not going to fucking happen.

Ever.

Ignoring the way her beautiful eyes grow large, I step between her legs, my hands balled into fists. It's all I can do not to reach for her. Biting off every word, I make myself clear. "There is no longer a choice."

"You knew." She leans away, supporting her weight on her arms. "You knew this could happen."

Feigning ignorance isn't going to work. Not with me. I pin her with a stare. "So did you."

She blinks. Emotions play over her stunning features. She's expressive, my kiska. It has always been easy for me to tell what she thinks. That's one of the things I love so much about her. With Katerina, I don't have to worry about manipulations and games. She's honest and straightforward. Maybe that's what the problem is. She's too honest, too good, to accept the ugly parts of my world.

An internal battle wages in her eyes. Yes, she knew what she was getting herself into when she agreed to move in with me. I've told her in not so many words that I'm a bad guy. True, I left out the gritty details of what goes on behind the closed doors of my empire. No one gets to where I am without blood on his hands, but there's no point in burdening her with that fact.

"I…" She wets her lips with the tip of her tongue. "This isn't what I expected."

Placing my palms on either side of her body on the table, I close some of that unwanted distance. "We won't be hiding forever."

"It's not the running or the hiding."

My voice is gruff with the need clawing inside me. "Then what is it, kiska?"

Her features contort, the brave mask she's wearing collapsing. "It's being treated like a possession."

The hurt etched in her expression hits me straight in the heart.

I get it. I'm not a foolish or insensitive man. Katerina is independent. Up until now, she's made all her own decisions. She's used to running her life and taking charge. In her relationship with her mother, she seems more of the adult, taking responsibility for her ailing parent, and as a nurse, she's used to making decisions that mean the difference between life and death. Locking her up and taking away everything that gives her life meaning isn't ideal, but it's not for forever. It's temporary and for her own good. She'll understand eventually. She loves me. She told me so once, and I'm determined to hear those sweet words again. I'll do whatever it takes to get them.

Except letting her go.

I've never begged for anything in my life, not even for bread when I was starving. She's the first one to bring me to my knees. Pressing my forehead against hers, I say raggedly, "Let me touch you, kiska. Please."

A sob catches in her throat. She shakes her head, brushing our hair together. "This isn't me, Alex. This isn't who I am."

I clench my fingers so hard my nails dig into the table. "Tell me what to fucking do."

"If you can't give me freedom, give me time," she says, gripping my wrist and moving it away to break the cage of my arms. "I need time and space."

When she ducks under my arm and slides from the table, I don't stop her. When she runs from the room, all but fleeing from me, I don't go after her. I don't acknowledge how much it hurts that she treats me like an enemy. Instead, I go in search of a bottle of vodka and give her the time and space she wants.

7

CALIFORNIA, THE UNITED STATES

*O*leg Pavlov presses the phone to his ear and walks to the edge of the terrace where he's out of earshot. He drums his fingers on the rail as he waits for the call to connect, inconspicuously checking to see if his bodyguards are in place. Assured that they're in position, he takes a handkerchief from his pocket and wipes the sweat from his brow.

What is taking the assassin so long? Acid burns in his stomach. This fucking ulcer is going to kill him.

Finally, Bes picks up.

Oleg cuts straight to the chase. "What did you do?"

"I do a lot of things on a daily basis," the assassin says smoothly. "You'll have to be more specific."

Oleg glances over his shoulder to where his family is having breakfast. Lowering his voice, he grits out, "Alex Volkov should be dead by now. Instead, he's running around St. Petersburg, very much alive." Despite the control he's forcing, his voice rises in volume. "And working very hard on finding out who's behind the assassination attempt."

When his wife, Annika, looks up, he gives her a smile, indicating all is well when nothing could be further from the truth.

"Oleg," she calls, "your breakfast is getting cold."

He raises a finger to indicate he needs another minute and turns his back on her. "Explain to me what the fuck you were thinking, stealing Katherine Morrell's key card instead of snatching the woman herself. All it accomplished was chasing Volkov straight to his army in Russia."

"Patience, old man," Bes says. "All in good time."

Facing the vista of the vineyard, Oleg says, "My patience is running out. So is your time."

"It will happen when I'm ready. We moved too fast the first time. That's why you failed."

"You mean *you* failed," Oleg says.

Bes laughs. "You gave the order. That failure is on your head, my friend."

Oleg clenches his jaw. "Do you have any idea what Vladimir is capable of?"

He's ignored two of Vladimir's calls already, saying that he was in public places and couldn't speak, but Vladimir expects him to call back and soon. He'll want a report on what the fuck went wrong this time.

"I do, as a matter of fact," Bes says, his tone dry. "If you don't want the throats of your lovely family slit, I suggest you go back to your breakfast like your wife ordered, and let me get on with my job."

Oleg glances around, acid pushing up into his throat as he searches the faces of the tourists. The motherfucking assassin is watching him? *Oleg* is the one paying Bes. *He's* in charge. How dare that lowlife Russian sniper spy on him like he's the goddamn target?

"Have I made myself clear enough for you?" Bes asks.

"I'm the one paying you," Oleg says, fighting to keep the fear from his tone.

"Yes," Bes drawls. "But there's always someone willing to up the price."

Oleg grips the rail hard. "Listen to me, you lousy—"

"I'd be careful with the insults if I were you. I'm sure Volkov will pay handsomely to know who ordered the hit on him."

Oleg goes cold in the heat of the day. How the fuck did this happen? How did the power switch from him to the man he hired? Bes is a rat, a lowlife, a dirty son-of-a-bitch traitor. If Vladimir finds out Bes is threatening to sell them out, he—Oleg—is dead. Hiring an unreliable cleaner isn't something Vladimir will let go unpunished.

"What do you want?" Oleg bites out.

"Evidence."

Oleg drags the handkerchief over his face. "Evidence of what?"

"Evidence of the crime you and Vladimir Stefanov committed."

Oleg freezes with his hand in midair. "What did you say?"

"You heard me."

Impossible. "I don't know what you're talking about."

Bes laughs again. "You know exactly what I'm talking about."

"Listen here, you—" Oleg swallows the insult, remembering Bes's threat. "You know how the business works. Vladimir and I collaborated on many things."

"I'm talking about the reason you want Volkov dead."

Oleg tightens his fingers around the phone to prevent them from trembling. "How did you find out?"

"A man like me has his ways."

"Tell me," Oleg says, spittle flying from his mouth.

"It doesn't matter. All you need to worry about is delivering the evidence of Stefanov's culpability."

Oleg is all but shaking in his shoes. He can't believe his ears. "You've got to be kidding me."

"I never joke, Oleg. You should know that about me by now."

"Do you have any fucking idea what Vladimir will do to you if he finds out? To *me*?"

"What do you care about what happens to me?" Bes asks. "With regards to you, Stefanov will never find out. He'll be out of the picture before he has a chance to try."

"You want to bring Vladimir down?" Oleg casts a

glance at his family and waves at his frowning wife again. "Why?"

"Stop asking questions that don't matter."

It fucking matters, because if Vladimir goes down, so does he. Oleg swallows. "Who's paying you for the information?"

"Don't worry," Bes says. "I'll keep your name out of it. Give me what I want, and you can continue your wine tour with your perfect family."

Oleg feels like he may be sick. "What about Alex Volkov?"

"You uphold your end of the bargain, and I'll uphold mine. Deliver the information, and I'll deliver Volkov's head on a platter."

The line goes dead.

Lowering the phone, Oleg stares at the screen. He's shaking with fury. How dare that assassin threaten his family? He'll skin him alive. The only reason he's not retaliating right now is because he can't let Vladimir find out that Bes knows the truth. If Oleg kills Bes, he'll have a hard time explaining it to Vladimir. Vladimir is a highly intelligent and intuitive man. He'll see straight through a lie. Besides, hunting down Bes might take months. No, Oleg's best bet is to play along. He'll deliver the evidence and let Bes bring Vladimir down. Once Vladimir is out of the way, he'll kill Bes.

Taking a roll of Tums from his pocket, he pops the pill from its casing and slips it onto his tongue. The more he thinks about it, the more Oleg believes it will not only be the best solution, but also a blessing in disguise. Let Bes do him the favor of getting rid of the ever-present threat of Vladimir. And once Bes himself is dealt with, no one will ever know the truth.

When Oleg walks back to his wife and children, his heartburn is already fading.

8

KATE

*W*hen I wake up the next morning, the bed beside me is empty. A sliver of light falls through the crack in the bed curtains.

Pushing up on one elbow, I pull one curtain aside. Daylight spills through the windows. The bedsheets are wrinkled. I lay a palm on Alex's pillow. The fabric is cool, but his scent clings to the linen.

I drag a breath of cardamom and spices into my lungs. Even in his absence, his presence lingers in the room. The events of last night weigh heavily on my chest. Folding my arms around my knees, I take a moment to reflect on our fight.

He'd come to bed long after midnight with vodka on his breath. I pretended to be sleeping, but the soft "goodnight" he whispered told me he knew I was awake. He respected my wish and kept his distance, not touching me during the night. I was both grateful and disappointed, and there was a moment when I almost gave in. In the scary, lonely hours of the early morning, I wanted to snuggle against him and throw an arm over his waist. A part of me wanted to anchor him to the bed, to prevent him from going out there, where it's dangerous. But another part of me couldn't—can't— forgive him. I don't know how to make peace with our new circumstances. I don't know who I'm supposed to be any longer. Our roles have changed, and I've yet to figure out where and how I fit into his life.

Am I his girlfriend or his prisoner?

Does he see me as a woman he cares about or merely his possession?

Ugh. I need to think, but my mind is clouded with confusion and emotions. Climbing from the bed, I go to the bathroom. The cupboards are stocked with all my usual brands of toiletries, and a box of contraceptive pills waits on the vanity. I pull out the sheet of pills. The pills have been popped out on the days of the month that have passed. It's not a new box. Alex thought about everything when he instructed Marusya to pack. I take today's pill and have a quick shower, which doesn't clear my head as I hoped it would.

The closet is stocked with many of the clothes Alex bought for me in New York, including formal wear and evening dresses. Thank goodness Marusya packed some of my own outfits at the bottom of the bag. With the way I feel, I need clothes that are familiar and comfortable.

After dressing in a pair of jeans, a warm sweatshirt, and my sneakers, I venture downstairs. The only sounds that greet me are the dong of the grandfather clock, announcing that it's ten in the morning, and the clanging of pots coming from the back of the house.

Finding the dining room empty, I walk to the kitchen.

Tima stands behind the stove. Pots simmer on the burners, steam rising from their contents. The space smells starchy, like porridge and potatoes.

"There you are," he says, wiping his hands on an apron. "Take a seat." He motions at the kitchen table where fruit, rye bread, jam, and cottage cheese are set out. "I thought it would be cozier to have your breakfast here than in the stuffy old dining room."

Grateful for his consideration, I plop down in a chair. "Thank you."

He goes to a counter set with several urns and flashes me a smile from over his shoulder. "Tea, coffee, or hot chocolate?"

"Coffee, please." I need the caffeine to clear the cobwebs in my mind.

"One coffee with sugar coming up."

It's not surprising that he knows how I drink my coffee. He prepared only vegetarian dishes last night. Alex must've briefed him on my preferences.

When he places a mug in front of me, I ask, "What are you cooking?"

"*Borscht* with *pelmeni* for lunch and roasted lamb with potatoes for dinner. That's for the men. I'm making vegetarian versions for you." He goes back to the stove, picks up a bouquet of fresh herbs, and chucks it into one of the pots. "You can never start the preparations too early. I also made oatmeal porridge. Alex told me you like to have oatmeal for breakfast."

I cup the mug, letting the warmth seep into my palms. "That's very considerate."

He serves a helping of the porridge into a bowl and carries it to the table. "It's the least I can do." Pushing a small basket of berries and a pot of honey toward me, he studies my face. "How are you doing today?"

I shrug. "I slept well, and I'm eating like a queen."

"That's not what I meant. How are you feeling in here, where it matters?" He pats his chest.

Unable to lie to his face, I look away. "Good."

"Mm." He goes back to stirring the contents of a big pot. "Alex left you English books in the library. The cable isn't connected, but there are DVDs." He looks over his shoulder again and winks. "All the seasons of *Downton Abbey* in case you're in the mood."

I utter a wry laugh. "Alex disconnected the cable? What does he think I'm going to do? Send Morse code via the cable connection?"

Tima's smile is so wide his whole face looks like a piece of creased paper. "You're certainly clever enough."

"Ha. Technology and I aren't friends."

"If there's anything you want, you only have to say the word. Alex will send for it."

"That's good to know," I say with a bite to my tone,

even though my anger is already wearing off, leaving me with a confusing mess of emotions and the worry that Alex is an open target outside.

"I've known Mr. Volkov for some years now." Tima puts the spoon on a saucer, turns to face me, and crosses his arms. "I've never seen him as invested in anyone as he is in you."

I raise a brow. "Is that supposed to make me feel better?"

Leaning against the stove, he says with a sincere expression, "He obviously cares about what happens to you."

I consider that. Tima is kind, but I don't know him. I don't trust him yet. I'm not going to discuss my dilemma or my feelings with Alex's staff.

Another smile scrunches up Tima's face. "Eat up. Your oatmeal is getting cold. I'm sure you have better things to do than keeping me company in the kitchen."

Actually, no. What else am I going to do with myself? "Do you need a hand in here?"

His eyes grow round. "Absolutely not. Mr. Volkov will roast me like that lamb if I make you work in the kitchen."

I frown at the expression. I hope he means that figuratively, but after the last couple of days, it doesn't sound as farfetched as it should.

"On with dinner," he says, speaking more to himself than to me as he goes to the pantry.

By the time he returns with his arms full of ingredients, I've finished my oatmeal and coffee. I rinse my bowl and load the dishwasher while he whistles an unfamiliar tune.

"Thanks for the breakfast," I say on my way to the door.

He lifts his head and gives an absentminded wave before continuing to chop the stalks off a bunch of beetroot.

The sound of a vacuum cleaner comes from the front of the house. Making my way over, I spot Lena in the foyer, vacuuming with earbuds in her ears. She looks up as I mount the stairs, but she doesn't say good morning. In return, I swallow the greeting that was on the tip of my tongue.

For the rest of the day, I explore the house. I find the DVDs and books Tima mentioned in the library and manage to distract myself for a while, but the stories don't hold my attention. I'm too strung out to let myself get lost in fiction.

When I grow tired of reading, I pull on a T-shirt and yoga pants and go in search of the gym. A guard mans the door, but he steps aside for me to enter. A fancy sound system boasts a variety of music mixes. It's not complicated to figure out how it works. I select a lively pop compilation, surprised at Alex's taste in music. I expected him to be a jazz or classical guy, not a pop music fan. Maybe this is just the kind of music he listens to when he works out.

Choosing the treadmill, I set it on a comfortable

speed and run until my legs feel like jelly. It's a good feeling. I ran cross-country in high school and did a few 10Ks on my own in college, but I've been working so much in the past couple of years that I've let my fitness routine fall by the wayside. Now I realize how much I've missed it. The exercise doesn't expel my turbulent thoughts, but it does lessen some of my cooped-up tension.

Thoroughly exhausted yet satisfied, I pull on a swimsuit, rinse off in the pool shower, and drift in the warm water of the Olympic-sized pool. Condensation runs down the sides of the skylight that lets in the sun. The smell of chlorine reminds me of vacations when I was little. The pleasant association relaxes me further, and by the time I stretch out on a lounge chaise with a view of the indoor garden, some of my level-headedness returns.

Lena surprises me, entering with an infusion that she deposits on the side table before leaving quietly again. I pick up the delicate porcelain cup and sniff the herbal tea. It smells like lemon verbena. A taste confirms I'm right.

As I sip the tea, I try to put things in perspective. What Alex did hurt me. The blatant way he executed my disempowerment without considering my opinion angered me. Yet I can't say it shocked me. Not really. Looking back, I now see the signs clearly—the way he insisted I go out with him, how he wouldn't take no for an answer until he'd worn down my resolve, how he moved my clothes into his house without consulting me, and how quickly he convinced me to move in with him. Then there was the unsettling fact that he always knew my shift schedule at the hospital.

The truth is he's always been this way, and despite the blinders lifting from my eyes, I don't want him any less. One touch from Alex is enough to make my knees weak. It's always been the case, right from the start, and I doubt the visceral pull he exerts on me will ever change. Last night was proof of that. My body always tells the truth.

I care about him more than I've cared for any man. If I want space, it's not because he's made me a woman on the run or put my life in danger. The reason I need to slam on the brakes is that he believes there's nothing wrong with keeping me locked up as long as he's convinced that it's in my best interest.

Can I tie myself to a man who won't give me freedom? Maybe Dania, the daughter of his business partner, was right. Maybe I don't fit in Alex's world. How much am I prepared to accept? Can I make peace with letting him dictate my life? No. Like I told him last night, that's not me. Then how do I take back my power?

A shadow invades my sunny spot. I glance up at the skylight. The sun is setting. I check my watch. It's close to five, and there's still no sign of Alex. A shiver of unease runs down my spine. I hate being kept in the dark while anything can be happening out there.

Seesawing between worry and anxiety is exhausting. I've been lying here, thinking this thing through until my brain hurts, and I still haven't decided on a course of action.

Putting the empty cup aside, I get to my feet. I find a bathrobe in the adjoining bathroom and pull it on over my swimsuit. My hair smells of pool chemicals and my skin feels dry. I need a shower to rinse the chlorine from my body.

After I've had a warm shower, I moisturize my skin and brush out my hair. Remembering Lena's comment that Alex prefers to dress for dinner, I choose a blue cashmere dress. I don't care what Lena and Alex think about my attire, but being underdressed puts me at an unfair disadvantage, even if it's just in my own mind. After applying mascara and lip gloss, I'm ready.

At seven, I go downstairs. The big house is quiet. Alex and his most trusted bodyguards are still not home. Like the evening before, the table is set with a variety of dishes. I finish dinner in solitude, my only company the ticking of the clock.

Tima distracts me with his lively chatter, telling me the names of the dishes in Russian and explaining their ingredients as he serves dessert and finally clears the table.

Not ready to retire, I go to the library and curl up on a chair. Someone made a fire in the fireplace. I watch the shadows the flames draw on the wall and listen to the crackle of the wood. Soon, a warm glow spreads over my cheeks, and my eyes start to droop.

I give a start when the door suddenly opens. Alex stands in the frame, wearing a dark suit and a black button-up shirt without a tie.

"I didn't mean to frighten you," he says, studying me with cunning intensity.

Sitting up straighter, I rub my eyes. "I was dozing off."

He steps inside and closes the door. "I'm sorry I'm late. I had to take care of business."

I follow him with my gaze as he crosses the floor and comes to a stop in front of the fireplace. "Business as in work, or business as in finding out who wants you dead?"

"Both." He props his forearm on the mantelpiece and stares into the flames. "I hope the dinner was to your liking."

"It was delicious, thank you." The concern I can't shake compels me to ask, "What about your dinner?"

He takes a log from the basket and throws it into the fire. "I ate at the office."

"Oh. Do you have a private cafeteria for your employees?"

His lips quirk. "We do. But for the executives, we have a standing order from a catering company."

"Convenient," I say, studying my hands.

He turns to face me. "How was your day?"

I blink up at him. "Do you really want to know?"

He unbuttons his jacket and pulls it off. "Yes."

Not in the mood for small talk, I shrug. "Good."

He drapes the jacket over the back of the sofa and

walks to my chair. Towering over me, he asks, "What did you do?"

"Don't tell me you're interested in the meaningless actions that occupied my hours."

"Just because you didn't save lives today doesn't mean what we're doing here is meaningless."

"What *you*'re doing here, you mean."

He gives me a patient smile. "Is it wrong that I'm interested in how the woman I care about spent her day?"

There are so many things wrong with the way I spent my day that I don't know where to begin.

Dragging a chair closer, he sits down next to me. "Joanne called."

I sit up straighter. "What did she say?"

"Just that she wanted to talk to you."

"What did you tell her?" I ask, holding my breath.

"That you were at the spa and unable to take the call."

I clench my hands on my lap. "Lying comes easily for you, doesn't it?"

"You can speak to her if you behave," he says without missing a beat. "In fact, I think it will do you good."

My mouth drops open. I don't know if I should be grateful for the concession or upset that he's bribing me with selective contact with my friends.

Taking my hand, he rubs a thumb over my pulse. "I need you to think back to the night outside Romanoff's."

94

"The night when I got mugged?" I ask with surprise.

The line of his jaw hardens. "Yes, but I don't think it was a mugging."

I pull free from his touch as shock washes away the warmth of the fire. "You think it was related to the stealing of my card?"

"Maybe," he says with regret.

I gasp. "Why didn't you say so?"

"I didn't put two and two together at the time. The more I've been thinking about it for the last couple of days, the more it seems like a possibility."

Unfolding my legs from under me, I shift to the edge of the chair. "But why steal my handbag? Was that also some kind of warning, a message to you?"

When he only stares at me with violence brewing in his steely eyes, another truth hits me between the eyes.

"You don't think he was after my bag," I say, jumping to my feet.

"Katerina." Alex follows my pacing with his gaze. "I need you to think. Tell me anything you can remember about that night."

The memory isn't pleasant, especially given what I've just learned. "You were there. You saw what happened." More truths pierce me like arrows. "Did you even give a statement to the police?"

"My men do their job better than your police do theirs."

"Your men." Right. "What did they find?"

He scrubs a hand over his face. "Nothing. That means the police would've found even less. At the time,

I thought like you, that maybe it was just an unfortunate mugging, but now I suspect differently." Getting up, he walks over and grips my shoulders. "I didn't want to put you through this, not then and not now, but you have to think back to that night. What did he look like?"

I dig into my memory, trying hard to give Alex something. "He was stocky and big with a bald head."

"What else?"

"He…" I swallow when I remember the cruel smile he'd given me. "He had bad teeth—crooked and yellow."

"Did he say anything to you? Could you make out an accent of any kind?"

A shiver of repulsion runs over me. "He just laughed in a creepy kind of way, like he enjoyed scaring me."

Alex's nostrils flare. "Did he have any discernable marks, like a scar or a birthmark?"

It suddenly hits me. I motion to the top of my scalp. "He had a tattoo here."

"What was it?" he asks, urgency lacing his voice. "Can you recall if it was a word or a picture?"

"A picture." Now that I think about it, I can see it clearly in my mind's eye. "An eight-pointed star."

He lets me go so suddenly I stumble.

"Are you sure?" he asks, his gaze drilling into mine. "Are you sure it was a star with eight points?"

"Yes," I say through dry lips. "Why? What does it mean?"

"Nothing." Grabbing his jacket, he presses a chaste kiss to my forehead. "Go to bed. Don't wait up."

And he's gone, the door slamming behind him.

9

ALEX

*R*ushing out the front door, I run into Igor.

"I parked the car," he says. "Yuri locked up the garage. Do you need anything else before I head out?"

I pull on my gloves. "Where are the others?"

"Having dinner at the barracks."

"Get them." I make my way to the garage with long strides. "Take three armored cars and bring a dozen men. Yuri too."

He doesn't ask questions. He jogs around the mansion as I unlock the garage door by pressing my thumb on the wall-mounted fingerprint scanner. The roller door lifts. The garage houses the cars I use for the city as well as a motorbike and an off-road four-by-four.

A hidden button at the back opens a false wall panel. Behind it is one of the several weapon vaults on the property. A digital lock requires a retina scan and thumbprint. I open the door and step inside the walk-in safe just as Igor returns with Leonid, Dimitri, Yuri, and twelve of the men not scheduled for the night guard shift. Three cars with bullet-proof windows and reinforced bodywork pull up outside, their headlights illuminating the snow-covered garden.

I take an AK-47 from the gun stand and hand it to Igor. "Take automatic rifles and grenades. Smoke bombs too."

Leonid hands the weapons to the men who gear up while Dimitri picks three drivers. I instruct them where to go, and in under a minute, we're leaving the property in four cars.

Leonid and I sit in the back. Yuri drives and Dimitri rides shotgun. No one handles a car like Yuri. He can maneuver a Land Rover down a cliff at a forty-five-degree angle. I don't trust any other driver. Plus, he's good with a gun.

Our convoy slips smoothly into the sleeping streets of the upmarket neighborhood. I don't expect a war, but I take nothing for granted where these mother-fuckers are concerned.

The gang that uses the eight-pointed star emblem operates from a shady part of St. Petersburg. They're a bunch of lowlife scums who make their money by smuggling weapons and drugs, but they'll do any job for a price. They're not picky about the so-called free-lance work they take on.

After leaving the historical center behind, we head toward Kupchino and park at the back of a warehouse with an eight-pointed star painted on the wall. That's where the gang stores their merchandise. I came here a couple of times in my youth when I was running deliveries. The attached building serves as their clubhouse, with the kitchen as a sorry excuse for a restaurant.

I scan the surroundings before we get out. Nothing stirs. They're not expecting a visit. They won't even see us coming. At my signal, the men exit their vehicles. Half of them follow me while the other half surround the building. Leonid goes ahead to scout the area, his gun pointed in front of him.

For now, we benefit from the cover of the dark night, but as soon as we hit the area illuminated by the streetlights, we move along the side where there are no windows. The place is exactly as I remember. The stench of rotting food and the pungent smell of piss hang in the alley. The bulb above the door burns. Good. A grin of anticipation splits my face. That means the motherfuckers are home.

Footsteps fall on the cobblestones. Leonid's beefy face appears around the corner. He creeps up to me before saying in a hushed tone, "The warehouse and the back are empty. No one on guard. There must be at least ten of them inside."

I take my gun from my waistband and tilt my head toward the entrance. My men move ahead of me to the door. We pass a small broken window that's boarded up from the inside—the toilet window.

At the door, I stop to listen. The noises coming from inside are faint. The walls are thick. There's a distinct clanging of metal, pierced by the occasional boisterous laughter. The cockroaches are dealing as usual.

I hold up a hand, counting down on my fingers. Leonid screws a silencer onto the barrel of his gun. On three, he shoots the lock open. Four men cover him as he kicks in the door. The sturdy metal slab swings inward, hitting the doorman squarely in the face. He stands frozen, a look of surprise trapped on his features, but he's as good as unconscious on his feet. After another beat, he falls backward like a dead weight. Not taking any chances, Leonid plants a bullet between the man's eyes as he steps over his body.

The silencer ensures there's minimal noise to attract attention, but the open door alarms someone who comes out of the back room, zipping his fly as he walks. His eyes grow large when he spots us. He utters a cry, reaching for the gun in his holster, but he's dead before he has his hand on the shaft.

All hell breaks loose.

Men fire at us from the back, forcing us to take shelter in the kitchen. It would've been easier to drop a grenade in the back room, but I want the man who attacked Katerina alive.

Men in dirty aprons are skinning rabbits at a big table. They look at us as if we're ghosts. The shortest one drops his knife and raises his hands. The other two follow suit when Leonid rounds on them with his gun. An old woman with a nose and eyes buried in folded layers of skin shouts insults from the stove, waving a wooden spoon.

Gunfire sounds from the hallway. The acrid smell of gunpowder hangs in the air.

The cooks are workers. The men are part of the gang, but the old woman gets paid to prepare their meals.

"Go," I say to her, motioning at the back door next to a storage area.

Instead of running, she grabs a pot from the stove and flings it at Leonid. The boiling liquid barely misses his shoes. With the distraction, the bravest of the cooks grabs his paring knife and throws it at one of my men, who ducks. The knife falls with a clatter on the floor.

Pop, pop, pop.

The three men drop like flies, each with a hole between the eyes. The barrel of Dimitri's gun is smoking. The woman goes berserk, grabbing a steak knife and charging at me.

Really? A steak knife? For fuck's sake. Give me a break.

Pop.

She falls on the floor, next to her minions.

I lower my gun. I don't feel bad about shooting a woman. I gave her a choice. She made it.

More shots come from the back room. It sounds like fireworks on New Year's Eve. They're giving it their all. We're not here to take prisoners, and they know it.

"Cover me," I say to Leonid.

I stealthily approach the door and steal a glance around the frame. The hallway is empty. Our targets are in the back, trapped inside the room. There's no way out but through the door we used or through the one in the kitchen.

Leonid takes an automatic rifle from one of our men. He sends a spray of bullets at the doorway of the back room while I move down the hallway. A man who dares to stick his arm around the frame gets his hand shot off. A howl of pain lifts above the noise of the gunfight. Another man dashes forward, firing blindly, but he goes down before his bullets can do any damage.

My men follow on my heels. By the time we're at the door, the shooting from inside has stopped.

"We surrender," someone calls from inside.

"Come out," I say harshly. "One at a time. And don't fuck with me, or I'll brick up every door and window and let you rot inside."

We line up on either side of the hallway, our weapons aimed.

The first man steps out, his arms hanging loosely at his sides.

"Put your hands behind your head," I say.

He sneers and reaches for something behind his back.

A sequence of rapid gunfire goes off.

His chest explodes, the gun he pulled from his waistband falling with a clang on the floor.

"Hold your fire," someone shouts from the room. "We're out of bullets. Unarmed."

"Come out now and I'll finish you off quickly," I call back. "You know you're dying here today."

A man walks out with his hands in the air. He's as tall as he is square, his puffed-up muscles steroid-induced. He wears a black shirt and pants with Italian shoes, apparently trying hard to imitate a crime boss. His shaved head shines under the bulb that dangles on a cable from the ceiling. A black tattoo of an eight-pointed star sits in the center of his skull.

Every muscle in my body goes taut with a need for violence. It takes all my self-control and then some not to off him right away.

Stopping in front of me, he spits at my feet. "Fuck you."

Three of my men filter into the back room while the others grab the man. He struggles at first, until they've tied his wrists and ankles with cable ties. Then he lies grunting on the dirty concrete.

"What's your name?" I ask, suppressing an urge to kick in his teeth.

"Vadim," he says with defiant pride.

He's brave but stupid. If he had one clever brain cell in that thick skull of his, he would've never laid a hand on Katerina.

One after the other, my guards shove the men from the back room through the door. There are four of them—three older men and a lanky young one with a dark stain on the front of his pants. The old men leer as they're brought to stand in front of me. They're hardened, old-school gangsters. They're not going to bow to me or anyone else. Too bad I don't give a fuck about their resilience.

Vadim went after Katerina, and these men are culpable by association.

I give the order with a nod of my head.

My men know what to do. They take them to the kitchen to finish them off. Only because of their age do they get to die quickly.

"Leave this one," I tell the guards, motioning at the one who's pissed himself.

He stares at me with owl-sized eyes, shivering in his shoes.

I point my gun at the bald-headed piece of filth on the ground. "Tie his ankles."

In a few seconds flat, Vadim has a thick rope strung around his legs. He hurls insults as Leonid and one of the guards drag his heavy weight to the bathroom. I grab the arm of the thin guy, tugging him along.

The bathroom reeks of a blocked drain and over-flowing excrement. Brown water covers the floor. Vadim curses me to hell as they drop him face down in the water.

Turning his face to the side, he spits. "Go fuck your-self, you motherfucking fuck."

I go down on my haunches, studying his face with the passive curiosity of someone who's about to dissect an insect. He's red with fury, about to blow a gasket.

My voice is cold, collected. "You know why you're here, tied up like a dog and lying in shit and piss, don't you?"

His upper lip curls. "Because you're frightened."

I chuckle. "Do I look frightened to you?"

"You're scared of what's going to happen to you, Volkov. Admit it. I'm here, lying in piss and shit because you're a coward."

"Wrong answer." My manner is calm, not betraying the cold fury inside. "You're here, about to die, because you laid your filthy hands on my woman."

"The American chick?" He gives a taunting laugh. "If I were in charge, I would've used her up nicely before delivering her."

My vision goes hazy. The urge to rip out his windpipe is so strong I have to curl my fingers in a fist to prevent myself from acting on a whim. That will be too merciful for the piece of scum.

"Deliver her to whom?" I ask coldly.

He laughs. "If you think I'll tell you that, think again."

Straightening, I say to Leonid, "Let's get on with it."

"What are you doing?" Vadim shouts as my men drag him to the toilet stall.

He squirms like a worm, wriggling and spewing gibberish as they lay a metal pole over the stall and throw the rope tied to Vadim's feet over the pole. It takes two men pulling on the long end of the rope to hoist him up.

Hanging with his head down, he twists from side to side. "You think you'll break me with torture?"

He's not worth the time or energy of torture.

When they carefully lower him, he starts to beg. He

makes useless promises and offers futile bribes. His voice is an insult to my ears until his head dunks below the brown sludge drifting on the dirty water in the bowl. All that are left of his pleas are gurgles and another spout of indiscernible prattle.

I give it a few seconds before giving the signal. The men hoist him up until only his forehead touches the filth.

"Cut me down," he says, coughing up brown water.

I walk to his side. "What were you supposed to do with Katherine?"

"Take her to an address and leave her there." He gags and coughs again. "An apartment in Brooklyn."

The answer makes me as volatile as a volcano on the verge of erupting. "What's the address?"

"I don't know. I was supposed to call a number—a burner, I think—once I had the woman. Instructions with the address were supposed to follow."

"On whose order?"

He blows a string of snot from his nose. "Cut me loose."

I raise a hand. The men lower the rope.

"Wait," Vadim cries out. "It was Stefanov. Vladimir Stefanov."

My rage is so enormous it takes me a moment to digest the name. Vladimir Stefanov? One of the biggest bratva bosses in St. Petersburg? What the fuck is Stefanov's problem with me? We've never done business. We haven't even crossed paths.

"Why?" I grit out.

Vadim shakes his head, sending drops of filthy water flying. "I don't know. It's not my job to ask questions."

I believe him. Vladimir Stefanov is too high up in the hierarchy to share his plans or motivations with a lowly cockroach like Vadim.

I flick my fingers.

The men lower the rope. Vadim's head disappears under the slimy foam again. He makes ugly gargling sounds as he twists his upper body.

Gripping the neck of the piss-stained young man— the last enemy standing—in a fist, I push him closer and to his knees so he can witness what it looks like when a man drowns in shit.

He shakes and whimpers in my hold, slobber running from his mouth.

"You see this?" I say, pressing his face to the rim. "This is what happens to a man who touches my family."

He gags, trying to turn his face away, but I hold fast.

For such a big man, Vadim has a small lung capacity. Sadly, his fight lasts no more than a few minutes before his bulk goes still. The bubbling stops and the sloshing of the water over the sides of the toilet stills.

I let the fool on the floor go with a shove. The moment he's free, he scurries away on his knees and uses the wall for support to claw himself to his feet.

"You're the lucky messenger who gets to live another day," I say. "Go tell Vladimir Stefanov what happens to people who touch what belongs to me."

He backs up to the door, watching me like he expects me to say it was a joke, that I'm going to kill him after all.

"Go," I say icily, "before I change my mind."

He runs, tripping in his haste. My men don't laugh. The situation is far too serious. What could've happened to Katerina is no laughing matter.

Leonid covers his nose with a hand. "Do you want me to dump the body?"

"No." I spare the dead *ublyudok* one last look. "Leave him here." It will send a stronger message.

Dimitri lifts a foot and wrinkles his nose as he takes in the wet hem of his pants.

"Let's get out of this stinking hole," I say.

Our cleanup team is already getting rid of the other bodies and wiping away our tracks when we leave the building and walk into the night.

"What the fuck was that about?" Leonid asks in a lowered voice.

I clench my jaw. "I have no idea, but we're going to find out." And I know exactly who the best man for that job is.

Yuri gets my door.

"Put a man on Stefanov," I tell Leonid as I slide into the back. "I want eyes on him twenty-four-seven." Now that I've stirred up some shit—literally—Stefanov may get nervous. He may make a move that will shed some light on what the hell is going on.

"Do you want me to take him out?" Igor asks, getting in beside me.

"No." I rub a fist over my brow as I consider the implications. "Not yet. I first want to know what he's cooking up and who else is involved. Whatever he's planning, he might not be alone."

Yuri starts the engine and steers the car into the street.

"Home, Mr. Volkov?" he asks.

"The office." I need to change into clean clothes before I set foot in the house. I'm not facing my kiska smelling like filth. I keep a few changes of clothes at the office for when I don't have time to go home before business dinners.

Taking my phone from my pocket, I type up a message to Adrian Kuznetsov, the corporate spy, asking him to dig around and see if my name has blipped anywhere near Stefanov's dealings. As much as I despise Kuznetsov, if there's anyone who'll find something, it's him. After encrypting the message with a software application, I send it to Adrian's secure email address.

"What now?" Igor asks.

"For now, we wait," I say, repeating Dimitri's words from yesterday.

10

KATE

Something is wrong. I know it.

Kicking off the high-heeled shoes that pinch my toes, I pace the floor of the library. The fire has burned out. It's close to midnight.

Where is Alex? What's taking so long?

Whatever that tattoo means, it's important, or else he wouldn't have run out of here like his life depended on it. He clearly expected trouble because he left with enough men to fill four cars while I helplessly watched their exodus through the window.

I consider calling him for the tenth time, but I don't pick up the phone on the desk. If he's in the middle of something dangerous, the last thing I want is to distract him. Instead, I keep watching the windows. I've opened all the curtains so I can keep an eye on the driveway.

Being shut in the house and not knowing what's

going on is driving me crazy. My stomach is tied in knots.

Movement at the gates draws my attention. Two guards run to the gateposts and stand at attention, one of them talking on a two-way radio. A car's headlights appear. They shine through the bars as the car comes to a stop in front of the gates. Rushing to the window, I grip the windowsill and crane my neck for a better view. The large gates swing open, and a convoy of cars enters.

Not bothering to pull on my shoes, I run to the entryway. As usual, a guard stands in front of the door. It's another reminder that Alex doesn't trust me. The knowledge chafes like a rough rope that's been ripped from soft palms. Whereas he betrayed my trust, I don't deserve his circumspection. I'm not stupid enough to run and put my own life and the lives of everyone I love at risk. I might not trust him with my freedom any longer, but I do trust him with my life. If there's anyone who's ruthless and powerful enough to protect me, it's Alex Volkov. But he is human, a man of flesh and bone, and very much vulnerable to bullets and blades.

My nerves are wreaking havoc on my emotions. I need to make sure Alex is okay.

"Please open the door," I say to the guard.

He stares straight ahead.

"Open the door," I demand in a firmer voice.

Just as I'm about to squeeze around him and do it myself, the door swings inward, letting in a dusting of snowflakes with a flurry of wind. The guard steps aside. When Alex enters, my chest deflates with the breath I was holding. My relief is so great I sag in a spell of weakness, feeling much like I do after an adrenaline crash.

Igor, Leonid, and Dimitri pass behind Alex, making their way around the house, but all my attention is focused on him. For a moment, time stills as we stand frozen, our gazes locked with awareness and knowledge running between us like electric currents.

He could've been killed.

For every minute he's out there, there's a possibility he may never return. Do I want to waste our time together on nursing my anger and protecting my pride? The man I met in New York City was only a part of the complex puzzle that is Alex Volkov. He's so much more than the sophisticated oil tycoon with an unexpected caring side. There are layers to him I'm just beginning to uncover. The man standing in front of me now is one-hundred percent the Russian oligarch who's both admired and feared. This is his home. His history lies here in this palace, in this city, along with everything that shaped him into the man he is. Here, I have an opportunity to *really* get to know him, this dangerous man I gave my heart to. All I have to do is embrace the twisted chance fate has given me.

My throat closes up with fear. Ignorance is bliss. As much as I care about Alex, there's a good probability I won't like the full truth about him. If I push for it, I'm walking off a cliff, falling into an abyss of darkness. I have no idea what awaits me there, but once I open that door, there's no turning back. I'll either love him more or hate what I find.

This could be a new beginning or the end.

The insight is terrifying. If we make it through this, we'll make it through anything. If he's willing to trust me with my freedom and I can make peace with every hidden part of him, our relationship will be built on a rock. Together, we'll be unshakable. However, if our foundation crumbles, I won't have a choice but to walk away. I've done it once, and I'll be strong enough to do it again.

There's only one problem with that scenario. Now that I know Alex better, I suspect I never truly walked away in New York. He was always pulling the strings. Every move he made was perfectly orchestrated. Even when he gave me freedom, he was reeling me in. That freedom was nothing but an illusion.

No, he'll never let me go. If our relationship comes crashing down, there will only be one choice.

I'll have to run.

I tremble a little as insight after insight hits me like a tornado and the verity settles like broken branches in the destruction it leaves behind.

"You can go," Alex says to the guard, holding my gaze as he pulls off a pair of black leather gloves.

The guard salutes and closes the door behind him when he leaves. The click of an electronic lock sounds. The door must be fitted with an automatic locking mechanism.

Alex studies me with unsettling attention as he takes off his boots. "Why aren't you in bed?"

His manner is cool, my earlier rejection sounding like a bee sting in his tone. The distance he keeps is what I wanted a few hours ago, but everything is different now. My insight has brought me to another choice.

I rub my arms. "I was worried sick."

The cold fire in his blue gaze warms a few degrees. "As you can see, I'm fine." A smile plucks at his lips as he unbuttons his coat. "But your concern flatters me—not that I want you to worry."

Stepping closer, I study him for signs of injuries when he takes off his coat. Besides his slightly tousled hair, he looks just like he does when he leaves on a normal workday for the office. "Where did you go?"

"To deal with business," he says, turning his back on me to hang his coat in the closet.

"It has something to do with that tattoo. Did you find out something?"

Facing me slowly, he says, "Quite a lot, actually."

"What?" I ask through parched lips.

He only continues to look at me.

"What, Alex? Tell me. Please don't keep me in the dark. I can't stand it. You have no idea what it feels like to be locked inside, not knowing what the hell is happening and going out of your mind with worry."

He rests his hands on my shoulders in a soothing gesture. "You have an army of men to protect you.

Nothing is going to happen. You don't have to worry about anything."

I twist out of his hold. "Stop patronizing me. How would you feel if you were in my shoes? Would you enjoy it if I locked you in here and went out to where someone wants to kill me without telling you what's going on? Would you be able to go to bed and have a sound night's sleep without knowing whether I'm okay?"

"Katyusha." He doesn't touch me again but beseeches me with his eyes instead. "I'm sorry for making you worry. I understand that this situation isn't easy on you."

I suck in a breath, trying not to cry. I'm not usually a tearful person, but I'm not myself. The current circumstances are getting the better of me.

"Wait for me in the library," he says. "I need a shower. Then we'll talk."

I don't argue. I go back to the library and pace the floor while I wait. Not ten minutes later, he joins me. His hair is still damp, and he changed into a pair of dark pants and a white shirt.

"Come," he says, draping an arm around my shoulders and leading me to the sitting area facing the fireplace. "You need a drink."

He gently pushes me down onto the sofa while he goes to the liquor tray. After pouring a stiff shot of vodka, he carries the glass to me. "Here."

Obediently, I take a sip. "What happened?"

In a blink, he clams up again, a closed-off look coming over his features.

"Please, Alex. Tell me."

"You don't know what you're asking."

"I'm asking you to show me the respect I deserve." Unwaveringly, I hold his gaze. "If you can't give me freedom, at least treat me like an equal in this."

He works his jaw from side to side. "I'm protecting you."

"You're not protecting me by cutting me out of parts of your life. You're keeping me ignorant."

A spark flashes in his eyes. "Are you sure you want to go down this road? There's no returning from this, Katerina."

I swallow. "I've already come to that conclusion."

Silence.

"Don't you believe I deserve your respect?" I ask softly.

"Fine." He takes a step forward, putting us so close that our knees touch. His eyes gleam as he stares down at me. "If you want enlightenment, that's what you'll get. Just remember, your judgment won't change a thing." Placing emphasis on the words, he says, "You're staying."

I've already come to that conclusion too.

A beat passes. When I don't take the opportunity he offers to back out, he gives a resigned nod. "The tattoo you recognized belongs to a gang that operates from a shady district in St. Petersburg," he says.

My mouth goes dry. "You went there."

"Yes," he replies in a level tone.

Our fingers brush as he takes the glass from my hand. I wait quietly for him to continue, unable to look away from his face as he brings the glass to his lips and takes a generous swallow of the liquor.

After another sip, he still says nothing, so I ask, "What did you find?"

Hardness fills his eyes. "The man who attacked you."

My heart thumps with loud beats. "He's here, in Russia? What did he say?"

Alex clenches his jaw. "That Vladimir Stefanov hired him for the job."

"To snatch me?" I still find it hard to believe that someone was planning to abduct me just a few blocks from where I work. Well, where I used to work. "Who is Vladimir Stefanov?"

He hands the glass back to me. "One of the bratva bosses who runs the underworld here."

I drink on autopilot, needing the fortification of the alcohol. "Why?"

"I have no idea." Muscles bunch in his temples. "But I'm working on rectifying that."

A mafia boss wants Alex dead. This is bad, much worse than the rival he imagined. I don't have first-hand knowledge of mafia workings, but I've read enough articles to know you don't want to get on the Russian mob's bad side.

I swallow hard. "Where is he now, this man you interrogated?"

"Dead," he says without batting an eye.

Dead.

The word refuses to register. I'm unable to process it. I stare up at his strong, masculine features as the truth I begged him for wars with denial in my chest.

He regards me with a mocking smile, wordlessly daring me to give sound to the thought in my head. That smile says he expected my judgment, and even so, he has no regrets. He's not sorry for what he's done.

"Say it, Katyusha," he says with narrowed eyes, his tone dangerous despite the endearment.

"You…" My voice is hoarse. I'm breathless with the realization.

"Killed him," he says, finishing what I'm unable to say.

My shock is palpable. It's charcoal black, a smoky odor that hangs in the air over the embers of the dead fire. My boyfriend—if that's what he still is—has killed a man. It's not the first time either. He's much too collected for someone who's committed his debut murder.

"He was a bad guy, Katerina," he says, a warning sharpening his gaze further.

The words slip from my tongue before I can stop them. "Like you?"

His eyes scrunch in the corners as his smile widens.

I didn't mean for that to sound like the judgement he so obviously expected from me, but the world I grew up in is a far cry from his. The people from my world have an inborn objection to killing. Not to mention, the oath I took to save lives won't let me justify taking one.

"Say it," he says again. "Tell me I'm a cold-blooded murderer and a monster. That's what you're thinking."

It's not. I clench my fingers around the glass. I don't know *what* I'm thinking. I thought *shady business dealings* involved handing money under the table to secure a few deals, not this. Yet despite what he's admitted, I can't label the man who conquered my heart a monster. The man who worshipped my body is not cold-blooded. The man who's paying for my mother's treatment isn't an uncaring psychopath.

"What's the matter, Katyusha?" Despite his arrogant smile, a flash of vulnerability passes over his face. "If you can't handle the truth, you shouldn't have asked for it."

"Shouldn't you have delivered him to the police?"

"Sometimes, my beautiful kiska, you can be so naïve." He leans down, resting one hand on the armrest of the sofa and brushing a curl behind my ear with the other. "But that's what I love about you."

"The police—"

"Are corrupt in my country." He straightens. "The bratva owns them."

"All of them?"

"Most of them. More often than not, they act as double agents, not only reporting back to the underworld bosses but also conveniently losing evidence or witnesses."

My throat tightens. "The police in the States—"

"The bratva has government officials from all over the world in its pockets. So does every man with enough money," he says in a harsh voice. "Same goes for successful Russian companies. Connections are essential both for success and survival. I don't trust anyone but myself. It would be stupid to do so." He leans closer again, resting his palms on either side of me on the sofa and trapping me between his arms. "I killed that man not because he was a threat to me, but because he touched you. And I'll kill any other man who lays a hand on you. I'll kill any motherfucker who as much as tries. Understand?"

I flinch at the outburst, my heart crumbling even as conflicting emotions battle inside me.

Alex killed to protect me. I can never condone his behavior, but yes, I understand what he's telling me. He's saying that this is his world and I'm a part of it now, whether I want that or not. He's reminding me that I no longer have a choice. That I never had one.

It's a lot to take in, but I did ask for it, and I don't shy away from the facts.

In the space of two days, I've come to realize that the assault on Alex's life isn't over. I've learned that my life is in danger, and therefore the lives of anyone connected to me. I've had my freedom and my choices stripped away. Most importantly, I've come to understand that Alex won't let me go. Not now, and not ever. And the part that hits me the hardest?

This isn't love for him. It can't be. At best, it's obsession.

Alex straightens. "If you have nothing to say, I suggest we go to bed. It's been a long day."

It has been. My head feels on the verge of exploding. But caring for someone can't be switched on and off with the press of a button. The nurse in me has to ask, "What about you? Are you all right? Did you get hurt?"

He smooths a palm over my hair and rubs a curl between his fingers. "Do you know why I was so attracted to you that first day when I saw you fighting to save Igor's life? Apart from the fact that it was impossible not to notice such a beautiful face and the alluring body under your clothes."

At a loss for words, I can only stare at him.

"You were so focused, so dedicated," he continues, "that you didn't even notice the other people in the room. You only had one goal, and that was to save the life of a critically wounded man. Gunshot wounds are related to criminal activities more often than not. You didn't ask what Igor had done. You didn't care if he was a bad man deserving of death. You saved him without casting judgment. As I watched, I wondered if you were some kind of angel." His gaze is intent on my face. "You fascinated me, Katherine Morrell. That kind of goodness was new to me." Slowly, he traces the line of my jaw. "Do you want to know something else? I was jealous of Igor. I was jealous of the dedication and care you gave him. I wanted you to care for *me*. I wanted the angel all to myself. I needed to know if you were for real." He gives me a soft smile. "And then I took you to dinner and to bed and discovered that's just who you are—pure and beautiful."

My breath catches at the admission. He's placing me on a pedestal, raising me to a level I don't deserve. "I'm not an angel, Alex."

"Maybe, but you're real." He runs a thumb over my lips before pulling away his hand. "Even now, hating me, you're real. You don't pretend to be someone you're not."

I want to say that I don't hate him, but he swivels on his heels and walks out of the room, leaving me with blood on my conscience and the sweetest declaration of obsession.

11

ALEX

*A*part of me hoped I'd never have to expose Katerina to every facet of my life. I wanted her to have the good and pretty portions I worked so hard at building. She doesn't deserve the ugliness, but it's part and parcel of who I am. If I'm keeping her, which I am, it's unavoidable that I peel away every rotten layer and give her the truth. She may hate me, but I'll work hard on winning back her affection.

She *will* give me her love again. I'm a determined man. Once I set my sights on a goal, I never fail to achieve it. I've worked for everything I have. My company, my properties, this palace... nothing was handed to me on a silver platter. I broke my back to build an empire from scratch. I earned every penny with my own two hands. Yes, these hands are dirty, but that's the price for living my lifestyle and not bending a knee to either of the forces ruling my country: the government and the bratva. Yet I've never worked harder for anything than I have for Katerina. I've pursued her with everything I've got. I've gone after her with every resource at my disposal, using every tactic in the book. I'll be damned if I lose her now.

I roll my neck to alleviate the stiffness of my muscles. After changing into pajama bottoms, I walk barefoot into the bedroom. The bed curtains are pulled closed. I slip a finger into the opening and lift the left one. The bed is empty. My kitten is probably hiding somewhere in the house, appalled at the prospect of sleeping next to a murderer.

I drop the curtain and leave the room. I meant it when I said I understood that the situation is hard on her. I said I'd give her space, and that's what I'll do, even though every cell in my body demands I take her to bed and make her say things she can't possibly mean, things I desperately need to hear.

All in good time.

At the study, I punch in a code on the electronic pad mounted on the wall to unlock the door. Until I'm certain Katerina won't run or call the police or the embassy, I'm keeping my laptop and cell phone locked away when I'm home.

Making myself comfortable in the swivel chair behind my desk, I pour another shot of vodka from the bottle Lena left for me and wake up my laptop.

A message from Adrian awaits me.

That was quick.

I upload it to the decryption app and read the text. Adrian did some digging into Stefanov's dealings as I requested. There's no mention of Vadim or the gang. Nothing out of the ordinary jumps out. I check the list of Stefanov's recent movements that Adrian attached. Stefanov had met with Oleg Pavlov, a bratva boss who's big in Moscow, in St. Petersburg a month before the assassin took a shot at me and a day after the event. On both occasions, they met at a club that Stefanov owns near Detskiy Severny Beach. There's no information about the business they discussed, but in between those dates, Stefanov also showed up at Oleg's house in Moscow. I look more closely at that date. It was a couple of days after Katerina was attacked near Romanoff's.

Dread slithers down my spine at the memory. If Katerina hadn't walked into the restaurant that night… If I hadn't been there, having dinner with Mikhail… I can't even think it. I can't put into thoughts what could've happened, never mind into words.

Leaning back in my chair, I take a swig of the vodka as I consider the information.

Vladimir Stefanov and Oleg Pavlov.

The names are familiar, even though I've never had the unpleasant experience of crossing either's path. Like every businessman with a certain net worth in Russia, I know who they are. That's not the familiarity I'm referring to, though. There's something else, a faint memory at the back of my mind. It's a niggling aware-ness, like a word you can't remember that's hovering on the tip of your tongue.

And then it comes to me.

My mind flashes back to the apartment on Vasilevsky Island where I grew up. I remember myself at fourteen, lying on my bed and reading a comic book I'd smuggled into the house. My father didn't want me to read those books. He'd said the pictures would make me too lazy to read.

The hushed voices of my mother and father came to me through the thin walls of my room. They were having an argument. It was rare for them to fight, so rare that I pricked up my ears. That's when I heard them—those names.

Stefanov and Pavlov.

My mother whispered them frightfully. My father replied in a soothing tone, and when he repeated the names, his voice was harsh. A moment later, the sound of pots came from the kitchen where my mother was making *solyanka* for dinner, and the smell of my father's cigarette reached me from the balcony.

Eager to know Batman's fate, I went back to my reading.

The ping of my phone brings me back to the present. I pick it up and check the screen. It's the head of the cleaning team, letting me know the job is done. Vadim's body should be discovered not long after daybreak when his cronies come to collect the goods for their daily deliveries. Stefanov will get my message soon.

Good. I can't wait.

Drumming my fingers on the desktop, I knock back the rest of the vodka. The alcohol slips smoothly down my throat, warming my stomach and loosening my tense muscles. Why did my parents fight about two bratva bosses? My father was a high-ranking police officer. He never discussed work at home, at least not when I was around. Was he a bought man? Did Stefanov or Pavlov own him? Is that why my mother was upset? Because he'd sold information to them? I can see how that would've upset my mother. She was a good woman, a humble person who believed in right and wrong. Corrupt cop is not the image I have of my father, but I was just a kid. I was more interested in forbidden pop culture and in saving enough money for a skateboard than I was in my father's job.

Unable to think about my parents without experiencing the pain that tears my heart out of my chest, I push the nostalgia aside.

How do the dots connect? Is there a link between my parents' conversation and the events of the last couple of months? What's the likelihood of the same names popping up then and now? Stefanov paid Vadim to kidnap Katerina. Did he also pay the man who stole her key card? It's a logical deduction. That means Stefanov most likely paid the assassin who tried to kill me. But why? What does it have to do with my parents, if anything? How does Oleg Pavlov fit into the picture? His meetings with Stefanov around the time of the attacks on Katerina and me could be a coincidence—it's very likely that the two bratva bosses do business together—but the fact that my father mentioned them both raises a big red flag.

I don't have the answers, but I will find them. And when I do, I'll make Stefanov and every man involved in his scheme pay.

Firing up the encryption app, I send another message to Adrian, instructing him to keep sniffing for information on Stefanov and to do the same with Pavlov. I put a handsome sum of money for bribing informants at his disposal and log into my bank account to pay him for the job he's done. Nothing motivates like prompt payment. He'll drop whatever else he's working on to get me the information I need.

The earlier adrenaline has yet to work itself out of my system. I'm too hyped up to be able to sleep. To use the time productively, I take care of the red tape surrounding Katerina's leave of absence. Once all the paperwork is out of the way, I schedule an email to be sent to Joanne at a reasonable time in the morning, asking her what time is convenient for Katerina to videocall her. I might be ruthless, but I'm a man of my word. I said my kiska could have a reward if she behaves, and now that she knows there's no way out, she'll behave if it means that she can speak to her friend. Call it manipulation, but I'm not forcing Katerina's compliance to make *my* life easier. I'm doing it for her. The sooner she adapts to her new situation, the sooner she'll be happy again.

I'm not optimistic about uncovering anything via the hospital security camera tapes. Nevertheless, I log into the real-time workflow to check on the team's progress. As I expected, they haven't found anything.

Hopefully, I'll learn more soon, either from Adrian or the man I've put on Stefanov's tail.

I type a command, telling my security chief, Nelsky, to shut down the search and instead focus on obtaining information on Stefanov and Pavlov's personal and professional operations. I want the blueprints of their homes and their offices. I want to know how many men they have on site and with what weapons they're armed. I want to know how many kids they have, where they go to school, where they keep apartments for their mistresses, what cars they drive, and what their wives eat for breakfast. I want to know every-thing right down to the brand of their underwear. I want to know their strengths but mostly their weak-nesses. I want to know where their protection is breachable. They may seem untouchable, but if you look hard enough, you'll always find a vulnerability.

Standing up, I stretch. Killing Vadim hasn't appeased my fury, not by a long shot. I need a stren-uous workout in the gym. Until I can lay my hands on Stefanov, the punching bag will have to do.

My phone rings just as I reach the door.

It's Igor.

I take the call with, "Yes?"

"I thought you'd like to know that Stefanov is having the house watched. There's a man outside. He's discreet, but we picked him up via infrared."

"Are you sure he's Stefanov's?"

"Yeah. We used a night vision camera and ran the face recognition program."

I smile grimly. We're already like old-time enemies, Stefanov and I, having eyes on each other. I can't wait to crush that motherfucker like a bug under my shoe. "Keep tabs on him."

"Already doing it. He entered a building across the river. He's making himself comfortable on the top floor as we speak."

"Good. Let me know if more men join the party," I say before ending the call.

It's never difficult to smoke termites from the woodworks. You just have to light a fire underneath them.

12

KATE

*D*rowning in guilt over being an accomplice to murder, I spend another two hours in the library. My mind goes round in circles until my brain feels like mush and I can't think anymore.

In the end, Alex gave me an easy out by taking away my choices. There's nothing I can do while being locked up and cut off from the rest of the world—for now, at least—and in a way, I'm grateful. Even if I had access to a phone, I could never tell on Alex. I'd sooner die than send him to prison—but this is not even an option right now. There's no one to call, no one to turn to. I can't trust anyone, not even the police. What's unfolding is bigger than I could've imagined. Two deadly forces are at war, and I'm caught in the middle. All I want is for Alex to get out of this alive. Selfishly, I just want this to be over so we can go back to our lives. I want to work and do what I do best—care for the sick and injured. Most of all, I want to be there for my mom when she comes home from the clinic.

Rubbing the heels of my palms over my eyes, I get up from the sofa. I'm tired, but I doubt I'll be able to sleep. Despite my mental exhaustion, I can't shut down my brain. Tonight's events keep running through my mind.

Maybe some warm milk will do the trick.

Lost in my thoughts, I make my way to the kitchen. As I turn the corner, I bump into a hard chest.

Gasping, I stumble back a step. Strong hands clasp my upper arms to steady me. Off balance, I stare at the naked chest at my eyelevel. A manly dusting of dark hair covers powerful pecs. Broad shoulders and well-cut muscles look as if they were carved from stone. Pajama bottoms ride low on slim masculine hips, exposing the deep lines of abs angling down to the groin. A thicker triangle of hair showing just above the elastic hints at what lies below the thin cotton of the pants. The fabric molds around a heavy cock, drawing a perfect outline of its impressive length, thick girth, and the groove that runs around the head.

Tearing my gaze from the sculpted body in front of me, I finally meet Alex's eyes. He stares down at me with heat sizzling in his blue irises, but his features are schooled.

"Alex," I say, cringing inwardly at how breathless my voice sounds.

He raises a brow. "Looking for something?"

I wet my dry lips. "I was going to warm up some milk."

A hint of sympathy warms his tone. "Are you having trouble sleeping?"

"Like you, it seems."

Crossing his arms, he takes a wide stance. "I need a workout. I was just on my way to the gym."

He's occupying all the space in the hallway, blocking my path. My pulse spikes, partly in anticipation and partly with a need to flee. My body is interpreting our positions as those of a hunter and his prey, and it likes the idea a little too much. It warms to the scenario, sending all of the heat straight to the juncture of my legs.

"I'll just…" Swallowing, I point toward the kitchen.

"Do you want me to get that?"

I blink, struggling to focus through the fog of desire that's invaded my senses. "W-what?"

Lustful intent narrows his eyes. In a low voice, he asks, "Would you like me to warm up some milk for you? I can bring it to the room."

"Oh, no." My reply is rushed. "I'll just, um, you know." Taking a breath, I pull my lecherous self together. "Do you want some?" When the icy blue of his eyes darkens a shade, I add hastily, "Milk. Do you want some milk?"

"Sure," he says slowly. "Why not?"

"Okay."

I move to the left, all but running in my haste to escape his presence. At the same moment, he takes a step to let me pass. The breath leaves my lungs with an *oomph* as our bodies collide for a second time. Like earlier, he catches me, testing my balance with his hands on my waist. I should pull away, but I don't. He should let me go, but he holds on.

Carefully, as if not wanting to scare me with a sudden movement, he wraps his arms around my body and pulls me close. His size and power envelop me, sheltering me from the harshness of our reality. How I've missed the warmth and safety of his embrace. Some of the tension leaves my body as I press my cheek against his chest and absorb the welcome relief of the security he offers. I didn't realize how much I needed the comfort of his touch until now.

Gripping my chin, he tilts my face. When he lowers his head, I don't turn away. I close my eyes and do the scariest thing I've ever done in my life. I step off into the abyss and tumble into the darkness—for better or for worse.

"Katyusha," he says in a rough voice, dragging his lips over my jaw to the corner of my mouth.

The kiss he plants there is dry and light. I've missed how warm and hard his chest feels against mine. I've missed dragging my hands through the soft strands of his short hair. Wrapping my arms around his neck, I act on the fantasy. A groan escapes from deep in his throat as I close my fingers and pull his hair gently in the process. The pressure of his hand on my lower back increases, arching my body as he draws me to him and rubs against me.

The hardness that grows against my hip makes me utter an involuntary moan.

"Yes," he growls, cupping my ass and pressing me tighter while he spears the fingers of his other hand through my hair.

In contrast to the roughness with which he palms my ass cheek, his hold on my nape is tender. Burrowing my face in his neck, I inhale deeply. His skin smells like a seductive mix of cardamom and musky man. His stubble pricks my lips when I bring them to his jaw. Trailing my hands over his shoulders and down to his chest, I trace the grooves that define his muscles. Under the solid slab of strength beneath my palms, his heart pounds with a wild beat. His callused palm catches on the wool of my dress as he smooths a hand down the outside of my thigh.

Skimming his fingertips over my nape, he brings his hand around and folds his fingers around my neck. The touch is possessive and tender. My breathing quickens as he aligns our lips, letting a second of anticipation pass before he presses our mouths together.

Fireworks explode in my belly. The house, the city, Russia, why we're here—everything vanishes as he parts my lips and slips his tongue inside my mouth. He drags in a breath, stealing my air. In response, I gasp into our kiss.

He sweeps his tongue over mine, teasing and testing. When I sag in his hold, all but melting against him, he pulls me closer by the gentle hold on my neck and kisses me with skillful precision. The strokes of his tongue are meticulous, designed to arouse, and he succeeds.

Every inch of my skin is on fire. The heat between my legs turns liquid. My breasts become sensitive and heavy. The way my nipples brush over his chest through the layers of my bra and dress makes me clench my thighs in need.

"Kiska," he groans between kisses, bending his knees and pulling me between his legs.

His erection rubs against me, stimulating just the right spot. Pinpricks of pleasure pierce my clit through my underwear. If he carries on like this, he's going to make me come right here in the hallway.

"Alex," I breathe, pushing on his chest.

He tightens his hold on my ass and neck, preventing me from pulling away, but he does slow the sensual assault of his mouth.

Brushing his lips over my ear, he murmurs, "I need this, Katyusha. How much, you have no idea."

I need him too. I was a fool to think I could fight him. He warned me it was a game I couldn't win, and as always, he was right. I'm a second away from surrendering.

"Let me take care of you," he says in a husky voice. Seductively, his soft lips press the words against my ear. "Let me remind you how good we are together."

I don't need a reminder. I remember only too well.

At my silence, he straightens to look down at me. The intention that sparks in his eyes is no longer out of control. It's more calculated but no less heated. The steely blue pools harden with determination as he holds my gaze, measuring my reaction while he slowly drags his fingers over my collarbone and down my chest. When he reaches the upper curve of my breast, my breath catches. Satisfaction bleeds into his expression. He studies my face with hooded eyes as he continues south, brushing his knuckles ever-so-lightly over my nipple. The tip pebbles into a hard point. Goosebumps run over my body, contracting my skin from the crown of my head to my toes.

The look of satisfaction on his face transforms into victory.

The test is over. The results are indisputable.

He's won.

Offering me a hand, he says, "Come with me."

This is moving faster than I anticipated—we still have a lot to talk about—but I've already made the decision. What's the point of delaying the inevitable?

Reaching out slowly, I place my palm in his. He folds his warm, dry fingers around mine and leads me to the staircase in the foyer. He climbs the steps confidently, like a man who knows he'll be obeyed.

My surrender doesn't come without a price. Shame and wounded pride squeeze my chest as I follow him into the bedroom. My only consolation when he turns me around and pulls down the zipper of my dress is that he'll make me forget.

"I want you," he says roughly, kissing the arch of my shoulder.

I close my eyes, focusing on the sensation of his lips on my skin while blocking out everything else.

He unclasps my bra with efficient, economical movements. A soft click later, the cups give. The temperature in the room is comfortable, but my nipples tighten as the fabric falls away. I stand dead still as he pushes the sleeves of my dress and the straps of my bra down my arms. I don't even dare to breathe. When the dress pools around my waist, he cups my breasts.

The feel of his warm, hardened hands on my naked skin is almost too much. I utter another gasp when he rolls my nipples between his fingers until they extend. Tipping back my head, I steal a glance at his face. He's watching the work of his hands, teasing me with light caresses by drawing infinity patterns around my nipples. He writes invisible words on the tops, sides, and undercurves of my breasts until my clit is swollen and throbbing with need. Too soon, he flattens his palms over my ribcage and drags them over my belly. I bite off a moan when he slips them under the dress.

Dipping both hands inside the elastic of my underwear, he pushes it down along with the dress. The fabric makes a rustling sound as it hits the floor. I'm left standing naked in front of him, his thin pajama bottoms the only barrier between us. He emphasizes that fact by pulling my back against his chest and letting me feel the hot, hard cock between his legs.

"Katyusha," he whispers, placing his hands on my

hips and turning me to face him. "Tell me you want this."

It's not my desire as much as his need to hear the words that makes me give him the truth. "I want you."

I've scarcely uttered the words before he dives for my lips. The earlier tenderness is gone. He claims my mouth with a kiss that devours. Gripping my jaw between the splayed fingers of his broad hand, he walks me backward to the bed while he eats my mouth as if he's starving for my lips.

My knees fold when the backs of my legs hit the mattress. I plop down onto the edge. He comes after me without breaking the kiss, pushing me down at the same time as he crawls over my body. Pinning me down with his fingers locked around my jaw, he tangles our tongues with the fervor of a deprived man. Breathing hard, I trail a hand over his chest, dragging my fingers through the coarse hair. A moan escapes my lips when he diverts to my neck and trails kisses over all the sensitive spots along the arch.

Catching my wrist, he guides my hand to his cock, showing me what he wants. I oblige, stroking his length through the cotton of his pants before squeezing my fingers around his girth. His flesh is hard and hot. Unable to resist, I slip my hand underneath the elastic and close my fingers around the thickly veined velvet skin. A groan reverberates in his chest.

He gives me another second to catch my breath before he goes back to kissing my lips while I work his pants over his hips. Supporting his weight on one elbow, he lifts his hips to help me finish the task. Finally naked, he stretches out on top of me, pressing the lengths of our bodies together. He's hard in all the right places, the personification of virile strength. I need the promise he presses between my legs, but I also need so much more. I need him on more than a physical level.

My jaw aches from our almost violent kissing when he tears his lips from mine to drag them over my body. He doesn't pause at my breasts or at the dip of my navel. Instead, he slides down my body, kneels on the floor, spreads my thighs, and goes straight for my pussy.

Holding my gaze, he licks my folds from top to bottom. The pleasure arches my back. Like earlier, when he caressed my breasts, he teases me by tracing the outline of my entrance with the tip of his tongue, avoiding the spot where I need his touch the most. After every full circle, he licks a little harder and goes a bit deeper, slowly driving me crazy. By the time he's tongue-fucking me, I'm shaking with need. When he finally draws my clit into his mouth and sucks softly, it only takes a few seconds before I come.

The orgasm spreads like languid heat from the center of my legs through the rest of my body. It creeps over me unhurriedly. The pleasure ripples like shockwaves after an explosion, rolling out in slow-motion and leaving goosebumps in its wake.

With one last, long lick, Alex raises his head to look at me. Pressing the pad of his thumb to my clit, he massages in a circle. Immediately, the ebbing need starts to build again. I always believed multiple orgasms were a myth, but Alex has proven me wrong. It's almost too much. I'm oversensitive. Instead of fighting it, I throw back my head and let go. Relaxing my hips, I lie still for him, letting him manipulate my body into another climax.

It takes longer than the first time, but when my release hits, it's quick and intense. The brutal pleasure makes my thighs quake. I'm still riding the high when he says in a hoarse voice, "Move up for me, kiska."

I do as he says, scooting to the middle of the bed. My back has barely hit the mattress before he's crawling over me again, his cock brushing over my inner thigh. Reverently, he kisses my belly and trails soft kisses on the undersides and upper curves of my breasts, working his way to my nipples. The reward for my patience is a sweet kiss on my left nipple. He circles the tip with his tongue before sucking on it with the same gentle treatment he gave my clit, while bringing a hand to my other breast to roll the nipple between his fingers.

I moan when he sucks a little harder. As if I haven't just had two orgasms, my folds swell with arousal. My sex clenches around nothing, begging to be filled, but Alex isn't to be hurried. He moves to the other breast, kissing and grazing my nipple with his teeth while laying a hand over the abandoned one. With his tongue and fingers, he works me into a frenzy, preparing me to take him.

He lifts his head to look at my face as he fists the base of his cock and aligns it with my entrance. Needing to hold onto him, I grip his shoulders.

"Tell me," he says hoarsely, parting my folds with the broad head of his cock. "Tell me if it's too much."

My answer is to wrap my legs around his ass. We've waited two days, and now that I've decided to take this step, I want all of him. He advances cautiously, driving an inch into me. My inner muscles clench involuntarily around the intrusion, but I make a conscious effort to relax and let him inside.

He moves with excruciating gentleness, giving me a few seconds to adapt after every inch he claims. Holding back takes its toll on him. It's evident in the sheen of sweat on his forehead and in the utter concentration etched on his features. When he's finally so deep inside me that our groins are flush together, he cups my face and kisses my lips. The kiss is sweet. It's both a tender compensation for and a subtle warning of what's to follow.

Even two days apart was too long. Alex is too virile, his appetite for sex too insatiable. Framing my face between his palms, he holds my gaze as he pulls out until only the head of his cock is wedged between my folds. He holds still for a second before sliding back in. In spite of his size, my body accommodates him without difficulty. My arousal is slick, aiding his movement. Plus, he took the time to prime me. The stretch is intense enough to be just a little scary. If he's not careful, he can tear me. The tinge of apprehension fuels me with adrenaline, increasing my tolerance threshold, and when his control finally slips, I'm ready.

As if sensing my final surrender, he pulls out and thrusts back. My skin tingles as his cock slides over ultra-sensitive nerve endings. Oral sex with Alex is great, but nothing beats the feeling of him filling me inside. Perspiration beads on his skin as he gives a few softer strokes. His hips fall into a rhythmic pattern, rocking our bodies together. The coarseness of his pubic hair brushes over my clit. The pressure of his groin on the bundle of nerves quickly makes my need climb again. I've never wanted to come so badly.

Wrapping my arms around his neck, I roll my hips to urge him on. He clenches his teeth, trying to hold still when I pull him deeper with my inner muscles.

"Katerina," he warns.

I lift my hips, taking him faster and breaking his pace.

He lets loose with a growl. Pinning my waist to the mattress with his large hands, he keeps me still and pounds into me with a harsher rhythm. With every thrust, the breath leaves my lungs. The roughness is delicious, taking me to the crescendo I crave.

He punches his hips until his face contorts into a mask of tormented pleasure. Raggedly, he orders, "Come for me one more time, kiska."

The sensual sound of his accent washes over my ears. The musky smell of man and sex intoxicates my senses. The connection between us is more than a joining of our bodies. It goes deeper than the heat that coils through my insides, but the pleasure momentarily overpowers all else as my body erupts into flames. The fire incinerates everything, burning away the barriers and protection around my heart, leaving me open, vulnerable, and susceptible to Alex Volkov's loving.

Because it *is* love, but only on a physical level. Even in the midst of mind-blowing sex, I'm lucid enough to understand how this works. I told him I was falling in love with him. He never reciprocated the words. His declaration is to empty his seed in my body, pumping until he's dry and I'm dripping with his release. It's a stamp of possession in the most primitive of ways, an instinctive act of a male leaving his mark.

Panting, I internalize the thoughts that take over as the sensations subside. I'm falling for him a little more every day. The web draws tighter, and like a trapped fly, I'm stuck here with nowhere to go. I have no way to protect myself from being consumed. Alex, on the other hand, doesn't have to suffer that sensation of slow suffocation. He already owns me wholly. He has me right where he wants me.

In his bed.

In Russia.

Pushing up onto one arm, he brushes the hair from my face. His voice is soft. "You're quiet."

"Exhausted," I reply honestly.

He searches my eyes. "What are you thinking?"

"That we didn't use protection."

"You're on the pill."

"Yes, but still."

"We're both clean."

I blow out a breath. "I know." It just seems more intimate and risky. It's a commitment without the safety net of love.

He gives me a surprised look. "You want to go off the pill?"

"No," I exclaim. "Of course not."

"Because if that's what you want—"

"It's hardly a subject up for discussion."

His eyes narrow minutely. "You're right. This isn't the moment. We should wait until after I've dealt with Stefanov."

What? Does he seriously think my refusal is only about the threat on our lives? Pushing away from him, I sit up. "I need a shower."

"Later." He catches me around the waist and drags my back to his chest. "I'll wash you myself, I promise. Stay like this for a while."

"I'll soil the sheets."

"Fuck the sheets. I like the idea of my cum inside you." Pressing a kiss to my ear, he whispers, "Way too much."

The implications of his words make me tense. I'm already a prisoner, not only of Alex but also of my own heart. I won't become a prisoner in blood too.

He curves his body around mine, trapping me in a comfortable but dangerous cocoon. We breathe in tandem while our hearts beat with different tunes. The darkness envelops us as he reaches over and closes the bed curtains.

We lie like that for a long time, awake and slumbering, at peace and at war. We're on the same side but at opposite ends of the spectrum. Even the arms he folds around me are a contradiction in terms. Depending on the perspective I choose, he's either imprisoning me or keeping me safe.

In truth, it's both.

He tightens his hold, pulling me closer, and I lay my hand over his where he cups my breast. Neither of us says the words the other wants to hear.

13

ALEX

*T*he gnawing worry is always present in the back of my mind, even in my sleep, but I wake feeling a little more at ease. The reason is the woman I'm spooning from behind, the woman I'll give my life to protect. Her close proximity calms me. As long as her slender body is pliant and warm against mine, no one can touch her. In the circle of my arms, no one can harm her.

Already hard, my cock rests snugly against the crease of her ass. For a moment, I fantasize about an ass wank, as dirty as the idea may seem, but I wore her out last night. The stress of our fucked-up situation is a lot for a delicate, kind-hearted woman to handle. The filth of the world hasn't desensitized her conscience, the way it has mine. She's like the angel on my parents' grave, a compassionate innocent who saves lives without asking questions. The hell I dragged her into is no doubt exhausting on both a physical and emotional level. She needs her rest.

Reaching for the bed curtain on my side, I pull it open. The room is dark. I check my watch. It's after ten. Even at this time of the year, the sun is up by now, but the heavy curtains in front of the windows keep out the light. I disentangle myself carefully from Katyusha and get up quietly, taking care not to wake her. The darkness is so thick I have to feel around to find my pajama bottoms on the floor. After pulling them on, I use the light of my phone so I don't bump into the furniture on my way to the bathroom, where I grab a robe.

I tie the belt around my waist as I make my way to the kitchen. Tima glances up when I enter. A knowing smile flashes over his face as he shifts his gaze from my unclothed state to the clock on the wall. I never sleep in. It doesn't take a genius to put two and two together, but he's wise enough not to make a comment. I have a high regard for his culinary skills, but my private life is none of his fucking business.

"I left breakfast in the warming drawer," he says. "Omelets with cheese and grilled tomato for the little rabbit."

I narrow my eyes at the term of endearment.

"I look out for her when you're not home," he says, pouring coffee into two mugs. "She could do with a little friendly company."

Only the fatherly way he says that prevents me from planting my fist into his face. Yeah, I'm a jealous asshole, possessive enough not to trust a sixty-year-old cook.

After Tima has set the omelets, quartered oranges, and coffee on a tray, I carry our breakfast back to the bedroom. The path to the sitting area is clear. I make it there without falling over anything and deposit the tray on the table before opening the curtains. Sunlight pours inside. The bright rays catch dust particles in the wedges they cut through the room. The sky is such a brilliant blue that it momentarily hurts my eyes. The thick blanket of snow that covers the ground sparkles like glitter. It's a glorious winter day, a good day for being outside.

The thought knocks my heart off kilter, punching me with an unpleasant dose of guilt. My world turns askew. I've always condemned keeping birds and animals in cages. Knowing I'll be walking through the door into the beauty of the winter's day while keeping my biggest treasure behind the lock of a gilded cage only adds to the weird notion that the pieces of my life are misplaced.

Misplaced, but for a good reason. Neither of us likes this situation, but it's necessary.

Tima is right, however. Katerina needs company, stimulation, and friends. The current arrangement is hardly healthy. Not to mention, I'm not being a good boyfriend. It's her first visit to Russia, and she hasn't seen anything apart from the inside of this house. It bothers me to restrain her freedom, but I'm afraid to let her out. Although… maybe if I plan it to the last detail and take the utmost precaution, I could show her some of the sights. She gave me a huge concession last night, letting me touch her while her heart is still unhappy with me. It's only fair that I show her I'm making an effort too.

To say I'm relieved at finally having access to her body again is an understatement. It's not just the physical relief of blowing off sexual steam. Reclaiming what belongs to me on every intangible level is much more important. I want everything—her body, her thoughts, and her love. She still feels betrayed. I get that. Which is why taking her outside of these walls will be good for both of us. One, it's important for her mental health. Cabin fever has never been conducive to anyone's wellbeing. Two, it will help me get back into her good graces.

The more I think about it, the more the idea grows on me.

The object of my thoughts stirs. A soft sigh escapes her lips as she turns on her back. Her dark hair splays over the white pillow, the waves looking soft and silky. However, the usual glow of her golden skin is absent. She looks so fragile, so utterly vulnerable as she lies there, a tiny shape under the mountain of blankets covering the king-sized bed, that I almost go back on the promise I've just made to myself to take her out.

Her long lashes lift. Blinking, she takes in the room. Her rich hazel gaze settles on me.

I feel the smile that stretches my lips somewhere behind my breastbone. It drifts to the cavity between my ribs and settles there with bittersweetness. "Good morning, my love. I brought you breakfast."

Clutching the sheet to her chest, she sits up. "What time is it?"

"Don't worry about the time. You needed your rest." I pick up the tray and carry it to the bed. "Tima made omelets."

"That smells good," she says with a weak smile.

"You must be starving." Heat shades my voice as I add, "After last night."

A flush works its way over her cheeks. She's not shy about sex or her body. What bothers her is her surrender. I know my kiska well enough to understand that she feels like she's lost a battle. Well, too bad. Our relationship isn't a war she should be fighting.

Balancing the tray on one hand, I put a plate and mug on the nightstand on her side. She watches me with her lip caught between her teeth, her waves deliciously untamed. I've always found a woman who's just woken up sexy. There's something alluring about that natural beauty before it's been touched by brushes and makeup, and there's no woman sexier or more alluring than my Katyusha, even when she's scrunching the sheet in her small fist as if her honor depends on it. We finally took ten steps forward last night. I'm not going to let her hide from me now and take us five steps back.

Hooking a finger into the sheet between the curves of her breasts, I tug gently. She holds on, clenching her fingers tighter. I don't let her off the hook. This isn't a war. There's nothing to lose. I'm not stripping her of her dignity or pride. I simply want things between us the way they used to be. I want her to be comfortable with her nakedness around me, like she'd been the morning after the very first time I'd claimed her.

After another beat of me tugging and her pulling, she lets go. The fabric slides over her breasts and pools around her waist, unveiling her like a stunning life portrait. Unabashedly, I stare at her curves and the pert pink nipples that top them like cherries. My cock comes to life, tenting my pajama bottoms and showing her in no uncertain terms what she does to me.

Her gaze moves south. She only graces my erection with her attention for a second before she focuses on my face.

My smile is like a door hanging on one hinge—crooked and unstable. I have a good mind to forget about food and have her for breakfast, but in the light of day, she's skittish. The moon was kind. It let us hide in the shadows and commit sins we can't face under the judgment of the sun. That's all right. I have patience, a lifetime of it where she's concerned.

"The food is getting cold," I say, breaking the tension by walking to my side and getting in under the covers next to her. I move carefully, making sure I don't topple the tray, and when I'm settled with my back against the headboard, I balance the tray on my lap.

She gingerly reaches for the plate on her nightstand. Once she's installed herself comfortably, I hand her a fork.

"Thank you," she says, watching me from under her lashes.

I choose a safe topic to keep the conversation light. "I told Tima you like omelets."

She takes a bite and hums her approval as she chews. The simple fact that she's enjoying the food warms my chest.

"Tima said he's cooking vegetarian portions for me," she says. "You don't have to cater to me. I'm used to adapting."

"You're my guest, Katyusha."

Her hand stills midway in the air, the fork hovering in front of her mouth. Too late, I realize my mistake. That was a bad choice of words.

Instead of commenting, she takes another bite, brushing the ugliness aside as if pretending it's not there will make it vanish.

Eager to maintain a pleasant mood, I say, "I'd like to take you sightseeing today."

She looks at me quickly. "Really?"

Her enthusiasm makes me grin. "I promised to show you St. Petersburg, didn't I?"

Her slender throat bobs as she swallows. "What about safety?"

Brushing a curl behind her ear, I say, "Don't worry. I'll take care of the security."

As I dig into my omelet, I make a mental note to tell Dimitri to plan a route and scout the roads in advance.

I'll have to station men on every corner and have snipers on the roofs. It'll be a mission to organize, but nothing is too much effort for her.

"Thank you," she says with a small frown, as if she's doubting my motive.

I can't resist kissing her cheek. "You're welcome."

The fact that she doesn't flinch or pull away further warms my heart.

Glancing at me, she asks after another forkful of omelet, "Will you show me where you grew up?"

The request catches me off guard. I expected her to ask about the Peterhof Palace or the Fabergé Museum, the usual tourist sights. "Why do you want to see that?" The prospect of going there tightens my stomach, not that there's anything left to visit.

Fiddling with her napkin, she averts her eyes. "I thought it would be good to, you know…"

"Good to do what?" I ask gently.

"To get to know you better." She shrugs. "There are many things about you I don't know."

She sounds almost guilty and definitely apprehensive. She tries to hide her reaction, but she's not a natural liar. There's something more to delving into my history than she's letting on. Even so, *getting to know me* hints at making an investment in our relationship, which I like.

Scratching my jaw, I consider what to tell her. I don't normally talk about my parents, but she deserves the truth.

I finish the last bite on my plate, knowing I'll lose

my appetite once I delve into the past, and set the plate aside. "I grew up on Vasilevsky Island, but there's no point in going there. There's nothing left of where I used to live."

She frowns. "Why? Was your building demolished?"

"No." Strain locks my jaw.

Her brown eyes soften. "You don't have to talk about it. I didn't mean to pry. I just wanted—"

"No," I say again. "You're right. You'll never have the opportunity to meet my parents like I did with your mother. It's good that you're asking."

She waits quietly.

"There was a gas leak in our building," I continue. "The whole top floor blew to pieces."

"Alex." Gasping, she lays her hand on my arm. "Were they…?"

"Yes."

Empathy fills her tone. "I'm so sorry."

"Eleven people were killed. I was at school when it happened."

A man from my father's unit relayed the news to me in the headmaster's office. With a stony face and factual words, he told me I was going to live in an orphanage. In just a few seconds, he condemned me to one of the cruelest systems in my country, one that was notorious for preying on the children it was supposed to protect.

I may have been more interested in comic books than in asking my father about his day, but at fifteen years of age, I knew enough to understand my fate. The bodies of children who'd been in the system turned up only too often. Every time my father opened a new case, my mother would light a candle. I could tell how many kids had died by the number of evenings a candle burned in the windowsill.

"I can't even imagine how hard that must've been for you," Katerina says, squeezing my arm.

"There was nothing left of my home. I couldn't go back to pack a bag. They took me straight to a halfway house, a dump on the smelly side of the Neva River's banks. The first night, I ran away."

She makes a small sound of distress. "You ran away?"

"What else could I do?" I don't give her the colorful details of the future that would've awaited me as a so-called system child.

Staring at me in shock, she asks, "All alone?"

"I was fifteen, man enough to brave the streets and earn a living."

She trails her fingertips over my forearm. "How?"

Her intention is to provide comfort, but my body heats at the innocent touch. Even the subject isn't enough to turn me off when she puts her hands on me. "I was lucky enough to secure a job as a delivery boy in a pharmaceutical company. The job can be dangerous. Delivery boys are often attacked, and the pharmaceuticals they transport stolen for the black market. Not many people have the stomach for it. I was good at defending myself, and the head of the division took notice. He favored me with extra work. It allowed me to save enough money to enter a business school at the age of nineteen. When I graduated, I landed a job in an oil company."

"What happened then?"

Many years of bitter determination and back-breaking work. Taking my mug, I watch her from over the rim as I drink my coffee. "What do you want to know?"

"How did you end up as a powerful business magnate who speaks several languages?"

I smile. "Do you think because of my background I can't be an educated man?"

A flush darkens her cheeks. "That's not what I meant."

"It's all right." I finish my coffee. "You're not the only one who's asked me that question. I worked my way up and made a few good investments. I parlayed those funds into searching for oil in an area of Siberia that my employer had dismissed but that I thought held a lot of promise. I was right. I struck gold, discovering a large oil reserve. That allowed me to start my own oil company and then branch out from there."

She regards me with fascinated interest. "What about learning to speak all those foreign languages? Did you also go to language schools?"

"I've always enjoyed reading, and I pick up languages quickly. A crash course usually does the trick."

She pulls her hand away from my arm and drops it

in her lap. "Your parents would be proud of what you've achieved."

I doubt that very much. My mother would be horrified at the crimes I've committed to get to where I am, but as long as I'm at the top of the food chain, I'm willing to make the sacrifice.

Handing Katerina a wedge of orange from the tray, I say, "I have some arrangements to make before we can go out. How about we have lunch in the old city and visit a few sights around there? I want to be back before sunset."

"Okay." Either excitement or relief brightens the honey flecks in her eyes.

"Given the time difference, you probably won't speak to Joanne until tonight," I say.

She bites into the flesh of the orange. "You'll really let me chat with her?"

"I can do better than that." Catching a drop of juice that runs down her chin with my thumb, I bring the pad to my mouth and lick it clean. "How about a video call?"

Her eyes grow large. "Really? That's not too risky?"

"I just need some time to put a few measures in place." With a warning, I add, "It won't happen every day."

"Thank you," she says, looking almost like the Katerina of old.

The fact that she's thanking me for a call that should be her right to make says a lot about how twisted this situation truly is. Not wanting to linger on that fact, I lean over and kiss her lips. They're sticky with sugar and taste of winter fruit. We never did have that shower I promised her. Like a selfish bastard, I didn't want to wash the stamp of my possession off her body. If anything, I want to come all over her and rub my cum into her skin.

The smell of citrus explodes in the air as she bends the peel to eat the orange. I put my mug aside and then do the same thing with hers before leaving the tray on the floor. The widening of her gaze when I take the peel from her hand and carelessly discard it says she knows what's to follow even before I pin her down.

14

KATE

*A*fter we shower together, Alex leaves me to get ready while he takes care of the arrangements for our lunch and tour of the city.

As I brush out my hair in front of a mirror, my cheeks heat at the recollection of how we spent an hour after breakfast in bed. The sex had been down-right wicked. A lot of dirty Russian words and loud moaning had been involved. I hope the walls are thick.

I haven't forgiven Alex, but I can't deny that I need him, now more than ever. I can't help but enjoy his company both in and out of bed. What's the point of running from the truth? I can't pretend he doesn't affect my feelings.

What he told me about his past has shocked me. I can't imagine how tough it must've been to survive on his own at such a young age. To achieve what he has, and with no support, took an enormous amount of self-drive. My respect for him has multiplied tenfold. I can only admire his determination, intelligence, and skills. Not many people, if dealt the same cards, would end up where he has. His sad but victorious history only confirms what I already know.

Alex never gives up. He always gets what he wants.

My hand shakes a little as I set the brush aside. I'm both excited and nervous about getting out of the house. Living in constant fear is new to me, and I've yet to learn how to deal with it.

A knock on the door startles me from my thoughts.

"Katyusha?" Alex calls. "We're good to leave a little earlier. We can go as soon as you're ready."

"I'll be down in ten minutes."

"Take your time."

Not wanting to make him wait, I quickly grab some clothes. In five minutes, I'm dressed in a pair of jeans, a wool sweater, and boots. When I come down the stairs, Alex is talking on the phone in Russian in the foyer. A few guards buzz around, carrying laptops and other equipment outside. Lena stands quietly next to the coat closet.

Alex has his back turned to me, giving me time to study how well his body fills out his clothes. A black button-up shirt stretches over his broad shoulders, and dark pants hug his sculpted ass. His bicep flexes under his shirt sleeve as he presses the phone to his ear with his left hand. A fancy watch and a chunky silver bracelet are visible on his wrist where the cuff has been pulled up. He looks like a walking billboard for a high-end men's designer clothing brand. A whiff of cardamom and cedar reaches me at the bottom of the staircase. He's such a perfect combination of everything that's deliciously male that it almost hurts to look at him.

Judging by his professional tone, he's discussing business. Spoken in his deep voice and with his commanding attitude, the foreign words sound sexy, even when they're work-related. Alex Volkov not only exudes power; he drips with sex appeal. It's not often that I have the chance to observe him unnoticed. I'm the one who's usually pinned under his dissecting stare. Making the most of the opportunity, I burn the incredible way he looks, sounds, and smells into my memory, so I can enjoy the stolen moment again later.

My steps are quiet on the carpet. I stop at a distance to give him privacy to finish his call. As if sensing my presence, he turns. A steely gaze collides with mine. The blue of his eyes warms several degrees as he takes me in from top to bottom. His visual evaluation contracts my skin as if he were running his fingertips over my body. The heated appreciation he shows for everyone present to see sends sparks to my belly. He finishes his conversation with a few short commands, sounding as in charge as ever while simultaneously devouring me with his stare.

Only Alex can direct his attention to two places at once and control both with precision and power.

Ending the call, he pockets his phone. "Ready?"

Sexual tension runs thick in the air. Our awareness of each other is visceral. It always has been, right from the start. Alex is an incurable disease. No matter what happens, I'll never get him out of my system. He's gotten too deeply under my skin.

Not trusting my voice, I nod.

Lena takes my coat from the closet and hands it to Alex. He helps me put it on before taking his own.

When we've finished pulling on our scarves and gloves, he offers me his arm. "Let's go."

The guard at the door opens it to let us out. Five cars are on the driveway. Men in dark coats wait next to the cars. They're dressed casually, presumably to blend in on the streets, but when the man in the front bends to get into the car, his coat falls open, revealing a gun in a body holster.

Alex and I get into the car in the middle. Yuri is in the driver's seat. He gives me a nod in the rearview mirror as he starts the engine. Alex says something to him in Russian, at which he pulls off.

Two cars lead the convoy, and two tail us. Alex takes my gloved hand in his and keeps it on his lap, caressing my knuckles with his thumb, but his attention is aimed outside. Tension fills the car as he keeps a vigilant eye on the surroundings. My muscles tighten. He wasn't this preoccupied on the drive from the airport to the house.

"Is something the matter?" I ask.

Turning his face to look at me, he makes a visible effort to relax his features. "Everything is fine."

I search his eyes. "Really?"

"I'm just being careful. How does your saying go? Better safe than sorry."

Why do I get the feeling there's something he's not telling me? "If the risk is too big, we can stay at home. I don't mind."

His expression softens. "We're fine. It's a beautiful day to be out. You deserve it."

Do I? Then why do I suddenly feel so guilty? I don't want to be the reason Alex risks our lives. I don't want him to get killed just because I couldn't handle a little claustrophobia.

"Alex?" I close my fingers around his hand. "Let's turn back. There's so much to do at home. There's a gym and a pool and a sauna. I haven't even explored the home theater yet. And Tima's cooking is better than any restaurant's, right?"

"Hey." He brushes his knuckles over my cheek. "Don't worry, kiska. I'd never take an uncalculated risk, not with your life."

"I don't need to go out and see the sights. I'm happy to—"

"Shh." Leaning over, he kisses my lips. "I want to do this. Now just relax and enjoy the day. That will make me very happy."

Not wanting to throw the enormous sacrifice back into his face, I shut my mouth and try to show him the gratitude he deserves.

"Excuse me," he says, taking his phone from his pocket. "I have to make a couple of calls."

For the rest of the drive, Alex is occupied on his

phone. From the firm tone of his voice, it sounds as if he's giving instructions. He could be talking to someone at his office, but my guess is the calls have something to do with securing our safety.

When we park in the old city, the men accompanying us get out first. Half of them clear a path while the other half surround us as Alex helps me out of the car.

Despite the army of men and the disconcerting meaning of their presence, I pause on the sidewalk to take in the scene.

The clear blue sky forms a perfect backdrop for the historic buildings. I read up on St. Petersburg after Alex first suggested bringing me here. The domed towers are a distinguishing characteristic of Russian Revival architecture. The colors are so vibrant they look like icing sugar on cupcakes. St. Petersburg on a clear winter day is magical.

Wrapping my arms around myself, I brave the icy breeze as Alex shelters me against his body and leads me down the street. While I stare at the gorgeous buildings, he sweeps the surroundings, his gaze alert.

After a short walk, we reach the Church of the Savior on Spilled Blood. With the snow covering its domes, it looks as if powdered sugar has been sifted over a rainbow cake. It's breathtakingly beautiful. Alex takes a selfie of us in front of the church that he sends to Joanne and my mom before we continue on our exploration. By lunchtime, we've visited the Palace Square, the State Hermitage Museum, and St. Isaac's

Cathedral. Since my face and feet feel frozen, I'm grateful when we enter a warm restaurant and take a table next to the window. It doesn't surprise me that the restaurant is empty.

"Did you book out the whole place?" I ask Alex when he seats me.

He offers me a smile as he takes the chair opposite me. "I like my privacy."

"So you've said," I say, studying him as he picks up the menu.

Our dining alone has more to do with keeping us safe than wanting privacy, I'm sure, and the fact that he's downplaying it to put me at ease only makes me appreciate his effort more.

"Would you like me to order for you?" he asks. "We could share a selection of starters if you'd like."

Holding out my hand, I say, "I'll have a shot at it."

A broad smile warms his face as he hands me the menu. "I admire your eagerness to learn."

The double meaning of his words sends heat to my cheeks. He taught me dirty Russian words in bed this morning, and I'm still marveling at how much power an ill-pronounced *"ya hochu tvoy chlen"*—"I want your cock"—had on him. When I repeated the phrase he'd whispered in my ear, he turned animalistic. The memory alone is enough to turn my underwear damp despite the fact that we're in a restaurant.

Pushing the erotic flashback aside with effort, I skim over the dishes listed on the menu. I've studied enough Russian words in New York to order mushroom *pelmeni*, which are dumplings served with sour cream.

Alex gives me an approving look. "Great choice. I didn't know you were improving your Russian on the sly."

I brush it aside with, "I've picked up a few words." I don't tell him I was planning on ordering a self-study course before we left New York. I'm not ready to admit how serious I'd been about us before he shoved me onto a plane. He has enough power over me as is. He doesn't need an ego boost.

"I'm impressed anyway," he says, ordering the meat *pelmeni* when the waiter comes to our table.

The boiled dumplings are soft on the outside and fluffy inside. The tangy sour cream complements the savory flavor of the mushrooms perfectly. After a steaming cup of Russian Earl Grey tea, I'm fortified and ready to brave the cold again.

We spend the rest of the afternoon shopping. Alex takes me to a few boutiques, all of them suspiciously empty of customers. He twists my arm into letting him buy clothes for me and gifts for my mom and friends at home. At his insistence, I select a miniature Fabergé egg replica encrusted with rubies for my mom and one with emeralds for Joanne—never mind that I have no idea when I'll be able to give it to them. He loads armfuls of hand-painted matryoshka dolls into one of our guards' arms for my colleagues at the hospital and pays for everything with his credit card. When we finally make our way outside with a pile of parcels, the sun is almost setting.

The drivers have been following us, the cars always parked nearby on the curb. Alex steers me to the car Yuri is driving and helps me into the back while the men load our parcels into the trunk.

Once we're settled inside, I turn to him. "Thank you, Alex. That was an amazing experience."

"You're welcome." He puts an arm around my shoulders and pulls me against him. "I'm glad you enjoyed it."

His smile is warm, but the tension doesn't leave his features. Even as he presses a kiss to my forehead, his attention is trained outside, as if he expects trouble at any moment.

Lena greets us as we enter the house, telling us that Tima has left refreshments in the library to hold us over until dinnertime.

"You go along," Alex says. "I'll be right there."

I stare after him as I remove my coat, unable to suppress my worry. Igor and Leonid enter with our parcels, carrying them upstairs. I haven't seen much of the guards since we arrived in Russia. They stay in the barracks and don't talk to me when I'm with Alex. I linger, taking my time to remove my scarf and gloves.

When they come back downstairs, I busy myself with putting everything in the closet.

Leonid exits first. Just before Igor steps through the door, I put a hand on his arm, holding him back.

He frees himself carefully. "Is there something I can do for you, Kate?"

"Alex has been very tense this afternoon," I say, keeping my voice down. "Has something happened?"

He glances at the top of the stairs. "Nothing's happened. He's just taking the necessary measures to make sure it stays that way."

"It went all right today, didn't it?"

"Surprisingly."

I swallow. "Did you expect trouble?"

"It would've been foolish not to."

"Then why did Alex risk going out?"

"It was a calculated risk," he says in a level voice. "If something were to have gone down, you would've been well protected."

"But you didn't like the idea," I say, trying to read him.

"It's my job to protect both of you. I don't like taking any risks, no matter how small or well managed."

"What are you really saying, Igor?"

"This house is the best-protected place you can be. If I were you, I wouldn't ask Alex to go on another adventure."

"I didn't ask," I exclaim in a whisper. "It was Alex's idea."

"Yeah, well, maybe you should dissuade him of those ideas. I'm sure you can find effective ways of occupying him here."

I pull my back straight. "That was an inappropriate remark."

"If you don't want my opinion, don't ask."

He nods at the guard, who opens the door.

"Igor," I say when he steps through the frame. "What's gotten into you?"

He pauses on the threshold. "Look, we're all tense about what's going on. It's rubbing off on everyone, that's all. As I said, Alex wouldn't have taken the risk if he hadn't been damn sure he could protect you. It just took a hell of a lot of resources and energy that could've been better spent."

"Right."

"Ah, hell." He throws his hands in the air. "That's not what I meant."

"It's okay," I say, backtracking toward the hallway. "I get it."

"Kate." He tips his face toward the sky. When he looks back at me, his expression is composed. "I didn't mean you're not worth the effort. I only meant our priority needs to be catching the fucker who wants Alex dead."

"I couldn't agree with you more," I say, my stomach knotting at the reminder of the problem we're facing.

"Just forget I said it. You're caught in the middle of a war, and we don't even know what it's about. It's not your problem or your fight. We'll handle it."

"You're wrong," I say, a little too forcefully. "I'm a part of Alex's life, and that makes this my fight too, whether I like it or not."

"Leave the dirty work to us. We'll catch the bastard." Turning on his heel, he walks away.

The guard shuts the door behind him and takes up his position in front of it, making a silent but strong statement.

Contemplating Igor's words, I go to the library. Admittedly, I enjoyed the day and I'm more than grateful for Alex's consideration. Yet I can't help but agree with Igor. We should keep a low profile until we're safe again.

A tray with tea and delicate cakes is on the table in front of the fireplace. Someone made a fire. The flames leap up the chimney, radiating welcome heat. I pour a cup of tea and am about to take a seat when Alex enters, carrying his laptop.

"Joanne is available now," he says. "Would you like to chat with her?"

I nearly drop the cup in my eagerness. "I'd love to."

He puts the laptop on the table and activates the connection. A second later, my friend's face appears on the screen. From the logo on the wall in the background, she's in one of the meeting rooms at her office. It's almost six o'clock here, which means she must be on her eleven o'clock coffee break. Her red curls form a copper frame around her pretty face. There's a glow on her cheeks and a sparkle in her eyes when she leans closer to the screen.

"Hey," she says. "There you are, elopers."

"Jo." I take a seat on the sofa. With everything that's happened, it feels as if I haven't seen her in weeks instead of days. "How are you?"

Alex sits down next to me.

"Same old on my side. The question is how are *you*?" She looks from me to Alex. "How's Russia? Thanks for the selfie, by the way. The scenery is spectacular." Winking, she adds, "You could've told me about your plans."

"It was a surprise for Katerina," Alex says, resting a hand on my knee. "She didn't know."

"Wow." Joanne makes big eyes. "That's a biggie. Careful, Alex. You'll win the boyfriend of the year award."

He clears his throat. "How's Ricky?"

"Busy. He has an exhibition coming up in the new year. We hope you'll be there."

"We'll try our best to make it," Alex says.

She turns her attention to me. "When are you planning on coming home?"

I glance at Alex.

"We're playing it by ear," he says. "Katerina has been working too hard. She's taking a much-needed leave of absence."

"Really?" Joanne says, not hiding her surprise. "And the hospital let you?"

"I was heading for burnout," I say, cringing inwardly at the lie. "It was either granting me extended leave or accepting my resignation."

She blinks. It's the first she's hearing of my supposed burnout. I can almost see the wheels turning in her head, the suspicions forming. But then she must decide I've simply been swept off my feet because she says with a sly smile, "I'm sure they don't want to lose you. And you're right. You deserve the break. What about Thanksgiving and Christmas? Will you be spending the holidays there?"

"We haven't discussed that yet," Alex says.

If she notices that he keeps his answers vague, she doesn't comment. I'm guessing she's decided we're madly in love and doesn't want to get in the way of that. Instead, she splays her hands and asks cheerfully, "So, are you having fun?"

Infusing my tone with as much excitement as I'm capable of, I tell her about the sights I've visited and the food I've tried.

Joanne grins. "You make it sound so beautiful. Russia is definitely going on my bucket list."

"You and Ricky will have to come visit." Alex draws patterns around my knee with his forefinger. "There's plenty of room here for you to stay."

Goosebumps run over my skin, making me shiver.

Her grin widens. "That's very kind. We'll definitely consider it." Then she glances at something to the side and her face falls. "Oh, shoot, I have to go to a meeting. I'll call you again soon."

"Sure," I say, already regretting having to say good-bye. "Don't work too hard."

"Send me more pictures." She blows me a kiss before the screen goes black.

There's a moment of silence, during which I process a strange sense of loss. A part of me already feels disconnected from my old life.

Alex closes the laptop.

"Thank you," I say, keeping my tone upbeat. He has enough on his plate. He doesn't need an emotional girlfriend too. It's probably just PMS.

"You're welcome, my love."

We sit like that for a moment, neither of us saying anything.

"Would you like a cup of tea?" I ask to break the silence.

"No, thanks. I have to get back to work." He stands. "I have to attend a function in a couple of weeks. It will be a formal affair. I'd like you to come."

Igor's words still ring clearly in my mind. "I don't know, Alex. Do you think it's a good idea?"

"I wouldn't have suggested it if I thought it was a bad idea," he says with a quirk of his lips.

I leave my untouched tea on the tray. "Maybe it's best if I stay at home."

He narrows his eyes, giving me one of those piercing looks that sees right into my soul. "It'll send the wrong message if I go alone."

"What message?"

"That I don't respect you."

I blink. "Why would people think that?"

"When a man keeps a woman in his house but

175

doesn't show her off in public, he's telling the world what her place in his life is in no uncertain terms."

"That she's his mistress?"

"Exactly. You're not a dirty secret I have to hide."

"My reputation is hardly worth your life." Or our lives, for that matter. "In general, do you have to go?"

He nods. "Not going will make me look like a coward. We can't let our enemy think we're scared. That's what he wants. I'm having the gala venue secured. I'll have men there before, during, and after the event. Besides, a lot of powerful government officials and private sector leaders will be attending. The security will be top notch." When I don't reply, he says, "Aside from the fact that I refuse to hide with my tail between my legs, my presence is imperative."

My hands turn clammy as I think about everything that can happen at a public event. "Why? What do you mean?"

"I'm in the process of entering into a joint venture with a company that manufactures small, portable nuclear reactors. If the Russian government gives the green light to this technology, we'll be able to provide clean, affordable energy to many of the outlying communities here and in the neighboring countries. This gala will bring together the key players in the energy sector and their decision-making government counterparts. If all goes well, it will speed up the approval of this technology."

Of course. Now that I know he grew up on the streets, I understand why this is important to him.

There's more to this event than advancing his business agenda. It's evident from the passionate way he talks about it.

"All right," I say, not that I really have a choice. Pretending to give me one is just a way of soothing my bruised feelings. It's like inflicting a cut and making it better by sticking on a Band-Aid.

"Good." He offers me a disarming smile. "I'll make sure you have an appropriate dress."

15

ALEX

The morning is gray. I open the bedroom curtains wider. Thick clouds hang in the sky. Snow is forecasted from late morning onward. The river looks dark in the grainy black-and-white picture of the cold day. Just as well I took Katerina out yesterday when the weather was clear.

In the garden, the men are doing their rounds. I probably shouldn't stand naked in front of the window.

Turning my back on the monochromatic winter image, I face a much prettier view. My kiska is sleeping on her stomach with her small hand on my pillow. The covers have shifted down, revealing the golden skin of her naked back. My cock hardens even though I had her less than an hour ago. I'd woken her at nine with my face buried between her legs. I'd been gentle, knowing she was half asleep. The sex was sweet. Vanilla. But I'm far from sated. My body demands more. With her, I always need more.

My plan was to go downstairs in search of breakfast. I have meetings scheduled at the office. After taking the day off yesterday, there's a lot of work to catch up on. I really should go get our breakfast, but instead, I walk over to the bed. With every step, lust heats my veins. By the time I reach the edge of the mattress, my body is primed with wicked intentions. I want to bury myself so deep inside her that there will be no question as to whom she belongs. I want to pummel her pussy until I've eradicated this need that consumes me. The satiation will only last half a day before I'll need her again, but at least it will afford me a few hours to focus on work.

I pull the covers slowly from her body until she lies exposed in front of me. Her legs are slightly parted, giving me a glimpse of the delicate pussy between them. Partly obscured, it's like a hidden treasure. The illusion of being unobtainable—out of sight and out of reach—makes it all the more alluring.

Climbing onto the bed, I crawl over her body. My cock pulses with need. The simple brush of the sensitive head over the silky skin of her inner thigh contracts my balls. The base of my spine tingles as my whole body tightens with pleasure. I straddle her hips and fist the base of my cock. A drop of pre-cum spills from the slit. Using it as lubrication, I rub the crest over the pink, plump folds between her legs.

Katerina stirs. She makes a sleepy sound, followed by a throaty moan as I get her wet. Her body responds beautifully. In an instant, she's slick. I wrap an arm around her waist and lift her lower body. Before she's fully awake, I'm already sinking inside her. Her body is supple and soft from sleep, her inner muscles easily letting me in.

Gasping, she gives me a startled look from over her shoulder. "Alex?"

I plant a reverent kiss on her spine. "Morning, kiska."

"What are you doing?"

I pull almost all the way out. "Isn't it obvious?"

She stretches around me, pretty like peaches and cream. Her back arches as I slam back in, her breath leaving her lungs on another gasp, but the moan she utters tells me she likes this.

Sliding out slowly, I admire the view. I like that she shaves. I like to see everything. From this angle, she's more open to me. I can watch as well as touch. Both her clit and rosebud asshole are accessible.

I cup her breasts and pull her into a kneeling position. Her nipples are already hard little pebbles, a telltale sign that she's turned on. I rub my palms over the tips, enjoying the slight weight of her curves for a moment before I smooth my hands over her sides to her waist to test her balance. When I'm certain she's stable, I start pumping my hips with an easy pace. Her body sways rhythmically to my beat. She's a beautiful instrument to play, and all her songs are mine.

Even at the slight escalation of my pace, pleasure already draws my cock harder. I thicken inside her as her inner muscles grip me like a velvet fist. I'm not going to last long. Slipping a hand around her body and between her legs, I pull back the hood of her clit with the pad of my thumb. I use my other thumb to press on her back opening, massaging with just enough pressure to add stimulation without risking accidentally hurting her by penetrating the tight ring of muscle.

"Alex," she cries out softly, sounding half panicked and half euphoric.

"Shh." I rub her clit and asshole with lazy circles. "I'm not going to take your ass. Not yet."

Her breath catches as she glances back at me, her eyes large with uncertainty.

If she's an anal virgin, she'll need a lot of preparation before she'll be able to take me. My pulse quickens at the idea of claiming that tight little hole, my lust burning out of control, but for now, I just let her get used to being stimulated on that forbidden spot.

When her moans get louder and she's scrunching the sheet in her fists, I pick up my pace and rub her trigger buttons harder. Our bodies rock in tandem as I thrust so deep that my groin spanks her ass. I move harder and faster, until the sound of our flesh slapping together drowns out her moans.

The way all her muscles pull tight is my cue that she's about to come. My release threatens to explode when she clenches around my cock, milking me, pulling me deeper. I grit my teeth, ignoring the raging need to spill already, and ride out her orgasm without breaking my speed. Only when she goes slack and collapses with her upper body flat on the mattress do I let go. The climax hits me like a cyclone. White-hot heat erupts as I empty my body inside hers. I pump until I'm dry before stretching out over her with my weight supported on my elbows.

Her panting is erratic, her ribs expanding and contracting with fast breaths. Brushing her hair over her shoulder, I kiss her nape and the arch of her neck. She smells of peaches. I can't resist sucking on the spot where her neck meets her shoulder, leaving a mark. My mark. If I could, I'd stay inside her and fall asleep like this, but I'm already late for work.

Regretfully, I pull out. She moans.

I kiss the shell of her ear. "Don't move."

Leaving her in a disarray of tangled, sex-drenched sheets, I wet a washcloth with warm water in the bathroom and carry it back with a towel. Once I've cleaned her up, I take out something I got for her from my dresser drawer.

I sit down next to her and show her the small box and the lube.

"What's that?" she asks with a frown, pushing up onto her elbows.

A wicked smile curves my lips. "I want your ass, Katyusha. I want every part of you." Lifting the lid of the box, I show her the silicone bullet with the sparkly head. "But I need to prep you before you'll be able to take me."

Her eyes flare. "Is that what I think it is?"

My smile widens. "A butt plug. You'll have to wear it all day. It will stretch you."

"I…" She wets her lips with the tip of her tongue. "I've never done that."

I brush the hair from her forehead. "Do you want to?"

She considers it for a moment.

"We don't have to do anything you're not up for," I say. "We can try, and if you don't like it, we'll stop."

"All right," she says slowly. "I guess."

Even spent, my cock twitches. "Kneel for me, kiska."

Obediently, she goes onto her hands and knees.

"That's good." I brush a hand over the firm curve of her ass. "Lean your upper body on the bed."

Watching me from over her shoulder, she bends her elbows and rests her cheek on her arm.

"Perfect," I say, caressing the other cheek.

The position pushes her ass into the air. Her globes are spread, giving me easier access to her virgin hole. Uncapping the tube, I lube the plug well.

"This is going to feel a little cold." I smooth a hand over her lower back. "Take a deep breath and hold it until I tell you to blow out."

She inhales deeply, looking a little frightened.

"This won't hurt," I say huskily, pressing the tip of the plug against her opening and letting her get used to the pressure. "Blow out now, slow and steady."

When she exhales the air from her lungs, I splay my fingers over her ass and spread her wider while applying a little more pressure.

"How are you doing?" I murmur, pressing harder slowly but surely.

Biting her lip, she gives me a nod.

"Words, Katerina."

"I'm good," she says in a breathy voice.

"Do you want me to continue?"

"Yes."

Gently, I twist the plug from side to side, stretching her sphincter until the ring of muscles gives and the toy pops inside. The white gemstone fits prettily in her crease, a jewel adorning a jewel.

"How does that feel?" I ask, stroking my palms over her ass cheeks.

"Strange." Her voice holds a curious tone. "Full."

Heat building at the base of my cock roughens my tone. "Wait until I take you while you're wearing that plug."

Her cheeks flush a little.

"It's so fucking sexy." I trace the outline of the brilliant stone. "Do you want to see?"

She nods.

I go back to the bathroom and return with a mirror. She cranes her neck for a look, her flush deepening as she studies the sparkly stone that adorns her asshole. I'm not into BDSM or anything like that, but I am an anal man, and without this preparation, I risk hurting, if not tearing, her.

After I set the mirror aside, I get back onto the bed and pull her legs straight so she's lying flat on her stomach. Ignoring my renewed need, I spend the next ten minutes massaging her shoulders, back, and buttocks to help her relax. When she's soft and pliant, I press a kiss to the top of her crease.

"Stay," I order. "I'll be back in a few minutes with breakfast."

As usual, breakfast waits in the warming drawer. Tima made *syrniki*. Served with sour cream, honey, and berries, the cottage cheese pancakes are my favorite. After feeding Katerina in bed, I rush through a shower and get dressed quickly. She's dozing off again when I kiss her goodbye. It takes much willpower to tear myself away from her and walk out of the room.

Igor and Leonid are waiting in the foyer when I get downstairs. Dimitri and Yuri are already in the car, the engine idling.

"Guard her with your life," I tell Igor. His orders are to protect Katerina when I'm not here.

He nods with a steely expression.

"Ready?" I ask Leonid.

He moves his jacket aside, showing me the pistol in his waistband.

We drive to my office in a convoy of five cars. I expect an ambush every minute we're on the move. I almost wish for it, just wanting to get the fight over with and kill the motherfuckers already, but nothing happens, and half an hour later, we arrive safely at my office building.

Grigori greets me with coffee and a stack of reports. A pile of contracts waits on my desk to be signed. Once he's briefed me on what I've missed in my absence, I spend the first hour catching up with the tasks on my priority list.

At noon sharp, Adrian calls on the secure line.

"What do you have for me?" I ask, swiveling my chair toward the window.

"Something big."

My body tenses with anticipation. "Go on."

"I've been keeping tabs on Oleg Pavlov, as you requested. A huge amount of money was recently moved from his bank account and distributed between various accounts. Some of those are offshore and others local. From there, the funds went dark. My finance expert managed to trace a portion of it. Some of the money ended up in Bitcoin and some in shell corporations. It's a real fucking maze. Whoever designed the system made sure we'd be taken on a wild goose chase." He pauses. "It turns out all the diversions lead back to one place, or should I say, one person."

"Who?" I demand.

"A hacker in Moscow. Goes by the name of Mukha. He's gone to great pains to keep his identity concealed. I'm afraid I don't have his real name for you yet."

A snowflake drifts down and sticks to the window. "What did Pavlov want with a hacker?"

"That's what I asked myself. So I did a little probing. I offered the money you provided. The fish took the bait. Apparently, Pavlov paid him to encrypt and deliver a file."

"What file?"

"He won't say."

"Then what information did my money buy?" I ask with impatience.

"He gave me the name of the person he delivered the encryption to. A certain Ivan Besov."

Turning back to my desk, I type a message to Nelsky, ordering him to run a background check on Ivan Besov.

"Guess what *my* hacker discovered when he followed Mukha's cyber trail?" Adrian continues. "Besov sent the file to Vladimir Stefanov."

I go still. "He did, did he?"

"Most certainly."

"In other words, Pavlov paid a hacker to deliver an encrypted file to Besov, and Besov delivered it to Stefanov."

"Correct."

I mull over the meaning of this. "What about Besov?"

"He's ex-military. He got kicked out on charges of torturing a political hostage. It looks like he took the fall for his team. The charges were dropped, but after that, he went on his own."

"What division?"

"Spetsnaz. Sniper."

The snow starts falling harder. "That would make a good assassin."

"My thoughts as well. He goes by the nickname of Bes."

Bes. Demon or evil spirit in Russian. How subtle. I hook a finger between my collar and my tie and pull on the knot to loosen it. "Any teammates we can question?"

"No." Paper rustles in the background. "He works alone."

A ping sounds in my ear.

"I've just sent you an attachment with the information I could gather on Besov," Adrian says. "He has an address in Moscow. If he's been traveling lately, he's been doing it with a false passport. According to his records, he's retired, living on disability payments, and he hasn't left Russia since his military missions."

A message from Nelsky pops up on my computer screen. I click on the attachment. It's a photo of Besov. He has green eyes and blond hair. The listed information says he's forty-two years old.

I fire off another message to Igor, instructing him to put a man on Besov and check out his address.

"You did well," I say, saving the file in a secret folder. "I want to know what's in that file Pavlov had Mukha send to Besov."

"Mukha won't give up the file. He's afraid of Pavlov and Stefanov. Understandably."

"Where are you now?" I ask.

"Still in Moscow."

"Can you trace the hacker?"

"It'll be tricky, but I can try."

"Do it. In the meantime, offer him double the money for the file. Promise him however much he wants, but get me that file. I need it decrypted."

"Are you sure this is the route you want to go? Pavlov and Stefanov are dangerous men."

A slow smile curves my lips. "So am I."

16

KATE

*E*very time I move, I'm aware of the toy inside my body. At first, the sensation is odd, but by late morning, I'm used to it. I almost forget about it until I sit down for lunch. The foreign pressure isn't uncomfortable. In fact, it's strangely arousing, serving as a reminder of Alex's intention.

The idea of anal sex both turns me on and scares me a little, yet I'm curious. I'd never been adventurous with my ex-boyfriends, and the fact that Alex is pushing my boundaries and is so at ease with kink thrills me. In my past relationships, I've often been the one to instigate sex. I love that Alex is taking the initiative and suggesting we try something new.

Since I've whiled away the morning by sleeping late and reading, I decide to spend the afternoon more productively in the gym. I don't mind walking or lounging with a butt plug, but I doubt running will be comfortable. After reading the instructions that came with the box, which are thankfully in English, I remove the plug and clean it with soapy water before putting it away. Then I pull on my exercise gear and grab a swim-suit on my way down.

Igor sits in a chair in the foyer, reading something on his phone.

"Hi," I say, not certain where we stand with each other after yesterday.

For a change, he smiles. "Good afternoon."

I stop in front of him. "Are you babysitting?"

He shrugs. "Duty calls."

"Lucky you."

"Alex said he'll be home for dinner."

I raise a brow. "I suppose the fact that I don't have a phone makes you the messenger too."

Lowering the phone to his lap, he says, "I'm not complaining."

"I do feel better knowing I'm so well protected," I say from over my shoulder as I continue on my way.

His chuckle follows me down the hallway.

Like the previous time, I select a lively playlist on the central sound system before hitting the treadmill. The running releases some of my tension and clears my mind. It's good to focus on the rhythm of my feet and forget about everything else. When my life returns to normal—when I go back to work—I'll make exer-cising a part of my daily routine again. I forgot how purging a strenuous workout can be.

After a half hour of running, I rinse off in the shower and do a few laps in the pool. When my skin starts to wrinkle, I stretch out on a lounge chaise under the skylight. It's snowing hard outside. It feels odd to lie in my swimsuit in an indoor garden while a snowstorm is raging on the other side of the windows.

Lena comes to ask if I'd like to use the *banya*, a Russian sauna. If so, she'll tell Tima to make a fire in the stove and heat the rocks. Not being a big fan of excessive heat, I decline the offer. Instead, I take a shower in Alex's bathroom. Stepping out of the shower, I wrap a towel around my body and take the sex toy from the drawer. I contemplate the box for a couple of seconds before making up my mind. As soon as I've made my decision, a pleasant wave of heat creeps over my skin. What I'm about to do feels forbidden and naughty. I use the lube from Alex's nightstand drawer to insert the plug like Alex had done this morning. Once it's fitting comfortably, I dress in a warm sweater and skirt and install myself in the library to watch a couple of episodes of *Downton Abbey*.

By teatime, I'm starting to feel restless again. I pass the time exploring the house in more detail, admiring the artwork and trinkets as I walk from room to room. The history of the palace fascinates me. I make a mental note to ask Lena about it. Maybe Alex can get me a book if an English translation is available.

I end my tour in the upstairs rooms. Standing in one of the luxurious lounges, I turn in a slow circle to take in the mural that runs around all four walls. The scene depicts a family out on a picnic. The clothes suggest an eighteenth-century period. From the quality of their attire, I'm guessing they're a wealthy, maybe even royal, family. The lady of the house is reclining on a chair while a woman in a housemaid uniform is serving her a cup of tea. The gentleman sits on the back of a stately black horse, his pose regal. Five kids of different ages are running after a puppy while three servants are chasing after them. A blanket is spread out on the grass, covered with grapes, bread, and wine. A richly embroidered tablecloth spills from an open wicker basket.

The detail is extraordinary. The fruit catches the rays of the sun, the fat grapes a translucent purple and green in the light. The craftsmanship of the painting is spectacular. I bet Ricky would love to see this. It's like being transported to the past. Did that scene play out here? The green lawn in the painting could easily be the palace garden in the summer. Alex did mention there used to be stables at the back.

An eerie quietness descends as I continue to study the mural. For a moment, it's just me and the family caught in the happy snapshot of a bygone era. A clock on the mantlepiece keeps time with a soft tick-tock. It's almost five o'clock and already dark outside. An inexplicable wave of loneliness washes over me. I feel suddenly isolated, alone with only the company of ghosts.

Needing a warm drink, I close the door behind me and go to the kitchen.

Lena is ironing table linen when I enter. Tima is presumably on his break. The kitchen is warm and humid from the vapor of the iron. The air smells like a mixture of starch and laundry detergent, transporting me to the weekends at my mom's place. Mom always did her ironing on a Saturday. Nowadays, that only happens if her health allows.

A pang of longing pierces me. I miss my mom.

"Can I get you anything?" Lena asks, glancing up from the hissing iron.

"I'm good, thank you." I walk to the fridge. "I just want to warm up some milk for a cup of hot chocolate."

She folds a napkin meticulously. "The cacao is in the top cupboard on your left, and the pots are underneath the sink."

After finding a small pot, I fill it with milk. "Would you like some?"

"No, thanks." She runs the iron along the seam of the napkin. "If you'd prefer to wait, Tima will be back from his break in ten minutes."

"I can make a cup of hot chocolate," I say good-naturedly. "It's not as if I'm doing much else."

She gives me a fleeting look before leaving the napkin on a neatly folded stack.

I turn on the gas and find a mug while the milk heats. "Have you been working here for long?"

"Since before Mr. Volkov bought the house."

Leaning against the counter, I shove my hands into the pockets of my skirt. "Do you know its history?"

"Some of it." She takes a napkin from a laundry basket and shakes it out. "The previous owner's wife made a study of the architecture and interior decorating. She collected every book on the subject she could lay her hands on."

"Are there any in English?"

She wrinkles her nose. "Only Russian, I'm afraid."

"Oh."

The iron blows out a billow of steam as she drags it over the napkin. "All the more reason to learn to speak Russian." With a haughty air, she adds, "That's if you're staying."

Not forever. At least I hope not. I have a job and friends in New York, not to mention my mom. I have a life there. The nagging uncertainty tightens my stomach anew.

Busying myself with spooning cacao and sugar into the mug, I hide my expression from Lena. My tremulous feelings must be showing on my face. A part of me isn't sure if Alex will ever let me go home. What if he's decided to keep me here indefinitely? As kind as he's being, I wouldn't put that past him. He's made it clear he won't let me go, and if he decides to stay here, which is a very real probability, my life as I knew it will be in the past. This is home for him, after all.

The burner makes a hissing sound when the milk boils over. I grab the pot from the stove and blow on the foaming liquid.

"Will you start entertaining soon?" Lena asks.

I turn my head to look at her. "What?"

"The previous owners used to throw the most wonderful parties. They had a charity ball every year.

The preparations took months. Mr. Volkov also entertains regularly, but mostly for business and on a much smaller scale. Of course, the previous mistress of the house was a direct descendant of Russian royalty, so they moved in circles that demanded lavish entertainment. Although, Mr. Volkov does mix with some families who have royal blood in their veins."

I pour the milk into the mug and carry the pot to the sink. "He does?"

"The Turgenevs, for example. Mikhail Sergeyevich Turgenev and his family are regular callers. Mr. Volkov is a close friend of the family. Maybe you met them in New York? Like Mr. Volkov, Mr. Turgenev has a house in America for business purposes. The family spends one month there every year. They returned shortly after you, I believe."

I still in the middle of rinsing the pot. "Dania Turgeneva? Those Turgenevs?"

"Ah." She gives an approving nod. "Then you did meet them."

"Briefly," I say, putting the pot on the drip tray.

"At least you already have a friend in St. Petersburg." She folds the napkin and sets it on top of the pile. "You should ask Mr. Volkov if you can invite Miss Turgeneva for tea. She's such a charming young lady and from a good family too." She gives me a sugary smile. "I'm sure he'll be happy to oblige, as close as they are."

No, thanks. Not after Dania told me she was destined to marry Alex.

Lena waves a hand in the air and says with a dreamy light in her eyes, "Those dinners are simply marvelous. That's when we take out the silver and crystal and polish everything to a shine."

So, Dania is a regular visitor. Why does that bother me? I've never been the jealous type, but then again, I've never dated a man like Alex, a self-made zillionaire who wants me to wear a butt plug.

Warmth travels to my cheeks, and not from the hot drink I'm sipping.

Lena's conversation has dried up. From the look on her face, she's still at one of those fancy dinners with the Russian royals.

I'm about to take my hot chocolate to the library when the door in the back opens and Tima enters from the mudroom.

Shutting the door, he rubs his hands together. "It's a blizzard out there." When his gaze lands on me, he smiles. "How's the rabbit today?"

His smile is contagious. My lips curve involuntarily in response. "I'm good, thanks."

Lena switches off the iron and picks up the laundry basket. As she walks from the room, she says with her nose in the air, "Dinner is served at seven sharp."

"Like every night," Tima replies, making a face behind her back.

I can't help the laugh that bubbles up in my throat. I catch it just before it slips out.

"Don't mind her," he says, taking an apron from a

hook and tying it around his waist. "She thinks her shit doesn't stink."

"Tima!" I say with a chuckle. "That's mean."

He winks. "It's true."

"She says she's been working here for a long time."

He takes a pan from the shelf and puts it on the stove. "She grew up in this house. Her mother was the housekeeper before her."

"Wow. She didn't tell me that. What about you?"

"Nah." He takes a knife from the block and pulls it through the blade sharpener. "She was here way before me. That's why she thinks she's the boss."

"How long have you known Alex?"

"A few years," he says evasively.

"How did you meet?"

"Let's just say our paths crossed when mine wasn't very straight or narrow."

Not wanting to pry when he's obviously not comfortable discussing it, I drop the subject. Being used to working with people all day, I miss human contact. I'm enjoying the company and I'm reluctant to leave, but I don't want to be under Tima's feet when he has work to do.

"I'll be—"

I'm about to say I'll be in the library when the door crashes open with a bang, and Igor and one of the guards rush through it.

Tima's hand tightens around the shaft of the knife. His stance is tense, as if he's ready to pounce.

My heartbeat spikes. Are we under attack?

"What's going on?" I ask Igor tensely.

The guard stumbles into the kitchen, clutching a towel that's wrapped around his hand.

Igor shuts the door. "He's hurt."

My professional side kicks in, and I drag a chair out by the table. The man looks as if he might keel over.

"What's his injury?" I ask as Igor helps him into the chair.

"He got cut," Igor says. "Knife."

"Let me see," I say to the man, unwrapping the towel.

"He doesn't speak English," Igor says.

I direct my question at Igor. "Do you have a first-aid kit?"

"I'll get it," Tima says, leaving the knife in the block and dashing down the hallway.

The blood has soaked through the towel. The man flinches when I pull the towel from his skin. Blood seeps from a diagonal cut in his palm.

"What's your name?" I ask as I take his hand to inspect the damage.

"Stepan," Igor says.

"It doesn't look as if any arteries are severed, but it needs stitches." Meeting the man's eyes, I say, "You're going to be all right."

"The sight of blood makes him..." Igor pauses. "How do you say? Woozy."

Tima returns with a first-aid kit that he leaves on the table.

"Can you walk to the sink, Stepan?" I ask. "I need to rinse off the blood."

"I'll help," Igor says.

Igor puts his arm around Stepan's shoulders and leads him to the sink as I go through the kit and extract a bottle of saline solution.

At the sink, I open the tap and hold Stepan's hand under the water. "I need some clean dishcloths."

While Tima opens a drawer and takes out a stack of cloths, I pour saline solution over the cut. When it's clean, I grab a dishcloth and wrap it around Stepan's hand to help stop the bleeding.

"That's good," I say in a soothing tone. "Now let's get you back to the table."

Igor helps him back into the chair as I drag another one closer for myself.

"Do you have a local anesthetic?" I ask.

Igor motions with his head toward the kit. "In there."

I position Stepan's hand with his palm facing up and his forearm resting on the table. "Keep pressure on the wound."

Igor does as I ordered, freeing my hands to find the anesthetic. I fill a hypodermic needle from the vial and tip my head toward the cloth. When Igor removes the cloth, I inject the anesthetic in the fleshy part of the man's palm.

"Take a clean cloth and press it on the cut," I say, looking for surgical thread and a needle.

Stepan is pale, appearing close to fainting.

"A soldier who's scared of blood?" Tima asks with a condescending smile.

"Only his own blood," Igor says, giving Tima a cold look. "Your blood, for example, wouldn't bother him."

"Hey." I give the men a stern look. "We're all on the same side. Igor, tell him he can close his eyes or look away."

Igor repeats the words in Russian as I prick Stepan's skin with the needle to test if the anesthetic has taken effect. He flinches.

"Does it hurt?" I ask.

Igor repeats the question before translating for me. "He can feel the sensation of being touched, but there's no pain."

"How did this happen?" I ask, pushing the needle through Stepan's skin at the top of the cut.

"Training," Igor says.

I lift my gaze to his fleetingly. "You train with real knives?"

"It would defy the objective to train with toy ones, wouldn't it?"

I bite back a retort. "What about Alex?"

"What about him?" Igor asks.

"Does he approve of this training method?"

"He's the one who insists on it," Igor says.

I gape at him. "That's dangerous. I can't believe he'd be so irresponsible."

Igor straightens his back. "He's not asking anything of us that he isn't doing himself."

The implication makes me go cold. "What? Does he train like this too?"

Igor's tone is indignant. "Of course he does. That's why we respect him."

Tima blows out a sigh. "If you've finished bleeding all over the room, I'd like to disinfect my kitchen. I have cooking to do."

"Sorry." I offer Tima a watery smile. "I should've taken him to the bathroom."

"Don't worry, my little rabbit," Tima says. "It's not your fault. These guys should know better."

Fear pools hot in my stomach as I go back to work. I knew Alex was working out, but doing combat training with his guards? With real knives? And who knows what other weapons?

"What's going on here?" a deep voice asks from the door.

I look up. The object of my thoughts stands in the frame, dressed in a dark suit and wearing a thunderous expression.

"Stepan is hurt," Igor says. "Knife wound."

"I can see that," Alex says, stepping over the threshold. "But what's he doing letting Katerina stitch him up?"

I blink up at him. "You'd rather Igor do it? At least I'm qualified."

"This isn't a fucking hospital." Alex stops next to the table. "The men know how to take care of their wounds."

Igor rubs a hand over his head. "I just thought—"

"That because she's a nurse you'll run a fucking sick bay?" Alex's voice is harsh.

"Alex," I say gently. "I'm happy to help."

"You're not here to work," he says, sliding a frosty gaze toward Igor. "And my men aren't here to put their paws on you."

"Enough." I tie a knot in the thread. "Instead of being angry about my assistance, why don't you hand me the scissors?"

Alex grudgingly obliges.

I cut the thread and give him the scissors with an overly sweet, "Thank you."

"We're talking about this in the library," he says with a tight jaw.

"After I've disinfected and bandaged the wound."

He crosses his arms, watching me with a broody expression, but he doesn't argue as I finish my work and tell Stepan to take a couple of painkillers and an antibiotic for good measure before going to bed.

Tima starts wiping the table with disinfectant as soon as Stepan stands. Igor has scarcely left with the patient before Alex wraps his hand around my upper arm and pulls me to my feet.

"Now we talk," he says in a dark voice, all but dragging me to the door.

"Wait." I dig my heels in. "I have to wash my hands."

He lets me, but the minute I'm done, he steers me to the nearest room and pushes me inside. It's one of the lounges close to the dining room. I walk to the center of the floor, creating some distance. He's unreasonably angry, and I'm upset. We both need space to cool down.

Watching me with gleaming blue eyes, he closes the door and turns the key.

The act makes my pulse jump. "What are you doing?"

"I don't like it when you touch my men," he says, advancing on me.

I crane my neck to meet his gaze when he stops so close our bodies almost touch. "It's my job."

His jaw bunches. "Not here it's not."

"I touch many men on a daily basis in New York," I say with barely suppressed frustration.

A muscle ticks in his temple. "That doesn't mean I have to like it."

I prop my hands on my hips. "You never said it bothered you."

"As I said, that doesn't mean I liked it."

"This is ridiculous. There's a difference between a caregiver's touch and an intimate touch. You get that, don't you?"

He gives me a hard smile. "It makes no difference to me what kind of touch it is. I don't want your hands on them." His voice lowers with dangerous intent. "And if I catch their hands on you, I'll chop them off."

Anger bursts through my veins, heating my skin. "I love my job. I'm good at it. You said so yourself. If you have a problem with my job, it's going to be a problem for us, and I mean a *real* problem." I add with emphasis, "A make-or-break problem."

"I do admire your skill and dedication." His words are softly spoken, but there's an edge to them. "I admire the profession you've chosen, and I respect your decisions. I'm not telling you that you can't do what you love. What I'm telling you, Katyusha, is that I don't like to share. I'll never like your hands on another man's naked torso or dick, no matter how professional the intention."

"You're jealous," I say, startled to realize just how much.

"Exactly." He splays a palm over my lower back, tugging me against him while he slips his free hand under the hem of my skirt to cup my sex. "*This*"—he squeezes—"belongs to me." Flicking my clit softly, he continues in a tone that leaves no room for argument. "Only to me."

A spark travels from my groin to my belly, but I can't let him sidetrack me with lust.

"No." I push on his chest.

He regards me with a mixture of surprise, anger, and disbelief, but he doesn't pull his hand away.

"We're not done talking." I grip his wrist and pull his hand out from under my skirt. "I'm not going to cheat on you. That's not my style. But I'm not taking orders from you." I point at the locked door. "If you can't accept that, you may as well walk through that door now. My job isn't up for discussion."

A quiet storm builds in his eyes. "Your job isn't the issue."

"Then what is?"

"My men," he bites out. "You're beautiful. They're horny. Put two and two together, and what do you get?"

"If you don't trust them, trust me."

Clenching his jaw, he says, "You're asking too much of me, Katerina."

I back up a step. "Is trust too much to ask?"

He stabs his fingers through his hair. "That's not what I'm talking about. I'm talking about not wanting them to enjoy your touch a little too much." The blue of his eyes turns cold. "If one of those motherfuckers gets an erection from looking at you, I'll chop off more than his hands."

"Alex, please. Stepan was in pain. I can promise you, turned on was the last thing he would've been while I was stitching him up."

"Just as well," he says, biting off every word.

I drop my hands to my sides. "I can't believe you. While we're talking about trust, why didn't you tell me you were training with your men?"

He frowns. "What does that have to do with anything?"

"You're training with knives, for crying out loud."

"Yes," he says, as if it should've been obvious.

"Someone got hurt today. *You* could get hurt."

"The point of training with actual weapons is making sure we *don't* get hurt."

"In a real fight, you mean," I say, hovering between anger and concern.

He closes the distance between us. "Precisely."

Hooking a curl behind my ear, he asks with a quirk of his lips, "Are you worried about me?"

"Of course I am," I say incredulously.

"Don't be. I know how to take care of myself."

"Then don't be jealous," I deadpan.

Folding his hand around my nape, he pulls me closer. "Are you saying you won't worry if I won't be jealous?"

"I'll try." I swallow. "Will you?"

He considers me for a moment. "What are you asking of me, Katerina?"

"I'm here anyway. I might as well put my skills to good use."

Studying me with a piercing gaze, he rubs a thumb over the back of my neck. "Are you bored?"

I shrug. "A little."

He nods. "Fine. I fight. You heal. Happy?"

"Was that so difficult?" I ask with a strained smile.

He smooths his palm up my thigh under the hem of my skirt. "You have no idea." Walking me backward to the couch, he adds in a soft, low voice, "But you know I'd do anything for you."

Our bodies are pressed flush together, his erection hard against my stomach. I slide my hands over his chest under his jacket as he tightens his grip on my hip. Holding my gaze, he follows the elastic of my thong with a finger, drawing a path from my side to my lower back. When he realizes my ass cheeks are bare, his gaze darkens. He caresses my left globe with a callused palm, his skin rough on mine. His movements are lazy and gentle, but intensity burns in his eyes.

My body tightens with anticipation, uncertain what to expect when he brushes a finger down my crease. Approval and heat wash over his features when he finds the jewel. I gasp as he presses on the plug, applying soft pressure.

"You've been a good girl," he says in a hoarse voice, lowering his head to mine.

I tilt my face up to give him easier access. He catches my lips in a searing kiss, eradicating our fight, truce, worries, and insecurities. None of those things matter when he reverses positions, sits down, and draws me onto his lap to straddle him. I forget about the imminent danger and the distant future, focusing only on the sound of his zipper as he pulls it down, and on the hot, smooth head of his cock brushing over my inner thigh.

Pulling my thong aside, he tests my folds with a finger. Satisfied that I'm ready, he lifts me to my knees and positions his cock at my entrance. He lets me take him at my pace, reading my face as I lower myself slowly.

The fullness is almost too much, the stretch of his cock with the added pressure of the toy unbearably stimulating. He presses a thumb on my clit, massaging until my inner muscles are supple enough to take him to the hilt.

"Wait," I say breathlessly, catching his wrist. "I'll come."

"Not yet," he agrees, cupping the side of my head and dragging me closer.

Pressing our lips together, he kisses me with a skill that makes my knees weak. He sweeps his tongue over mine and explores the depths of my mouth before gently nipping my bottom lip. The kiss is unrushed. He keeps still, giving me time to adjust to the new fullness and to enjoy the sensation of him filling me.

After a long period of kissing, he starts moving slowly. I grip his shoulders for balance as he rolls his hips. The sensation is so intense, the penetration so deep, that I throw back my head and moan. He picks up his pace, adding friction to the already overpowering pressure. This pleasure is different. It's darker. More devastating.

The faster he moves, the higher my need climbs. It rises to a crescendo, but I don't go over. I can't, not without some kind of touch on my clit. I slip a hand between our bodies, needing to get there like never before, but he locks his fingers around my wrist, preventing me from touching myself.

I'll go out of my mind if this intolerable yearning doesn't stop soon.

He rocks me faster but not harder, keeping the thrusting gentle.

"Alex. I need—"

The rest of my words are cut off as he slams up and steals my breath.

His voice is heated. "I know what you need."

Moving a hand around my body, he grips the

jeweled head of the plug and twists from left to right while pummeling my sex with shallow thrusts. That's all it takes. I break with a shudder, barely biting off a scream. Release tears through me like a violent storm. He follows a second later, his body going taut as he comes inside me. Instead of pulling out when he's empty, he makes me ride the aftershocks of my orgasm, prolonging them by keeping pressure on the toy with his palm.

I've never come like this, not with this much force and not from this kind of stimulation alone. Collapsing against his body, I rest my forehead on his shoulder and inhale the masculine aroma of his cologne. The familiar smell grounds me as much as his strong hands on my back.

"How are you doing?" he murmurs, nipping my earlobe.

"Mm." I'm not sure I'll be able to peel myself off his body, never mind rise to my feet.

"It's time for an upgrade," he says in a husky voice. "You're ready for a bigger size."

I don't have to ask what he means.

"Silicone or glass?" he asks, sending goosebumps over my arm when he sucks on the sensitive spot behind my ear.

"Silicone sounds softer." Just to tease him, I add, "I like red."

He chuckles. "A ruby it will be."

I pull away in surprise. "A ruby?"

He brushes the hair from my face. "What did you expect, my love?"

"Crystal?" I ask with a frown.

"Tsk." He shakes his head.

My lips part in disbelief. "You mean…?"

"A diamond, yes," he says. "You didn't think I'd put a common crystal in your ass, did you?"

The crass words shouldn't sound hot, but they heat my stomach.

"And just so we're clear," he says, gripping my hair in a tight fist. "I won't be walking through that door any time soon, kiska."

17

ALEX

A week passes with no action on the security front. Stefanov got my message for sure, the one I sent via that dead *ublyudok*, Vadim, but he's not making a move. He's biding his time, maybe waiting for a weakness to exploit. We're caught in a frustrating stand-off, each watching the other.

There's no new information from Adrian either. He's still trying to trace the hacker who calls himself Mukha. The guy—Mukha—is good. I have to give him that. Nelsky and my team are on his trail too, but they've come up with zilch. Adrian tripled my original offer to the hacker for the file he encrypted for Pavlov, and the pesky little fly said he'd have to think about it. He said if he were to hand the file over, he'd have to take on a new identity and disappear. He'd never be able to set foot in Russia again. Whatever is on that file is damn important, enough for the fly to be wary of selling it, even for three million euros, and enough for Stefanov to want to kill me.

What I still don't know is how Pavlov is connected to any of this. Like Stefanov, he's beefing up his army. You'd think they're preparing for war. My informants told me they've both ordered more weapons on the black market and hired more men.

As far as Besov goes, I'm almost a hundred-percent certain he's the fucker who took a shot at me, although I can't prove he was in the States when the shooting happened. According to the flight records I got from my contacts, Besov has been safely and soundly on Russian soil for years. That doesn't mean he didn't travel with a false passport. The man I ordered to watch Besov's apartment informed me that Besov isn't home. The neighbors said he keeps to himself and never speaks to anyone, but they haven't seen him in a good two months.

While I'm waiting, I use my restless energy to ensure that the upcoming event will be secure. The gala dinner will be held downtown in the Lion Palace Hotel ballroom. The event coordinator has provided me with the guest list. Stefanov and Pavlov aren't invited. The bratva bosses aren't the kind of influencers the government wants to associate with when it comes to nuclear power.

Since many government officials and leading businessmen will be attending, the security is already top notch, but I insist on putting extra measures in place.

For one, I want every person searched before they're allowed to enter the gala venue. The hall has a separate entrance from the hotel, which plays in my favor. It makes controlling who enters and exits considerably easier. I'm an important enough guest to get my specifications met to the last T. My money lines the pockets of many of the attendees, after all. The fact that Mikhail Turgenev and his family will be present further aids my efforts. Turgenev, who's a stickler for security, seconded my suggestions. He even asked to have walk-through metal detectors installed at the entrance.

We'll also have checkpoints set up and all vehicles searched for explosives before they'll be allowed to approach the hall through a cordoned-off one-lane street. Our carefully screened valets will park the vehicles in the underground parking lot that will be watched by a team of guards before, during, and after the event.

In addition, Mikhail and I will have the building surrounded. Our men will be stationed around the whole block, armed with automatic rifles, smoke bombs, and grenades. Of course, they'll be discreet. The general public won't even know they're there. My security chief, Nelsky, will monitor the movements around the hotel via satellite. We'll also have drones positioned at strategic coordinates, both to have extra eyes on the venue and for additional firepower if needed. Those drones are loaded with missiles that can flatten a ten-story building. Lastly, I'll have men on the floor who'll be connected to Nelsky and me via a central communication system. Any enemies stupid enough to target anyone at the gala will be squashed like insects before they come within a five-kilometer radius of the building.

This doesn't mean we're going to leave the house defenseless. Even though Katerina and I will be attending the gala with an army of men, enough of them will remain at my residence to hold down the fort there. I've also put extra men on the watch at Stefanov's, Pavlov's, and Besov's dwellings. If they move so much as a meter, I'll know about it.

Katerina is surprisingly accommodating about all the precautions. I expected her to complain and sulk about her loss of freedom, but she bravely carries the undeserved burden I've dumped on her shoulders. In turn, I bend over backward to fulfill her whims and wishes, even if it goes against every instinct I possess. Letting her play nurse to my men isn't easy for me. I explained to her in detail why it upsets me, but she makes an effort not to worry every time I put a foot outside the house—or she's simply not showing how much the concern affects her—and therefore I try to keep my jealousy in check.

The men flock to the house as if Katyusha lives there for their fucking benefit. Igor and Leonid transformed one of the lounges into a sick bay complete with an examination bed and medical equipment. The men come to her with everything from sprained ankles to headaches. Since my kiska seems to be genuinely happy to help and less stressed when she's keeping busy, I grind my teeth and bear the wimps' presence in the house. They never complained about a cut on a finger before. I suppose the novelty of Katerina's presence has yet to wear off.

I've never compromised for anyone before, but Katerina is a first for me in many aspects. Besides, the reward for my suffering is most effective. She's been more open with me during the last few days, her advances both sweet and hot.

I'll do anything if it means she'll give me access to her body and her heart.

WHEN I COME HOME FROM THE OFFICE ON FRIDAY evening, I go straight to the homemade clinic. The room smells of disinfectant as I open the door. It's empty. For once, there's no patient with a splinter in his skin to be pampered.

Urgency drives my steps as I walk through the house. I'm eager to see her. I left while she was still sleeping this morning and didn't get a chance to kiss her goodbye. Her laughter comes from the end of the hallway, the sound beautiful and clear. Tima says something in his baritone that makes her laugh more.

I follow the sound of their banter to the kitchen. Tima is scrubbing pots in the sink, and Katerina is leaning with her backside against the table. She's wearing a tight-fitting sweater and a skirt that hugs her thighs. Paired with high-heeled boots, the outfit looks sexy as hell. She's been mostly wearing dresses or skirts for the past week, and the reason heats my veins and sends blood to my groin.

"Alex," she says, offering me a smile. "Tima was telling me about some of your less appetizing local dishes."

Tima acknowledges me with a nod from over his shoulder. Despite the fact that I'm jealous of the attention Katerina gives him, I'm grateful to him for keeping her company when I'm working late. He doesn't have to hang around in the kitchen. It's long after his usual sign-off time.

Advancing toward her, I take in her shapely form. "Is that so?"

"*Keeshka*," she says with an adorable accent, wrinkling her nose. "Intestines stuffed with meat and meal? Or pig blood?" She shivers. "He told me it's one of your favorites."

"I'm an adventurous eater," I say, stopping short of her.

The huskiness of my voice must betray my lust because her throat bobs with a soundless swallow as she stares up at me.

Tima dries his hands on a dishcloth. "I'm done for the evening unless you need me for anything else?"

I don't break eye contact with Katerina. "We're good."

"Good night then," he calls on his way to the door.

It slams behind him with a bang, enclosing us in silence.

"How was your day?" she asks after a beat, her voice a little hoarse.

"Good." I lean my palms on either side of her body on the tabletop. "Yours?"

She wets her lips. "The usual."

I narrow my eyes at the act. Innocent or not, it makes me want to kiss her. "I hope you didn't overexert yourself."

"It will take more than that," she says, ducking underneath my arm and escaping to the other side of the room.

Her walk is unhurried, but she's running all the same. On top of sensing my desire, she must also know intuitively that I have special plans for her tonight.

Going on tiptoes, she opens the overhead cupboard. "I was going to make tea. Would you like some?"

Smiling inwardly at her futile diversion attempt, I stalk to my innocent little prey. She stretches to grab hold of the tin of tea. I reach over her and take the tin, making a mental note to tell Tima to put the refreshments on a lower shelf. The action puts our bodies together. Her back presses against my chest and her buttocks against my thighs. I put the tea aside and lean closer, capturing her between the counter and my body.

Like a cornered rabbit playing dead, she keeps perfectly still. Only her ribcage expands with fast breaths. She knows what I want, and it scares her.

I lower my head and inhale the fragrance of her skin before kissing her neck. She smells like my favorite dessert—peaches and cream. Despite her fear, she tilts her head, giving me better access. Splaying one hand over her stomach and the other over the curve of her breast, I hold her close as I kiss her neck slowly and meticulously. I pay extra attention to the part where her neck meets her shoulder, knowing this is an erogenous zone for her. When her skin turns red from my stubble, I kiss my way up the arch of her neck to the sensitive spot behind her ear. She moans when I graze her earlobe with my teeth. As I draw my hand from her stomach down between her legs, her nipple hardens under my palm where I'm fondling her breast.

She sags against me with her eyes closed and her lips slightly parted when I reach my destination. Cupping her pussy, I hold her in place while I slip my other hand between our bodies to explore the crease of her ass. The jeweled head of the butt plug is hard beneath my palm.

"Good girl," I whisper in her ear, pressing a rewarding kiss on her jaw.

She mewls when I press two fingers on the plug and apply gentle pressure. I've been patient. We've been playing with butt plugs for a week now, using a bigger size every day. I've stretched her carefully and fucked her roughly, and she's loved everything I've done. She's ready to take my cock.

I rub her clit with the heel of my hand to get her wet. She arches her back, pushing her ass harder against my palm. Using both hands, I play with her front and back, massaging her clit and asshole in circles. Her breathing quickens as I increase my pace. Just before she breaks, I stop.

Wrapping my fingers around her wrist, I say, "Come."

She follows me wordlessly to the bedroom. No one is going to disturb us, but I turn the key in the lock for good measure. I like my privacy.

"Strip," I say in a voice rough with desire, peeling off my jacket.

She holds my gaze as she undresses, dropping the clothes in a heap at her feet. I do the same, tearing out of my shirt and pants as fast as I can.

When we're both naked, she turns toward the bathroom, presumably to remove the plug. "I'll just be a minute."

I watch her cross the floor, admiring the sway of her ass and the red gemstone that peeks out from between her globes.

The wait almost kills me. My cock is hard and ready, a heavy weight jutting out between my legs. I fist the shaft and pump twice, catching the drop of pre-cum and lubricating the head. When Katerina steps back into the room, apprehension widens her eyes as she trails her gaze over the work of my hand.

"I'm not going to hurt you," I say, reminding her of my earlier promise. "If you tell me to stop, I will."

She swallows when I open the bedside drawer and take out the lube.

"Kneel on the bed like I taught you, Katyusha."

Her obedience warms me in all the right places

when she climbs onto the bed and kneels with her ass in the air and her elbows on the mattress.

I climb onto the bed behind her and spread her thighs to my liking. In this position, I have access to all of her body. Her asshole is nicely stretched, an inviting temptation. Arousal glistens on her bare folds. To be sure, I dip a finger between those plump lips. She's slick, as ready as I am.

Gripping my cock in a fist, I position the head at her pussy and part her carefully. She stretches around me, taking me easily as I slide in to the hilt. I hold still for a moment, giving her time to adjust while I uncap the lube and squirt a generous amount into her crease.

Using a finger, I spread the lube around her dark hole before working it inside. She clenches around the intrusion, her inner muscles gripping my finger tightly. I nearly come then and there, imagining what that tightness will do to my cock. As I start to pump with my cock, I do the same with my finger, synchronizing the pace to take her ass and pussy with shallow strokes.

She moans, letting me know she likes the double stimulation. I've taken her enough times while she was wearing a butt plug to get her comfortable with the feeling of being overfilled, and I've used my fingers to teach her how to enjoy having her ass played with. Meeting my undemanding pace, she pushes back with every thrust until I give her two fingers. I carry on like this for a while, slightly quickening the rhythm but keeping the thrusting in both holes gentle until she's so needy that she's grinding her ass against my groin.

I only pick up the pace when I'm fucking her back entrance with three fingers. Mimicking the pumping of my cock, I sink deeper and go harder to get her ready. When she arches her back and makes a sound that tells me she's close to coming, I give it to her, holding nothing back. She orgasms with a cry, her inner muscles clenching hard on my cock and fingers.

While she's supple inside and high on the euphoria of release, I pull out and align my cock with the pretty hole between her ass cheeks. I go painstakingly slow, applying steady pressure on the tight ring of muscle until it starts to give. She stretches perfectly, letting me in with little difficulty. Before she's come down from her climax, the head of my cock is buried inside her ass.

"How are you doing, kiska?" I ask roughly, rubbing my palms over her globes. It takes everything I have to exercise restraint, but I'd sooner die than hurt her.

She watches me from over her shoulder, her big brown eyes hazy with endorphins and her pupils already dilating with fresh need. "Good."

Dragging in a deep breath, I sink an inch deeper. Her ass grips me like a fist. She's velvet soft inside, the slick heat of her body milking me so hard I have to clench my teeth so as not to ejaculate before I'm fully sheathed. The alluring sight of her forbidden entrance swallowing my cock doesn't help. It's one of the most erotic images I've ever seen.

The preparations have paid off. She's taking me exceptionally well. Resting her cheek on her arm, she lies quietly and, like a good girl, lets me do the work. My skin is slick with perspiration from the strain of holding back when she closes her eyes and blows out a contented little sigh. Good. I couldn't have asked for a better reaction. I want her first time to be perfect. I want her to enjoy this as much as I do.

With every inch I drive deeper, my balls draw tighter. The pleasure is excruciating. The need to pump is all-consuming. I brush a hand over the delicate line of her spine and caress her back as I take my time to own this part of her. When I'm three-quarters in, it gets impossibly tight. I slip a hand between her legs and work her clit the way she likes. She softens with a whimper, and I slide all the way in.

Fuck. My groin is flush against her ass. So hot. So pretty. I wish I could film this to show my kitten how beautiful she looks. If privacy weren't as important to me, I would. As for me, the picture is burned into my memory. I'll have wet dreams about this for the rest of my life.

Wrapping my hands around her waist, I keep her still as I pull out an inch and sink back slowly.

The action makes her gasp. This is where it gets intense.

I bend down to plant a kiss on her back. "Do you want more?"

"Yes," she says in a shaky voice.

"Open your eyes for me, kiska. I want to look at you."

She obliges, lifting her eyelashes and giving me a

glimpse of those soft brown pools with the honey-gold flecks.

I pull out two inches before pushing back in. Her breathing picks up and her moans turn louder. I could drown in the noises she makes. The sexy sounds spike my arousal, and it takes every ounce of self-control not to move faster. I advance with herculean patience, taking care not to tear or hurt her. I'm well aware of my size and her small body.

A few more gentle pumps of my hips, and I'm taking her ass with long, slow strokes. She's panting now, her need evident in the crescendo of her moans. I could make her come quicker by playing with her pussy, send her tumbling over the edge by finger-spanking her clit, but for her first time, I want her to come from anal stimulation alone.

When I'm certain she's ready to take everything, I pivot my hips faster, taking her harder. She bites her lip and swallows her moans as she watches me obediently. Her eyes are like mirrors. A flinch tells me to slow down. A bat of her eyelashes tells me to move faster. The widening of those hazel pools tells me she's close.

So am I.

I go for the last sprint, keeping her in place with my hands on her hips as I increase the pace. My rhythm is grueling but controlled. I read her face as I slam my groin against her ass. Her expression is one of pleasure, not of pain. Intense pleasure. There are a million-and-one nerve endings in that part of her body, and I know just how to move to trigger them all.

One last thrust, and she comes with a soundless gasp. Her pretty lips part as her whole face pulls into a mask of ecstasy. It's my cue to let go. Hot ribbons of cum erupt from the sensitive crest of my cock, filling up her ass. The release is so powerful that, for a moment, I go weak.

Katerina's upper body collapses on the mattress. I follow her down, careful not to pull out too suddenly and hurt her. Supporting my weight on my arms, I cover her body with mine and kiss her shoulder. It takes a few moments before our breathing starts to calm, and I stay inside her, reveling at the possession. I've marked her in yet another way. Call me primitive, but it's hugely satisfying.

I brush a kiss over her temple. "How are you doing, my love?"

"Mm."

Her lethargic response makes me smile. "Take a breath and hold it. Blow it out when I tell you." I push up onto my arms. "Breathe out slowly, kiska."

I pull out gently as she exhales. Cool air washes over my cock. Already, I miss the heat of her body.

"Don't move," I say, caressing her firm globes as I get to my feet.

We need a shower, but it can wait a few minutes. I've thoroughly worn her out.

In the bathroom, I wet a facecloth and grab a towel. Gently, I clean her up. I even have enough brain cells left to call Lena and tell her to prepare a tray with the dinner and leave it in front of the bedroom door.

As I settle next to Katerina on the bed and pull her close, I can't help but bask in the knowledge that I own her on every physical level. It's only fair, seeing that she owns me, heart and soul. The words I never thought I'd say to any woman are on the tip of my tongue, threatening to spill over my lips, but she's already dozing off and this is hardly the moment.

I don't say things I don't mean. I don't make promises lightly. The day I tell Katerina I love her is the day I'll put a ring on her finger. The words are sacred. They deserve to be saved for a special occasion. And since she may not be on board with where I plan to take our relationship, she may need the consolation of those words when she realizes that in this matter also, I'm not giving her a choice.

18

KATE

*O*ne day rolls into the next, and before I know it, it's Thanksgiving. Nobody celebrates it in Russia, of course—it's a purely North American holiday—but I can't help thinking about the big home-cooked meal I'd be having with my mom if it weren't for the fact that she's at the treatment center while I'm halfway across the world. Worse yet, I might not see her for Christmas.

Alex must notice my mood because he encourages me to call my mom that evening, something I'm always more than happy to do. He has Lena make a cup of hot chocolate for me and then considerately gives me privacy.

By now, he trusts me enough to believe I won't ask my mom to contact the embassy or something along those lines.

Once I'm settled on the sofa with the cup of hot chocolate in my hands, I dial my mom.

"Hey, honey," she says, sounding out of breath. "How are you?"

"We're good. More importantly, how are you?"

"Great. We've just finished an aerobics session in the heated pool. The water is marvelous. Oh, and guess what? I'm losing more weight. My pants are so loose I'll have to go on a shopping spree soon."

I smile at her enthusiasm. "How's the treatment going? Are you feeling an improvement?"

"Absolutely. The diet makes a huge difference. I love the holistic approach here. It makes so much more sense than simply swallowing a few pills. I'm doing an electronic detox at the same time, and a break from social media is doing me wonders." She lowers her voice. "I dare say, I love the doctor the most. Dr. Hendricks is a charming man, not to mention brilliant. He's done so much for people suffering from my condition."

"Yeah, well, it's okay to admire him. Just don't take it beyond the professional."

She utters a forced little cough.

"Mom!" I press a hand to my forehead. "Please tell me you didn't."

"We haven't taken things to a physical level if that's what you're worried about. We felt we should wait until after the treatment. It wouldn't be professional, you know, to take it further now."

I leave my drink on the coffee table and shift to the edge of my seat. "You make it sound serious."

"Don't worry, honey. We're just enjoying each other's company and having fun. I'm not planning on marrying him."

"Still, I don't think it's a good idea to flirt with the staff."

"We're only getting to know each other." She clears her throat. "In fact, he'd very much like to meet you and Alex when you come for Christmas."

I take a deep breath. "About that… We may not be back before Christmas after all."

There's a moment of silence on the line. "That's a long break from work you're taking, honey," Mom says finally. "Is something wrong?"

Crossing my fingers, I say, "Not at all. Alex is just very busy with some projects here, and I don't want to return to New York on my own."

"Ah. Well, don't worry about it, honey. I completely understand, although I was looking forward to seeing my future son-in-law."

I cringe. "Mom."

"He's serious about you, Katie. Anyone can see that."

"Do you need anything?" I ask, eager to change the subject. "Snacks? Toiletries? I can arrange for an internet delivery."

"That's sweet of you, but I have everything I need."

"Okay. Let me know if—" I catch myself. "Send a text message to Alex if you're running short on something."

"Will do. I miss you, honey."

I swallow down an untimely sob. "Miss you too, Mom."

Before she can hear the emotions tearing up my chest, I hang up.

AS THE DAYS MARCH ON AND CHRISTMAS APPROACHES, I feel increasingly homesick. No matter what I'm doing, my mind often drifts off to nostalgic memories of the holiday. On Christmas Eve, my mom and I would take a taxi to Manhattan. We'd brave the cold to admire the Christmas lights and the giant tree at Rockefeller Center before having a special dinner at home and exchanging gifts.

Fortunately, the winter holiday spirit isn't lacking in Alex's house, even though I've learned that Russians celebrate Christmas on January 7th, as per the Eastern Orthodox tradition. Since that's considered a purely religious holiday, a lot of the Christmas traditions I'm familiar with—the tree, the gifts, the decorations—are instead part of the New Year's celebration in Russia. Thus, the cookies Tima has been baking, the ones that fill the kitchen with the aromas of cinnamon, raisins, and vanilla, are for the New Year's celebration, not Christmas. So is the tree with delicate glass ornaments that Lena has put up in the foyer, as well as the pine branches and red ribbons she's tied around the balustrades. The pantry is stocked with cured meats and pickled fish for the men's New Year's Eve party rather than for Christmas lunch. Decorations have also gone up in the street, but they're not visible from Alex's bedroom windows. I have to climb up to the top floor to get a peek at the fairy lights that span across the road along the river. The lights aren't colorful, like the ones back home, but white, depicting snowflakes, Christmas trees, and reindeer.

Not wanting to add to Alex's problems by burdening him with my depressive mood, I keep my feelings to myself. I can't say he's not accommodating. He lets me speak to Joanne, June, and my mom on the phone every week. It helps, but I still miss them. I can't shake this weird sense of sadness.

It's not that I'm bored. There's plenty to occupy me in the house, and Alex's guards keep me busy. More often than not, their ailments are minor, but I welcome the visits. It provides me with human contact, even if our different languages don't always permit communication. Sadly, my Russian isn't improving much. I asked Tima to teach me a few words, but with all the conjugations and male or female nouns, the language is much more difficult to master than I imagined. I try to stay positive, but even the walls of a palace can get to be too much after several weeks.

Alex is late for dinner almost every night. He's a workaholic, but he's also putting a big effort into finding the man who's threatening his life. He refuses to tell me much, always answering my questions with vague answers. Since he's also focusing a lot of his attention on preparing for the gala dinner, I don't bother him with selfish requests to go outside. We'll attend the ball soon enough.

In the meantime, I content myself with walks in the garden. At first, the heavily armed men unsettled me. Their weapons made me nervous. With time, I got used to the guns. The automatic rifles slung over their shoulders don't shock me as much as they did initially.

Three days before the party, a team of people arrive first thing in the morning for a dress fitting as well as a makeup and hairdressing trial. To my dismay, Lena is present to act as translator, her condescending smile never slipping.

The dressmaker, a middle-aged woman with exotic features, shows me three evening gowns to choose from. The first is white and figure-hugging with diamante detail, and the second is a red dress with a low back and wide skirt. Both are gorgeous, but the third is my favorite. The cut is simple. The skirt is long with a slit on the side that ends just above the knee, and the sleeves are off-shoulder. The pale pink fabric has a beautiful pearly shine. Crystal beads have been sewn onto the bodice, artfully creating delicate flowers.

The dressmaker suggests that I try on all three dresses, but I already know which one I want. She helps me put on the pink dress and positions me in front of the full-length mirror. The dress looks as if it were made for me. The only adjustment necessary is taking up the hem a few inches. She pairs the gown with high-heeled silver sandals and a matching clutch bag. The outfit is perfect.

After pinning the hem, she helps me remove the shoes and the dress. I put on a robe over my underwear and install myself in front of the mirror in Alex's dressing room for the makeup trial that follows next.

The makeup is heavier than what I usually wear, but the black eyeliner, smoky eyeshadow, and nude lipstick are suitable for a formal evening. The hairdresser takes my hair up in soft curls, leaving a few tendrils to hang down my neck. When the makeup artist and hairdresser are done and ask if I'm satisfied with the end result, Lena translates my answer, telling them I'm very happy. They both wear broad smiles as they pack up their equipment.

Lena stands at attention like a drum majorette in the dressing room while they clip their cases closed. She watches my reflection in the mirror as I wipe off the makeup with cotton swabs. I don't want to be rude, but the way she's studying me makes me uncomfortable.

"I won't keep you any longer," I say, trying to dismiss her politely. "Thanks for translating."

She lifts her chin. "I suppose grace is inherited and can't be learned."

I pause with my hand in midair. "Excuse me?"

The ladies wave and take their leave. A guard waits outside the door to escort them downstairs. If they're insulted about having their cases and persons searched before entering and exiting the house, they don't show it.

When it's just Lena and me, she says, "The white gown and subtler makeup would've been more appropriate."

I pull my spine straight. "I liked the way I looked."

"Well." She sniffs. "Just make sure you don't embarrass Mr. Volkov." She adds with meaning, "The whole of Russia will be watching the event."

"You can go now," I say in a firm tone, no longer making an effort to be polite.

"You're not done yet." She waves a hand toward the door. "What about the beautician?"

My smile is tight. "I'll manage."

"As you wish," she says, turning on her heel and leaving.

I'm definitely not Lena's choice of a partner for Alex. I suppose not being from royal ancestry doesn't help.

The beautician has already set up her makeshift salon in the indoor garden next to the pool. She gives me a wax and a full-body exfoliation before treating me to a massage. After a manicure and pedicure, I'm ready for the upcoming party.

It's not quite noon, but the sky is gray and it's snowing outside. Once again alone in the big house with no patients to treat, I put on my swimsuit and do a few laps in the pool. When I surface for air after swimming underwater, I come face to face with a pair of fancy black dress shoes.

I trail my gaze from the shoes to the dark suit pants and button-up shirt until I meet Alex's handsome face. With his hands shoved into his pockets, he's in a relaxed stance, but the underlying tension is ever-present in his body.

Propping my forearms on the edge of the pool, I smile up at him. "Hey. Playing hooky from work today?"

His smile is faint in return. "Having fun?"

"Just keeping fit. Or trying to, at least."

His smile doesn't widen at my attempted humor. Offering me a hand, he says, "I'm sure your fitness is great."

I close my fingers around his and let him pull me out. He takes the towel I left on the chaise lounge and wraps it around my shoulders.

Rubbing the towel over my arms, he says, "Katyusha, there was an incident with your mom."

I freeze. "What?"

"You don't have to worry. She's fine. She just had a little setback."

"Setback?" I take a step sideways, escaping his touch. "What kind of setback?"

"She had a dizzy spell and fell, but she didn't hurt herself and nothing is broken. The doctor examined her. Her blood pressure is fine."

A hollow feeling settles in the pit of my stomach. "Why wasn't I told?"

"I'm informing you now," he says in a reasonable tone.

Anguish and helplessness mix together, turning into anger. "When did you find out?"

"An hour ago. That's why I came home. I left the office as soon as I received the news."

I take another step to the side, creating more distance between us. "You could've called me. You *should've* called me. Immediately."

"Katyusha." He raises his hands. "I thought it was better to tell you in person."

"If I had a damn phone, this wouldn't have been an issue. I would've known an hour ago." I march toward the door. "I want to speak to her."

Before I've made it halfway across the floor, he grabs my wrist and spins me around to face him.

"You have to calm down, Katerina. I know this is upsetting for you—"

I yank my arm from his hold. "You have no idea how this is for me."

He narrows his eyes. "As I was saying, I know this is upsetting for you, but she's in good hands. It was probably just a little low blood sugar from adapting to the new diet."

"You don't know that. It could be a more serious problem. I want to speak to her, Alex." I make my voice hard. "Now."

He clenches his jaw. "It's not even five in the morning there. She's sleeping. You'll speak to her later today."

"Now," I repeat. Unable to go to my mom or to offer my help is bad enough. His attempt to keep me from speaking with her makes me feel just a little hysterical.

"Katerina," he says harshly, grasping my shoulders. "Get ahold of yourself."

"No." I twist out of his grip. "I want to see her. She's my mother. Don't you get that? She's the only family I have."

"Katyusha," he says in a gentler tone, reaching for me again. "Don't upset yourself so much, my love."

I backtrack to the door. "She's sick. She fainted. She *fell*, for crying out loud. I'm not going to sit here like a pampered princess while my mom needs me."

The blue of his eyes hardens like glittering gemstones. "You'll stay here or wherever I decide to keep you safe, and you'll do as I say. That's the only choice you have in this equation, kiska."

The harsh words are like a blow to my head. We've been doing so great, getting along so well, pretending that everything is normal. Yet it's not. And I can't do anything about it.

Spinning around, I run for the door. To my relief, he doesn't follow. He grants me the reprieve of solitude as I lock myself in the library and come to terms with the truth. Over and over, I come to terms with it. *This is no honeymoon*. No matter how great or adventurous the sex, no matter how well he treats me, there are limits to this arrangement, and only one person makes the rules.

Alex. He holds all the power.

Now that I'm slightly calmer, however, I have to admit he's right about the hour. I'm not going to call my mom at five a.m. and wake her if she's sleeping. I don't have a choice but to wait until it's later in the morning in the States, at least nine or so.

A knock comes from the door.

"Katyusha?" Alex calls. "Come have lunch. You have to eat."

I have a good mind to throw a vase at the door, but he's right again. Starving myself isn't going to change anything.

Taking a few deep breaths, I get my emotions under control before unlocking the door. He stands on the threshold like a king, regal and imposing, his large frame dominating the space.

"I want to see her, Alex," I say quietly. "I want to examine her for myself."

"That's her doctors' job and what I'm paying them for," he says in an uncompromising tone. "This discussion is over." He holds out a hand. "Now come dress and have lunch with me."

He's not giving me a choice. Nothing has changed since we arrived in St. Petersburg. Maybe it will never change.

I don't accept his proffered hand. Gritting my teeth, I go upstairs, change, and join him for lunch in the dining room.

Our meal progresses in silence. He tries to draw me into a conversation a couple of times, asking about the dress rehearsal and if I like the ball gown, but when he remains unsuccessful at getting a response, he eventually falls quiet.

He does wait with me in his study until the clock strikes four p.m. He works while I pace the floor. The minute the grandfather clock announces the hour, he connects his laptop and activates a video call.

When my mom's face comes onto the screen, I collapse onto the sofa in relief at how well she looks. Her cheeks have a healthy glow, and her blond hair is prettily styled. She's wearing her favorite blue sweater and a lighter blue silk scarf that brings out the color of her eyes. Judging by the painting behind her on the wall, she's sitting in the lounge.

"Mom, hi." I swallow to contain my emotions. "How are you?"

"Katie," she says with a broad smile. "Alex. How good to see you."

I glance up to find Alex behind me, leaning with his arms on the backrest of the sofa.

"So," my mom says. "How are you two doing?"

I wave a hand. "Never mind us. Are you all right? I had such a fright. What happened?"

She utters an embarrassed laugh. "I didn't want to worry you. It's nothing. I told the doctor he shouldn't even have called you."

"Of course he had to," I exclaim.

"I got up to pee at night and tripped over the dresser, that's all."

Narrowing my eyes, I study her face. She looks thinner, some of the roundness of her cheeks gone. "They said it was a dizzy spell. Are you eating enough?"

"The dietician is excellent." My mom adjusts her

scarf. "I'm eating more than enough, and the food is delicious. The doctor already ran a few blood tests, and everything looks fine."

"Okay," I say slowly, unable to shake my concern.

"These things happen," my mom says. "I'd taken a hot bath earlier in the evening, and I might've under-eaten a bit at dinner. It's possible my blood pressure might've been a bit low. In any event, they're monitoring me like a baby, so you can enjoy your vacation without any worries." She gives me a bright smile. "Speaking of your vacation, how is it going?"

"Great," Alex says. "Although, we haven't gotten around to as much sightseeing as we'd like."

My mom winks. "I understand. You're not getting out of the bedroom a lot, are you?"

"Mom!"

"I still have plenty to show Katerina," Alex says, not missing a beat at my mom's remark. "I want her to get to know my home country."

"Understandably." Mom checks her watch. "I'm afraid I have to go. I have a checkup with the doctor in five minutes."

"Let me know how it goes," I say. "And please take care of yourself."

"I will." She blows us a kiss. "Thank you for checking on me. Speak to you later, kids."

At *kids*, Alex chuckles. She's my parent, but she's only seven years older than Alex.

When the screen goes black, he leans over me to close the laptop.

"Thanks," I say, rubbing my palms over my thighs. "You didn't have to be here for this." He could've gone back to the office to work in peace.

"It was the least I could do," he says, squeezing my shoulder. "Now I'm going to get some more work done, and then we'll grab dinner."

My mom texts Alex after her checkup and cheerfully informs us that she's as healthy as a horse. Still, I worry about it all through dinner, and then I can't fall asleep at night. Alex does his best to wear me out with mind-blowing pleasure, but for once, even that doesn't help. So after I toss and turn for two hours straight, I get up. To my surprise and over my protests, he gets up too, and then he stays up with me, quietly working on his computer next to me while I watch some *Downton Abbey* in an effort to take my mind off things.

By three a.m., I'm completely exhausted, but my mind is still churning. To calm myself, I ask Alex to text my mom again, to check if she's had any other spells and he does. Mom replies right away, assuring me that she's perfectly fine and has had a great day.

Alex watches me with compassion. "Now that you've seen for yourself that there's nothing to worry about, let's get some sleep."

There won't be much sleep for him. He's up every morning at six to work out until seven before leaving for the office at seven-thirty. Sometimes, he exercises in the gym, and at other times, he spars with his men in the barracks. My stomach is always tied in knots when he's training with them, knowing how quickly an accident with a blade can happen.

Coming around the sofa, he sits down next to me. "Katyusha." He waits for me to look at him before he continues. "I know this isn't easy for you."

"My mom…" I swallow the lump in my throat. "She has no one but me."

"I know," he says, brushing a strand of hair behind my ear. "That's why I'm taking you to see her for Christmas."

"You are?" I ask with surprise.

"Yes, kiska."

"When did you decide this?"

He simply looks at me.

Ah. He's made a spur-of-the-moment decision to soothe my bruised feelings. He's made it all by himself without discussing it with me—not that I'm unhappy about the prospect. My battered ego doesn't want me to accept the olive branch he's offering, but if it means I'll get to see my mom, I'll gladly lay down my pride.

"Thanks," I say in a detached tone, pushing to my feet. "That's very generous of you."

The text reply from Mom has comforted me, yet something inside of me still feels broken. It feels as if I've been violated, which is exactly the case. My free will has been stripped away, and Alex won't let me forget it. His actions keep on reminding me of my inferior place in his life.

He follows my progress with a dark gaze as I walk out of the room, but like earlier, he doesn't come after me. He lets me go to bed alone. And when I wake up the next morning, he's already gone.

19

ALEX

I'm like a wounded bear at the office. Even Grigori stays out of my way. It's more than the lack of sleep. My kitten is docile—for now—but she's angry with me. She's unhappy about the choices I'm taking from her hands, and when she's upset, so am I, especially since I'm the reason she's upset to begin with. This whole damn situation is driving a wedge between us. I'm worried that by the time this nightmare is over, that wedge will have settled for good.

No matter. I'm nothing if not dedicated and resilient. I'll work hard to win back her adoration. Once she's taken my surname, I'll have all the time in the world to obtain that goal. In a few months from now, when we look back on all of this, she'll see that I was right. She'll understand that I acted in her best interest. Eventually, she'll forgive me.

My phone rings on the way from the boardroom to my office. It's Adrian. Igor follows closely behind me, keeping up with my long strides as Adrian tells me there's still no answer from Mukha and no sign of him either. The hacker is practically a ghost, untraceable and nonexistent as far as his trail goes.

I hang up with a curse and slam a palm on the door of my office. Igor catches the door before it bangs against the wall.

"Alex," he says as I plop down in the seat behind my desk.

The rare use of my first name makes me look at him. "What?"

"You're not your usual self."

"No shit." I push on the thumbprint scanner to open the wall shutter. "And your point is?"

He advances to my desk. "You need to remain level-headed. You have to keep your wits about you if you're going up against Stefanov."

I boot up the wall-mounted computer screen. "Three fucking weeks and we're not making any progress."

"It's more than the lack of progress," he says, giving me an even look. "You're upset because of Katherine."

I narrow my eyes. "Careful, Igor. I owe you for saving my life, but don't think for one second that gives you the right to put your nose in my private affairs."

He's undeterred. "Her stress is rubbing off on you."

Indeed. I'm not an unfeeling monster. I know how tough the news about Laura was on my kiska.

"There was an incident with her mother yesterday,"

I say, wiping a hand over my brow. "Everything is fine now. She'll come around."

"This has been going on since way before yesterday. She's in the dark. Put yourself in her shoes. Imagine how she must be feeling."

"Are you the expert on Katerina's feelings now?" I ask in a tight voice.

"She's not stupid. She's picking up on things. She asked me about you the day after you took her sightseeing."

"Is that right?" If Igor is discussing me with *my* woman behind my back, I swear I'll break his face. My tone is cool. Shrewd. "Asked you what exactly?"

"Why you were so tense."

I curl my fingers into a fist on the desktop. "If you told her someone is watching the house…"

I don't finish the threat. Igor knows me well enough to understand what would happen to him if he'd been so stupid. Katerina has enough to worry about. I'm not dumping information on her that can only give her nightmares and more sleepless nights.

He raises his hands. "I didn't tell her anything."

"But?"

"Maybe you need to share more with her."

He's really starting to get on my nerves. "Like what?"

"You haven't told her about Stefanov and Pavlov. You need to tell her what's going on. What if she gets it into her head to run?"

"There's a damn good reason for not telling her," I

say, slamming my fist on the desk. "And it's none of your business."

He backtracks a step. "It's your call. I just thought—"

"Don't fucking think where Katerina is concerned. That's my job."

He drops his hands. "Whatever you say."

"Is that the reason why you insisted on accompanying me to the office today? To chew off my ear about how I treat my girlfriend?"

He shakes his head. "Alex."

"Mr. Volkov," I grit out. There are limits to what I'll tolerate. Katerina is definitely off limits.

"Mr. Volkov," he says, giving me a wounded look. "Leonid was long overdue for babysitting duty."

Looking at the door pointedly, I say, "I have work to do."

He nods. "If you need me, I'll be checking on the man who's watching Stefanov's house."

"You do that," I say in a frosty tone.

The minute he's closed the door behind him, I pop in my earbuds and dial Krupnov, the most prestigious jeweler in Eastern Europe. Katerina isn't going to run. She's too clever to attempt something so foolish—not to mention, my staff and the guards won't let her. Yet Igor's words have ignited a spark of unrest in my gut. All the more reason to follow through sooner than later on the decision I've made.

Just when I think Krupnov isn't going to pick up, he answers with a haughty, "Good morning."

"Alex Volkov on the line."

"Mr. V-volkov," he says, sounding flustered. "What an honor."

"I need a ring."

"Of c-course," he stammers. "What kind of ring?"

"An engagement ring. Send me a few designs."

"Y-yes. Absolutely. As you may very well know, all my rings are custom made, each one unique. There are no two of the same in the world."

"I don't need a sales pitch, Krupnov. If I'm calling you, it's because I've already made up my mind."

"W-well, yes, sir. It's just that I'll need to meet the lady to design a ring that will match her p-physique as well as her character. I don't have to tell you that w-women can be very particular in their tastes."

I pull up the forecast for the joint venture. "I want a diamond, the biggest one you have." Opening the spreadsheet, I glance over the figures. "And rubies. The best quality ones you can find. Set the stones in white gold. I'll send you the size."

It shouldn't be too difficult to obtain that. I can measure one of Katerina's rings. She has a ring shaped like a rose that she wears on her right hand. Her left ring finger should be no more than half a size smaller than her right. Or better yet, I can buy her a new ring and use the excuse to measure her finger.

Suddenly eager to set my plan in motion, I ask, "How long will it take you to design?"

"F-for you, sir, I'll put the job in the front of the queue."

I tap on the button to bring up the cost sheet for the construction of the new reactors. "How long, Krupnov?"

I'll have to move some funds around and liquidate a couple of other investments if I'm to put this much into the joint venture, but this is important to me. I know what it feels like to be poor and freezing. I send an email to my CFO with instructions to start the liquidation process.

"The d-design can be ready in a week's time, provided that you approve and don't w-want to make changes, but it will take me longer to make the r-ring. All my designs are hand crafted with—"

"Delivery date?"

"How about V-Valentine's Day?" he asks uncertainly. "It's always a g-good date for an engagement."

"New Year's and not a day later. I trust I can rely on your discretion?"

"Y-yes, Mr. Volkov. Of c-course, Mr. Volkov."

"And Krupnov?"

"Yes, Mr. V-volkov?"

"If it's not the prettiest ring that's ever been made, I'll kill you."

He gives a high-pitched laugh.

I hang up just as the door opens and Dania Turgeneva walks into my office.

Minimizing the screen, I watch with wary surprise as she crosses the floor. She's dressed in a red two-piece suit with matching heels. Her dark hair is drawn back in a high ponytail, and the makeup on her face is flawless.

It's not the first time she's been here, but she's never walked into my office unannounced. She's also always accompanied her father. The fact that she's here alone tells me this isn't a business visit.

"Alex Volkov," she says, stopping in front of my desk with her hands on her hips. "How un-neighborly of you to be back in St. Petersburg for three weeks already without so much as a call."

Manners dictate that I stand. "I've been busy."

"So I've heard." Her red lips stretch into a smile. "Lena told me you have a guest."

"Lena, huh?" I round my desk and indicate the sofa in the sitting corner. "I didn't realize the two of you were so friendly."

She sits with a graceful movement and crosses her legs. "I called your house to invite you to dinner." She shrugs. "Lena answered."

I take the chair facing the sofa. "I see."

"Friday night," she says, tapping her long, red fingernails on the armrest.

"I'm afraid that won't be possible."

She gives me a sly look. "Lena already told me you have nothing planned."

"Lena is my housekeeper." I add with an unfriendly smile, "She doesn't plan my agenda."

"Playing it safe?" She raises a brow. "Everyone knows about the attempt on your life. Is that why you keep your girlfriend locked up in your house?"

"Obviously, Lena talks too much." I make a mental note to reprimand Lena when I get home.

She waves a hand. "Don't blame poor Lena. It's pretty much common knowledge in town. You know how fast news travels, especially when you book out restaurants and boutiques for your girlfriend." She pauses with a dramatic air. "Or shall I say soon-to-be fiancée?"

If she weren't the daughter of a business associate whom I happen to respect and admire, I would throw her out of my office and have her escorted from the building.

Instead, I give her a hard look. "Have you been eavesdropping, Dania?"

"I was about to knock." She makes big eyes. "I couldn't help but overhear. Krupnov, mm? You're not playing around."

"Is there a point to this visit?" My calm voice doesn't betray my impatience. "I have a busy morning scheduled."

"I'm just a little surprised. I mean, you? Engaged?" She laughs. "Love has never been high on your priority list. Are you even capable of the feeling? I know you better than anyone, Alex Volkov. You've never said *I love you* to anyone." She gives me a polished smile. "But maybe I'm old-fashioned. Maybe in your book, marriage doesn't require love."

My jaw flexes. "I do love Katerina, very much, and I'll tell her so in no uncertain terms when I put that ring on her finger."

She gasps. "You haven't told her?" Her gaze narrows as her lips part wider. "You haven't said the big L-word yet. My, oh my. Are you sure you're doing the right thing? If it's that hard to say, maybe you don't feel as strongly about her as you should."

She couldn't be more wrong, but how I feel about Katerina is none of her damn business. "My feelings are none of your concern." I lean closer. "And if you mention a word to anyone and spoil the surprise, you will sorely regret it."

"Shame on you, Alex." She clicks her tongue. "How long have we been friends?"

I stand. "Not long enough to cross the line you're crossing now."

"Oh, calm down. I'm not going to tell anyone, if that's what you're worried about. I'll keep your little secret. I'm shocked at the bold step, that's all." She irons an invisible crease from her pants with a palm. "Are you sure it will be a good surprise for… What's her name again? Kate, right?"

"Katerina," I say through clenched teeth. "Katherine."

"Are you sure Katherine will say yes?"

My reply is filled with calculated determination. "Oh, she will."

Dania gets up. "A word of advice? Make sure she still feels the same as she did in New York before you pop the question." Winking, she adds, "This is Russia. Things are different here than in America. Not everyone can adapt to our way of living."

Our way of living doesn't refer to how we do things in our motherland. It refers to the kind of men Mikhail and I are, to the things we do to survive. Dania grew up in this world. Katerina didn't. That's what Dania is implying.

"Grigori will see you out," I say evenly. "Give my apologies to your father for not being able to make the dinner."

For a second, the well-practiced act Dania puts on for the world cracks, and a flicker of concern slips into her dark eyes. Going on tiptoes, she kisses my cheek. "Do take care, Alex. I hope you're making progress in tracking down whoever wants you dead."

"I am," I lie.

"You know my father would gladly help."

"I can take care of myself."

"Promise me you'll be careful."

"I promise."

She bites her lip, regarding me quietly for a moment. "You know, Alex, you and me—"

"There is no you and me, Dania."

Money is as important to her as it is to her father. She's always been more interested in my wallet than in my heart.

She puts on a fake smile. Just like that, her mask is back in place. "I suppose I won't see you before the party then. Papa is going to extreme measures with security. I guess the reason is you."

"I guess," I say, shoving my hands into my pockets.

Flashing me another practiced smile, she walks to

the door. "Don't be a stranger, Alex," she says, pausing in the frame. "Papa considers you a friend."

I follow her with my gaze as she walks through the foyer and past Grigori's desk.

The minute she gets into the elevator, my assistant rushes over.

"I'm sorry, Mr. Volkov. I told her you were busy, but she wouldn't take no for an answer," he says before closing my door with an apologetic expression.

I blow out a breath to rid myself of the lingering annoyance and sit back at my desk. No one says no to Turgenev's daughter. Certainly not my assistant, who's considered way beneath her in the power hierarchy. She's her daddy's princess, and a spoiled one at that, one who's used to getting her way.

For once, though, Dania Turgeneva isn't getting what she wants. She's not getting my money or my status, and she's taking it surprisingly well. Then again, I've been very clear about my intentions. Perhaps she finally understands that there's only one woman destined to be Mrs. Volkova.

2 0

KATE

*T*he same team of women arrive on the afternoon of the gala to help me get dressed for the event. Thankfully, this time, Lena isn't present.

I'm ready half an hour before the time Alex said we needed to leave. A guard escorts the women downstairs while I add the finishing touches by dabbing on perfume and putting on the ruby earrings Alex gave me in New York.

By six, I go in search of Alex, who dressed in one of the other rooms to give the women space in his. The hallway I pass through is quiet, not a sound coming from behind any of the closed doors. Not knowing which suite he's using, I make my way to the foyer.

Since the incident with my mom, the atmosphere between us is still strained. Neither of us has brought up the argument again. We're maintaining peace by avoiding the subject. Alex came home late the following night, and we had dinner as if nothing happened. Later, in bed, we made love like he hasn't shattered my life and like the world around us isn't falling apart.

As I near the end of the hallway, voices drift from downstairs. I pause on top of the landing. Alex and a man I haven't met are conversing in the foyer. Alex is wearing dark suit pants and a fitted waistcoat over a white shirt. With his dark brown hair brushed back and his shoulders impossibly broad, he looks danger-ously handsome. Intimidatingly so. The thin, short frame of the man facing him only aids in emphasizing Alex's formidable strength and size.

I haven't made a sound, but Alex pauses mid-sentence and glances toward where I stand. The blue of his eyes heats a shade as he trails his gaze over me.

"Katerina," he says in a deep voice, pronouncing my name with that Russian accent that always makes it sound exotic. "I'd like you to meet someone."

I pay closer attention to his guest. Like Alex, the man is dressed in a dark suit, but a less formal one. He's holding a metal case the size of a briefcase in one hand and a cane in the other.

Alex leaves the man standing there and climbs up the stairs to meet me at the top. Catching me off guard, he lowers his head and plants a kiss on the shell of my ear. It's a tender but possessive kiss, one that unmistak-ably stakes a claim.

"You look beautiful," he says softly enough only for me to hear.

It's not so much the words as the admiration in his eyes that gives weight to the compliment.

He offers me his arm. When I've placed my palm on his forearm, he carefully leads me down the stairs. I'm used to walking in heels, but I appreciate the gentlemanly gesture.

"This is Mr. Krupnov," he says when we reach the bottom of the staircase.

The man puts the case down and rushes over as fast as his cane allows. Extending a hand, he says in a heavily accented English, "A p-pleasure to meet you."

"Likewise," I say, accepting his handshake.

Placing a hand over mine where it rests on his arm, Alex smiles down at me. "Shall we go to the lounge? I have a surprise for you."

I look between Alex and the man, a tinge of nerves sparking in my stomach. Under normal circumstances, I like surprises, but with the situation we've found ourselves in, I've learned to be cautious. I don't like the disadvantage of being in the dark.

"Please follow me," Alex says to Mr. Krupnov, leading the way to the lounge.

Once inside, we stand stiffly in the center of the room while the man leans his cane against the sofa and places the case on the coffee table. When he clips it open, my breath catches. Rows of rings set with gemstones of all the colors of the rainbow fill the case. The designs range from elaborately bulky to plainly elegant.

"Choose one," Alex says, motioning at the box.

The craftsmanship of the rings is exquisite. I don't doubt each one costs a fortune. Of course, Alex can easily afford the whole case of rings. What bothers me isn't the price of the gift he's proposing but the reason for it. I've learned that Alex never does anything without a careful calculation.

"It's not my birthday," I say.

Alex gives me a crooked smile. "I'm well aware."

"Then why?"

He raises a brow. "Do I need a reason?"

I study his face, but his expression gives away nothing.

"I c-couldn't help but notice your earrings," Mr. Krupnov says with a wink. "May I suggest the ruby ring?" He picks up a golden ring with a big ruby in the center and smaller ones surrounding it. "This o-one is a classic design. Q-quite timeless."

"Try it on," Alex says.

When I don't move, Alex snatches the ring from Mr. Krupnov's palm and takes my hand. Holding my gaze, he slips it over my ring finger.

I look down. Wow. The somewhat old-fashioned design transforms on my hand, the tier of rubies taking on a three-dimensional effect as the gemstones catch the light and come to life as if each of them has a heartbeat.

Alex twists the ring to test the fit. "It's a little loose."

"T-that's not a problem." Mr. Krupnov takes a finger gauge set from his pocket. "I c-can easily adjust the band." He gives me a questioning look. "If t-this is the ring the lady likes? M-maybe you'd like to t-try some others?"

The ring is perfect, but I say, "I can't accept this. It's too much."

"We'll take it," Alex says.

Mr. Krupnov jumps on the sale. "I-I'll just take the young lady's finger sizes, and y-you'll have the ring by n-next week."

"Alex," I protest.

He gently wiggles the ring from my finger and hands it to Mr. Krupnov before kissing my hand. "I won't hear any arguments on the matter."

"Why?" I ask as Mr. Krupnov takes a notebook and pencil from his other pocket.

Alex presses a kiss to the corner of my lips. "Because I can."

Just like that, the discussion is over. Mr. Krupnov takes the measurements of my fingers and scribbles them in his notebook. He asks on which finger I'd like to wear the ring, writes that down too, and then he takes his leave.

When we're alone, I feel compelled to say, "Thank you," even though Alex didn't give me the option of refusing his gift.

He frowns. "You don't look happy. If you don't like that ring, I'll get you another one."

"The ring is gorgeous."

"Then what's the matter?" he asks, taking my hand.

"I'm not used to receiving gifts that must cost more than what I make in a year."

Resting a hand on my hip, he tips up my chin with a finger. "Get used to it."

I'm about to press him more for the motivation behind the sudden gift, but he stills me with another kiss on my lips.

"We'd better go." Tension flows into the set of his shoulders. "We can't be late. I want to get to the venue before everyone else."

Right. Because it's dangerous to go outside.

My stomach muscles knit into a ball when he leads me to the foyer where Lena waits with our coats and my clutch bag. Alex helps me into the tailored white evening coat before pulling on a stylish jacket and his own coat. Steering me outside, he helps me into the car idling in the driveway. As usual, Yuri drives.

We make our way to the old center of the city in a convoy of cars. Alex wears an earpiece and constantly communicates in Russian while checking his phone. After forty minutes, we arrive at a roadblock. Yuri lowers his window and says something to the man who approaches his window. Immediately, the boom gate lifts.

My stomach tightens further as I take in the men in combat gear armed with rifles who are lined up on either side of the road. It's as if we're entering a war zone. At the end of the block, we arrive at a stately building with columns in the front. It's snowing softly. The flakes are illuminated by the golden lights shining from the impressive façade of the former palace that has been turned into a hotel. Lena proudly told me that the venue had been the residence of Princess Lobanova-Rostovskaya in 1820.

We enter a heavily guarded underground parking garage. From there, an elevator with a thumbprint scanner takes us to the ballroom. Alex's bodyguards follow us to the hall, staying no more than a step behind. Alex hands in our coats at the coat room before wrapping an arm around my waist and keeping me close to him.

As we're the first to arrive, the hall is empty of other guests. Round tables are set with brocade tablecloths and gold-trimmed crockery. Some waiters are polishing crystal glasses and golden cutlery, while others are aligning the place settings. The centerpieces are flower arrangements of white lilies and peonies that perfume the hall with their sweet scents. The flowers must've been cultivated in hothouses or flown in from a summer region for the occasion.

When Alex has done a round of the room with me in tow, he leads me to our table and seats me.

"Champagne?" he asks as a waiter appears with a bottle.

"Thank you," I say, nodding at the waiter.

Not long after, the guests start arriving. Within minutes, the hall is brimming with women in gorgeous dresses and men in fancy suits. Alex is holding my hand under the table, but he's still busy on his phone, talking in rapid Russian. I don't mind. I'm entertaining myself by people watching.

The first guests to join our table are an elderly lady

with a red sequined gown and a gentleman with a silver waistcoat and bowtie. Alex introduces them to me as the Dyatlovs.

Mrs. Dyatlova tells me to call her Elvira. Her British-accented English is impeccable, which she attributes to the years she studied in England. Mr. Dyatlov, on the other hand, has to rely on his wife's translations to follow our conversation and soon gives up, launching into a discussion with Alex in Russian instead.

The next invitees to arrive are a couple who look to be in their early forties. Mrs. Feba Zykova is a lively woman who explains that she owns a textile factory, while the subdued Mr. Zykov is in the import and export business. What kind of import and export, his wife doesn't say, and he doesn't seem to speak the best English either. Alex no doubt made sure the women at our table are fluent in English, a consideration I'm very grateful for.

Elvira gives me tips on sights to visit. I let her talk, not telling her I probably won't be able to visit any of the museums or ballets she recommends. Alex is still talking to the men, but he keeps a point of contact between us with his hand on my knee. The touch is both reassuring and possessive.

When Elvira stops talking to take a sip of water, Alex leans over and whispers in my ear, "Not too bored yet?"

I turn my face toward him. Like always, I'm hyper-aware of his presence. The smell of his spicy cologne and the electrifying touch of his fingers on my knee overpower my senses. It's impossible to stare into his eyes and not drown in those vivid blue pools. His lips quirk as his eyes crinkle in the corners. He knows the effect he has on me. With a single look, he renders me defenseless. The attraction between us is as strong as the first day we met. If I weren't so level-headed, I would say running into each other on that day was fate. But that would mean that Igor had been shot for the sole purpose of bringing Alex and me together. Ironically, it would mean that the very reason we're here in St. Petersburg and in this horrifying situation—the fact that someone is trying to kill Alex—is what's responsible for driving us into each other's arms. In some way, I'd have to be grateful to Alex's hunter. If not for him, we never would've met.

"Good evening," a polished female voice says.

I look over at the guests who have arrived at our table and freeze. Dania and her father, Mikhail, stand on the opposite side. My spine goes stiff as I recall my conversation with Dania at the cocktail party in New York, when she told me she was destined to marry Alex.

Dania and Mikhail do the rounds to say their hellos. Dressed in a white gown with a flowing skirt, Dania looks like a Disney princess. Her black hair forms a stunning contrast with her blue eyes and pale skin. Her makeup is light and youthful, giving her an innocent look. Virginal, almost. Classically beautiful. She looks like perfect marriage material, and from the way the men in the room are staring at her, she's undeniably desirable too. Is this what Lena was trying to tell me? That I haven't dressed the part? That I have no idea what I'm up against or how to fight the subtle war for a man's attention?

I steal a look at Alex while Mikhail shakes his hand. At least he's not gawking at Dania like the other gentlemen.

"I'm so glad we're at your table," Dania says when it's our turn to exchange a greeting. "I was looking forward to seeing you when I heard you were in St. Petersburg."

To my dismay, she takes the empty seat next to me. Mikhail installs himself in the available spot on Alex's right.

"How are you, Dania, darling?" Feba asks with affection. She's speaking English, no doubt for my benefit. "It's been ages."

Dania waves a hand. "I've been traveling nonstop. You know how Papa's business takes us around the world."

"I hope you'll pay us a visit now that you're home," Feba says.

"We should organize a lunch," Dania says. "Women only." She winks. "I could do with a break from the company of businessmen."

"I didn't know you were so involved in your father's business," Elvira says with a tinge of disdain. "How's your mother?"

Dania meets Elvira's gaze head-on. "You know how

Mama is. Unfortunately, always intoxicated." To me, she says, "In case you haven't heard the gossip yet, my mother is an alcoholic and not seen in public much."

That shuts Elvira up. The men are still engrossed in their conversation. Mikhail doesn't show any signs of overhearing what has been said.

"To answer your question about my involvement in the business, Elvira," Dania says sweetly, "as you know, I'm the only child. One day, I'll take over."

"More likely, your future husband will," Elvira says.

"How about meeting up at Chekhov's next week?" Dania asks, looking around the table. "They have a new chef and the reviews are outstanding." She turns in her seat to face me. "Kate, you have to come. I can introduce you to some friends who'll help you pass the time while Alex spends all those long hours at the office. Everyone knows what a workaholic he is. If you enjoy the opera and ballet, you must join me at my monthly culture club."

"That will be marvelous," Feba says. "I know you young people prefer the nightclubs, but if you'd care to spend a couple of evenings in an old lady's company, I'd love to introduce you to some of my artist friends. They make for the most entertaining company."

I'm about to make up an excuse of why I won't be able to accept the invitations when Alex says, "I'm afraid that won't be possible."

Dania gives him a wide-eyed look. "Really, Alex. This isn't the Middle Ages. I'm sure Kate is capable of making her own decisions." She fixes her gaze on me. "Aren't you, Kate?"

Alex tightens his fingers on my knee. "Katerina and I still have a lot to see."

"Yet you've done nothing but work since you've been back, as I've seen for myself when we met yesterday," Dania says with a reprimanding frown. "You're not planning on keeping your girlfriend all to yourself, are you?"

I tense even more. They saw each other yesterday, and Alex didn't mention it to me? Then again, why would he? He calls the shots. He only shares with me the facts he deems necessary.

"You know how it is," Alex says with a strained smile.

Dania bats her eyelashes. "Actually, I don't."

The smile on Alex's lips turns cold. "We're like newlyweds." His tone carries an unspoken warning. "Still on honeymoon."

Elvira gasps.

Feba picks up a menu and fans her face.

Apparently, sex before marriage is frowned upon by the older company at our table. Or at least discussing it is.

Dania's grin is smug. "You don't protect a lady's honor, do you, Alex Volkov?"

Mikhail clears his throat and reprimands, "Dania."

"Just watching out for my fellow sisters." Cupping my hand, Dania continues, "Don't let him boss you around even before he's put a ring on your finger.

You're allowed to be your own person. We've moved with the times in Russia, you know."

I pull my hand away. "Thanks, but I'm too busy to accept any invitations at the moment."

"Busy doing what?" Dania asks. "Sitting home alone all day?"

"Nursing," I say in a tight voice.

"Nursing," Dania says slowly. "Yes, of course. You're a nurse in New York. Alex mentioned something like that. Who are you nursing?" She scoffs. "His bodyguards?"

Under the table, Alex squeezes my knee so hard it almost hurts, but his grip on the stem of his water glass remains light.

"Excuse me," I say, pushing to my feet. "I have to powder my nose."

Alex stands too. "I'll accompany you."

"To the ladies' room?" Feba exclaims, fanning her face faster.

"Please, Alex," Elvira says with a wink. "There are limits even for honeymooners."

Alex's polite humor is all fake. "No one has ever accused me of not being a gentleman."

"I'll accompany her," Dania says, getting up. "If it makes you feel better, Alex, my bodyguards can stand guard."

"Sit, Alex," Mikhail says, placing a hand on Alex's forearm. "Let the women be women and do whatever women do in the ladies' room."

"Gossip," Dania says conspiratorially.

I have no desire to let Dania accompany me to the bathroom. Going there is just an excuse to escape, but everyone is staring at Alex, Dania, and me now, waiting for Alex's call. He's already made me look like someone incapable of making her own decisions. He's announced to the whole table that we can't keep our hands off of each other when the older women have made it clear the subject is taboo in a public conversation. They already have a negative impression of me. If Alex insists on walking me to the bathroom, it will only make matters worse. After what was implied, they'll no doubt think we're going together to have a quickie.

A tense moment passes as indecision plays on Alex's face. I know how worried he is about our safety, but thanks to the measures he put in place, the hall is like Fort Knox.

"We won't be long," I say, taking back the only power I can as I push back my chair.

My heart keeps time with heavy beats. A second passes, then another, and then Alex slowly sits down, but not before catching the gaze of Igor, who stands not far away from our table.

Beyond relieved, I excuse myself and walk away. Dania hooks her arm around mine like we're friends, chatting amiably as I follow the bathroom sign to the end of the hallway.

I don't hear a word she says. My mind feels as if it's been stuffed full of cotton. All I can think about is how humiliated I feel, even though I logically know that wasn't Alex's intention. He was only trying to keep me safe, but in doing so, he told me and everyone else that I can't go anywhere without his consent.

"Hey." Dania nudges my shoulder when we enter the ladies' room. "Are you all right? You look pale."

I go to the vanity and face my reflection in the mirror. My cheeks are indeed pale despite the makeup and the natural olive tint of my skin. Taking a bronzer from my clutch, I brush a little over my cheekbones.

"Is Alex treating you well?" she asks, smoothing a hand over her perfectly styled hair. It's caught in a ballerina bun at the nape of her neck.

"I know what you were doing out there," I say, giving her a hard look. If she thinks I'm going to play her games when we're alone, she'd better think again.

She pats her hair. "What I was doing was looking out for you."

I chuckle humorlessly. "Is that right?"

"Look," she says with a sigh. "Alex told me what's going on when he reached out to me yesterday."

He went running to her with our problems? I don't believe that for one second. I study her face in the mirror as I take a tube of lipstick from my bag. "And what might that be?"

"He told me about the shooting in New York. He's worried."

"Damn right he's worried. Someone is trying to *kill* him."

She leans her backside against the vanity. "He can

ANNA ZAIRES & CHARMAINE PAULS

take care of himself. He's worried about *you*. You're a weakness."

I inhale sharply. "I didn't ask for this to happen."

"No." She gives a wry smile. "That much is clear. You're not here of your own free will. You're nothing but a prisoner. Sadly, now you're keeping Alex a prisoner."

I gape at her. "What?" Has Alex told her he's all but kidnapped me? Or is she just guessing? And what does she mean by that last bit?

She shrugs. "Alex feels responsible for you. He has to stick around now until he's certain you're safe. You're not doing him any favors by hanging around."

She is just guessing about my status, I'm almost sure. Either way, I have no reason to hide the truth. "Like you said," I say, capping the lipstick and dropping it in my bag, "I don't exactly have a choice."

"What if you did have a choice?"

I still. "What's that supposed to mean?"

"What if you could get away?"

I don't like the way this conversation is going. "I won't do that to Alex."

"Do what? Give him a chance to hunt his attacker without you being a ball and chain? You're not only hampering his efforts. You're also significantly reducing his chances of getting out of this alive."

Clenching my fingers around my bag, I turn to face her. "What are you trying to say, Dania?"

"If Alex were with me, like he's supposed to be, my father would've long since gone after my fiancé's attacker. By now, the threat to my future husband would be nonexistent."

My grip tightens. "Bullshit."

"You don't realize how powerful my father is." Her expression is rueful. "It's safe to say we're not going to be friends anytime in the future. The one thing we have in common is that we both care about Alex. It's the only fact we agree on, am I right?"

"Exactly." I narrow my eyes. "What point are you trying to make?"

"Hanging on to him is a selfish move, Kate. You're not from our world. I told you that once already, and if you didn't believe me then, look around you tonight. Look at the people at our table. Do you think you fit in? You can't even speak our language. If you cared about Alex at all, you'd set him free and let him live the life he's destined to live, a good and long life. My father can make that happen. Once we announce our engagement, my dad won't leave a stone unturned to get the man who threatens his future son-in-law and therefore his only daughter's future."

"You're delusional," I say, making to walk away.

She locks her fingers around my wrist, holding me back. "Is this the kind of life you want? Forever under Alex's thumb? Doing as he says and only going where he lets you—*if* he lets you?"

I pull free. "You don't know anything about Alex and me."

"And you don't know how it works in our world, but I think you're beginning to realize that St. Petersburg isn't New York. You won't have a job here and go out to meet friends. Once Alex ties you to him for good, you'll be like a bratva wife. You won't have a say. Your opinion won't matter. You'll be lucky if you ever see your family again."

That strikes a nerve, a painful one, but I pull my lips into a mocking smile. "And it will be different for you?"

"It will be, because my father is Mikhail Turgenev, and I'm the sole heir to his business." Giving me a pitiful look, she asks, "Who is *your* father?"

The arrow hits me straight in the heart. Not knowing my heritage has never bothered me before, and I hate that this woman has the power to make it matter.

"One more thing you need to know about Alex," she continues, "is that he doesn't fall in love. Ever."

Of everything she's said, those words hit me the hardest. "You don't know that."

My mask must be slipping because her expression turns full of pity. "Why do you think he's never told you that he loves you?"

Her statement stabs like a knife into my stomach. It takes everything and more not to show her how much it hurts. Lifting my chin, I say in my most confident tone, "You don't know that either."

She crosses her arms and cocks a hip. "Oh, but I do darling." The pity in her regard intensifies. "He told me so himself yesterday."

If she'd impaled me on a sword, she couldn't have

tortured me more. Not sparing her another glance, I walk out of the bathroom.

Igor and a few guards I don't know are waiting outside. Dania exits on my heels, smiling as if butter won't melt in her mouth.

The guards follow us quietly back to the hall. Alex and Mikhail stand when we arrive at our table. Two waiters jump to action, pulling out our chairs. The appetizers have been served. The others wait until Dania and I have been seated before picking up their eating utensils.

"Is everything all right?" Alex whispers in my ear, rubbing a thumb over my shoulder.

A shiver runs down my arm. "Yes." I force a smile. "Perfectly."

"I was starting to miss you," he says in a husky voice.

"Wine?" Mikhail asks.

"Vodka, please," Dania says.

Feba gives her an approving nod.

Mikhail flicks his fingers, at which a waiter approaches and pours vodka for Dania and wine for me. Mikhail goes on about the sweet wine that's paired with the starter, but I tune him out. All I can think about is Dania's cruel words.

There's a kernel of truth in Dania's argument. Two, actually.

One: will I forever be Alex's puppet? He likes being in control. Will he let me have my life back when all of this is over? And two: am I harming Alex by being in his life? Igor implied I was the reason Alex risked our lives by taking me sightseeing. True, Igor believed I'd selfishly asked Alex to take me out, but even though I actually suggested we stay home, Alex still took the risk for my benefit, and that makes me responsible. In an indirect way, my presence is having a negative impact on Alex's life. What if I *am* making him weak? What if his obsession with me is making him more of a target?

Throughout the five-course dinner, the questions keep churning in my head. I don't remember what I eat and drink, or what the women talk about. When it's time for the keynote speech about nuclear power, Alex considerately translates for me, whispering what is being said in my ear.

The content of the speech goes in one ear and out the other. What sticks is my growing conviction that this potential joint venture is important to Alex because he believes in affordable heat for everyone, including the less fortunate communities.

It feels like forever before we say our goodbyes, which takes a good hour as Alex has many people to greet. At last in the car, I relax marginally for the first time.

"What's wrong, kiska?" Alex asks, draping an arm around my shoulder.

I make another brave effort to smile. "Nothing."

He pulls me closer. "You barely said two words during dinner."

I escape his piercing gaze by looking through the window. "It was difficult to follow the conversation."

Gripping my chin, he turns my face back to him. "The conversation was in English. That's why I made sure the women seated at our table were fluent in your mother tongue."

"Thanks for that," I say with genuine gratitude.

"It's only normal." He searches my face. "There's something else you're not telling me." Narrowing his eyes, he asks, "Did Dania say something to you in the bathroom?"

"Actually, yes." I study him right back. "She said she saw you yesterday."

"She did," he says slowly, a question in the admission.

Then she wasn't lying about that. "She said I'm your weakness."

In the soft, interior light of the car, his blue eyes darken. "You are." Tracing the line of my jaw with his thumb, he says in a low, deep voice, "The only one I've ever had."

I drag in a breath. "If I make you weak—"

His tone turns harsh. "Don't you even dare say it."

"I was just—"

He splays his fingers over my cheeks, pouting my lips, and growls, "I'm not letting you go. Not now. Not ever. Do you understand?"

The truth twists inside me, cutting a little deeper.

"This isn't love," I whisper. "This is obsession."

His blue eyes glimmer as he narrows them another fraction. My heartbeat picks up. The man looking at me is a predator with incredible intelligence and cunning human insight, one of the most business-savvy and intelligent people in the world. He's got power in spades, both the natural kind some men are born with and the kind that comes with money. He's the most powerful person I know, in fact, and he's observing me like a hunter who has no intention of letting his prey get away.

His voice is dangerously soft as he drags his hand down to my neck. "It doesn't matter what you call it. You're mine, and your life is here now." Locking his fingers around my neck, he holds me in a possessive grip. "It will be a happy life if you don't fight it so hard."

I swallow, my throat moving against the pressure of his palm.

Lowering his head, he brushes a question over my lips. "Is that clear, Katyusha?"

"Yes," I say, not daring to breathe.

I know where this is going when he pushes me down, yet I don't stop him. There's only a partition between us and Yuri, but it's not the only time he's taken me in a car. When my back hits the seat, I don't utter a protest. The taste of defeat is bitter in my mouth, but I try to take my loss without letting him see my tears. My stomach clenches with anticipation as I wait for the moment he slays me.

He doesn't make me wait long. Planting the gentlest of kisses on my lips, he dips a hand under my skirt and between my legs. My underwear is no match for his strength. The lacy fabric gives with a tearing sound that mixes with my gasp just before he forcefully sinks two fingers inside me. Barely giving me time to drag in air, he finger-fucks me with harsh strokes.

My body bows to his rhythm, responding with pleasure. He nips my bottom lip and feeds me tender Russian words as he spanks my clit with the heel of his palm while curling his fingers inside. It's a battlefield, and the war is over before it's even begun.

I come in seconds, surrendering like a beaten enemy. It doesn't matter that my release locks every muscle in my body with excruciating ecstasy, or that he presses sweet praise with kisses to my neck for my record-breaking performance. It's a loss all the same.

Because that's how it works in war.

There are only two outcomes, only two sides.

If you're not the winner, you're the loser.

21

ALEX

*I*t's quiet at work, the building deserted except for me, Igor, and a few bodyguards. The sky outside is still dark. A vista of city lights spreads out below my office window, twinkling on a blanket of snow. The streets aren't buzzing with the morning rush hour yet. I'm the first one in, which gives me time to catch up before everyone demands my attention.

Settling behind my desk, I study the report in front of me. The gala was a big success. Many influential business players pledged their support for nuclear power. The pressure is on for the government to give the green light to the new technology. As usual, there's a shitload of red tape, but it's only a matter of time.

I close the report and pull up my emails. After scanning through them, I file the less urgent ones in a folder for later and open the most important messages. The first is from Konstantin Molotov, checking on how the gala went and informing me about a few kinks his engineers have worked out in the latest version of the portable reactors. Konstantin is the brains behind the technology, and though we have yet to formally sign the papers for the joint venture, my engineers and I have been working with him for several months as part of our due diligence process.

The Molotovs are a powerful, well-connected family from Moscow. Their wealth and position in society go back generations, all the way to Czarist Russia. Konstantin Molotov is the oldest of four siblings and is widely considered to be a tech genius, while his younger brother, Nikolai, runs the business side of things—or did until recently. The youngest Molotov brother, Valery, seems to be managing most of their holdings now, though Nikolai is overseeing this particular project despite the fact that he recently married an American woman and is currently residing in a small mountain town in Idaho, in the States.

I reply to Konstantin, telling him that the event went well and that we're one step closer to getting government approval for his technology. Of course, all of this is predicated on the joint venture going through. If the Molotovs back out at the last moment or try to screw me over in any way, it'll take just a few words whispered in the right ears to choke the project with red tape. Naturally, I don't say that to Konstantin. I don't need to. He understands perfectly how things work in our world.

I'm about to launch into a review of the new safety

regulations we're implementing at one of my oil wells when the screen of my phone lights up with a call. I usually send my calls to my voicemail until later in the morning, using the only time I have without interruptions from my employees constructively, but one glance at the caller ID and I take the call.

"Alex," Adrian says. "My apologies for the hour, but I know you're an early riser, and I figured you'd want to hear this without delay."

I tighten my grip on the phone. "Tell me you found Mukha."

"I did. It wasn't easy, but my hacker finally discovered a loophole in Mukha's cyber tracks. We planted a bug in the electronic currency I sent him as payment for the information he gave me. The bug piggybacked on the currency all the way to the Cayman Islands and back to Russia. It turns out he pays for his mother's care at a nursing home in Moscow. I paid her a visit."

"Spare me the details," I say with impatience. "Where is the son of a bitch?"

"He's renting a house on the outskirts of Moscow. I'm on my way there now."

I sit up straighter, anticipation tightening my gut. "Pay him any price he wants for that file, and if he's still not willing to sell, get the information any way you have to." I put emphasis on the next words. "At any cost."

"Understood. I'll get back to you tonight."

The line goes dead.

Finally. It's about time. If all goes well, by nightfall, I'll know the reason Stefanov wants me dead.

22

RESIDENCE OF VLADIMIR STEFANOV, ST.
PETERSBURG

*V*ladimir bounces his leg under his desk. He feels especially on edge tonight. Alex Volkov knows he's behind the assassination attempt. That's the message Volkov was sending by letting Vadim's head soak in a toilet bowl full of shit. That's why Volkov is having his house surveilled. The only reason Volkov hasn't struck yet is because he doesn't know why Vladimir tried to put a bullet in his brain. The only people in the world who do know that are Oleg and Vladimir himself.

Oleg is the weak link. Why else did he run like a dog with his tail between his legs to hide with his family in California? The only thought soothing Vladimir is that this mess will soon be over. Before the clock strikes twelve, one more nagging worry will be something of the past. At last, he'll be able to seal that closet full of skeletons and let it sink to the bottom of the Neva River with the bodies he plans on dumping there.

As it turns out, Oleg Pavlov arrived a short hour ago at the airport and should be ringing his doorbell just about—

Ding dong.

Now.

Inwardly, Vladimir smiles.

For security reasons, his study is soundproof, but he's left the door open so that he can follow the sound of the footsteps as they advance.

Oleg's voice bounces off the arched ceiling of Vladimir's stately home. "How's the family?"

"Good, thank you," Vladimir's wife, Galina, says. "How about Annika and the children?"

"All good," Oleg replies in a strained tone.

Galina enters the study, followed by Oleg. "I'll leave you to your business."

"Galina," Vladimir says. "Go buy us some of that Napoleon cake that Oleg likes so much. The one from the bakery in Nevsky Prospekt."

Her smile is uncertain. "That's so far away. It'll take me an hour or more in the traffic. I'll just go to Lastochka."

"No." Vladimir's double chin quivers as he shakes his head. "That one is no good. Go to the one I told you. Tell the owner I sent you."

"All right," she says with a nod, giving Oleg a tight smile as she leaves the room.

Oleg's shoulders sag in obvious relief. Vladimir knows how Oleg's mind works. Oleg thinks that if Vladimir is sending his wife to buy him some cake, he has nothing to be worried about. He's less nervous about why Vladimir ordered him to fly all the way here from California. He feels exactly the way Vladimir wants him to—safe.

"Sit," Vladimir says jovially, motioning at the chair facing his desk.

Oleg pulls on the knot of his tie as he takes a seat. "What's so urgent that it couldn't wait until after my vacation?"

Vacation, his *zhopa*. After selling Vladimir out to Bes, Oleg was hiding in a hole like the rat he is.

Vladimir studies him with a sly gaze. "We have a problem."

Oleg sits up like a stick man. "What problem?"

"Volkov is on to us."

Oleg pulls on his tie again. "He is? How do you know that?"

Vladimir flicks the picture of Vadim's body across the table. For the purpose of setting today's plan in motion, Vladimir kept the news of Vadim's murder to himself. Better to catch Oleg off guard.

Oleg blanches as he studies the photo. It's not a pretty sight. "How do you know it was Volkov?" he asks, turning the photo upside down.

Vladimir points at the photo. "Because that's the man I sent to grab Katherine Morrell."

"I knew it." Oleg shifts to the edge of his seat, his voice growing in volume. "It was a mistake to interfere."

Vladimir adopts the appropriate hard look. "Are you criticizing me?"

"No, but…"

"But what?" Vladimir asks harshly.

Oleg clears his throat. "When did this happen?"

"Not that long ago," Vladimir says. "I asked you to come the minute I found out. But that's not all. Volkov is having your house watched as we speak. He probably had a man on your tail in California too."

"What?" Oleg's voice turns shrill. "How did he find out?"

"Who knows?" Vladimir shrugs. "What matters is why he came back to St. Petersburg."

Oleg's Adam's apple bobs as he swallows. "Why's that?"

"To start a war. We have to prepare. We need to get our men ready."

"*Mudak*." Oleg drags a hand over his balding, liver-spotted head. "When do you think he'll attack?"

Vladimir doesn't miss the slight shaking of Oleg's hand. "Today. My informants tell me his men are arming up. You have to call your most trusted men here for a meeting. There's no time to waste."

"What about Bes? I need to tell him about Volkov's plans."

"Bes is wasting time going after the woman. He

didn't get the job right the first time. And not the second time either, for that matter. It's up to us now."

Vladimir can almost see the gears turning in Oleg's head. He thinks Vladimir doesn't know that he's a traitor. He thinks Bes wants to fuck them both over, but he can't tell Vladimir that without admitting his betrayal. He thinks like Vladimir expects him to, and when he opens his mouth, he utters the words Vladimir predicted.

"We have to deal with Bes. He insults us. It's not good for our reputation."

Inwardly, Vladimir grins. "In good time. Our priority is Volkov. If we don't act fast, we'll both be dead tonight."

Sweat beads on Oleg's forehead. He takes a handkerchief from his pocket and dabs at his brow. "How much do you think Volkov knows?"

Vladimir puts on a grave expression. "It's hard to say."

"How did he find out?" Oleg asks again, blinking a couple of times. "Only you and I know the truth. That means the traitor is Bes." He mans up, saying with bravado, "That's double the reason to kill that no-good assassin now." As he says this, Oleg almost looks relieved. In his mind, killing the assassin will take care of all his problems. Little does he know.

"We need to destroy all the evidence that can point a finger at us," Vladimir says. "I got rid of everything on my side the same day Volkov escaped from foster care."

Of course, he did nothing of the kind. Just like Oleg, he kept the evidence locked in his safe as insurance for the day he needed something to blackmail Oleg with. The only one who knows Vladimir never burned the evidence is himself. "Do you have anything that'll incriminate us?"

"No," Oleg says, averting his eyes briefly before meeting Vladimir's gaze again.

Vladimir smiles. Oleg has just given him a valid reason to off him. No one in the bratva will blame him for executing a traitor.

"Call your men." Vladimir checks his watch for dramatic effect. "We need to ambush Volkov before he makes it out of his house. If he catches us here, we're fucked."

Oleg clutches the armrests of his chair. "Between your men and mine, he'll be outnumbered."

"He's got Turgenev on his side, remember?"

"*Mudak*," Oleg says, now sweating so profusely that dark patches stain his shirt around his armpits.

Pushing to his feet, Oleg takes his phone from his pocket and dials his second-in-command with a swift instruction to bring the highest-ranking men in his organization to Vladimir's stronghold of a house. Fast.

"Let's drink to our victory," Vladimir says when Oleg ends the call, producing a bottle of vodka.

Oleg looks aghast. "You know it's bad luck to drink before the deal is done."

"Come on," Vladimir says with a mocking smile.

"We have to behave like victors, not losers. Besides, we'll catch Volkov by surprise. He won't expect us to storm his house. He'll expect us to hide in our fortresses where we're best protected."

Oleg wets his lips. Hesitantly, he takes the glass Vladimir offers.

They drink a toast, and then another. Oleg's men arrive just as they finish the third. The five men who rank highest in his organization are his cousins, an uncle, and a nephew.

Vladimir gets to his feet with effort, his joints groaning under his weight. His words are loaded. He chooses the right expression to go with them, enjoying the little drama he's putting on. "Let's go talk where it's safe."

The men nod in unison. Vladimir sweeps his study daily for bugs, but the opposition and the clean players in the police force always find new ways. Their latest favorites are drones.

Vladimir leads the way. His men wait outside the door to his study. They let Oleg and his men pass, discreetly covering Vladimir's back before following the entourage to the basement.

Like the study, the basement is soundproof, but for a different reason.

Vladimir walks down the well-lit stairs to where a guard stands at the bottom. Taking his gun from his waistband, he hands it to the guard, who places it on a table where a bottle of vodka and shot glasses are set out to look like a preview to a celebration.

"Gentlemen," Vladimir says, motioning at the table for them to disarm as well.

One by one, they lay their weapons on the table.

When the guard pats them down for concealed guns and knives, Vladimir says, "My apologies for the necessary precautions, but you know how heated we men can get when the testosterone levels run high."

Everyone laughs at that, except Oleg's uncle. He glances at Oleg. "I don't like this."

Lowering his head to Oleg's ear, Vladimir says in a conspiratorial tone, "I don't need to remind you that Volkov could already be on his way here as we speak. We have one shot at taking him out. If we fuck it up…" He leaves the sentence hanging, letting Oleg imagine the worst.

Oleg commands his uncle with a flick of his head. Like the rest of the men, his uncle disarms and hands over the gun strapped to his ankle.

"Through here." Vladimir motions at the door down the hallway that his guard opens. "I have a surprise waiting for you."

Oleg tenses at *surprise*. "What's inside there?"

Vladimir gives him a pat on the back. "Go see for yourself."

Oleg's uncle is the lamb who sacrifices himself for the slaughter and goes in first. Sticking his head back around the frame, he says with a frown, "It's a woman."

"A woman?" Oleg asks, sounding confused.

Equally baffled, the uncle replies, "Handcuffed."

"Go on," Vladimir says, hardly able to contain the spark of excitement igniting inside him.

Oleg catches that spark. His eyes gleam with wicked intent as he forgets to be frightened and goes inside to see which whore Vladimir is gifting him and his men. He's done it before. It's only natural that Oleg believes the lie.

When Oleg and his entire crew are inside, Vladimir's men pick up their guns and follow. The guard locks the door.

Oleg blinks at the fearful woman in the cheap, revealing clothes who's handcuffed to the metal frame of the bed. Her thin arms and legs are dirty, and her bleached hair is oily. Usually, they go for high-class hookers, and they like to play dress-up. Oleg's favorite is a dominatrix uniform and a whip.

"Why is she dressed like that?" Oleg asks, wrinkling his nose. "She looks like a whore you snatched from a street corner." He turns on his heel. "What's going on, Vlad?"

Vladimir's men pull their guns.

Oleg raises his hands, palms out. "Vladimir." His voice trembles. "What are you doing?"

"On your knees," Vladimir grits out. "All of you."

When they don't react, Vladimir takes a gun from one of his men and slams the weapon against the side of Oleg's head.

Oleg drops to his knees.

"Down," Vladimir says, pointing the barrel between Oleg's eyes.

One by one, Oleg's men kneel.

Good. They should be crawling in the dirt at his feet.

"Fucking traitor," Vladimir says. "Did you think I wouldn't find out?"

"Please." Oleg cowers with his hands in front of his face. "Bes blackmailed me. He said he'd kill my family if I didn't give him the information." When Vladimir only grins, Oleg cries out, "He tricked me."

Vladimir sneers. "I know that, you motherfucking stupid idiot."

"He told you," Oleg says, tripping over the words. "It's Bes who told you. He's playing us, Vladimir. He's playing both of us."

"Do you really think I'm dumb?" Vladimir caresses the trigger with his finger. "It was a test. *My* test. One you failed miserably."

"Vladimir," Oleg begs.

And that, very fittingly, is the last word he says.

Vladimir pulls the trigger.

The whore screams as Oleg falls backward like the dead weight he is.

All hell breaks loose. Oleg's men try to disarm Vladimir's guards, but it's nothing but a futile show of bravery. They die like they should, with bullets in the backs of their heads.

Executed.

Wiping blood splatters from his hand, Vladimir says to his man in charge, "Clean up this mess and shut that woman up."

"Gladly," the man says, aiming his gun between her eyes and pulling the trigger.

The high-pitched screaming stops.

Finally. Sweet silence.

Vladimir climbs over the bodies, making his way to the door. "Next," he says to himself, looking back at the massacre from the doorframe, "is Volkov."

23

KATE

*W*hereas the gala dinner pleased Alex, it had the opposite effect on me. Dania's words repeat in my mind as I go downstairs for breakfast. Alex may never let me have a life again, and he may never love me. The more I think about it, the more I'm convinced that love isn't part of the equation. Would he have ripped me from everything and everyone I care about if he truly loved me? I doubt that. Love is selfless. Obsession, on the other hand, is selfish.

Whatever the case, I'm powerless to change my circumstances. My hands are tied.

"Why the long face?" Tima asks when I walk into the kitchen. "Didn't you enjoy the fancy party last night?"

I give him an honest smile. "Not exactly."

He's the only person in St. Petersburg around whom I can relax. For everyone else, I have to wear a mask. I don't trust them with my feelings. Sadly, that includes Alex.

"Were the women bitches?" he asks, putting a bowl of oatmeal in front of me as I take a seat at the table.

"Only one woman in particular."

Crossing his arms, he regards me with a sympathetic smile. "Let me guess. Dania Turgeneva."

I give him a surprised look. "How did you know?"

"I've observed her when she's come here with her father. She's been giving Mr. Volkov strong signals."

I pull the honey closer. "What kind of signals?"

"The signals a woman gives a man to let him know she's available and willing."

"Ah." I consider that as I dribble honey over the porridge. "She told me that she and Alex were promised to each other, like in an arranged marriage."

"Ha." He snorts. "I'm sure she and her father would like that."

I dip the spoon into the porridge, scooping up a helping of nuts and berries with the oatmeal. "Then it's not true?"

"If it were, you wouldn't be here." He winks. "Don't listen to anything Miss Turgeneva says. Jealousy makes you nasty. Isn't that how the expression goes? Besides, Mr. Volkov has never called her kiska. He's never used that term of endearment for anyone else."

I looked up the word. It means kitten. At first, I thought it was derogatory, like reducing a person to a pet, but then I read that the term is used affectionately for someone you care about, especially by a man for his female partner.

"Thanks," I say with a grateful smile, and I don't only mean for the reassurance and the breakfast. Because of him, the kitchen has become my refuge in the house.

"Eat up," he says with a mock-stern expression, just like my mom used to do when I was little.

I still can't believe Alex is taking me to see her for Christmas. It feels unreal, and I'm worried that he'll change his mind if something happens on the security front.

Tima goes back to preparing the lunch, letting me finish my breakfast in silence. When I'm done, I rinse my bowl and carry a mug of coffee to the library, where a fire is burning as usual. For a moment, I'm undecided about how to occupy myself. There aren't any men with ailments knocking on the door this morning. I've almost caught up with all the seasons of *Downton Abbey*. My job always kept me busy. I relished the time I had off, using it to either see my mom and my friends or to recharge by vegetating on the couch. Since we've been here, I've been mostly vegetating, and it's getting monotonous. The only positive about having so much free time is that my exercise regime is back on track, but right now, I don't feel like working out or swimming.

I settle on the sofa with a book, but by the time I've finished my coffee, my mind is drifting again. I can't stop thinking about what Dania said, that I'm hampering Alex's efforts to find the man who's trying to kill him. What if she's right? What if he's using most of his resources to protect me instead of tracking his enemy? Is he doing either of us a favor by keeping me here?

The answer is a tough one to face because I care. And because I care, the truth hurts.

I MUST'VE DOZED OFF BECAUSE I WAKE UP ON THE SOFA to find myself covered with a blanket. The book I've been reading has been placed on the side table. Someone considerately left a bookmark to keep my place.

Blinking, I sit up. I'm not wearing my watch, but I can guess the hour by the fact that the curtains are closed. It must be dark outside already. Lena always closes the curtains when the sun sets. I've slept from this morning straight through the afternoon. We came home late last night, and I didn't sleep much when we went to bed. I tossed and turned, mulling over the scene with Dania in the bathroom and the way Alex had proven his possession of me in the back of the car.

I throw the blanket aside and stand. My stomach grumbles, reminding me I skipped lunch. I'm about to make my way to the door when it opens and Alex enters.

"You're awake," he says. "I was just coming to check on you."

I look at him with surprise. What is he doing home so early? He's still dressed for the office in navy blue suit pants and a white fitted shirt. He never arrives before dinner.

"What time is it?" I ask.

He checks his watch. "Just after five."

"Why are you home so early?" Concern tightens my stomach as I recall the incident with my mom. "What happened?"

"Nothing," he says with a smile, closing the door before crossing the floor. "You don't have to worry." Staring down at me, he cups my face. "It seems I've been neglecting you if you think something must be wrong for me to be home early."

I study him with uncertainty. "It's just not like you."

His smile turns sweet. "It won't always be like this. I know I've been at the office a lot lately, but the preparations for the gala and the due diligence for the joint venture have been consuming a lot of my time."

"And finding the man who wants you dead," I say, my body automatically tensing at the thought.

Regarding me with a soft light in his eyes, he caresses my cheek with his thumb. "That's why I'm early. We made a breakthrough today."

My breathing quickens. "You did?"

"You remember the informant you met at the cocktail party in New York?"

"Adrian? The man you said I shouldn't trust?"

"Yeah, that one. He got me some information that will shed light on what's going on."

I swallow. "Should *you* trust him?"

"No. He's a man with no loyalty who's on no one's side. His only alliance is with money, but the information he delivers is always good. That's why he's built himself a solid reputation as an informant."

"I see," I say, even though I don't. I wouldn't trust someone like that, but I suppose Alex is experienced in unorthodox matters and has better judgment than I do. "When will you know?"

"Tonight, hopefully," he says with a gleam in his eyes.

The knowledge seems to excite him, but it only stresses me more.

"Hey, relax," he says, dropping his hand to my shoulder and massaging the tense muscle. "I'll take care of everything." Lowering his head, he adds in a soft voice, "I'll take care of you."

He sweeps his mouth over mine, barely brushing our lips together. He's testing the waters, gauging my reaction. We didn't make love last night, and it wasn't because he thought I was tired and he was being considerate. It was because of the way he took me in the car—with dominance and possession. It was meant to prove that he owns me. It wasn't an exchange of mutual desire or an expression of affection. It was a punishment. A lesson. He wanted the message to sink in. He wanted me to remember that leaving isn't an option. Not today, not ever.

I bend backward, putting distance between us before he can deepen the kiss. I still feel bruised inside about last night, not only because of how he treated me in the car but also because of what transpired at the party. I'm feeling all kinds of confused. I'm a mess, and burying my head in a fog of lust won't help me find clarity.

Alex locks his fingers around the back of my head, keeping me in place as he homes in on his target and claims my lips, not taking no for an answer. When I push on his shoulders, he grips my wrist and walks me back to the sofa.

Turning my face sideways, I whisper in protest, "Alex."

"Tell me you want me," he says, releasing my wrist to splay a large hand over my lower back. He presses our bodies together, letting me feel the hardness between his legs. "Because I sure as hell want you."

The words shouldn't ignite a spark in my belly. They shouldn't heat my body and make me wet, but I can't help my reaction to him. In a carnal way, the physical affection is a balm for my bruised feelings. I do need some kind of care. Despite my mind telling me this isn't wise, my heart wants him to hold me. Especially now. Especially after last night.

"Katyusha," he murmurs, nuzzling my temple. "I'm not going to force this if you don't want it, but you're torturing me."

I let last night happen because some battles aren't worth fighting. This time, it's not about choosing my battles wisely but about needing a substitute for love. When he touches me, he not only makes me forget. He makes me believe that what's between us goes deeper than purely physical need. That's why I don't object when he pulls down the zipper of my skirt and pushes it over my hips. When he reaches for the hem of my sweater, I lift my arms obediently. Item by item, he strips me until I stand naked in front of him.

Even though the room isn't cold, I shiver a little. He must've stoked the fire when he covered me with a blanket. The flames are burning high. The warmth leaves a pleasant glow on my skin. He trails a gaze over me, taking me in from top to bottom. The heat in his eyes warms me more than the fire, the desire he shows openly making electric sparks run through me. With a single step, he closes the distance between us, grabbing me so suddenly that a gasp escapes my lips.

Framing my face, he kisses me savagely. Abstaining last night has made him even hungrier than usual. He peels out of his jacket without breaking the kiss, devouring my mouth as he unbuttons his shirt and yanks the hem from his pants. His buckle makes a clinking sound, and then his belt is undone. He's already toeing off his shoes while he's unzipping.

A moment later, he's naked too, towering over me with his perfect body and masculine strength. There aren't any barriers left between us, at least not of the physical kind. On an emotional level, there are plenty, but he doesn't give me time to ponder them. He goes straight for the kill, dipping one hand between my legs while cupping a breast with the other as he resumes kissing me.

I expect him to be impatient, but the man consuming me with practiced skill is someone who's always in control. Parting my folds with a finger, he tests my arousal and groans when he finds me wet. My nipple hardens against his palm as he gently kneads the curve and starts moving his finger with leisurely strokes.

Lifting his hand from my breast, he closes his fingers around my neck and uses the leverage to pull me flush against him. The stance presses my breasts flat against his chest. Letting my lips go with a nip, he searches my eyes to study the havoc he's wreaking when he sinks two fingers deep inside.

My inner muscles clench around the intrusion. A spark of nervous excitement ignites in my belly when he tightens his fingers marginally around my neck.

"*Skazhi mne trakhnut' tebya,*" he says against my lips, a phrase he's taught me in bed. *Tell me to fuck you.*

"*Ya khochu chtoby ty trakhnul menya,*" I say in my broken Russian. *I want you to fuck me.*

A predatory look mixes with male satisfaction in his eyes. When he pulls his hand from between my legs and applies gentle pressure on my shoulder, I go down on my knees willingly.

His cock is jutting out proudly, heavy and hard. Gripping the base, he says in a lust-roughened voice, "Lubricate it well, kiska."

I understand the warning. I know what he wants.

He stands stoically when I wet my lips and stretch them wide to accommodate his thick girth. Relaxing my jaw, I take him into my mouth. He watches with unwavering attention as I trace the crest of his cock with my tongue before sucking him deeper. Supporting the back of my head with one large hand, he holds the root of his cock in the other and pushes toward the back of my throat.

I breathe through my nose as he slides in and out. He's not going deep enough to make me gag. He pivots his hips with an easy pace, taking my mouth with slow, shallow thrusts. When I'm moving to his rhythm, he lets go of his cock to caress my cheek. The touch is soft and appraising, encouraging me to swallow.

He never forces me to take more than I can handle. He's not suffocating me or stretching my throat painfully, but my eyes nevertheless water from the effort. Sucking him off is a turn-on, making me even wetter. He's showing the utmost constraint, not losing an ounce of control, yet the earthy taste of his precum on my tongue tells me he's not unaffected by my performance.

Gripping his thigh for balance, I caress the heavy sac between his legs. A slick drop of salty liquid squirts onto my tongue. His expression remains stoic, but the line of his jaw hardens as he grits his teeth.

I double my speed, taking him faster. I want him to give me his power. I want him to lose this round and come in my mouth, but he has other ideas. He twists my long hair around his fist and carefully pulls back my head until his cock slips from my lips with a pop.

He looks down at the result of my work. His cock is

slick and wet. Taking a cushion from the sofa, he dumps it on the rug in front of the fireplace.

When he catches my gaze again, his eyes are ablaze and his voice thick with lust. "Get on your hands and knees for me."

He grips my elbows and pulls me to my feet to facilitate my compliance. Not that I need any coaxing to do as he says. Facing the roaring fire, I kneel on the cushion and brace my palms on the rug.

"Keep your knees pressed together," he says behind me.

I follow that order too.

He smooths a hand over my spine, starting at my lower back and ending between my shoulder blades. "Now place your elbows on the floor."

I bend my arms and support my weight on my forearms. The position puts my ass in the air, presenting both my openings for his use. I know what's coming. We've done this enough times before. All I have to do is place my cheek on my arm, close my eyes, and let him manipulate my body. Alex likes to be in control, but he's not a control freak in bed. When I need to take charge, he encourages me to do so. He loves it when I'm on top. But tonight, I need this. I need to escape, and I can only do it when he pushes my boundaries until the world around us no longer exists.

Something hot and velvety brushes over my clit, making me jerk. I open my eyes and lift my head to look back at him from over my shoulder. He's rubbing the head of his cock over my clit, massaging in circles with just the right amount of pressure. I bite my lip, fighting the pleasure that already curls in my belly like the lick of a flame. I don't want to come too soon, but it's no use. I agreed to be played like an instrument when I kneeled in a submissive position, and Alex will wrench the reactions he wants from my body at his will and pace.

Tonight, he wants me to come fast. Parting my folds with his thumbs, he slides his cock slowly inside. My toes curl from the stretch. The pleasure is different than earlier, but it's no less intense. He moves with lazy strokes, giving me time to adjust, and when my inner muscles soften around the intrusion, he thrusts deep and fast.

Perspiration beads on his forehead. His powerful chest is magnificently defined in the light of the fire. Deep shadows run over his face and the grooves of his biceps as he grabs my hip in one hand and slips the other between my legs. I want to watch the spectacular show, but when he rolls my clit between his fingers, my body arches with pleasure. My neck can't support the weight of my head any longer. I drop my face back onto my arm, experiencing the tightening of my muscles with every nerve ending in my body.

I don't have to tell him when I come. I'm clenching hard around him, every part of me locked in ecstasy. Before the climax has released me from its grip, he's pulling out, leaving me empty, but not for long. A familiar pressure builds around my back entrance. The orgasm ebbs, leaving my body boneless and supple in the aftermath. That's the moment he chooses to enter me, using my arousal as lubrication. I take him without difficulty, my ass stretching to accommodate him the way it's been trained.

This pleasure is different too. It's darker. It doesn't come without pain, but the discomfort only fires up my nerve endings anew, turning every inch of me hyper-sensitive to his movements and touch. I dig my nails into the scratchy wool of the rug as he sinks so deep that his groin is cushioned between my cheeks. My breathing is hard and fast, the way I suck air into my lungs uncontrollable. I inhale the smell of wool from the rug and smoke from the fire, every sensory detail imprinting in my mind. My need spikes, my sated body demanding release again.

When he finally starts pumping, my lips part on another soundless gasp. I swallow my moans as he slams into me, rocking my body to a much harsher rhythm. I'm experienced enough in our anal play to take it. I crave it, even. The pain intensifies until it becomes muddled with the pleasure, and I can't tell if I'm flying or falling. The only awareness left in my consciousness is the extreme need to come.

Orgasming like this is much more powerful. It feels deeper. It lasts longer. When I finally break, a wave of intense pleasure tears through me. Like a violent ocean, it rips me apart, slams me to pieces on the rocks and washes the devastation ashore. My mind is half present and half floating, only partially conscious of Alex still thrusting between my ass cheeks. He says something in Russian, but my mind is too mushy to translate the words. He shoves one last time before he freezes, his taut body locked deep inside mine. Warm liquid fills my insides, bathing my stretched skin and leaving a slight sting.

All my energy depleted, I can only kneel there and let the strange hybrid of pain and pleasure rack me. He leans over me, covering my back with his chest, and kisses my neck. He keeps me warm with his body and asks something—how I'm doing, I think. Unable to scrounge up enough strength to answer him, I let him stroke my side while I pretend I'm safe in the cocoon of his arms. He tells me how well I did, adding more words of praise, but I can only internalize the sensations and another kind of sting that reverberates in my heart.

"Stay," he says, pressing a kiss to my temple.

I flinch when he pulls out. I must be really tired because despite the fact that I slept all day, my mind is already going hazy again. I barely focus on Alex as he crosses the floor, grabs a box of tissues from the coffee table, and kneels behind me. After cleaning me up, he takes the blanket from the sofa, drapes it around me, and lifts me into his arms.

"Where are we going?" I ask as he carries me out of the room.

Undeterred by our lack of clothes, he makes his way to the closest bathroom, which is the one by the pool. Fortunately, we don't run into anyone on our way.

His aftercare is gentle. He washes my hair and body

in the shower before patting me dry with a soft towel. When we're both wrapped in fluffy robes, he carries me to his bedroom and puts me to bed with an instruction to rest while he fetches dinner.

I can't stand it. I can't stand the uncertainty. Against my better judgment, I open my mouth, but I *need* to know. I have to know if Dania was lying.

"Alex?"

He stops in the frame and turns to look at me.

I brace myself for humiliation. "Do you—"

The phone rings shrilly on the nightstand.

Frowning, he walks over and lifts the receiver. "Yes?" His voice carries a hint of irritability.

His frown deepens as he listens. After a moment, he says with a clenched jaw, "I see."

He lifts his gaze fleetingly to mine and catches me watching. Turning his back to me, he continues in a tight voice, "That won't be necessary. I'm no longer at the office. I'll call you back in five minutes." The phone makes a click as he returns the cordless receiver to the base.

I clutch the blanket to my chest. "Is everything all right?"

When he faces me again, his expression is schooled, but the worry lines are still visible around his eyes. "There's been a complication. I'm afraid I won't have the information tonight on the man who's hunting me."

A stone drops in my stomach. "I'm sorry."

He gives me a strained smile. "It's not your fault. I'll

get dinner, but I won't be joining you. I have to deal with this."

I swing my legs over the side of the bed. "I'll get the dinner."

"No," he says in a commanding tone. Softer, he adds, "Stay in bed, my love. You need to rest."

"Is there anything I can do?" I ask, the lethargic effect of my orgasms vanishing as fear brings a fresh wave of tension.

"No, but thanks." He checks his watch. "You wanted to ask me something before the phone rang."

I pull up my knees and hug my legs. "It's nothing important."

"We'll talk about it later."

I nod, though I have no such intention. My courage has already failed me, and in light of that telephone call, we have much more serious matters to worry about than whether Alex loves me.

24

ALEX

*T*ima is still in the kitchen when I go downstairs. I instruct him to prepare a tray for Katerina and a sandwich for me. While he's getting our dinner ready, I grab a T-shirt and a pair of sweatpants from the closet in the gym and get dressed. The food is ready when I return to the kitchen.

After delivering the tray to Katerina, who's already half asleep in my bed, I leave her with a kiss and go to my study. A gourmet sandwich and a glass of water is set on the desk. I dial Adrian and finish the sandwich in three large bites while I wait for him to answer.

He picks up after several rings.

"What the fuck happened?" I ask, chugging back the water.

"Someone other than us wanted to find Mukha. He was already dead when I got there."

"Fuck." I scrunch the napkin in my fist. "How?"

"A bullet in the back of his head."

That has a ring of Vladimir Stefanov to it. It's his favorite style of execution. He likes to shoot between the eyes, but when his men follow orders, they do it the dishonorable way, by not looking the person they're killing in the face.

"I managed to sweep the place before the police got there," Adrian continues. "There was no sign of a computer or laptop. All his equipment had been cleared out. If Mukha had made a hard copy of the file, whoever got to him took it."

I grit my teeth. "In other words, it's a dead end." Literally.

"Pretty much," Adrian says with resignation. "Is there anything else I can do for you?"

"Not for now." I push away from the desk and stand. "Keep your ear to the ground. If you happen to stumble upon anything useful, I want to know about it."

"I'll do that," he says before ending the call.

Fuck.

I slam a hand on the desk. Mukha was my only lead to what's brewing with Stefanov. There's still no sign of Besov. According to the man who's watching his apartment, he hasn't returned home. That leaves me with one alternative—a last resort. I'll have to get the information from Stefanov himself. I'm not opposed to the idea of torturing the motherfucker, but I won't be able to trust the filth that comes out of his mouth. I was hoping to have the information before taking him on. If he's going to such lengths to hide it, there's a good chance he may not spill the beans even when I pull off his fingernails one by one.

Walking to the window, I draw back the curtain. It's dark, and snow is falling in the yellow glow of the powerful spotlights that illuminate the garden. On the opposite side of the river, someone is sitting in a room on the top floor of an apartment building with a pair of binoculars, reporting the activity in my house to Stefanov right this very moment. The idea makes me want to go out there and slit the cockroach's throat before dumping his body on Stefanov's doorstep and getting the fucking information I want. However, if I've learned anything in life, it's that you win a war with patience and not with impulsive actions. There's still time. Stefanov hasn't made a move yet. I'll give it until after Christmas, until we've visited Laura in the States. After that, the gloves will come off.

I drop the curtain and dial Nelsky. It's after working hours, but my security chief takes my calls twenty-four-seven.

He answers in a shaky voice. "Mr. Volkov?"

"What's the status on finding that file?"

He swallows audibly. "Nothing yet, sir."

My temper ignites. "What the fuck am I paying you for, Nelsky?"

"We've tried, sir. Our hacker can't find anything."

"Is the hacker even worth the fucking space he's taking up in my office?"

"He's good, sir." If anything, he sounds uncertain. "The best."

"Then he'd better prove it. Get me something, or don't come into the office when I'm back next week."

"Yes, sir. Thank you, sir. We'll work around the clock."

"You do that," I grit out before stabbing the red button to end the call.

Too on edge for sleep, I open my emails on my phone. There's a message from Konstantin Molotov. His brother Nikolai is finally ready to sign the papers formalizing the joint venture. The only catch is that he wants to meet me in person to do so, which means coming to his remote compound in Idaho. Nikolai is cc'd on the email, so I reply, thanking Konstantin for the introduction and suggesting that Nikolai and I meet the day after Christmas. Katerina and I will be in America anyway, and I might as well kill two birds with one stone.

Nikolai replies promptly, confirming the meeting and saying that he'll send directions and safety instructions.

Good. Like me, he must be a stickler for security. Then again, in our position, we don't have a choice. We haven't gotten this far by not watching our backs.

I go to the liquor tray, pour a double shot of vodka, and down it in one go. Another double later, I barely feel a buzz. What I need is a good sparring with the men.

I may not be any closer to having the information I want, but file or no file, before the New Year, Stefanov will be dead. That's a guarantee.

25

KATE

*O*n the morning of Christmas Eve, Alex wakes me early. He rushes me through a shower and breakfast, and forty minutes later, we're boarding his private plane with the gifts he'd insisted I buy for my mom and friends when he took me sightseeing and visiting boutiques. We'll be spending the night in Deep Creek, where Alex made reservations at a B&B. He must've booked out the whole place, seeing that Igor, Dimitri, Leonid, Yuri, and four other men are traveling with us.

I sleep for most of the flight, getting in some quality rest thanks to the comfortable bed in Alex's bedroom cabin. Being the workaholic that he is, Alex uses the time to catch up on business.

He wakes me up for the landing just before four in the afternoon. Like when we were arriving in Russia, he's constantly talking on a satellite phone, presumably making sure we're safe. Four cars are parked outside the private hangar our plane taxies into. The armed men exit the plane first. When they've checked the cars and the hangar, Alex and I get into a car with Yuri. Sandwiched between two cars in the front and one at the back, we make our way to Deep Creek.

From town, it's a short drive to the clinic. The modern building sits on a few acres of land near a lake. Snow covers the ground, and the blue lake is frozen, forming a beautiful picture.

My mom is waiting in the lobby when we arrive. Dashing across the floor, she pulls me into a hug.

"Katie." After kissing my cheek, she holds me at arm's length. "Look at you. You've lost weight." Her brow furrows. "Are you eating enough?"

It's hard to contain my emotions and not burst into tears. "More than enough. I'm so happy to see you."

"Me too." My mom turns to Alex. "This is the best gift ever."

Alex bends down to kiss her cheek. "You look great, Laura. It's good to see you."

My heart warms as I take her in. She indeed appears trim and fit. Her skin has a healthy glow, and her eyes are sparkling.

"Wow," I say. "Look at *you*."

Raising her arms, she twirls in a circle. "What do you think?"

"Mom, you look amazing."

"Thank you," she says, beaming. "I'm so much better already. I still have a few painful spells, but it's nothing compared to how it used to be. I'm agile again. It's amazing to do normal chores without discomfort."

"I'm so happy for you." She deserves this and so much more.

She smooths a hand over her dress. "All because of you, Alex. I can never thank you enough."

"No thanks needed," Alex says with a warm smile.

Mom glances over his shoulder at Igor and Leonid, who stand just inside the door. "Are they with you?"

"Yes," Alex says. "Don't worry about them. Traveling with bodyguards is protocol for me."

Wait until she sees the men outside. At least their guns are concealed under their jackets. I don't even want to know how Alex got the clinic to allow weapons inside.

"Really?" Mom tilts her head. "Does that mean you're a kidnapping candidate, as in getting captured for ransom?"

"Not likely," Alex replies with a chuckle.

"We brought some Russian food made by Alex's chef," I say quickly to change the subject. "I hope you like it. We thought it would be cozier to have lunch here than somewhere in town."

"Not much in town is open tomorrow," Alex adds.

My mom throws an arm around my shoulders. "There goes my diet."

"Don't worry." Alex picks up the cooler bag at his feet. "I instructed my chef to only use ingredients that are allowed in your eating plan."

"How considerate of you." Mom flashes him a smile.

"Just as well. Otherwise, I'll be in trouble with William."

"William?" I ask as she steers us toward the elevator.

The glow on her cheeks deepens to a flush. "Dr. Hendricks."

I make big eyes. "You're on a first-name basis?"

Lowering her voice, she says with a glint in her eyes, "We're on first base too."

"Mom!" I whisper-exclaim.

She winks. "I have a surprise for you." She ushers us into the elevator when the doors open. "You don't have to go to the B&B in town," she continues. "Someone pulled out of the program—family emergency—so there's a vacant room. William suggested you stay here to spare you the traveling to town and back. No charge."

The elevator stops on the second floor.

"That's very kind of him," I say, glancing at Alex, "but we don't want to impose."

Alex holds the door for us. "Katerina is right. We should probably stick to the plan and sleep in town."

"Nonsense." Taking my arm, Mom leads me down the hallway and says over her shoulder to Alex, "He wouldn't have offered if he didn't want to."

She unlocks the door at the end and goes inside ahead of us. "These rooms are a bit smaller than the ones on my floor, but they're still comfortable. What do you think?"

I look at Alex for an answer. He's put a ton of security measures in place. Changing everything will take major reorganization.

He surprises me by saying, "It looks great. If you're sure it's not an inconvenience to the management, we'll gladly stay."

"Great," Mom says. "That settles it then."

"I'll let Yuri know to bring our bags up," Alex says.

I look around as I unbutton my coat. The room is cozy. Despite the sleek, modern look of the building, the focus is on comfort inside. A double bed and nightstand take up one half of the room, and a desk, bar fridge, sofa, and coffee table the other half. The colors are neutral, soft shades of beige with accents of green. A large window frames the lake against the backdrop of the mountains, allowing for plenty of light.

"You can unpack your things here," Mom says, indicating a small dressing room that connects to a bathroom.

I hang my coat on the hook behind the door and unwind my scarf. "Some of the food needs to go in the fridge. I'll start with that."

Alex carries the cooler bag Tima had packed to the desk.

"Let me give you a hand." Mom takes the frozen dishes from the bag. "What's all this?" she asks, bringing them to the fridge. "Your chef shouldn't have gone to so much trouble, Alex."

"It was no trouble," he says, removing his coat.

"A lot of people didn't want to interrupt their treatment and decided to stay here over Christmas," Mom says as she stacks everything neatly in the fridge. "We're having a special dinner tonight."

"That's very thoughtful of the staff," I say, handing her the last plastic container.

She shuts the fridge and walks to the sofa. "They're all amazing. Everyone here is so kind." Sitting down, she looks between Alex and me. "What about you? How is St. Petersburg? Tell me everything."

Smiling, I take a seat next to her. "I've already told you everything on the phone. What about your apartment? Is your neighbor taking good care of it?"

She pats my hand. "Everything is fine at home. Are you sure you can't stay longer?"

"I'm afraid not," Alex says, taking his phone from his pocket. "I have some business obligations in Russia."

Mom grimaces. "I'm not complaining. I just can't believe you flew all this way for a couple of days."

"I took the liberty of booking one of the private lounges for our lunch tomorrow," Alex says. "I hope that will do."

Mom clears her throat. "Speaking of lunch, William suggested we have lunch at his place instead of in the visitors' lounge. He reckons it will be more comfortable for us."

I steal another glance at Alex. "What about his family? I don't want to put him out."

"He's a widower." She crosses her legs. "His kids are grown up and are visiting their in-laws upstate this year, which means he'll be alone for Christmas too."

"Oh, I'm sorry he lost his wife," I say. "Did it happen a long time ago?"

"Five years. It was a drawn-out illness." Blowing out

a sigh, she gives me a sidelong glance. "I think it was very difficult for him and the kids."

"I can only imagine."

Alex types something on his phone. "Give me his address. I'll get my driver to program his GPS."

More likely, he'll make sure the surroundings are safe.

"I'll send you a text message with the directions when I get back to my room." A smile softens my mom's pretty features. "You must be tired after the long trip. Do you want to catch a nap before dinner?"

"I actually slept a lot on the plane," I say, "but a shower will be welcome."

She gets to her feet. "I'll leave you to get settled. Shall we meet around seven?"

"That sounds good," Alex says, pocketing his phone.

"Just knock on my door when you're ready," Mom says on her way out. After giving us a wave, she disappears with a bounce in her step.

"She really does look good," Alex says after closing the door behind her.

Walking to him, I wrap my arms around his waist. "Thank you, not only for the visit but also for doing this for my mom."

He kisses the top of my head. "I already told you, Katyusha, your family is mine."

I melt against him, unable to help myself. When he's kind like this, it's difficult to remember that he holds my free will hostage.

THE DINNER IS A JOVIAL AFFAIR. THE DISHES ARE PLANT-based, low in saturated fat and sodium, with plenty of vegetables and whole grains. The menu theme is Mediterranean, which includes a spread of baked artichoke, ratatouille, sundried-tomato-and-chickpea stew, and a delicious gazpacho of melon, garlic, basil, and mint. The dessert is strawberry soup served with paper-thin, dairy- and gluten-free ginger tuiles.

Dr. Hendricks—or William—isn't there. My mom says he wants to give us time alone to catch up. From how much she talks about him, it seems they spend quite a bit of her free time together.

We meet the other patients staying here for Christmas. The group is diverse, with men and women of all ages. Living together for a few weeks has created a camaraderie that's obvious in their banter.

Megan is ten years older than my mom and is originally from Hawaii. George is a veteran who owns a cattle farm in Texas. Daphne is forty and is opening a florist shop in the new year. I enjoy the lively conversation and meeting new people. It's a welcome change from my isolation in Russia. For a few hours, I forget about the awful reality of Alex's life and how it has impacted mine.

After dinner, we have homemade, alcohol-free ginger beer in the lounge by the Christmas tree, while Daphne plays the piano and George has us all in stitches with his impersonation of Billy Mack's

"Christmas Is All Around" from the movie *Love Actually*.

By bedtime, my stomach hurts from laughing.

I give my mom a hug when we arrive at our room, still wiping tears of laughter from my eyes. "I had so much fun tonight."

Alex regards me with a warm curve of his lips. Even he had a few laughs.

"So did I," Mom says.

"Alex and I have a gift for you."

"Oh, honey. You shouldn't have." Waving a hand around the space, she says, "This is already too much, and your visit is the best gift I could've asked for, not to mention how costly and tiring the trip must be for you."

Taking her hand, I open the door and drag her inside. "Come on."

"You didn't think we'd come empty-handed?" Alex asks with a chuckle, following us inside.

"Shall I close my eyes?" she asks with a squeal.

I laugh. "It's wrapped. You can look." Taking the first gift from my bag, I hand it to her.

She shakes it and turns it on all sides. "What is it? I have no idea what to guess."

"Open it," I urge.

She tears away the wrapping paper and lifts the lid of the box. "Oh, Katie," she exclaims, pulling out the cashmere sweater. "This is gorgeous. And blue, my favorite color."

"I'm glad you like it. It's from a boutique in St.

Petersburg."

She hugs first me and then Alex. "I love it."

I hand her the second gift. "This one is from Alex."

She leaves the sweater on the desk to tear the gift paper off the box. When she lifts the lid and unties the strings of the velvet bag, she gasps. "My goodness. This is gorgeous. Look at the detail."

"It's a Fabergé replica," Alex says. "Unfortunately, it's not the real thing."

"I love it." She lifts the delicate egg from the box and studies it in the light. "Are those...?"

"The gemstones are real," Alex says. "It's a collector's piece, part of a limited edition. The valuation certificate is in the box."

"Oh, my." She gapes at him. "I can't accept this."

"Now you sound like Katherine," he says with humor. "Of course you can. I insist."

"This is beautiful." She puts it back in the velvet bag before carefully returning it to the box. "Thank you, Alex."

"It's given with much pleasure," he says warmly.

"I can't thank you enough." My mom's eyes glitter with tears. "Not only for the gifts, but also for taking such good care of my daughter."

Alex doesn't move a muscle. His reply is smooth, practiced. "She takes good care of me too."

Some of my excitement evaporates. The lies we're feeding my mom are a damper on my short-lived giddiness. I feel despicable, like a traitor, but how can I destroy her illusion if she's doing so well and looking so much better? How can I tell her the truth if it will crush her? No, it's better that she believes the lies, no matter how awful telling them makes me feel.

Patting my cheek, she says, "I should let you catch some rest. Good night, kids. Thanks again for spoiling me."

"You're welcome, Mom," I say, my throat clogging up with darker emotions.

She turns at the door. "The best gift is still having you here."

Not trusting my voice to speak, I blow her a kiss before she shuts the door.

Shit. I'm a horrible person, deceiving my own mother like that. This isn't how she raised me. Living with Alex is forcing me to become someone else, and I'm not sure I like that someone.

Turning toward the window, I hide my expression from Alex, who thankfully busies himself with taking off his jacket. I don't want him to see what will be written openly on my face—that right now, I despise both of us.

I take in the moonlit scene. It's stopped snowing. The landscape is a clean white of fresh powder glittering under the lampposts of the garden. Pristine. Not murky and full of dirty lies. There are no other buildings nearby, but I nevertheless close the curtains. With everything that's going on, I'm becoming paranoid.

I jump when Alex touches my shoulder.

"Hey," he says, twirling me to face him. "Why so on edge suddenly?"

"Is it safe to sleep here?" I can't hide the strain in my voice. "I don't want to bring the danger straight to my mom."

"Everything is taken care of," he says in a placating tone, rubbing my arms. "The men are on watch, and we have satellite surveillance."

"What about the lunch at Dr. Hendrick's house?" I ask, not reassured.

"I've already sent Dimitri to check things out. I won't take any risks, Katyusha."

"Okay." I bite my lip. "I'm happy to be here, more than you can ever know. I just—"

"Leave the worrying to me." He squeezes my biceps. "The only thing I want you to do is enjoy the time with your mom."

"You're right." My smile is halfhearted. "I should make the most of it." Although it's easier said than done.

He studies my face. "You looked happy tonight. Carefree."

"I was." I consider how much to tell him. I don't want him to think I'm ungrateful. "It was fun. It made me forget."

Regret flashes in his eyes, but it's gone in a blink. Pulling me closer, he says, "I know how to make you forget."

His mouth is on mine before I can reply. He spears his fingers through my hair, strokes his tongue over mine, and, as promised, takes me to a place where danger doesn't exist.

26

ALEX

*T*he vibration of my phone on the nightstand wakes me. I'm a light sleeper. It's part of my conditioning to always be alert. Reaching out for the phone, I check the screen. Nelsky. It's barely five o'clock here but noon in Russia.

I untangle myself carefully from Katerina. Her features are illuminated by the faint blue light from the electronic thermometer on the fridge. She looks peaceful in her sleep. Vulnerable. Sparing her beautiful face one last glance, I get up quietly and go to the bathroom, where I close the door before flicking on the light. It's safe to talk in here. Dimitri swept the rooms for cameras and listening devices while we had dinner last night.

My gut draws tight with anticipation as I take the call. Nelsky wouldn't call me at five in the morning for frivolous reasons.

"I hope I didn't wake you, sir," he says with a soprano pitch to his voice.

"What's going on?" I ask, facing my reflection in the mirror.

"We found it, sir."

I go still. Time stops ticking.

"Sir? The file. We found the file."

My heart goes into overdrive, thumping with triumphant beats in my chest. "Where?"

"In iCloud, sir. Mukha hid a copy there, maybe to use as insurance if his life happened to be at risk."

Much good it did him.

"It wasn't easy," Nelsky continues, "but our hacker eventually unraveled enough cyber threads to lead us there."

"I assume you already downloaded it and wiped the original."

"Yes, sir. We couldn't risk someone else finding it."

"Good work," I say, keeping my voice down so I don't wake Katerina. "Send it to me."

He coughs. "There's still one little hiccup we have to deal with before I can send it, sir."

I clench my jaw. "What hiccup?"

"The file is encrypted and we can't break the code." He adds hastily, "Not yet."

"Fuck," I say under my breath.

"I'll let you know as soon as there's an update."

"Do that." I scrub a hand over my face. "No matter what time of the day or night."

"Yes, sir."

"And Nelsky?"

"Sir?"

"You're not fired."

He utters a nervous laugh.

I end the call.

Taking a few long breaths, I process the news. The file is in my hands. At last. If that hacker I'm paying a fortune per month is worth his salt, I'll have the information soon. Though I have a feeling I'm not going to like what I'll find.

I switch off the light and go back to bed. The mattress dips when I get in next to Katerina.

Frowning, she blinks her eyes open. "Alex?"

My name on her lips warms my chest and hardens my dick. I wrap my arms around her and kiss her forehead. "Go back to sleep, kiska."

"Is everything all right?"

"Yes."

The lie comes easily. If the price for her tranquility is an untruth, I'll gladly carry the burden of that sin.

Her voice is croaky with sleep. "Where did you go?"

"I just went to the bathroom for a sip of water."

"There are bottles in the fridge." She snuggles closer to me, nestling under my arm. "Do you want me to get you one?"

The offer warms me in a different way, a way I seldom, if ever, experience. No one else tries to take care of me without expecting something in return.

"No, kiska," I say in a soft voice, tightening my arms around her. "I'm good."

She settles with a sigh, resting her cheek on my chest. She's cute when she's like this—half asleep and not yet remembering to be angry with me. Now that I finally have that fucking file, her negative feelings will soon be a thing of the past. I'll tie her to me in every way imaginable. She'll never be able to get away, but I'll make her so happy she'll be too delirious to realize how effectively I'm spinning my web around her. And even if she does, she'll be too ecstatic to mind. I'll give her everything her heart desires, everything a man with money and power can. Not that material things are that important to her. Sure, she likes pretty dresses and shoes and even the jewelry she says is too expensive. But what she really wants are the simple things—a job she enjoys, a happy home, friends, a family.

I'll give her a family.

Soon.

As soon as I've eliminated the threat on our lives.

The thought alone makes me hard. My semi-erection turns into a full-blown hard-on that tents my pajama bottoms. Sliding a hand along the curve of her spine, I push up the silk camisole top of her sleep set. She presses closer, throwing her thigh over mine.

The non-verbal permission is all I need. There's a sudden fire in my veins, an urge to plant my seed deep inside her. It's different than the desire I always feel for her or the compulsive necessity to show her constant affection. It's more primal and, at the same time, more of a conscious decision. This isn't an impulse. At the back of my mind, I've always known that this is where we're heading. And now that my mind and body have taken notice of my resolve, I'm impatient to chase that goal.

I slip a hand under the elastic of her shorts and trace the crease of her ass before cupping a cheek. She arches her hips, rubbing the sweet spot between her legs against my thigh. She's so wet I can feel her arousal through the fabric of my pajama bottoms. The fact that I arouse her, that her body is making all that cream and honey for me, satisfies a primitive side of me I didn't even know I possessed.

Locking my hands around her small waist, I lift her on top of me so that her body is stretched out on mine, her thighs straddling my hips and her breasts flattened against my chest. I drag her up a little, sliding her silk-covered pussy over my rock-hard cock. When she lifts onto her arms, the extended tips of her breasts brush over my chest through the silk of the camisole. I grab her face between my palms and kiss her hard, too hard maybe, but she kisses me right back, tangling her tongue with mine. The depth of her mouth is sweet, her moans an aphrodisiac.

When I grip the elastic of her pajama bottoms, she closes her legs so I can shove the shorts over her hips. I leave them just under her ass, too eager to reach my destination to undress her completely. Straining up, I don't break the kiss as I slide a palm over her globes and between her legs. I curl a finger to part her folds. She's not just slick. She's dripping wet. For me.

I'm eager to sink inside her, but I want to see what I

do to her first. Slowing the kiss, I press our lips together one last time before I roll her off me and sit up against the headboard. She gives me a confused looked as I move the covers aside.

"Come here," I say, pointing at my lap.

She grabs the elastic of her shorts, making to remove them, but I shake my head and switch on the bedside lamp for a better view.

"Put your pussy in my lap, kiska." My voice is dark with lust. "I want to see it."

She looks uncertain.

"Ass up," I say, making sure my instructions are clear.

She bites her lip, considering the order for a moment before asking, "You're not going to spank me, are you?"

Amused, I raise a brow. "Not unless you want me to. Do you?"

"No," she says quickly.

"Then lie down."

She looks at my groin, where the head of my cock is pushing through the elastic of my pajama bottoms and pressing against my stomach. "Don't you want to take those off?"

Her eagerness makes my lips quirk with satisfaction. "In a moment."

Slowly, she executes the order, watching me warily as she drapes herself over my lap so that her pussy is cushioned on my legs and her ass is in the air. There's something perverse about her being presented like this, with her shorts around her thighs and her ass naked. I like that she doesn't wear panties under those silky pajama bottoms. I like that I can see everything from this angle.

Flattening a palm on her lower back, I stroke her soft skin. Her body breaks out in goosebumps when I caress her firm globes. Her bare pussy glistens with wetness, the plump lips swollen and pink. I trace the seam slowly, making her shiver. She bends her elbows and rests her cheek on her arm, watching me, but she can't see how erotic the sight is when I part those pretty lips in the V of two fingers to reveal the little pearl hidden underneath. I draw the thumb of my free hand over the button. Even the light touch makes her jerk. She clenches her ass cheeks when I apply firmer pressure.

I tear my gaze away from the work of my hands to gauge her expression. Her eyes are closed and her lips slightly parted, her breaths coming rapidly. Focusing my attention between her legs again, I rub faster while applying more pressure. She lifts her ass a little, the involuntary movement giving me better access, enough to gather some of her slickness. Keeping her open between my fingers, I turn my other hand palm-up and sink two fingers inside her. She looks so hot with her ass in my lap and my fingers in her pussy that a hot jet of precum erupts from the tip of my cock.

I never thought I'd get off on pulling down a woman's shorts and making her come in my lap with my fingers, but here I am, ready to ejaculate in my pants, because this isn't any woman. This is *my* woman. I don't break the pace of my fingers as I lift my other hand and suck my thumb into my mouth. I lubricate it well before pressing on her back entrance. The tight ring stretches easily, letting my thumb in to the knuckle. It only takes a few pumps before she gets to where I want to bring her. I nearly explode when she comes with a cry, squeezing her inner muscles around my fingers. If it's not the hottest thing I've ever seen, I don't know what is.

Aftershocks are still racking her body when I peel the shorts from her legs. I take just enough time to push my own pants over my hips before lifting her into a sitting position so that she straddles my thighs. Fastening my hands around her waist, I help her onto her knees. I hold her in place with one hand and grip the root of my cock with the other to position it at her entrance. She does the rest of the work, lowering herself over me. With every inch I sink into her, my balls draw tighter. I'm not going to last long, but that's not the point. That's why I took care of her pleasure first.

She leans back, rocking gently while resting her hands on my legs. Her nipples are hard points visible through the silk of her camisole. Her curves bounce with her movement, the fact that they're hidden somehow making the sight hotter. I home in on the triangle between her legs, on how her pussy stretches to accommodate my cock.

That's all it takes. I grip her waist to hold her in

place and pivot my hips, taking her with harsh thrusts. Sweat beads over my body as I pound into her, taking everything that belongs to me. The foreplay has been too much of a turn-on. Long before I'm ready, the release builds at the base of my spine. Two more thrusts, and sweet, agonizing pleasure pumps through my body and blows my mind. I'm breathing hard, lost in the moment, forgetting crucial details such as being alert.

Wrapping my arms around her, I press her to my chest. I'm reluctant to pull out. My body is sated. It should be satisfied at stamping my possession on her, but now that the idea of earlier has taken root, it wants more. I want everything with her, including the family I never thought I'd have. I won't rest until it's done, until I've bound her to me with no option of escape. Before that can happen, I need to put a ring on her finger. The one I brought with me isn't the one that will tie her to me yet, but for now, it'll do.

Reluctantly, I move her aside. Sex with Katerina is always hot, but our morning sex is especially intense. After cleaning her up, I coax her into having a shower with me, and then I take her back to bed. It's still early, yet neither of us is tired enough to drift back to sleep.

After pulling on a pair of sweatpants and a T-shirt, I get two cups of hot carob almond milk from the vending machine in the hallway and carry them back to the room.

She gives me a smile when I offer her the drink. "You always spoil me with breakfast in bed." Teasingly, she adds, "You do realize I've gotten used to it and will now expect it for life?"

For life. Fuck, yeah. "I can live with that."

I leave my drink on the nightstand and get the gift-wrapped box from my bag. Getting back into bed next to her, I say, "Merry Christmas."

Biting her lip, she looks at the box I leave on her lap.

"Hey." I brush a strand of hair from her face. "What's wrong?"

Her smile turns sad. "I didn't get you anything. I would have, but…"

She doesn't say it's because I took away her access to her money and her freedom to go where she likes.

"We don't celebrate Christmas in Russia on this date." It's a poor excuse, a feeble attempt at brushing away the hurt that underlies the unsaid, but I tell myself this situation is only temporary. "Besides, I don't need anything."

She looks at me quickly. "That's not the point. Giving a gift isn't about offering something the recipient *needs*."

My words are gentle, soothing. "I know, my love." My smile is a consolation. "But I appreciate the intention. That's all that matters."

Judging by the pleat between her eyebrows, she disagrees. Not wanting to spoil the aftermath of our amazing sex with an argument, I opt for changing the subject. "Aren't you going to open that? I know you already know what it is, but it seemed like an appropriate time to give it to you."

"Thank you," she says, making a good effort to not let me see the sadness that remains in her eyes.

I keep my tone light. "Open it first before you thank me."

She tears away the wrapping paper and opens the lid of the box. "It really is exquisite."

I lift the ring from the box and take her hand to slide it onto her finger. "Rubies suit you."

"So that is what the ring is for? For Christmas?"

"Yes," I say, another lie sliding smoothly from my tongue.

"You shouldn't have."

"I wanted to." And that's not a lie.

"Thank you again." She holds her hand to the light, studying the ring.

"You're very welcome again."

"What about the gifts we brought for Joanne, June, and the girls at the ER?" Hope sounds in her tone. "Are we making a detour via New York?"

"No." I try to deal the blow with gentleness. "Leonid already mailed the gifts yesterday from town."

"I see." She nods a couple of times. "That was a good idea." Leaving the paper cup on the nightstand, she gets out of bed.

"Katyusha."

"I'm going to get dressed," she says, not looking at me. "My mom always gets up early. I'd like to have breakfast with her."

It takes every ounce of willpower I possess and more not to go after her, but my gut tells me to give her a moment. As close as we were during sex, she's pulling away from me again. Her behavior only confirms what I already know. Katerina isn't a woman I can buy with gifts and keep happy by showering with jewelry.

What she needs are things money can't buy, such as the freedom I can't give her yet... and that I'll never be able to give her if she doesn't say yes.

27

KATE

*A*lex just gave me an enormous gift, but instead of making me happy, it reminded me of what he'd taken away from me. I'm not ungrateful. I just can't forget that in reality I'm nothing but a prisoner, as Dania so kindly reminded me.

Determined not to let my sadness ruin what little time I have with my mom, I get ready and go downstairs at seven to knock on her door. She opens it wearing a pretty red dress and matching jacket. Red looks good on her. The color compliments her complexion and brings out her blond hair and blue eyes.

"Morning, honey," she says, drawing me into a hug. "Merry Christmas. Where's Alex?"

"Merry Christmas, Mom." I kiss her cheek. "Alex is taking care of something work-related. He's having breakfast in the room and will catch up with us later."

She runs her gaze over my jeans, sweater, and Uggs.

Planting a fist on her hip, she says, "We need to go shopping."

I lift a finger. "Oh, no. I'm not walking into that trap again."

The last time my mom took me shopping, we spent hours trying on clothes. I had blisters on my feet by the time I finally managed to drag her home. To add insult to injury, she convinced me to buy a short black dress that'd cost an arm and a leg and that I've never had the courage to wear.

Gasping, she grabs my right hand. "Look at that. This ring is gorgeous." She meets my gaze with a twinkle in her eyes. "Let me guess. Alex?"

I nod. "My Christmas gift."

"That man is something else. I'm happy for you. You deserve it." She hooks her arm through mine. "Come on. Let's have breakfast, and then I'll take you on a tour."

Some of the heaviness pushing me down vanishes. Her enthusiasm is contagious.

"Let's," I say. "It might be the mountain weather, but I'm starving."

In the dining room, we take a small table on the closed terrace. With the view of the lake and the sun filtering through the window, it's gorgeous. While we sip a delicious brew of carob and cinnamon, my mom fills me in on her treatment process. I feel a little guilty about enjoying the breakfast of frozen berries and vegan yogurt, knowing Alex's money is paying for it, but I brush the thought aside. He's told me repeatedly he wants to do this. At first, I thought it was because he loves me, but now I know better. Alex is a very generous person, and he likes to give gifts. That's what this is—an enormous gift. Although for a man as wealthy as Alex, the price of this treatment must be small change. I was a fool to see more into it.

"Did you hear what I said?" Mom asks.

I pull myself back to the present with an internal reprimand. Now isn't the time to let my mind drift. "I'm sorry. I was daydreaming."

"Mm." She gives me an approving look. "Someone is in love. I asked if you'd like to see the rest of the place after breakfast."

"Sure." I finish my drink and pick up my fork. "I'd love to."

After we're done eating, my mom takes me on a quick tour, showing me the parts I didn't see during my first visit, including the gym, the heated pool, the yoga and meditation rooms, the dietician's office, the lecture hall where they have educational sessions, and the physiotherapy wing.

The physiotherapy treatment includes massages and mobility exercises, Mom explains. Next to the wing where they do the treatments is a small beauty salon where patients can have a haircut or a manicure. Most patients stay for a couple of months, which makes such a service necessary.

At the end of the tour, Mom checks her watch. "Oh my goodness. Look at the time. We'd better go grab the food you brought."

Alex is working on his laptop at the desk when we get to our room. After he and my mom exchange Christmas wishes, we get the dishes from the fridge while he packs up his laptop and locks it in the safe. Just before twelve, we make our way downstairs.

Dr. Hendricks waits in the deserted reception area. Tall and dark-haired, with gray creeping into his sideburns, he's a handsome man who looks both smart and relaxed in a button-up shirt and a pair of chinos. At our approach, he straightens from where he was leaning on the counter. When his gaze falls on my mom, his green eyes go wide.

"Laura." He crosses the floor and meets us halfway, taking the shopping bag from my mom. "You look amazing."

"Thank you." A flush darkens her cheeks. "This is my daughter, Kate, and her boyfriend, Alex."

"Kate." He extends a hand, shaking first mine and then Alex's. His smile is warm, his eyes friendly. "It's good to meet you both."

"Thank you for inviting us to your home, Dr. Hendricks," I say.

"Please, call me William. Thank you for accepting." He reaches for the shopping bag I'm carrying. "May I?"

We load everything in his car while he asks how our flight was. Alex replies with a vague answer, not mentioning that we came by private plane. As William helps my mom into the passenger seat of his car, he tells us about the local attractions in the nearby Smoky Mountains in case we decide to return in the summer.

He looks up when Alex's guards get into their cars, but he refrains from asking questions as Alex and I head to our car. Mom must've already briefed him about Alex's so-called protocol.

William's vehicle takes the lead, and we follow. I look around as we exit the clinic grounds. Where are the men watching out for my mom? Alex said she wouldn't even know they were there. Are they hiding out somewhere in a nearby cabin, or are they keeping tabs on her via satellite? Maybe both.

We take a road that snakes up the mountain. From there, the drive only takes fifteen minutes. William's house is a modern structure situated on an outcrop with a view of the lake and the mountains. While my mom unpacks the grocery bags, he takes Alex and me on a tour. The house is small, but the rooms are spacious and the minimalistic furnishings create an unobstructed flow between the living area, dining room, and kitchen. Two upstairs bedrooms share a bathroom and balcony. My favorite part is the outside terrace that overhangs the slope.

We stop at the rail to admire the view. Alex leans one elbow on the rail and drapes his other arm around my waist. As always, his closeness seduces my senses, making everything else seem insignificant. Not even the view can compete with him, although the vista is magnificent.

"This is spectacular," I say.

"I'm glad you like it," William replies. "I had the

house built five years ago when I moved here from Oakland."

Alex casts a practiced glance toward the horizon, his blue eyes alert as he takes in the surroundings. Seemingly satisfied with his visual evaluation, he checks his phone before saying, "I'll go check if Laura needs help in the kitchen."

"Kate?" William says when Alex is gone.

I abandon the vista to look at him.

"I want you to know that you have nothing to be worried about where your mom is concerned. We like each other." A smile appears on his lips. "A lot. I love her optimism and her zest for life. She's an amazing woman. I also realize she's a bit of a free spirit, so I have no intention of rushing her into anything."

He seems so sincere I can't help but believe him. "That's good to know."

"When I take my vacation this summer, I'd like to visit her in New York City. I was hoping we"—he waves between us—"me and you, could also get to know each other better. I know you're busy. Your mom has told me about your job."

I return his smile. "I'd like that."

"Great." He utters a soft laugh. "I don't want to give you the wrong impression, like I'm rushing things when I said I wouldn't, but my kids will be in Florida. Maybe we can all go down there and spend a weekend together? I'd love for both you and your mom to meet them. And Alex, of course."

Brushing the windblown wisps of hair off my face, I

say, "I'll keep that in mind when I plan my summer shifts." That is, if I'm back at work by then. "I'm sure I can finagle a long weekend."

"Wonderful." He raps the rail. "Shall we go inside where it's warm?"

When we get back to the kitchen, my mom and Alex have finished unpacking the bags.

"What do you think?" she asks under her breath as William pours us organic grape juice while Alex keeps him company.

"He seems really nice," I say sincerely.

She's all but glowing. "I knew you'd like him."

"Here you go," William says, handing us each a glass of juice. "Homemade from Californian grapes."

We spend an agreeable half hour together, sipping our drinks in the kitchen while we warm up Tima's dishes and William adds the finishing touches to the ones he prepared. I listen attentively as he tells me about the program and its development. On a personal level, everything regarding Mom's welfare concerns me, and on a professional level, I find the medical information fascinating.

Our lunch stretches well into the afternoon. It's dusk when we finally thank William, say our goodbyes, and drive back.

Despite the amiable afternoon, I can't shake my tenseness when we arrive at the clinic. Knowing me as well as she does, my mom picks up on it.

"Is everything all right?" she asks as we enter the foyer.

"Yes," I say, smiling for her benefit. I hate myself for lying to my mom. "Everything is perfect."

Surprisingly, I sleep well and wake up rested the following morning. I thought the anxiety would keep me tossing and turning all night.

Other than opening my eyes, I don't move. Alex is lying on his back, still asleep. I use the opportunity to study him. His face doesn't carry the tenseness that strains his features during the day. For once, he looks relaxed. Stubble darkens his jaw. His eyelashes are long for a man, softening the straight, harsh lines of his strong bone structure. He looks vulnerable in his sleep. The way my heart squeezes reminds me just how susceptible I am to him.

Trying to be quiet, I slip out of the bed, but the minute I stand up, Alex opens his eyes. The unguarded smile he gives me is my undoing. His blue eyes are soft with sleep yet piercing as he evaluates me. A feeling like a flapping of wings stirs in my chest.

"Sleep well?" he asks in a bed-sexy voice.

"Yes, actually." I glance at him from under my lashes as I dig through my bag for clothes. "You?"

He shifts up and rests his head on the headboard to watch me. "Like a baby." His lips quirk. "Like always when I sleep next to you."

My gaze is drawn to the sexy curve of those lips. My reply is meant as a clever comeback, but my voice sounds embarrassingly breathy. "With the emphasis on sleep. I'm surprised you didn't jump on me when we went to bed."

That quirk stretches into a lazy smile. "You sound disappointed."

Rolling my eyes, I head for the bathroom.

"Katyusha."

I stop in my tracks.

His voice is apologetic. "I wish we could stay longer, but we have to leave today."

I didn't expect otherwise, but the news is nevertheless disappointing. "When?"

"After breakfast."

I nod. "I'll be ready."

When I've finished getting dressed in the bathroom, I step back into the room. Alex is on the phone, speaking to someone in Russian. He's still in his pajama bottoms, pacing the floor. I can't help but stare at the broad, well-defined expanse of his chest and the flat ridges of his stomach.

He places a hand over the microphone of his phone. "You go ahead, my love. I'll follow later."

Igor is waiting outside our door to escort me downstairs. I find my mom on the terrace having breakfast.

"There you are," she says when she notices me. "Where's that sweet man of yours?"

"On the phone. He'll be down shortly."

"He sounds like a workaholic." She scoots to the side. "I hope you don't mind that I started breakfast without you, but I thought you might sleep in."

Taking the chair next to her, I say, "Alex doesn't want to get home too late. I'm afraid we have to leave after breakfast."

"He's very conscientious."

If only she knew.

I'm half done with my breakfast when Alex arrives. The minute he walks through the doors, everyone looks. He has that effect on people. It's not just his imposing height or potently masculine features. It's the self-assured way he carries himself.

He offers us a smile and makes his way over. Despite the friendly gesture, the tension is back on his face. The square line of his jaw is more pronounced from the way he always clenches it a little, and his eyes are tight with awareness. He seems permanently vigilant, forever on his guard.

"Good morning, Laura." He takes in my mother. "You look beautiful. I really like that new hairstyle on you."

She pats her hair. "Why, thank you. What a charming man you are. Have a seat."

When he puts a hand on my shoulder, my body takes notice. Awareness tingles in my nerve endings and travels down my arm as goosebumps run over my skin under my sweater.

"If you don't mind, I'll grab a quick breakfast in the lounge," he says. "I have business to take care of. Besides, I robbed you of Katerina yesterday. You deserve to have her all to yourself this morning."

He gives my shoulder a squeeze before walking off.

"Oh, my," Mom gushes. "That man is perfection. Could he be any more wonderful?"

Great. Now she's in love with the idea of Alex and me. I bite my lip. What if things don't work out? She'll be so disappointed, and I can never tell her the truth.

"What's with the long face?" she asks, taking my hand.

I shake myself out of it. "I'll miss you."

"I'll be home before you know it."

I blow out a shaky breath, not telling her there's a good chance I may still be in Russia at that time. "Just enjoy the time you have left here. You deserve it."

"I have to admit, this feels more like a vacation than a treatment. I'm having so much fun with the other patients, and then, of course, there's William."

I nod. "He wants us to meet his children in Florida this summer."

Concern plays over her face. "Are you okay with that?"

"Of course." Again, provided I'll be back in the States. I push the disturbing thought aside. "He seems serious, but he told me he won't rush you into anything." My experience with Alex makes me say, "Promise me you won't make any rash decisions."

"You know me." She lets my hand go with a squeeze and pulls the juice closer. "I may be impulsive, but I take my time before committing to anything."

I don't want her to think I'm against her having a long-term relationship with William. "I only want you to be happy."

"I am," she says with an easy smile. "That's all I've ever wanted for you too, Katie. I'm truly happy you've finally found your match."

Avoiding answering, I take the juice she poured and hide my face behind the glass.

When it's time to go, she sees us off. We say our goodbyes, my mom hugging both me and Alex and making him promise not to work too hard. She waves until we turn the corner.

It's then that the emptiness hits me.

It's then that I think that maybe I should've run when I had the chance.

28

ALEX

*W*e fly to a small private airfield in northern Idaho, where I leave a disgruntled Katerina on the plane with enough men to guard her. I don't tell her where I'm headed or about the contract I'm about to sign with Nikolai Molotov. If I did, I'd have to tell her why I'm not taking her, and I don't want her to worry about the fact that I don't trust Nikolai. Though I've been working with Konstantin for months and have no reason to think his brother wishes me harm, I don't put my faith in anyone I don't know personally.

I don't leave until we've set up perimeter alarms and Igor has satellite surveillance running on his laptop. A secure connection feeds the information to my phone. No one besides me, Igor, and the pilot knows our flight schedule. It's unlikely that anyone will come looking for us here, but I repeat my instructions, commanding the men to guard Katerina with their lives. Igor assures me he'll follow protocol the minute he picks up any movement close by, meaning he'll send a reconnaissance team to find out who's on the way. The pilot is ready for takeoff in case of an emergency. His order is to leave immediately if there's any threat. I can always find my own way back. I know how to take care of myself.

The drive to the compound is tense. Yuri is behind the wheel and Leonid rides shotgun. It's a cold, gray day with fog hanging thick in the air. I can barely see ten meters ahead.

As we get higher into the mountains, I call Igor. "How is she?"

"Still angry," he says in his gruff voice.

"She'll get over it." Even though I can see for myself on my phone, I ask, "How about the surveillance?"

"Everything is running smoothly."

The words don't reassure me. I don't like being away from my kiska.

Leonid glances at me from the front passenger seat when I end the call, his beefy face pulled into a frown. He doesn't like the fact that I'm practically keeping Katerina prisoner. My men respect her. They've taken a liking to her. Well, tough luck. I'm not taking risks with her safety. Leonid and everyone else can go fuck themselves.

I address Yuri in a terse tone. "How much farther?"

He shoots a quick look at the GPS. "Ten minutes."

The road zigzags up the mountain. Exactly ten minutes later, we arrive at a stately metal gate. At our approach, the heavy gate slides apart, revealing more dense woods and a narrow, unpaved road.

Why would Nikolai Molotov hide out here in the middle of nowhere? I suppose the isolation allows for heightened security measures, even more than my St. Petersburg residence. Maybe I should build myself a compound in the middle of nowhere too and keep Katyusha there. For her safety.

Yuri pulls up to a modern house. The lights shine golden through the vast windows. All those windows give me an uneasy itch that crawls between my shoulder blades. With no blinds or curtains, the occupants are sitting ducks, an easy target for any stalker or assassin. If Nikolai Molotov's reputation for being a mistrustful son of a bitch is true, the glass is bullet-proof. Still, I've never liked feeling exposed.

The front door opens, and Molotov himself steps outside.

Leonid gets my door. He follows with Yuri as I make my way over and shake Molotov's hand.

Molotov ushers us inside and invites my men to have refreshments in the kitchen while he and I go to his study.

"In here," he says, standing aside for me to enter.

The vista behind the window is hidden by the fog. A few floodlights color the footpaths of the garden with an emerald light. The view must be spectacular on a clear day.

"Sit," he says, leading me to a round conference table near his desk.

When I'm seated, he takes a bottle of vodka from an ice bucket and pours two shots. "I believe you have an assassin on your tail."

I regard him from under my eyelids. "News travels fast."

"In our circles." He places a glass in front of me and takes the chair behind the desk. "Are you making headway in finding the man who wants you dead?"

Inhaling deeply, I exhale through my nose as I consider him. Like I said, I don't trust anyone, not easily. "As a matter of fact, yes."

When I don't elaborate, he asks, "And who is this person who wants you dead, if I may ask?"

My smile feels flat. "You may not."

"May I ask why then?" He traces the rim of his glass. "Power?"

"Power is always a good motive for killing."

A grin slides onto his face. He knows I'm not going to tell him anything. "What's with the evasiveness?"

Impatience slips into my tone. "What's with the curiosity?"

"I like to know with whom I'm doing business." Leaning back, he studies me with an inquisitive look. "Not so long ago, you were parading a woman around New York City, a woman you took to Russia with you. Katherine Morrell, am I right? It was all over the gossip magazines."

I tighten my grip on the glass. "If you value your life, you won't speak her name again."

"It's like that," he says, giving not only his agreement

but also his understanding with a nod. "What happened? Did your hunter go after her to get to you?"

If I clench the glass any harder, it's going to break.

"Ah," he says when I don't answer. "I see that I'm right."

Narrowing my eyes, I say in a calculated tone, "You seem very interested in matters that don't concern you."

He regards me for a moment, both thoughtful and attentive. "You have a lot of enemies."

I raise a brow. "So do you."

"This joint venture will guarantee you an alliance with my family. To a certain extent. Is that the real reason for your interest in Konstantin's project?"

"It will also secure you an alliance with me. Is that why you're signing the papers?"

He smiles at my comeback. Silence stretches for a beat before the tension gives and a more amiable atmosphere settles.

"What's with the questions, Nikolai? I thought you were happy with my terms. Do you have doubts?"

Pulling his glass closer, he says, "Just making sure you'll stay alive for the project to actually get off the ground."

I give him a cold look. "I have no intention of dying."

"Good." He raises his glass. "To our mutual objectives."

I clink my glass against his. "To the joint venture."

We throw back the liquor in unison. When I put my

empty glass aside, he takes a folder from the drawer and slides it over the desk.

I flip back the cover. As I read the contract, he pours more vodka. Satisfied that everything is stated as we agreed, I take a felt tip pen from my pocket and sign my name.

"This warrants another toast," he says.

After he signs, we drink twice more. When he lifts the bottle for a fourth round, I get to my feet.

"I'd better get going." I button up my jacket. "We have a long trip ahead."

He follows suit. "There's plenty of room here if you'd like to stay over."

"Thanks, but I'd prefer to get back."

Coming around the desk, he says, "I'll walk you out."

We go via the living room where Yuri and Leonid are watching television while stuffing their faces with a spread of snacks.

At the front door, I pause. "Tell me something, Nikolai."

He waits.

"What is a man who supposedly loves the opera more than anyone doing out here in the wilderness?"

His eyes tighten. "I like fishing."

Right. Does it have anything to do with the young American wife he took not so long ago? Either way, every man is entitled to his secrets, so I leave it at that. I'm halfway to the car when he speaks.

"It's my turn to ask you something, Alex."

Pausing, I face him.

"Why did you choose Konstantin's project?" he asks. "There are a hundred other investments with a much lower risk profile."

"Because everyone deserves affordable power."

He utters a low laugh. Yuri and Leonid join in. So do I. Let them think what they will. They don't need to know I mean it. As far as my reputation goes, I'm heartless.

Just as we get into the car, my phone rings.

It's Igor.

Every muscle in my body goes rigid. I take the call even before Leonid has closed my door.

"What's wrong?" I ask, my voice tight.

"Everything is fine here," Igor says. "Kate is safe. Something went down in St. Petersburg." He pauses, the silence grave. "I got word from our man who's watching Stefanov's house. I thought you'd want to know."

"Hold on." I put my phone on speaker for Leonid's benefit. If shit is going down, it will save time if I don't have to repeat the message. "What happened?" I bite out as we clear the gates of Molotov's property.

"Stefanov executed Pavlov and wiped out his whole senior commanding team."

What the fuck? "He did what?"

"That's not all." Another pause. "He decapitated the body and delivered a headless corpse to Pavlov's doorstep, apparently to send a message."

"What message?"

"He claims Pavlov betrayed him," Igor says. "Sold him out."

Leonid catches my gaze in the rearview mirror. "Stefanov is cleaning up after himself."

Exactly my thought.

"What did our man see?" I ask.

"He says Pavlov arrived first and later his under-bosses. He didn't see them leave, but their cars were driven away. That's when he suspected something was happening. Soon after, the bodies were carried out of the house in broad daylight for all to see. He reported it to your man in charge, who sent a drone. He's got footage of the body being dumped on Pavlov's doorstep."

That's a strong message to send. Everyone in Russia will think twice before double-crossing Stefanov. He may have set up the massacre to look like a justified bratva execution, but the fact that he silenced Pavlov means he's getting nervous.

Good.

I have a feeling more action is about to go down.

I can hardly wait.

29

KATE

e arrive back in St. Petersburg with the same strict security as before and make it to Alex's house with no incidents. Lena and Tima welcome us in the foyer. I convey my mom's and William's thanks to Tima for the food and excuse myself to have a shower.

When I come downstairs for dinner, Alex calls me into the library. I enter cautiously. He's sitting on the sofa with his laptop on the coffee table in front of him.

"Is anything the matter?" I ask.

Steepling his fingers, he gives me an examining look. "Not at all. Why would you think something is wrong?"

"Because you're being hunted by a killer? Because my mom is sick, and lots of bad things can happen while I'm not there? Because you look serious, and that always means bad news?"

His mouth tightens. "You're exaggerating."

I walk to the sofa. "Then what is it?"

"Joanne sent you a message to say Merry Christmas."

I tense. The fact that Alex is filtering my messages is wrong on so many levels. My voice comes out harsher than I intend. "How kind of you to convey the message. I hope you told her Merry Christmas from me too?"

His blue eyes narrow marginally, but he smooths it over with a smile. "How about telling her yourself?"

I glance at his laptop. "Now?"

"If that's fine with you. She's available. They visited Joanne's parents in Hudson for Christmas Day but returned home this morning. She's saving her vacation time for warmer days."

"Wow." I utter a laugh. "You know more about my friend's life than I do these days."

"Katerina," he says with a frown.

I shrug. "It's true. So? What did you tell her?"

"I told her we flew out to see your mom, but that we had to return straight away due to my business obligations."

"I see." My smile is wry. "Is there any point in me talking to her then? Since you've already told her everything you want her to know."

He gets to his feet. "Why are you so agitated about this? I thought you'd be happy to speak to her."

"You know what will make me happy? Reading the messages she sends me without having them censored and relayed by you."

He rounds the sofa. "What's wrong with you?"

"What's wrong with me?" I backtrack a step. "What's wrong is *you*."

I turn for the door, but he grabs my wrist and hauls me back. "Katyusha. This isn't like you. I thought we had a good time in Deep Creek. I thought you were happy to see your mother."

"I was happy to see her. Very. I already told you that."

"Then what's gotten into you?"

"Everything," I say, pulling free of his hold. "This." I wave around the room. "The fact that you lock me up here and filter my messages. And how about the fact that I don't have a life any longer? You land your plane in the middle of Idaho and leave me there while you do whatever the hell it was you did there. I don't know how you justify that behavior to yourself, but it's not okay, Alex."

His frown deepens. "I had a business meeting. That's all."

"It doesn't matter why you went there. What matters is that you're selective with the information you share with me. How do you expect me to trust you if you read all my emails but keep me in the dark about your affairs?"

He watches me quietly, his eyes gleaming with anger, but I'm too upset to care.

After a terse moment, he says, "I apologize for leaving you in the plane. It was for your safety. It won't happen again."

It's not even about having been stuck in a plane in

the middle of the woods. To be honest, I haven't been myself since we left Deep Creek. My emotions are all over the place. This whole crazy situation is getting to be too much. The uncertainty is killing me.

Taking a few deep breaths to calm myself, I say, "I didn't mean to lash out at you like that."

"I understand." He wraps his arms around me and drags me against his chest. "It will soon be over, kiska."

I crane my neck to look at him. "Will it? Why? What's going on?" What isn't he telling me?

He kisses my forehead. "Do you want me to postpone the call with Joanne until you feel more like yourself?"

"No," I say quickly, freeing myself from his embrace and brushing my hands over my hair. "I'd like to chat with her."

Giving me another piercing look, he goes back to the sofa, takes a seat, and wakes his laptop screen to connect a video call. I sit down on the edge of the seat next to him.

Three seconds later, my friend's face fills the screen. "Katie! How good to see you." She's walking through a spacious room with raw brick walls. "You too, Alex. Merry Christmas again." She plops down on a brown leather sofa, folding one leg under her, and puts the laptop on a coffee table.

"Thank you," I say with a genuine smile, some of my tension lifting. "Merry Christmas to you too."

Ricky waves from behind an island counter stove

where he's stirring something in a pot. "Merry Christmas, guys."

"We're at Ricky's place," Joanne says. "He's renting a loft apartment in the Meatpacking District." She smiles at him from over her shoulder. "He's cooking."

She's wearing makeup, and her hair has been blow-dried straight. I can count on one hand the number of times I've seen her without her spiral curls.

"You look amazing," I say.

"Thank you." A blush colors her cheeks. "It's a special occasion."

Ricky comes around the counter carrying a bottle of wine in one hand and two glasses in the other. "Once you two are done with your honeymoon," he says, taking a seat next to Joanne, "I'll invite you for dinner too."

"We'd like that," Alex says.

Ricky winks as he pours the wine. "I'll hold you to it."

"How's your mom?" Joanne asks. "I can't believe you flew all the way to North Carolina and didn't stop over to see us."

Alex throws an arm around me. "As I said in my text message, duty called."

"You work too hard, Alex." Joanne takes the glass Ricky offers her. "Coming from me, that says a lot."

Alex chuckles. "It's a busy period. It will calm down after the new year."

Joanne takes a sip of her wine. "Back to your mom, Katie. What's new?"

"She's feeling so much better," I say.

"That's awesome." Joanne snuggles closer to Ricky. "I'm glad to hear that."

"How about your parents?" I ask.

She shoots Ricky a puppy-eyed look. "They're doing fine. It really went well."

I look between them. "What went well?"

Ricky cups Joanne's knee. His smile is all teeth. "I decided to do it the old-fashioned way and asked Joanne's dad for permission to marry her."

"What? You got engaged?" I gape at Joanne. "That's fantastic! Congratulations. Is this what tonight is? A celebration dinner?"

Joanne glows. "We wanted you to be the first to know before we tell everyone else."

"Congratulations," Alex says. "That's very good news."

Placing a hand over my heart, I say, "I'm so happy for you. When's the big day?"

"Soon," Ricky says, his gaze heating as it lands on Joanne.

"I know it's rushed," she says, "but we know we're good together. Why wait?"

"Why indeed?" I utter a shriek. "My best friend is getting married! I can't believe it."

She shifts deeper onto her seat and rests an arm on the backrest. "Ricky wants to elope. I think we should have a small, intimate ceremony."

Joy warms my chest as I study their happy faces. "I'm sure you'll work it out."

"I hope I can count on you," Joanne says. "I'd love for you to be my bridesmaid."

"Of course," I say on impulse. "It will be an honor." Belatedly, I glance at Alex and bite my lip, realizing I've just made a promise I may not be able to keep. The thought is a damper on the happy mood. Not wanting to spoil the moment, I quickly change the subject. "When are you going to choose the ring?"

"We're not getting rings," Ricky says. "We're getting tattoos. It's a cliché, but it seems like the right choice for us."

"Good for you," I say with a smile. "This is a wonderful Christmas surprise."

Joanne makes a face. "My mother is disappointed that I've decided against a ring and a big wedding."

"She respects your choice," Ricky says. "She just needs a little time for the idea to grow on her."

"Tell us about your visit to Deep Creek," Joanne says.

Ricky holds up a finger. "I'm going to give the sauce a stir, but I'm listening."

While he goes back to cooking, I tell them about the clinic and my mom's progress, but I refrain from mentioning William for now. There's no point in bringing him into the conversation unless their relationship, which is still in an early stage, lasts beyond the treatment center. I've learned my lesson with getting my hopes up too soon. My mom is a butterfly. Not many men hold her attention for long, and then there's her illness. Like her ex-boyfriend Martin, most men bail when times get tough.

Too soon, Alex checks his watch. "I'm afraid we have to leave you. We're about to have dinner, and we don't want your lunch to get cold."

More accurately, he wants to make sure we don't stay on the call for too long. It's one of his security rules.

"It was good to see you," Joanne says, unfolding her leg from under her. "We'll call you again soon."

"I'd like that," I say. "I want to know everything about your plans for the wedding."

After saying our goodbyes, Alex ends the call.

He regards me solemnly for a heartbeat before saying, "I'm sorry you can't be there for Joanne. I know you would've liked to help with the wedding arrangements."

I sit with a stiff back, waiting for the real blow.

His tone is regretful. "It pains me to say this, Katyusha, but we may not be back in time for the wedding, not if they tie the knot soon."

I turn my face to look at him. "You took me to see my mom for Christmas. I'm not asking to be there to help my best friend with her wedding preparations, but why can't we attend her wedding?"

"*If* they decide to have a ceremony."

"Hypothetically speaking then."

He blows out a sigh. "I'm sure they'll postpone the big day if you ask them to."

I stare at him with parted lips. "Are you for real? I'm

not going to ask Joanne and Ricky to postpone one of the most important days of their lives to accommodate *me*. How selfish do you think I am?"

A moment of silence passes as he studies me quietly before saying, "Suit yourself, but there will be no more traveling until the end of January."

I jump to my feet. "The end of January? That's more than a month away."

He regards me with an expressionless face. "I'm aware of the timeline."

"And when we get to the end of January, will it become the end of February?"

A muscle ticks in his temple. "It will be as long as it takes."

I utter a laugh. "You're unbelievable."

He gets up. "This is a difficult time for both of us. Don't make it harder than it already is."

Tears burn at the backs of my eyes, but I blink them away.

"If at all possible, you will be there." He takes my hand. "There are things that need to happen first, things that will compromise our safety if I don't deal with them first, and when I've taken care of them, we may have to lay low for a while."

"That's what you keep saying."

Wrapping an arm around my waist, he pulls my body flush against his. I lean back, but not far enough to escape his lips. He slants them over mine in a searing kiss, sending an instant fire to my lower body.

I push on his shoulders, fighting for distance until he loosens his hold.

"Katerina," he says, fixing me with a predatory stare.

"No, Alex." I grip his wrist and remove his arm from around me. "This time, you don't get to kiss yourself out of a fight."

Not sparing him another glance, I walk out of the room, my heart aching—and not just because I might not be able to attend my best friend's wedding.

ALEX

I'm up early the following morning. I had trouble sleeping because my kiska is angry. She told me goodnight and let me kiss her, but the message came through clearly when she turned her back on me and went to sleep.

After blowing off some steam in the gym, I have a shower and inform Tima that I'm staying home and will be around for lunch. I instruct him to prepare something special for Katyusha, one of her favorite dishes, and then I go to my study to get some work done.

I've barely settled behind my desk when Igor raps on the open door.

"Enter," I say, waving him inside.

"There's been a development you should know about," he says as he approaches my desk.

I give him my full attention.

He stops behind the visitor's chair. "Stefanov has

put a price on Besov's head. Word has just been put out. The news is circulating in the bratva circles."

"Interesting." I rub a thumb over my lips. "What's his reason?"

"Stefanov claims Pavlov sold him out to Besov. According to him, Pavlov is a traitor and Besov a blackmailer."

"This drama is getting more intriguing by the minute."

It doesn't take much to connect the dots. Stefanov and Pavlov were in cahoots. One or both of them ordered the hit on my life, hiring Besov for the job. Stefanov has already killed Pavlov. Now he's putting a target on the assassin's back. If the price is high enough, someone will eventually find Besov and deliver his head on a platter. Stefanov is silencing everyone who was involved in his scheme to get rid of me. The only loose end left is me, which can only mean one thing. He's getting ready to come after me.

"Tell the men to be extra vigilant. I have a feeling it won't be long before Stefanov strikes."

Igor nods and leaves briskly.

I unlock my laptop screen with my thumbprint and pull up my emails. A call comes in from Nelsky. Since I'm back from the States, he reports to me on a daily basis.

I take the call from my laptop, which is connected to my phone. "You'd better have something for me."

"As a matter of fact, I do, sir."

I freeze with my fingers over the keyboard. "Did you crack the code?"

"Ten seconds ago, sir."

My body tenses with anticipation. "Did you have a look at the contents?"

"No, sir. I'm sending an encrypted file to you now."

A message from Nelsky pops up in my inbox. "Got it. I'll call you back if I have further instructions."

I end the call and download the message in the encryption application that descrambles the code. It's a security tape recording of a man tied up in a chair, his face beaten to a bloody pulp. I barely recognize the symmetrical features and square chin, but I do recognize the round table with the checkered tablecloth and the wooden bowl with fruit.

Our kitchen.

My father.

An untimely flashback hits me in the gut, a memory of coming home from school to the smell of my mother frying *blini*. I can see her smile as she told me to wash my hands.

"An orange first," she said, ruffling my hair as I stuffed a *blin* with honey into my mouth after washing my hands at the sink. "What are oranges for, *malysh*?"

"For not catching a cold," I replied dutifully with a full mouth, taking a seat at the table.

The lines around her blue eyes softened. "And why is that?"

I rolled my eyes. Could these questions have been any more basic? "Because they have vitamin C."

She put an arm around me, hugging me to her waist. "Good."

The scratchy fabric of her apron felt abrasive against the first man-scruff on my cheek. She smelled of frying oil and soap. I hugged her back, but then embarrassment made me pull away.

"I'm too old for hugs," I said in a gruff voice.

She patted my cheek. "You're right. You're almost a man now, my Sasha."

My chest swelled with pride. "I'm Alex. I'm too old for Sasha too."

"Alex," she agreed gently.

The memory fades, and my chest squeezes with pain. Had I known what would happen the next day, I would've hugged her longer and told her I loved her.

Snapping out of the past, I force my attention back to my laptop, pain and anger mixing to create a violent cocktail in my blood.

On the screen, two men face my father. Both are fat around their waists and flabby in their arms. My father, a police officer who regularly encountered the worst of humanity, had security cameras in the apartment, just in case. The men must be unaware of the hidden cameras because they turn their backs on my father, revealing their faces.

My pulse jumps.

Vladimir Stefanov and Oleg Pavlov.

Putting his head close to Stefanov's, Pavlov says, "He's not going to talk."

Stefanov grins. "Oh, he will." He faces my father

again. "Tell us what evidence you have against us and where it is, and we'll let your wife and son live."

My father spits blood on the floor. "I have nothing. You're wasting your time."

Stefanov flicks his fingers at Pavlov. Pavlov walks somewhere, disappearing from view. A moment later, he's back, dragging a chair with him.

My heart stops.

My mother sits in the chair, her hands tied behind her back. He leaves the chair next to my father's so that their shoulders are touching. My mother cries softly, but she doesn't scream.

"You'll talk," Stefanov says. "Or you'll watch her die."

"She has nothing to do with this. Please, let her go," my father begs, a desperate entreaty in one eye and the other one swollen shut.

Stefanov bends down, putting him and my father at eye level. "Talk."

Pavlov grabs my mother's hair, fisting her dark curls in his fingers. She whimpers when he raises his other arm, poised to strike, but she doesn't cower.

"Stop," my father cries out. "Stop, please! I'll tell you."

"Where?" Stefanov demands.

"In the bathroom. There's a loose tile on the bath. It's behind the piping."

"Go," Stefanov says to Pavlov even as the latter hurries from the room. Then to my father, "You thought you could blackmail me?"

"No," my father says with disgust. "I was going to hand it over once I knew whom I could trust."

"Not very clever." Stefanov shakes his head. "I own the police force."

"Not everyone," my father says bravely.

Pavlov returns with a plastic bag dangling from his fingers. "Got it. He's got photos of us meeting with his superior and documents proving we pay him."

Stefanov nods. "You did the right thing, Viktor. Now you and your family will live. I'll even reward you handsomely for the trouble. Is there anything else you'd like to give me? For every other piece of information you hand over, I'll double the price."

My father's head drops. "No."

"I think he's telling the truth," Pavlov says.

Stefanov's voice is clear, his command cold. "Turn on the gas."

My mother blinks. Her head turns as she follows Pavlov with her gaze to the stove. "No." The whispered word is filled with dread.

Pavlov turns on the gas.

Stefanov takes a lighter from his pocket and lights the fat white candle that stands on the table, the one my mom used to save electricity.

"No," my mother cries.

"You said you'd let us go," my father yells, drops of blood splattering from his mouth onto his vest.

"The boy is almost fifteen," Pavlov says. "He'll be a problem for us later."

"No!" my mother says.

"Don't worry about the kid." Vladimir walks to the door. "He'll end up in the system. He'll be lucky if he survives."

"Goodbye, my friends," Pavlov says in a mocking tone, following in Stefanov's footsteps.

My parents sit side to side, facing each other. My mother gives my father a tremulous smile, and then the screen goes dead.

I clutch the edge of the desk so hard my nails leave imprints in the wood.

I see my surroundings through a haze of red.

Pavlov and Stefanov owned my father's superior at the police force. It's a pity that son of a bitch is long since dead, or I would personally torture him into his grave. I'd bet my left arm he was the one who pulled the security tape from the remote feed and handed it over to Oleg Pavlov. Pavlov then gave the tape to Besov via Mukha, who encrypted the file.

Why did Pavlov hand the tape to Besov? There can only be one reason. Besov threatened Pavlov's life. Besides me, who else would've wanted that tape? Stefanov. It's evidence connecting him to the murder of my parents. He would've wanted to make sure it never fell into my hands. I'd bet my right arm that Stefanov ordered Besov to threaten Pavlov for the evidence. The minute Stefanov had the file, he killed Pavlov. Now he's getting rid of Besov, and then me. Nice and clean.

One question remains. How did Stefanov find out who I am? Volkov is a common surname in Russia, and

Alexander is a popular first name. After I dodged the system, there's no way he could've kept track of me. If he had, he would've killed me a long time ago. No, he must've found out recently that I'm the son of the couple he killed in cold blood, not long before Besov took that shot at me. I imagine his surprise when he discovered I didn't die in the system after all. It must've been his worst nightmare come true, learning that I've become one of the most powerful men in this country. He knew that if I ever found out about the murder, I'd come after him with everything I've got.

The cold rage doesn't show in my voice as I get to my feet, grab my phone, and dial Igor. "It's time," I say when he picks up. "We're going in."

"Don't you want to wait for Stefanov to make the first move?" he asks.

"It's no longer necessary." I walk from the office with long strides. "I got the information I wanted."

"I'll brief the men," he says with resignation.

I hurry to the back of the house, taking the shortest route to the barracks to weapon up, and nearly knock Katerina off her feet as she comes out of the kitchen with a mug in her hand. I grip her elbows to steady her, making sure I haven't accidentally burned her with the hot liquid.

"Alex," she exclaims as she stares up at my face. "What's wrong?"

"Nothing," I say, moving her aside. "Stay in the house. No walks in the garden today. I'll be back in a few hours."

"Alex," she says again, leaving the mug on a hallway table to run after me.

I don't slow my stride. "Katerina, not now, please."

Tima looks up from the stove, his face serious for once.

Taking Katerina's arm, I lead her back to the kitchen. "I have things to prepare, and I don't need you in the middle of it." Cupping her jaw, I plant a chaste kiss on her lips. "Now be a good girl for me."

She blinks, watching me with slightly parted lips and a frown as I turn on my heel, but I can't worry about her now.

Stefanov's time on Earth has come to an end. He will cry for his mother before I'm done with him.

"*W*ait," I call, going after Alex again.

"For crying out loud, Katerina," he all but growls. "Go to our room and stay there."

Catching up with him, I grab his arm. "Tell me what's wrong."

He spins around and says with narrowed eyes, "Don't make me tell you twice. If you can't follow the order, I'll lock you in there myself."

He'll what? This is taking the game to a new low.

I pull my back straight. "*Your* room, you mean, because it's never been *ours*."

He casts a glance at Leonid, who passes us in the hallway with brisk steps. When Leonid is out of earshot, Alex says in a low voice, "I don't have time for word games." Pulling free from my grasp, he continues on his way.

I jog ahead and stop in the doorframe of the

kitchen, blocking his way. "If you're planning on leaving this house, you'll have to go through me first."

"Katerina." He clenches his jaw. "I'm not going to lay a hand on you with force, so please step aside."

When I don't move, he reverses direction, heading for the front of the house.

I stand frozen to the spot, gaping. What's gotten into him? I understand that he's under enormous stress, but that's not a reason to behave like a jerk. I want answers, but now is obviously not the time to press him.

Dragging in a few deep breaths, I bite my tongue and march to the stairs as Alex crosses the foyer. Just as I reach the bottom of the staircase, the door flings open and Igor enters. Alex pauses in his stride.

"You have visitors," Igor says, closing the door behind him. "Mikhail and Dania are at the gate."

Alex pinches the bridge of his nose and tilts his face to the ceiling. "Fuck. What shitty timing."

Igor shifts his weight. "Shall I tell them to come back later?"

Alex blows out a sigh before facing Igor again. "No." His jaw bunches as he looks at the door as if he can see through it. "Mikhail will consider turning them away an insult. Let them in." Looking at me from over his shoulder, he tells me with a tight expression, "You'd better hang around for a while longer before you go to *our* room."

I ball my hands into fists. I'm getting tired of being

treated like Alex's subordinate. He may be one of the most powerful men in the world, a self-made oligarch, but I'm still my own person. I've worked hard for my independence and confidence. I won't let him undermine those qualities just because he has more power than I do.

Before I can open my mouth to argue, Igor opens the door, revealing four cars pulling up in the driveway. Like us, Mikhail and Dania travel with bodyguards. A man exits the first car to open the back door of the second vehicle. A slender, pale leg is exposed as Dania gets out, her skirt riding a little too high. She unfolds her body gracefully and brushes a hand over her hip to straighten her skirt. Dressed in a red figure-hugging two-piece with matching heels and a fur coat draped over her shoulders, she's the epitome of elegance. Her stance is regal as she waits for her father to come around the car. Surrounded by men in black combat gear with caps depicting a labyrinth logo, which I presume to be Mikhail's emblem, they make their way to the door.

It's too late to escape, not that I'd leave her alone with Alex. I trust her as far as I can throw her. Her bathroom speech still rings clear in my mind.

Alex extends a hand when Mikhail reaches him. Except for the stiffness of his shoulders, he doesn't betray his stress. His face is composed and his manner controlled—a practiced mask. "Mikhail. This is an unexpected surprise."

Three guards stay outside. Four step inside the

house before Igor closes the door. They stand at attention near the entryway, blending in with the furniture.

Mikhail shakes Alex's hand. "You couldn't make it to dinner, and we haven't heard from you since." His lips tilt as he casts a sideway glance at his daughter. "Dania insisted we check on you. She was worried." Dipping his chin, he studies Alex. "We both were."

"We were in the States," Alex says. "I told you."

"Yes, yes." Mikhail pulls off his leather gloves. "However, you didn't tell me that you're back."

Lena appears on cue, rushing across the foyer to take Mikhail's gloves and coat.

"Dania," Alex says, acknowledging her with a nod, but he doesn't kiss her cheek when she tilts up her face.

I don't miss the minute tightening of her eyes.

"I hope you don't mind the uninvited visit," she says, smiling sweetly up at Alex.

"Not at all," Alex says, returning her smile. It doesn't reach his eyes. "You remember Katerina."

Dania and Mikhail turn their attention to me.

Mikhail gives me a critical once-over, taking in my oversized off-the-shoulder sweater and leggings. "Of course. How are you, Kate?"

Lifting my chin, I walk over with a straight back. "I'm good, thank you for asking. How about you?"

Raising his arms, he says with a condescending tilt of his lips, "As you can see."

"It's lovely to run into you again," Dania says to me. "You look…" She trails a gaze over me. "Nice?"

"Thank you," I say, matching her sugar-sweet tone. "You look… formal? Are you on your way to an event?"

Lena, who's taking Dania's coat, smothers a snort. When Alex gives her a hard look, she quickly busies herself with hanging the coat in the closet.

Dania chuckles. "This is my day wear, darling."

Alex holds out an arm, indicating the formal lounge. "Shall we?"

He leads the way.

Looking around, Dania falls in behind him. "Not much has changed around here. It's about time a woman redecorated this stuffy old place."

"Dania," Mikhail says with reprimand. "Alex will think you're insulting his taste."

"I know Alex's taste," she says, swaying her hips as she follows him into the lounge. "It's modern, like his house in New York."

The jab hits me hard, just as she intended. It's meant as a reminder that she's seen the inside of his house, and more specifically, the inside of his bedroom. It was before he knew me, but still. If I could claw her eyes out right now, I would.

"Would you like a drink?" Alex asks, motioning for them to take a seat on the sofa. "Vodka?"

"Tea for me, if you don't mind," Dania says, sitting down next to her father. "I'm parched."

Alex takes a seat on the couch and pulls me down with him. To Lena, who stands in the doorframe with her hands folded in front of her, he says, "Tea and vodka, please." Looking at me, he asks, "What would you like, Katyusha?"

"Tea is fine, thank you," I say.

"You know which tea I like, Lena," Dania says. "That lovely licorice and verbena homemade brew of yours."

"Yes, ma'am," Lena says before leaving the room.

Dania addresses me. "Tell us about your trip to the States."

Not in the mood to discuss my family or personal life with them, I answer vaguely, "It was great."

Alex stretches his arm across the backrest and brushes a finger over the naked skin of my exposed shoulder. "Too short, I'm afraid."

We make small talk for another few minutes, and then the discussion turns to business, which excludes me from the conversation.

Lena arrives with a tray that she puts on the coffee table. She pours herbal tea from a small porcelain teapot for Dania and offers me a cup of Earl Grey. After serving everyone a slice of Tima's almond cake, she leaves.

Alex pours the vodka and hands Mikhail a glass. It seems early for drinking hard liquor, but I know it's a Russian custom. Mikhail drones on about the business while we finish our tea. He's in the middle of a sentence when Dania interrupts him by standing abruptly.

Placing a hand over her stomach, she says, "I don't feel well. Kate, can you please accompany me to the bathroom?"

"Of course," I say, already on my feet.

The men stand, their brows pleated.

"Shall I call a doctor?" Mikhail asks.

"It's just a little nausea, Papa."

I rush after Dania as she hurries to the door.

"Katerina is a nurse," Alex says. "She'll let us know if we need to call."

Dania knows her way around the house. She runs for the guest bathroom, banging the door against the wall as she opens it.

I follow and close the door for privacy. Her face is pale and sweat beads on her forehead. She looks like she's on the verge of vomiting. Just in case, I open the toilet lid.

"How do you feel?" I ask. "Only nauseated or do you also have stomach cramps?"

"Listen to me," she says, startling me by grabbing my shoulders. She continues in an urgent tone. "We don't have much time. In a moment, I'm going to be sick. *Really* sick."

I lean away, taking in her feverish face. "What are you talking about?"

"The tea. Lena slipped something into it."

"What?" I exclaim.

She gives me a shake. "Listen to me. This is your only chance to escape." She tips her chin toward the toilet stall. "There's a bag behind the door. Get changed. Soon, there will be mayhem. It'll look as if I'm dying. They'll think it's poisoning. My father is going to rush me to the hospital. I'll get into the car with him.

While everyone is distracted, get into the second car. My bodyguard is the driver. Lie down in the back. He'll take you to the airport. Lena packed you a bag. It's already inside the trunk with money and a false passport."

Too shocked to find words, I can only stare at her.

"It's your only chance of getting away," she says, letting go of my shoulders. "I'm not going to poison myself twice for you."

"What about you?" I ask, battling to process what's happening. "What did Lena give you?"

"Don't worry about me," she says, wiping her brow with the back of her hand. "It was a small dose. I'll survive."

"I can't believe you did this," I say, shaking from head to toe. "It's so dangerous and irresponsible."

"Don't let it be for nothing." She pushes me toward the toilet. "Go. Hurry. We're running out of time." When I don't move, she says, "It's now or never, Kate. Do you understand what I'm saying?"

My brain goes into shutdown mode, even as my training dictates that I assist her. When her shoulders curl inward and her chest heaves, I take her arm.

"Come," I say, leading her to the toilet. "I'm calling Alex."

She shoves me away. "Take the fucking bag, Kate. Don't be an idiot."

I look at the bag in the corner behind the door. "How did it get here?"

"My bodyguard smuggled it to Lena," she says,

kneeling in front of the toilet. "Does it fucking matter how it got there?"

Brushing her hair over her shoulder, I say, "I can't just leave you like this."

She utters a laugh. "I'll have enough people worrying about me. All you—" Violent retching cuts the rest of her sentence short.

I hold her hair as she empties her stomach. When the worst of it is over, I run for the door.

A knock falls on it as I'm about to reach for the handle.

"Katerina?" Alex calls. "Is everything all right?"

"No," I say, opening the door.

Alex and Mikhail stand on the threshold, their faces tense with worry.

"It looks like poison," I say in a shaky voice. "She needs to get to a hospital."

"Breakfast, Papa," Dania says meekly from the toilet. "*Blini.*"

Mikhail utters a string of expletives.

Alex says tersely, "I'll call an ambulance."

"No." Another heave racks Dania's body. Sucking in a breath, she says, "I want you to take me, Papa. I don't trust the ambulance."

"Tell your driver to start the engine," Alex says to Mikhail. "I'll tell my men to make sure the roads are clear. You'd better call home on your way and take samples of the breakfast. Maybe sweep the kitchen."

Mikhail gives a nod before running down the hallway.

"Can you hold down the fort here while I check on security?" Alex asks me, his words quiet but rushed. "I'll send Igor to carry Dania to the car."

My stomach twists as I nod. "Of course."

Offering me a fleeting smile of gratitude, he follows on Mikhail's heels.

Another bout of vomiting leaves Dania slumped over the toilet. There's not much I can do for her other than holding her hair out of her face. If the dose of poison she took isn't lethal, it'll work itself out of her system in a few hours. However, they'll still have to monitor her at the hospital to check for organ or nervous system damage. They'll probably pump her stomach to be on the safe side and hook her up to a glucose IV while running tests. After overnight observation, they'll discharge her and send her home. Her life will return to normal, and her suffering will have been wasted.

I look between her and the bag.

"Fuck you, Kate," she says, her chest rising and falling with rapid breaths. "I'll kill you if I went through this for nothing."

Shit. I don't know what to do. She's right about one thing. This is my only chance. There won't be another opportunity. The house is in chaos and I'm caught in the maelstrom, forced to make a rash decision.

Instinct kicks in, survival mode taking over. I drag the bag from behind the door to the vanity area of the bathroom. My hands shake as I pull down the zipper and take out a black T-shirt, a puffy jacket, a pair of combat pants, and a cap with a labyrinth logo.

Am I really doing this? I'm not thinking logically any longer. Pure adrenaline dictates my behavior. I yank off my sweater and drag the T-shirt over my head. I don't bother to remove my leggings. I only kick off my sneakers before pulling on the too-big combat pants. I'm in the middle of bundling my hair under the cap when the door swings inward.

Fright freezes me in place. If Alex catches me, I don't know what he'll do to me. I only know that it's too late. I'm guilty. I've been from the moment I unzipped the bag.

Lena steps into the bathroom.

I blow out a breath, nearly collapsing with relief.

"Come on," Lena says, taking a pair of combat boots from the bag. "Igor is on his way. You have to hurry." She hands me the boots and shoves my sweater and sneakers into the bag. "Put them on in the next room. I'll hide your clothes and take care of Dania."

I hesitate.

"Now, Kate," Lena says in a stern voice, prompting me to action.

I act on autopilot, taking the boots and peering around the open door. There's a commotion in the foyer, men running in every direction. The front door stands open. Mikhail is in the entrance, pulling on his coat while barking something in Russian to one of his men. Alex has his phone pressed to his ear, presumably alerting the security at Mikhail's house, or maybe he's warning the hospital of Dania's arrival.

Quietly, I slip around the frame and enter the deserted summer lounge next to the bathroom. It's one of the many rooms we don't use. I press my back against the wall behind the door, taking a deep breath as footsteps fall hard in the hallway. Scraping together all the courage I possess, I put on the boots. My hands tremble so much when I tie the laces that the effort is messy at best.

Igor's voice booms from the bathroom next door. He's saying something in Russian. Lena replies. Ducking my head, I hide my face behind the visor of the cap and scoot around the frame. My heart beats with deafening thumps in my chest as I walk briskly down the hallway.

Caught up in the havoc, no one looks up as I fall in line with two men carrying rifles. Igor comes out of the bathroom, carrying Dania in his arms. Alex ends his phone call and hurries toward them. Mikhail follows.

I use the opportunity to slip through the front door. Alex's men are carrying metal detectors and guns inside. After what's happened, Alex will make sure our security hasn't been breached. I walk toward the cars in the driveway, my heart threatening to burst from my chest with every step I take. It's too late to turn back. By taking action, I'm collaborating with Dania. Alex may even think I concocted this plan, but there's no time to ponder the possible consequences. There's only one way forward, and it's getting out of here. I'll figure out the rest when I'm on American soil.

The back door of the second car is open. The man next to the car gives an almost undetectable nod as he meets my gaze. I glance over my shoulder. No one is watching. I slide into the back, facing straight ahead. The man shuts the door. When nobody shouts and nothing happens, I slide down the seat and lie down flat. There's a blanket on the floor sticking out from under the passenger seat. I cover myself, not daring to breathe.

Mikhail's voice reaches me in my hiding place. Footsteps crunch on the gravel. When my lungs start burning, I realize I've been holding my breath. I inhale the scent of the leather seat and a feminine perfume that sticks to the cashmere blanket. The wool tents slightly with my exhale, the scratchy fibers tickling my nose.

Don't sneeze, Kate. Please, don't sneeze.

The engine starts. The car rolls forward slowly. I count the seconds. After fifteen beats, we pick up speed. The faster we go, the more my pulse quickens.

The man says something in Russian.

Syad', it sounds like. *Get up* or *sit up*.

Pushing the blanket aside, I stare at the sky through the window. The day is overcast. It looks as if it's going to snow. I straighten. We're still in the city, in a neighborhood I don't recognize, but there's a signpost with an airplane symbol up ahead.

I glance through the back window. We're not the

only car on the road, but I don't see any of Alex's familiar black cars. We're not being chased.

The interior of the car is warm and the jacket I'm wearing is thick, but I still shiver. Instead of relief, an inexplicable sense of loss assaults me. I feel adrift. Lost. Torn and confused. I've yet to process what I've done. It was a spur-of-the-moment decision, not something I planned. And the stress is far from over. Nothing's resolved until I set foot in that plane. At that point, I'll be free. That's what I have to focus on.

Holy shit.

Dania did it.

I made it.

I rub my palms over my face. I still can't believe I'm out of Alex's stronghold.

Turning my face toward the window, I stare out with an unseeing gaze. My thoughts are focused on the future, on what I'll do when I get home. I'll let Alex know I'm safe. He deserves that much. But I'll make it clear that I'm not prepared to be a prisoner any longer. While he deals with his assassin, I'll disappear, take some time to think everything through. In the meantime, I'm not going to dwell on why Dania helped me. She didn't do it for selfless reasons, that's for sure.

The driver steps on the gas as we approach a traffic light. It's green for us. A pair of headlights advances from the crossing, heading toward the red light, but the car doesn't slow down.

Blinking, I frown. Too late, I realize he's not going to stop.

"Look out," I yell, trying to warn the driver.

He yanks the wheel to the right.

The car smashes into us from the side, hitting the passenger door in the front. The airbags pop. Metal crunches and glass cracks as the momentum pushes us over the tarmac. My body is thrown violently against the door as our car folds around a lamppost.

Every bone in my body aches as I blink in shock, struggling to process what's happened. The driver of the car who hit us gets out. He walks around our car toward the driver's side. The window has exploded from the impact. The lamppost obstructs the door, and the other side of the car is banged in so badly that I'm not sure he'll be able to open the door. He'll have to call the fire brigade to cut us out.

He stops in front of the broken window.

"Help us," I croak, wiping away something wet that runs over my cheek. I'm trembling all over, the cold from the outside somehow already inside my body, the chill encasing my insides, scrambling my thoughts.

He offers me a smile. Taking a gun with a silencer screwed onto the barrel from under his coat, he pushes the gun against the airbag and fires a shot. A scream catches in my throat. A car pulls up next to us, presumably to offer assistance, but the driver's eyes go wide when he sees the gun. He pulls off without a word.

I scoot to the other side, yanking on the door with shaking hands, but it's stuck.

The man puts two fingers on the driver's neck, checking for a pulse.

Oh God. Maybe he just shot the airbag to deflate it.

I raise my hands, my stomach roiling with a mixture of terror and hope. "Please." Does the man even understand English? "Please, don't hurt us."

Aiming the barrel at the driver's temple, the man pulls the trigger.

32

ALEX

Igor takes the front steps two at a time and stops next to me where I stand on the porch. Flanked by Dimitri and Leonid, we watch Mikhail and his entourage leave.

"Poisoning?" Leonid says. "Who would want to poison Dania Turgeneva?"

The cars clear the gates. I follow their speedy departure with a thoughtful gaze. "Whoever he is, he's a dead man."

"You bet." Dimitri shakes his head. "No one messes with Mikhail's princess. I can't believe someone was so stupid."

"What about the operation?" Igor asks. "Do we still move out?"

"No." I shove my hands into my pockets. "Let's wait until there's news about Dania. It would be disrespectful to launch a full-blown war if Mikhail's daughter is dying. We should wait until Mikhail knows more about the poisoning and how it happened."

"What about Kate?" Igor's brows pull together. "Does she have any idea what kind of poison it may be?"

"We haven't had time to speak yet," I say. "Keep alert and double the guards around the house. Let me know if you pick up anything on satellite. I'm going to talk to Katerina."

The men nod in unison. I leave them in charge of the security and go back inside the house. The door clicks shut behind me, the electronic pad beeping as the lock activates. Two men guard the door. Another stands near the hallway.

"Anything?" I ask as I approach him.

"No, sir," he says, looking straight ahead. "The downstairs rooms are clear. We're checking upstairs as we speak."

I have the house swept on a weekly basis and immediately after I've had visitors. I trust Mikhail, but it can't hurt to be cautious. Especially in light of what has transpired.

Making my way past him, I go to the guest bathroom. A smell of bleach hangs in the air. Lena is mopping the floor. She looks up when I stop in the doorframe.

"Have you seen Katerina?" I ask.

"No, sir. Maybe she went upstairs."

On my way to the lounge, I check the library and my study. Both rooms are deserted. The lounge is empty. I try the room Igor converted into a makeshift clinic, but when I don't find her there either, I make my way upstairs.

The house is big. Three men are sweeping the second floor. I pass them in the hallway and open *our* bedroom door.

Empty.

Crossing the floor with big strides, I enter the dressing room.

No sign of her.

I knock on the bathroom door. "Katerina?"

No reply.

A bad feeling grows in the pit of my stomach. I open the door, already knowing what I'll find.

Nothing. No one.

Fuck.

I yank my phone from my pocket and dial Igor, already running for the stairs. When he picks up, I bark out, "Katerina is gone. Search the house, the garden, and the barracks."

"Yes, sir."

"You," I say, pointing at one of the men guarding the front door.

He jumps to attention.

"Did Miss Morrell leave the house after Mr. Turgenev and me?"

"No, sir."

"Fuck," I mutter under my breath, racing for the kitchen.

"What's going on?" Tima asks when I skid to a stop

in the middle of the floor.

"Is Katerina here?"

"No," he says, frowning.

Still clutching my phone, I spear my fingers through my hair. "She's gone."

His face collapses, his eyes and mouth drawing down. "How long?"

"Not more than ten minutes."

He moves a carving knife aside and leans his palms on the counter. "She could be hiding in the house."

"I'm having the property searched."

"If she's not..." He looks at me from under his eyebrows.

"Then she slipped out while the emergency with Dania was unfolding." I feel sick merely saying those words.

"She couldn't have walked through the gates. The guards would've noticed."

I grit my teeth. "They also would've noticed if she'd gotten into one of the cars. She must be in the house."

He sucks air through his teeth.

"What?" I ask.

"If she's not in the house and nobody saw her leaving, you have to assume she left with Mikhail."

I slam a fist on the table. "Mikhail would never do that. He knows I'd kill him."

"What about Dania?" Tima asks, his eyes narrowing into slits.

"Dania was puking out her lungs."

"There's something wrong with this poisoning

scenario." Straightening, he crosses his arms. "I've administered a few poisons in my day, and I can tell you that if Dania had been poisoned at breakfast, the symptoms she was having wouldn't have kicked in three hours later. They would've manifested almost straight away."

I still. "Are you saying she was poisoned here?"

"It couldn't have been the cake. Lena brought four empty plates back to the kitchen, so you all ate the cake, right? What did Dania drink or eat that no one else did?"

I slide my gaze toward the drip rack where the teacups and teapot are stacked. "Herbal tea."

The knowledge sinks into my gut like a stone. I know it instinctively as I walk to the drip rack and lift the teapot to peer inside.

"Lena washed it already," Tima says. "She cleans the porcelain with bleach to remove the tea stains."

"Thereby removing all traces of the contents inside," I say slowly, uncontrollable rage unfurling in my chest.

He gives me a level look. "Exactly."

My voice is calm, not betraying the violence flowing through my veins. "Bring her here."

Tima rounds the counter and walks down the hallway.

I dial Igor.

He answers with, "There's no sign of her yet."

"Check all the passenger manifests for domestic and international flights. I want men at every station and airport in St. Petersburg. Katerina may have left with Mikhail's entourage."

"Fuck. I'm on it."

Next, I dial Nelsky. "I want the satellite surveillance footage of my house from the last thirty minutes. Send it to my phone."

I cut the call when Tima leads Lena in by her arm.

She yanks her bicep from his hold and lifts her chin. "Is there something I can do for you, Mr. Volkov?"

I walk to the counter. "How long have you worked for me, Lena?"

"Since you bought the house, sir."

Taking the knife Tima was using, I study the blade in the light. "That makes it quite a few years."

"Yes, sir," she says, looking down her nose at Tima, who stands wide-legged in front of her, effectively blocking her path should she get it into her head to run.

"Are you loyal, Lena?"

She meets my gaze head-on. "Yes, sir."

"To whom?" I ask, wiping the knife on my sleeve.

She swallows visibly.

I approach her. "Were you loyal to the previous owners?"

"I was, sir," she says with a tremor in her voice.

"Why?" I ask, circling her.

"Sir?"

"Why?" I repeat, placing emphasis on the word. "What made you loyal to them?"

She blinks. "They were of royal descent. They were suitable inhabitants for this house."

I raise a brow. "And I'm not?"

She utters an uncomfortable laugh. "You're the new owner, sir."

Stopping in front of her, I look her dead in the eye. "Did you poison Dania?"

She blinks.

My patience is running low. "Did you or did you not put poison in her tea?"

No reply.

She utters a shriek when I fist my hand in her hair and push her to her knees. Stepping behind her, I pull back her head and press the sharp edge of the blade against her neck.

"Answer me, Lena, or I swear I'll gut you like a pig."

She grips my forearm and tries to pull it away. "Please, Mr. Volkov."

"Answer me. You know I never bluff."

"It was D-Dania's idea," she stutters out, spittle flying. "She told me to put the wormwood in her tea."

"Why?" I ask, pressing the blade until I draw a thin line of blood.

"Please…" Her throat works with a swallow, tears spilling down her cheeks. "She wanted to help Miss Morrell escape."

Rage blurs her features in my vision. "Did Katerina ask Dania for help?"

"I d-don't know," she blubbers.

I give her hair a yank. "Why did you do it?"

Tima regards her with disdain, his face pulled into an expression of disgust. "Because she's a royalist."

"Because Miss Turgeneva is a suitable mistress for this house," she cries out. "Please, I only wanted what's best!"

I let her go with a shove. "Lock her in the summer lounge. Take her phone and make sure she doesn't leave the room."

"With pleasure," Tima says as he grips her arm and pulls her to her feet.

I leave the task in Tima's capable hands and summon Yuri, Igor, and Leonid. On my way to the car, I inform Dimitri of the situation and put him in charge of the security at the house.

Leonid checks the GPS to find us the least congested route to the hospital while I dial Mikhail and tell him what I've learned.

We make it to the ER in record time. Mikhail waits outside Dania's private room, his cheeks colorless.

"How is she?" I ask, tilting my head toward the door.

"She'll be fine," he says with a troubled expression. "Let's not talk in the corridor. Best if we go inside."

Dania lies pale against the white sheets, her dark hair splayed over the pillow. She pushes up on her elbows when my men and I enter and her father closes the door.

"Alex," she says with surprise. "How nice of you to check on me."

I clench my jaw. "Cut the bullshit, Dania. Lena told me everything."

Her gaze turns shuttered. "I don't know what you're talking about."

I level a dark look at Mikhail.

"Dania," he says, "if you got yourself poisoned on purpose to help Katerina escape, you'd better tell us now."

"Papa!" She gapes at him. "Do you think I'd do this to myself?"

"I love you, princess, but this time you've gone too far. There's not a trace of poison in our house." He adds in an angry voice, "Which means you lied to me."

"Papa, I don't—"

He holds up a hand. "You've dishonored me and put a stain on our family name. If you don't tell the truth, you leave me no choice but to disown you. You'll be a nobody, out on the street alone, with no one to protect you and not a penny to your name."

A look of hurt flashes across her face. "Papa, please. You're the only one I have. Mama doesn't—"

"The truth, Dania, and think carefully before you open your mouth and tell another lie," Mikhail says.

Folding her hands on top of the covers, she looks desperately between me and her father.

"Tell us what happened," Mikhail says, "and I'll take responsibility for your actions."

She looks at the window.

"Dania," I say, my tone harsh. "You have no idea

what you've done. Katerina's life could be in danger this very minute."

When she still doesn't say anything, I walk to the door. "So be it. You've made your choice."

"Wait," she calls, glancing at me from under her lashes.

I pause.

"Fine. I told Lena to put a few drops of steam-distilled oil of wormwood in my tea. I was only trying to help Katerina." She gives her father an imploring look. "You have to believe me, Papa."

Mikhail utters a cussword. Dania jumps when he kicks the visitor's chair.

"How did you do it?" he asks with flaring nostrils.

"My bodyguard smuggled a uniform to Lena when we arrived at Alex's house. Kate changed in the bathroom. While everyone was distracted, she got into the car my bodyguard was driving."

I clench my hands so hard my knuckles make a cracking sound. "Where did he take her?"

She drops her gaze to her hands. "To the airport."

I grab my phone from my pocket, dialing Nelsky as I grit out, "Without a passport?"

Dania doesn't look at me. "I arranged for a false passport. Lena packed her a bag."

"Where is she flying to?" I demand.

"America, I assume," Dania says, finally meeting my gaze. "I left enough money in the bag to buy a ticket to anywhere."

"Fuck," I say, dragging a hand over my face.

"Our men are at the airport," Igor says, his phone already in his hand. "I'll let them know."

"This was a premeditated affair," Mikhail says through thin lips, looking at his daughter with disappointment.

Nelsky answers in a high-pitched tone. "Sir?"

"She's at the airport. Destination unknown." I don't elaborate. He knows what to do.

"I know my apology can't make up for what Dania has done," Mikhail says, turning toward me. "I'll give you access to all of my resources. I'll do everything in my power to help you find her. Rest assured, Dania will be appropriately punished." His gaze hardens. "As for Lena, I trust you'll deal with her."

My phone pings with a notification. I check the message. It's an update from Nelsky. The team is checking the satellite footage of the roads leading from my residence to the airport, but they haven't found anything yet.

I'm shaking with both anger and fear. I feel like strangling Dania and watching the life bleed from her eyes.

"If anything happens to Katerina," I say to Dania in a cold, dangerously quiet tone, "I will hold you responsible."

"Alex." Mikhail splays his hands. "Tell me what I can do to help."

"Nothing for now," I bite out, leaving the room and slamming the door behind me.

I'm halfway down the corridor before Leonid and Igor catch up.

"We'll find her," Leonid says. "If she's on her way to the airport, she won't get far. You have enough connections to prevent the plane from taking off."

Yes, I do. But even if she's already in the air, I'll find her, and when I do, there will be hell to pay.

33

KATE

My mouth is dry when I wake up. It takes a moment to focus my eyes. The room is unfamiliar. An overhead bulb throws light on the concrete walls and floor. The only furniture is the bed I'm lying on.

My stomach twists. What happened? Where am I?

I try to sit up, but my arms are stuck above my head. I can't move them. Craning my neck, I take in the handcuffs around my wrists.

In a flash, it all comes back—the accident, the man who shot Dania's driver and then injected me with something.

My pulse speeds up. What does he want from me? Either he's kidnapped me for ransom, or he's the man who wants Alex dead. If the latter is the case, I don't have to wonder hard why he took me. A shiver runs over my body.

Who is he? Being in the dark only makes my situation worse. Knowledge is power. Right now, I have no power. All I have left is control. Losing my calm isn't an option. I have to breathe and keep a level head to figure out a way to escape.

Deep breaths, Kate. In and out. Focus.

The sound of a key scraping in a lock comes from the other side of the door. I strain my neck for a visual to assess the danger. The door swings open, and a man I don't recognize enters. A waistcoat stretches over his corpulent torso. Thinning gray hair frames his round face. He watches me with narrowed eyes as he advances to the bed.

Whoever he is, this man is evil. It's evident in the excitement that flashes across his ugly features as he takes in my restrained position. I swallow hard, trying to hide my fear.

Towering over me, he says in a thick Russian accent, "You must wonder what you're doing here."

No longer able to support the weight of my head with my neck muscles, I let my head fall back on the mattress. "The question has crossed my mind."

He seems amused. "I have to congratulate you. You're very calm for someone in your situation."

I'm not, but I'm glad he thinks so. "Who are you? Where am I?"

"Vladimir Stefanov." He sits down on the edge of the bed. "You're a guest in my house."

I scoot to the other side of the mattress, as far away from him as possible, as more dread fills my veins. I've heard the name before. Alex told me it was Vladimir

Stefanov who'd hired the man to abduct me in New York. "What do want from me?"

"You're going to bring me Alex Volkov."

Even though it was the answer I expected, I go cold. "How?"

"A trade." He looks pleased with himself. "You for him."

My mouth goes dry. "How do you know Alex will do it? Who says he even cares that much about me?"

Stefanov chuckles. "Oh, he does. Why else did he come running to Russia to protect you when my hitman threatened your life?"

I suck in a breath. "My hospital key card. That was your doing."

"Yes," he drawls.

"Who took it?"

He raises a brow. "Remember Ivan Besov?"

It takes a moment before I place the name. When it comes back to me, I exclaim, "The man who fractured his wrist?"

"You were lucky that he slipped in the snow." Stefanov folds his hands over his stomach. "That part wasn't planned."

I go even colder as my suspicion is confirmed. When the attempt to kidnap me from the alley failed, this man, Stefanov, sent Besov to snatch me on my way to work.

How did Stefanov know I was on my way to the airport? My stomach turns over. Did Dania sell me out?

"How did you find me?" I ask in an unsteady voice. "Who told you where I was headed?"

"One of my men was watching Volkov's house from a building across the river. He spotted a small person getting into the back of a car and managed to take a photo. Imagine my surprise when it turned out to be you."

"You had us followed." Anger mixes with my fear. "You ordered the man who took me to crash into our car. We could've died in that accident." My voice escalates in volume. "He shot the driver."

Stefanov shrugs. "You didn't die."

"I'm an American citizen," I say, my heart thumping with a wild beat in my chest. "You can't just kidnap me in broad daylight."

"Maybe not in America." He grins. "But this is Russia."

My pulse goes into overdrive. "Alex won't let you get away with this."

"He will. This time, I'm not planning on failing."

Breathless with fright, I ask, "How is this supposed to work? What happens now?"

"Now we wait for Alex to arrive. And then…" He pushes a finger against his temple and makes as if to pull a trigger with his thumb. "Bam."

It takes everything I have to maintain my pseudo-calm. "Why? Why do you want Alex dead? What do you want? Money?"

He gets to his feet. "If it were about money, I could've simply traded you."

"Wait," I say as he walks to the door, but he leaves without sparing me another glance.

Horror washes over me as the situation becomes terribly clear.

Alex and I aren't leaving here alive.

34

ALEX

*I*t's been an hour since I left the hospital, and there's still no news about Katerina's whereabouts. I'm pacing my study, checking my email and phone every few seconds. The lunch Tima brought stands untouched on my desk. Mikhail won't let Dania's interference go unpunished, but I feel like killing her all the same. I'm still undecided about what to do with Lena.

A knock falls on the door. Leonid enters, his face somber.

"Any news?" I ask.

He shakes his head. "What about Nelsky?"

My phone vibrates in my pocket. I take it out and look at the screen. I've been sending business-related calls to my voicemail, preferring to keep the line open in case there's an update from one of my men.

My heartbeat picks up as I register the name on the screen.

"Have they found—" Leonid continues.

I hold up a hand to silence him. "It's Igor."

Leonid's expression goes tense, reflecting what I feel inside.

I swipe the answer button and put the phone on speaker. "Tell me you have news."

"She's not at the airport," Igor says in a rushed tone. "No one matching her description has checked in."

I assume she would've changed into normal clothes before entering the airport building. We don't know what she's wearing, but my men have her passport photo on their phones. They're questioning both passengers and airport staff, asking if anyone has seen the woman in the photograph.

"What about the parking lots?" I ask harshly.

"There was no sign of Mikhail's car." He pauses. "We did, however, find the driver."

I tighten my grip on the phone. "Dania's bodyguard?"

"Yes."

Exchanging a look with Leonid, I ask, "Where?"

"At the morgue."

My heart slams to a stop.

Leonid moves closer, his troubled look intensifying.

"I'm here now with one of Mikhail's men," Igor continues. "He identified the body."

My order is brusque. "Tell me what happened."

"Car accident, but that's not the cause of death. Someone popped him in the head."

"Fuck." Ice fills my stomach. This is my worst nightmare come true. If anything has happened to Katerina… I can't even think it. Rage burns like acid in my chest. "Any sign of Katerina?"

"No," he says with regret. "But we did find the bag with the clothes, money, and passport Dania had mentioned in the trunk."

Dania wasn't lying. My kiska was in that car.

"What about satellite footage?" I ask, clenching the phone hard. "Are there any witnesses to the accident?"

"No one reported the accident when it happened," Igor says. "A good half hour passed before someone called it in."

"Inform Nelsky." Covering the microphone with a hand, I direct the order to Leonid. "I want that satellite feed. Now."

He hurries to the door. "I'll let him know."

"Comb the area where the accident took place," I tell Igor. "Tell our men to start searching in a twenty-kilometer radius. Knock on every door and ask every person living in that vicinity if anyone has seen something. Don't offer money. They may spew bull-shit just to get the reward. Use fear instead." It's faster.

"Got it," he says and hangs up.

I shut my eyes briefly, praying I find Katerina before I have to make a call to Laura that will destroy her as surely as it will destroy me.

My phone pings a second later. I look at the screen, but it's not the satellite recording that I'm expecting from Nelsky. It's an image of Katerina lying on a cot in a cell, handcuffed to the bedframe. The text message is signed by Vladimir Stefanov.

Motherfucker.

Fury like I've never experienced rushes through my veins, even as fear rips through me, cold and terrifying.

Leonid walks back into the room. "Nelsky says you'll have the footage in five minutes." One look at my face makes him stop in his tracks. "What's wrong?"

I turn the screen of my phone toward him, shaking with rage as I show him the image.

He blanches. "Fuck."

"Weapon up." I clench my teeth so hard it feels as if my jaw is about to unhinge. "We're going after Stefanov. I'm bringing her back."

He pushes a hand on my chest as I take a step to the door. "It's a trap."

I grip his wrist and move his hand away. "Of course it's a fucking trap."

"Mr. Volkov," he says carefully, holding my gaze. "You have to consider the fact that she may already be dead."

Before he can blink, I grab him by the lapels of his jacket and smash his body against the wall. "She's alive and well." I need to believe that.

"For now, maybe," he says, unfazed by the violence. "Once Stefanov has you, he won't need her any longer. If we launch an attack on his house, what guarantee do you have that Stefanov won't slit her throat? He's not going to wave a white flag and simply hand her over. If he thinks he's going to lose, he'd rather take her with him to the grave than give her back to you."

That's not what I have in mind. I'm not going in guns blazing while hoping for the best.

Leonid must see the intention in my eyes because his jaw goes slack.

"You're going to suggest a trade," he says, sounding flabbergasted. "Your life for Kate's."

"What else?" I growl, letting him go with a shove.

"Think about it," he says, coming after me as I make my way down the hallway. "That's what Stefanov expects you to do. That's what he wants."

"Then that's what he'll get."

I send a text message to Dimitri, telling him to round up the men, all fucking two hundred of them. Then I fire off a message to Igor to bring him up to scratch and to inform him that our rendezvous point is Stefanov's house.

Outside, Yuri leans against the hood of my car. He straightens when I approach. I check that my gun is loaded and get into the car.

"Mr. Volkov," Leonid says.

I slam the door, cutting off further conversation.

Pounding a hand against his forehead, Leonid paces next to the car.

I wind down the window. "Are you coming or what?"

He drops his hand on his hip, regarding me with a defeated look. "I work for you because I respect you.

413

We all do—Igor, Dimitri, and every guard in your employ."

"Are you getting sentimental on me?" I ask with a cold smile.

"None of us is the leader you are. That's why you're the boss. That's why we follow your orders. If you die, everything you've built will be wasted."

It'll go to Katerina. I've already set it up with my lawyer. Not that I have any intention of making it easy for Stefanov. "I'm leaving. If you're coming, get in. If not, it was good to know you, my friend."

With a curse, he gets into the front passenger seat.

Yuri starts the engine. We don't speak during the ride. I stare through the window at the familiar landscape, but inside, my blood is boiling.

On the way, I get the satellite feed from Nelsky on my phone. I watch the accident happen with balled hands, from the point when the fucker hits their car to where he carries an unconscious Katerina to a truck parked half a block down the road. From there, he drives straight to Stefanov's house.

"*Svoloch*," I mutter under my breath, squeezing the phone so hard the plastic casing cracks down the middle.

"We're here," Leonid says, pulling my attention from the scene I'm replaying on my phone.

I glance up at the imposing gates of Stefanov's house. "Are the men on their way?"

"They'll be here in five minutes. They left shortly

after us." His gaze is pleading. "Don't go in there alone, Mr. Volkov."

If I don't, Katerina is dead.

Not bothering to answer, I dial Stefanov.

"Volkov," Stefanov replies in a jovial voice. "I was expecting your call."

My voice is tight with repressed fury. "I want to speak to her."

"Of course you do. Hold on."

Shuffling and footsteps sound, and then her sweet voice comes on the line. "Alex?"

I sag in my seat, physically weak with relief. "Are you all right?"

A choked sob.

"I'm coming for you, Katyusha," I say, my voice harsh as I imagine what Stefanov has done or could still do to her. "Hold on for me, my love."

"Don't," she whispers. "It's a—"

"As you can see," Stefanov's voice interrupts, "she's very much alive."

I'm going to crush that motherfucker. "How do you want the trade to work?"

"Come alone, unarmed, and I'll let her go."

Leonid, who's listening in on the call, shakes his head.

"Do I have your word?" I ask.

"I swear on my mother's grave," the fat bastard says.

In that case, "I'm here."

I end the call and hand my phone and gun to Leonid.

"Mr. Volkov," Leonid says with a plea in his voice as he takes the items. "Alex."

Opening the door, I step out into the gray light of the day. The snow has lifted momentarily. An eerie quiet has dawned on the landscape.

Leonid follows suit.

Four guards armed with automatic rifles walk through the gates toward us.

The one in the front says, "You're to come unarmed. No phone."

Raising my arms, I stand waiting, giving my consent to be searched. The man who voiced the command hands his gun to the one on his left before patting me down. When he's sure I'm not wired or carrying hidden weapons, he motions for me to walk ahead.

Leonid looks on with helpless anger painted across his face.

"Don't look at me like I'm already dead," I say, lightening the mood with a smile.

He doesn't reciprocate. He follows me with his gaze the way one would stare at a funeral march.

I don't hesitate. Leonid disappears from my peripheral vision as I walk through Vladimir Stefanov's gates.

35

KATE

The door rattles as it opens. A guard steps inside. I cringe on the bed when he approaches, flattening my body on the mattress. Without looking at me, he unlocks the cuffs around my wrists and stands aside. Another guard enters with a tray that he puts on the floor. Both men leave, and a second later, the sound of the key turning in the lock echoes in the space.

Rubbing my arms to get my blood circulation going, I push to my feet. The light in the room isn't overly bright, but it reaches far enough to illuminate the contents of the tray. They brought me food—a sandwich and a glass of water.

I'm not touching it. It may be drugged. Regardless, I'm unable to eat in the state I'm in. At least Stefanov doesn't want me dead yet. Otherwise, he wouldn't have sent food. He needs to keep me alive until he's lured Alex into his trap. In the long run, I'm dead, but Alex is still free. I just hope he's clever enough not to walk into Stefanov's trap.

I look around the room for a way to escape, but the only way out is through the door. I expect it to be locked and guarded. Nevertheless, as soon as the circulation has returned to my legs, I run to the door and feel the handle. The door doesn't budge.

My gaze falls on the tray. It's metal. I could whack someone over the head with it. If I hit hard enough, I could give my victim a concussion that would cause a blackout. Knocking out a guard will win me time, but I'll need more than a metal tray if I'm to make it over the threshold where another guard will be waiting.

I look around again. If there are cameras, they're well hidden. Still, I can't take any chances. I have to assume my kidnapper is watching me. In my circumstances, an aggressive outburst will be expected behavior.

Taking aim, I kick the tray with all my might. It goes flying and hits the wall with a thwack. The plate and glass shatter against the concrete. Water drips down the gray surface and the sandwich falls open, a slice of cheese on one side and the buttered side on the floor. Glass crunches under my boots as I walk over the mess and crouch down in the middle of it. Selecting the sharpest pieces of porcelain from the broken plate, I take them discreetly and hide them behind my back. Then I retreat to the far side of the room, sit down on the floor, and wait.

When the door opens again, I'm ready. I stand up,

holding the broken pieces of the plate behind my back, but instead of one guard entering to remove the spoiled food like I expected, four of them enter.

My heart hammers as I make myself small in the corner and keep quiet, trying not to attract attention to myself.

The man in the front looks at the mess on the floor before lifting his gaze to me. He speaks English with a strong accent. "That was a foolish move." His smile doesn't reach his eyes. "Who knows? It could've been your last meal."

I feel like stabbing him in the eye, but I bite my tongue and look away. I have to be patient and bide my time.

The one who addressed me stands guard as the others carry buckets and brooms inside. They throw water over the floor and scrub the mess away with the brooms. A smell of chlorine reaches my nostrils. Stefanov must be making sure no diseases break out in his prison.

Since they're not attacking me, I dare a glance at the guard who spoke English. "Where am I?" I look around. "What is this place?"

"You're in Vladimir Stefanov's house." He says it with glee, as if he wants the information to scare me.

It does. It also explains why they're cleaning up. Smells and infections spread fast.

They sweep up the broken crockery and the wasted food. When the floor is clean, they mop up the water, rinse the concrete with clean water, and leave with their buckets and brooms.

Once again, I'm alone. It's only then that I become aware of how much I'm shaking. It's a natural reaction to the shock, but I don't like it. In an effort to both calm and warm myself, I walk around and stretch my sore muscles.

My isolation doesn't last long. A sound at the door alerts me. Backing up to the wall, I grab my makeshift weapons as adrenaline floods my veins. A plan takes shape in my head. I'll ask them for a glass of water and stab whoever delivers it in the neck. I have no idea what waits behind that door, but I'll just have to take my chances.

A sliver of light falls over the floor through the crack as the door opens. I remain immobile, measuring the danger, but the man who enters isn't one of Stefanov's guards.

It's Alex.

Relief and fear war in my chest.

He stumbles as someone pushes him, and then the light from outside disappears as the door is shut.

At a loss for words, I stare at him. Despite the situation, the moment is sweet. I thought I might never see him again. In his long, tailored coat and fancy dress shoes, he looks as formidable as ever. His thick dark hair is brushed back. His long lashes dip as he takes me in from head to toe. Signs of strain are visible on his hard-featured face. His blue eyes are marred with worry lines, and the couple of days' worth of stubble that darkens his jaw sets off the paleness of his skin.

His voice is rough. "Did they hurt you?"

The rasp of that timbre is like water to my ears. "No."

He looks at me as if he may consume me. "Come here."

I don't hesitate. When he opens his arms, I lay my makeshift weapons on the floor and run into his embrace. His body is strong and warm, the heat emanating from him enveloping me. I inhale the familiar scent of cardamom as I burrow my face in the scratchy wool fabric of his coat. He lets me soak up his presence before holding me at arm's length.

He conducts another visual evaluation, scanning the length of me. "Did they touch you?"

"I'm okay." My voice is meek in the aftermath of my relief, even though that relief will be short-lived.

A muscle ticks in his jaw. "I'll kill them for taking you. I swear it on my parents' graves."

I swallow away the dryness of my throat. "Why did you come? It's a trap."

His smile is crooked. "Did you think I'd leave you here?"

Wrapping my arms around him, I press my cheek against his chest. I only give myself another second to be comforted by his presence before I pull away. "I'm sorry for running. I shouldn't have done that. Every-thing just happened so fast. There wasn't time to think."

A smile softens his features. "I understand why you did it. I put you in an impossible situation." Regret fills his eyes. "If not for me, you wouldn't be in this place."

"You're not angry with me?"

"I'm furious, kiska," he says in a low, rough voice. "You put your life in danger."

"Dania—"

"I know what she did. She admitted everything."

"Is she all right?" I ask.

The line of his jaw turns hard. "She'll be fine."

His face swims in my vision. "We're going to die, aren't we?"

Stroking his hands up my arms, he tightens his fingers on my shoulders. "I won't let you die, Katyusha." He pulls me close and crushes me against his chest. "I was going out of my mind with worry. You have no idea."

I free myself from his embrace and go to the corner. "Look," I say, lifting my weapons from the floor. "I managed to get these."

His gaze widens, then narrows as he walks over to me. "I can't decide if I should feel proud or spank you for even considering something so dangerous." Taking the shards from my hands, he studies them in the light.

"We can take them out when they open the door," I say hopefully.

"*We* will do nothing." He fixes me with a hard look. "You will stay in the corner, as far away from danger as possible. I'll take care of it."

Before I can argue, footsteps sound on the other side of the door.

My heart beats wildly. There's only one reason why Stefanov's men could be coming for us now, and it's not to bring us food.

ALEX

*V*ladimir Stefanov himself steps through the doorframe.

Hatred pushes up my throat. I want to pounce on him and slash him to pieces, but three guards armed with automatic rifles follow on his heels. If I were alone in this hole, I wouldn't hesitate to rip out his heart. But I have Katerina to consider. I have to protect her, which I can only do if she doesn't distract me by putting herself in danger.

Tilting my head toward the corner, I give her a wordless command. To my relief, she backs away slowly until the shadows swallow her shape. I take a breath and clear my mind, letting instinct take over. I need to focus on survival and not on the woman I love, because love is a potent reminder of everything I stand to lose.

I square my shoulders as Stefanov approaches,

discreetly sliding my hands behind my thighs to hide the porcelain shards.

His bloated face is smug when he stops in front of me. "I was wondering if we'd ever meet in person. If I were you, I would've hoped the day would never come."

I have a good mind to snap his thick neck, but that would be too easy. "You have me. Let Katerina go."

The layers of his chin quiver as he laughs. "You didn't think I'd let a witness walk away, did you?"

Gnashing my teeth, I hold back the violence that threatens to erupt. "A man who doesn't keep his word is a dishonorable man." Even in our unethical circles.

He curls a lip and says in a mocking tone, "I've been accused of worse."

My smile is cold. "No one wants to follow a dishonorable man."

"Who would they rather follow? You?" He laughs again, glancing at his men. At his cue, they all pipe up with chuckles. "In that case, they'd be following a ghost."

"Honor our deal and let her go. There's still time. In another minute, you won't have a choice any longer."

He scoffs. "Do you think you're in any position to negotiate?"

I close a step between us. "With the file that's fallen into my hands, I have *all* the power."

His gleeful expression slips. "What file?"

"Come on, Stefanov. You're a terrible actor."

His eyeballs bounce in their sockets. I imagine the gears turning in his head as he tries to figure out who betrayed him. He got rid of Oleg Pavlov, the only other man besides Besov who knew about their crime. He must come to the conclusion that Besov is the guilty party.

"You're wondering who gave it to me," I taunt.

"Gave you what?" he asks, keeping up the show.

My voice is cold, the hatred I feel for this man coloring every word I utter. "The video of how you killed my parents."

A gasp comes from the corner, but I tune it out. I need to focus on Stefanov. He's a snake at best, one who'll happily strike when my guard is down.

Fear creeps into his eyes, but he blinks it away quickly.

I laugh. "Did you think I wouldn't find out?"

He sneers. "It doesn't matter. You're a dead man anyway."

Stefanov isn't naïve. He knows I'd never trust him to keep his side of the bargain. He's prepared for a war, but it doesn't matter. My army is much bigger than the thirty men guarding my house. Stefanov won't know what's hit him. I'll burn this house to the ground before the day is over. He can stand there with his self-satisfied look, thinking the fifty men on his property will cut it, but soon, he'll beg for his life. Only before it comes to that, I need to know who betrayed *me*.

I watch him carefully as I ask, "How did you find out who I was?"

His grin says he's already savoring his premature

victory. "The grave keeper told me a man came to visit the graves. She took a photo and sent it to me."

"The old woman? You paid her to inform you if anyone visited the graves?" No wonder I felt like my parents were trying to warn me after I visited them that first time, shortly before I left for New York. I chuckle grimly. "I have to give it to you, Stefanov. You don't leave anything to chance."

He looks pleased with himself. "In case you'd grown up and were plotting revenge. I have to say, I didn't think you'd survive on the streets."

"I survived rather well," I say with a mocking smile.

He gives me a sly look. "Who told you? Who gave you the tape? Tell me now and I'll finish you quickly."

I don't fucking think so.

Pop, pop, pop.

Gunfire comes from upstairs.

It's the distraction I've been waiting for.

Stefanov gives a start. "What the—?"

Before he's finished his sentence, I have an arm wrapped around his throat, holding him like a shield in front of me while I push the sharp point of the porcelain against his neck.

"Drop your weapons," I say to the guards. "It'll only take a little pressure to make him bleed out like a pig."

"Shoot him," Stefanov yells.

The guards aim their guns, undecided. If they shoot at my hand, they'll put a bullet in his neck. They can't shoot at my head without going through his skull. They've been trained to protect Stefanov, and that training won't allow them to take an uncalculated risk.

"Shoot the woman," Stefanov says, gurgling as I tighten my grip.

"You shoot her," I say, "and your wife is dead."

On cue, a woman's shrill voice sounds from the top of the stairs. "Don't shoot, Vlad! It's Galina. Please. They have me."

Stefanov curses as footsteps fall on the stairs. A group of men filter through the door. They're armed to the teeth, carrying grenades, combat knives, and AK-47s. Dimitri follows with Galina, pointing a gun at the back of her head. Igor comes in behind them, wiping his brow with his sleeve when he spots me.

"*Yob tvoyu mat',*" Stefanov mumbles.

I address Igor. "Take Katerina. Get her out of here."

"I'm not leaving you," she says as Igor rushes over.

She's too brave for her own good.

"You heard Alex," Igor says. "Let's go, Kate."

"Let's fight it out," Stefanov says defiantly. "Man to man."

"Don't do it," Katerina cries out when Igor takes her arm and drags her to the door. "He'll fight dirty. Come with me, Alex. Don't let revenge muddle your decisions."

Her voice washes over me, the sweet sound grounding instead of distracting me. I've never been more present in the moment. My mind has never been clearer.

"I love you," I say.

She stills at that. Momentarily, so does Igor. It's not the place or time, but I owed her those words. I needed to say them before things got even uglier.

Giving up her struggling, she nods. With that single gesture, she offers me acceptance. Her trust warms my chest with pride. I came here expecting many reactions. At the top of my list was blame. It's my fault she's in this mess. But when she follows Igor past me, her soft hazel eyes are like mirrors, reflecting what I feel in my heart. Her lashes lower and lift. In one blink, she tells me everything I want to know. She tells me that she's mine, and that she'll love me regardless.

The hatred dissipates, turning into icy calmness. I'm cool and collected. The power I've given Stefanov by hating him vanishes. Just like that, he doesn't count any longer. His actions don't touch me. He's just a bag of filth that needs to be dealt with. A loose end that needs tying.

Even though I've acquired all this power and wealth, I've never felt truly happy or free. My past has always hovered like an invisible sword over my head. I've blamed myself for my parents' deaths. I've lain awake at night, thinking that I should've smelled the gas leak, that I should've told my father not to smoke in the apartment. I've beaten myself up for reading my comic books and not paying attention to a faulty stove that was right under my nose. Now, for the first time since my parents' death, I taste the sweetness of freedom as the shackles of my past fall away.

Dimitri pushes Galina to the center of the floor.

"The house is surrounded. Stefanov's men surrendered." He gives Galina a nudge. "Tell him."

"It's true," she says through her tears. "They've taken away all the weapons and locked everyone in the lounge."

"Casualties?" I ask.

"Two of Stefanov's men," Dimitri says. "We caught them by surprise."

Squeezing Stefanov's neck, I say to his men, "No one else needs to die. Lower your weapons."

Stefanov chokes out, "They'll kill you."

"You're outnumbered," I continue, ignoring him. "Don't be foolish. Put your weapons down. Unlike your ex-boss, we don't shoot unarmed men. I'll offer any man who pledges his loyalty to me a job."

Spit flies from Stefanov's mouth. "He's lying."

I press the point of the shard hard enough to break his skin. "Pavlov's family wants revenge. Not to mention Ivan Besov, on whose back you've slapped a target."

He goes quiet.

My chuckle is condescending. "By now, Pavlov's family has already retrieved Oleg's head from your freezer. You know that as well as I do."

He drags in a labored breath. "Kill me, and you're nothing but a cold-blooded murderer too."

I laugh coldly. "Which of us isn't? We all have blood on our hands. Still, no one wants to support a traitor." I turn to my men. "Take his guards upstairs and lock them up with the others."

Stefanov's guards don't argue. They walk from the room like a flock of sheep following their new shepherd.

When only Dimitri, Stefanov, and his wife are left, I address her. "Do you want to die with him?"

She shakes her head, making her blond hair fly to the sides. "No. Please, no."

"Piece of shit," Stefanov says under his breath. "Some wife you are."

She spits at his feet. "Damn you to hell, Vladimir Stefanov. May you burn there."

I nod toward the stairs. "Take her."

As Dimitri turns with his charge, Stefanov moves with startling agility for a man his size. Pulling back an arm, he slams an elbow into my stomach. The blow knocks the air from my lungs. The moment my grip loosens, he twists in my hold and plants a fist into my jaw. The force makes me stumble. Off balance, I barely have time to ward off the next punch he aims at my face.

Yanking the shard from my hand, he jabs it into my side where my coat and jacket have fallen open. The pain burns cold. It's a sensation I'm intimately familiar with. I was assaulted with various sharpened objects while I lived on the streets. I know how to block it out and use the adrenaline to focus on my opponent's moves.

Dimitri doesn't fire. Our fights are always fair. Stefanov takes a wide stance, breathing hard. He's severely overweight and unfit. He hasn't done his own fighting in years. In the second he catches his breath, I strike. Slicing with the other shard, I cut his face from his eyebrow to his lip.

Blood spurts over his eye. It looks worse than it is— a head wound always pisses blood—but he squeals like a pig being slaughtered.

Galina screams.

Stefanov comes for me, but the blood pouring over his face blinds him. He's stabbing at air. Grabbing his wrist, I squeeze hard enough to crack his bones. He utters a cry and splays his fingers, dropping his weapon.

"That's better," I croon, bending his arm behind his back.

Dimitri throws me a pistol.

I push the barrel between Stefanov's shoulder blades. "Walk."

We go up the stairs, following in Dimitri and Galina's wake. I move my coat away and steal a glance at my side. Blood drips through the tear in my shirt. The cut needs stitches, but it'll have to wait.

"Get everyone out of the house," I tell Dimitri. "Leonid will know where to take them."

While Dimitri and Galina go to the lounge, I shove Stefanov ahead of me to the kitchen. "Don't move. If I shoot you in the back, you'll finish your life in a wheelchair. I don't imagine it's the kind of life a bratva boss wants."

He says nothing, complying with silence.

I keep the gun aimed at his back as I go through the

drawers. It doesn't take me long to find what I need. It's a child's skipping rope, shoved into the drawer with crayons and pens. His daughters are in college. The skipping rope must be a keepsake. Good. That seems fitting.

I make quick work of tying him up in a chair. He regards me with hatred until I walk to the stove and switch on the gas. Then he starts to beg.

"No, please," he says, blinking away the blood that colors the whites of his eyes red.

I stop in front of him. "My father said those same words. Except he didn't beg for his own life, only for my mother's." I cock my head, studying his features so I'll always remember the look of defeat on his face. "You didn't show mercy then, but now you ask for it?"

"I have money," he says through slobber and tears. "Lots of it."

I bend down, putting us on eye level. "Do you think I need your money?"

"I have power. I can make anything happen. What do you want?" His manner turns feverish. "A nice big house full of women? You want men to kneel when you walk into a room? Say it," he urges, leaning toward me. "Say the word and it's yours."

"Spare your breath for the devil," I say with disgust.

"No," he yells as I take an ornate candle from a shelf and put it on the table in front of him.

The odor of gas already taints the air.

"Please, Volkov," he says, stumbling over the words.

I take the box of matches next to the stove. Pulling

one out, I bring the flame to the candle. The wick catches. An orange flame springs to life.

"I'm a father," he cries. "I have two daughters."

I don't listen to more. I throw the charcoaled matchstick over my shoulder as I exit the room.

Dimitri waits by the front door.

"Did you evacuate the house?" I ask.

He nods. "Leonid and the rest of your men drove the guards away, sir. Galina called her sister to fetch her."

I didn't give her time to take anything valuable from the house. Stefanov left me with nothing. His family will be left with nothing too.

"Where's Katerina?" I ask as I make my way down the driveway.

"She's waiting in the car," he says, lengthening his stride to keep up with me. "Igor is with her. Yuri is waiting by your car for your instructions."

My chest expands as I drag in a breath.

"Sir. Alex?"

The way he says my name makes me look at him. "What?"

He motions at my side. "You're bleeding."

"It can wait."

He knows when not to argue with me.

We stop outside the gates. Igor leans against the hood of the car, smoking a cigarette. I can count on one hand the number of times I've seen him smoke. I breathe even easier when I spot Katerina in the passenger seat of the car. She clutches the dashboard with both hands, her eyes brimming with tears. I need to get her out of here. She's encountered violence in her profession, but she hasn't experienced it firsthand. I just need a moment longer.

I turn around. Dimitri stands next to me, our backs straight and our faces solemn as we face the house. It's quiet, like when I arrived. The eeriness rides on the brilliant sunlight that's broken through the clouds. The rays make a fan of light, and then the gap closes and everything goes gray. The birds are quiet, as if they know.

Boom!

An explosion rocks the house, blowing the roof tiles into the air. Billows of orange burst through the windows, creating heatwaves over the white landscape. Flames leap into the air, their black-tipped tongues curling with smoke.

"Come on," I say to Dimitri. "There's nothing left here." Physically or emotionally.

"Do you want me to drive?"

"Go with Yuri and Igor. I'll follow." I need to be alone with Katerina.

"Straight home or via the hospital?" he asks, glancing at my side again.

"Home." Katerina can stitch me up there. "Meet us at the house."

"We'll start interrogating Stefanov's men," he says, already making his way to the car where Yuri waits. "We'll determine who'll come over and whom we need to get rid of."

Straightening, Igor puts out the cigarette and drops the butt in his pocket. He gives me a respectful nod before getting into the car with Dimitri and Yuri.

I stand in the road as they pull off, watching their car until they turn the corner. It feels a lot like the end, like closing a chapter that didn't end happily. After that last full stop lies hope. A new page. Time to let go of the past and move on.

Galina is on her own, but she has what my mother didn't have—her life and her children. How she builds her new future is up to her. In a warped sense, that has a ring of freedom to it.

I owe Mikhail a call to tell him what's gone down. But not now. I'll call him when we get home.

Impatient to be with Katerina, I close the distance with hurried steps. Even as I grip the door handle, sirens sound in the distance.

She gives me the minutest shake of her head, tears pouring down her face as I get in beside her.

I close the door and lay the gun in the console. "Hey." Cupping her face, I drag her closer. "It's over. You're all right. We're going to be fine."

A shadow that moves in the back catches my eye. In a flash, I understand Katerina's reaction, that slight shake of her head.

Someone is hiding in the back.

A man sits up. "Famous last words."

Fighting instinct takes over, but before I can dig my fingers into his eyes, he presses a gun against Katerina's temple.

My insides shake with fury. The sight of that gun against her head makes me want to break every finger of the hand clutching the gun before shooting out the man's brains.

Engulfed with helpless anger, I meet his gaze in the rearview mirror. He has square features and blond hair. I recognize him before he says, "The name is Ivan Besov. It's a pleasure to finally meet you, Alexander Volkov."

37

KATE

*T*he barrel of the gun is cold against my temple. I stare at the one Alex left in the console. How quickly can I grab it?

"Tsk, tsk," Besov says, reaching between the seats for Alex's gun.

"You're a dead man," Alex grits out.

Besov laughs. "In case you haven't noticed, I'm the one with the weapons."

Alex turns in his seat. "What do you want?"

Besov shrugs. "Nothing."

"Then why are you here?" Alex asks with a glacier stare.

"I never leave a job unfinished." Besov smiles at me in the rearview mirror. "And I never fail. It's not good for my professional reputation. Besides, you've been such a challenging prey. It'll be an honor to finally kill you."

Blinking back my tears, I glare at him. He must've slipped into the car while the action was going down in the house. Igor and I—everyone—had been too distracted to think about searching the cars. It wasn't until I was already inside the vehicle that I realized I wasn't alone.

"The police will be here soon," Alex says.

The lights of the sirens are already visible in the distance.

"Drive," Besov says, pushing the barrel harder against my temple.

Alex gives me a reassuring smile. His voice is soft. "Put on your seatbelt, Katerina."

It's easy to follow his order. It's always been easy to follow him. He's the kind of leader people trust.

He secures his own seatbelt before starting the engine. "Where do you want me to go?"

"Back to the main road," Besov says, lowering the gun to my side. "Left at the intersection."

Alex's knuckles turn white as he grips the wheel. His body is like a tightly coiled spring, but he drives smoothly, turning the car around and heading toward the main road. We go left just as the police cars round the bend and speed down the road.

I crane my neck to look at them as we drive in the opposite direction, my heart pounding. Maybe I can flag one of the men.

Besov nudges me in the ribs with the gun. "Eyes in the front."

Not having a choice, I face forward. Anyway, what

would I have said if the police had stopped us? Alex just blew up Stefanov's house. With Stefanov inside it.

The bleakness of our situation suddenly crashes down on me. We're screwed. Ironically, in the cell, I had hope. But out here? Our chances aren't looking good. We have no weapons and Besov, a skilled assassin, has two. Plus, Alex is bleeding. I glance at his side where his coat has fallen open. Underneath the jacket, his shirt is torn and soaked with blood. It looks like a stab wound. He needs stitches. If the bleeding doesn't stop, he'll soon be too weak to drive, never mind defend himself.

"Turn right here," Besov says.

The fancy neighborhood with the big houses makes way for apartment buildings. We cross a bridge and drive alongside the river. It starts to snow, flakes drifting down onto the windshield. Alex switches on the wipers.

We drive for another few minutes, following Besov's directions, until the buildings run thin and we finally leave St. Petersburg behind. We're on a road leading toward the countryside. He must be taking us somewhere isolated to kill us.

The silence in the car is stifling. The road runs straight for as far as I can see. Besov isn't giving directions any longer. With no witnesses around, he raises both guns, pushing one against my head and the other against Alex's.

Alex flexes his jaw, but he keeps his eyes on the narrow road, navigating us through the snowfall that turns into a storm as the wind picks up. The wipers make swooshing sounds, batting left and right as Alex puts them on maximum speed. Our visibility diminishes. The snow falls down harder, the flakes illuminated in the headlights of the car.

Trees dot the sides of the road. They quickly grow denser. We're entering a forest. Clutching the edges of my seat, I look at Alex. He's pale, a tell-tale sign of blood loss. Turning his head no more than an inch, he fleetingly moves his gaze from the road to my face.

"I love you," he mouths.

The words are silent, but their meaning is powerful. Charged.

Scraping together all the courage I can muster, I give him a smile. Our gazes lock. He's no longer focused on the road. It only lasts for a second, but I know instinctively that this is the moment our lives are supposed to flash in front of our eyes.

With a sharp movement, he jerks the wheel to the left. Our bodies are thrown to the side as the car skids across the road. The seatbelt cuts into my chest. I scream. I can't help it. At the same time, the momentum propels Besov through the air. Arms flailing, he hits the door, but not before a shot goes off.

Pain lances into my shoulder.

The car crashes through a barrier and barrels down an embankment. I'm tossed forward as the tires lose grip. We torpedo ahead, hitting a ditch at full speed. The thick snow breaks our velocity. My neck jerks violently as we come to an abrupt halt. The nose of the car dives, and the weight of the back pulls it over. The world tumbles past my window as we roll onto the roof. The crash jolts my spine. The car condenses, metal groaning and windows exploding.

Then silence.

I'm still for a moment. Disoriented.

It's snowing too hard to make out anything other than that I'm upside down, squeezed into a narrow space.

"Katerina!"

Alex's voice penetrates the strange numbness encasing me.

A warm hand touches my arm. "Katyusha, talk to me."

I force my vocal cords to function. "I'm…" I swallow. "I'm all right."

He utters something in Russian, a curse or maybe an exclamation of relief. "I'm unclipping your seatbelt. Brace yourself."

The clip makes a clicking sound. The breath leaves my lungs with an oomph as my back hits the roof.

"I'm coming for you," he says, unfastening his seatbelt before pushing himself through the window.

Dazed, I lie in the wreck. We've crashed. I scan the space in front of me. Besov is slung sideways, his neck bent against the window. The guns are no longer in his hands. They're nowhere in sight.

Pain burns in my shoulder. My left arm feels numb. Crossing my right arm over, I brush a hand over the aching spot.

It's wet.

I lift my hand to my face.

Blood.

I've been shot.

"Katerina," Alex says next to me.

I turn my head. He's kneeling in the snow, his face pinched into a mask of concern.

"Push your upper body through the window," he urges. "I'll drag you out."

I try to do as he says, but my left arm won't cooperate.

"Just a little more, my love." His tone is calm, but he can't hide the anxiety that shows through the forced tranquility of his expression. "I've got you."

Hooking a hand under my right arm, he pulls me through the broken window. The glass has shattered into tiny pieces, but the puffy jacket protects me against the roughness of their broken edges.

"You're going to be fine," Alex says, cradling my face in his lap.

"Alex." My voice is scratchy. "I've been shot."

His lips flatten. Chaos swirls in his icy blue eyes, telling me the truth even as he offers me a smile. "You're going to make it."

I moan when he lifts me into his arms and rises to his feet.

"Your phone," I say, breathing through the sharp waves of pain. "Call for help."

"I have to get you to safety first."

We must have a guardian angel, because the wind

stills to a breeze and the snowfall calms enough to allow visibility.

Sheltering me against his chest, he takes a step. The snow is so thick he sinks knee-deep. On the other side of the ditch, a field stretches out before the forest. He has to cross that distance before we can hide in the denser vegetation. We won't make it far like this, not with him wounded and carrying me while trudging through the snow.

"Put me down," I say raggedly. "Make the call."

He pauses, hesitates.

"You've lost too much blood. You can't carry me all the way there. The snow is too deep."

Indecision flashes in his eyes. He knows I'm right because after another second, he lowers me carefully. The snow is cold beneath me. Soon, my jacket will be damp. If I don't bleed out, hypothermia will set in. If the bullet has severed an artery, I'll need surgery and fast. The professional side of me calculates the risks on autopilot as he shrugs off his coat and lays it out like a blanket.

"No," I say through bloodless lips. "Keep it on. You'll freeze to death."

He flashes me a grin. "I'm used to this cold. I grew up in it, remember?"

I'm not from Florida either, but that doesn't make either one of us immune to simple science. Once his body temperature drops below ninety-five degrees, he's dead.

"Alex, please." I protest some more as he picks me up and lays me on his coat, but he's not to be deterred.

Crouching next to me, he brushes the hair from my face. "I can't leave you lying in the wet snow. You'll go into hypothermic shock."

A movement by the car draws my attention. Alex is partially blocking my view with his body, but when he straightens, I spot Besov climbing to his feet.

"Alex," I cry out, my insides turning to ice.

Following my gaze, he spins around.

Besov leans against the car, pointing a gun at Alex. Judging by the blood running down the side of his face and the way he sways on his feet, he's taken a hard knock. Alex positions himself in front of me, sheltering me with his body, but I see the horrific picture unfolding through the wide stance of his legs.

"You lose," Besov says, laughing as he aims the gun at Alex.

Alex charges.

My scream tears through the air.

Besov pulls the trigger, but his hand is unsteady and the bullet hits the snow left of Alex. Besov stumbles sideways. Before he's found his balance, Alex dives through the air. The gun flies from Besov's grip as both men go down. They roll through the snow, fists and elbows flying.

Ignoring my numb arm, I struggle to my feet. My boots sink into the snow. The messily tied shoelaces don't help. My feet fit loosely, slipping inside the oversized boots. The left one gets stuck in the muddy ground beneath the snow, and I go down face first. I push up onto my good arm, dragging myself off the ground. Male war cries and grunts come from where the men are fighting. I wipe the snow from my face and spit out the mouthful I've eaten before forcing my legs to move again.

Alex and Besov are trying to kill each other with their bare hands. They roll down a second embankment to the edge of a frozen river. Adrenaline pumps through my body, vanquishing the cold. I pick up my speed, my lungs burning from exertion, and in a few more steps, I reach the gun.

The metal is cold when I haul it up from the snow. The weight is heavy in my palm. I've never fired a gun, but my finger curls instinctively around the trigger. Bracing the arm on my injured side against my body, I run as fast as the snow allows while pointing the gun in the direction of the fistfight.

Both men are bleeding worse than before. A trickle of blood runs from Alex's nose, and Besov's eyebrow is split open.

"Alex," I scream when I reach the embankment. The snow is thinner here, almost iced. Before I can catch myself, I slide down the slope. My feet slip out from under me. Pain shoots up my spine as my tailbone hits the ground, but I don't let go of the gun. I grip it tightly, holding on for life and death.

"Alex!" I aim blindly in front of me.

The men don't stop. Grunts follow the dull thuds of their fists as they rain punches down on one another.

Alex is on top. He gets in a blow that sends Besov's face flying sideways. A jet of blood flies from Besov's mouth and paints a red streak over the snow. Besov jams a fist into Alex's injured side. Alex howls, his head thrown back. It gives Besov a chance to fling Alex around, reversing their positions. Cartilage cracks as he slams a fist into Alex's nose.

I don't have a clear shot. If I pull the trigger, I may kill Alex. Aiming the gun in the air, I fire.

Pop!

The gunfire echoes in the space. A flock of birds lifts from the trees in the forest and rises noisily into the sky.

Both men freeze. I slide to the bottom of the embankment on my ass, lifting my feet to prevent my heels from digging into the snow and stopping me.

With Alex momentarily distracted, Besov breaks free. Instead of running up or down the embankment, he beelines straight for the frozen river. When he's halfway across, far enough to feel safe from my amateur aim, he stops.

One of his eyes is swollen shut and his lip is split, but that doesn't prevent a mocking smile from curving his lips. "You may get away now, but I'll be back for you." His voice rings out over the expanse. "You'll never sleep soundly again. That's my gift to both of you." He blows me a kiss before resuming his escape, this time walking at a mockingly normal pace.

My vision goes hazy. It's like a scene from a movie where the bad guy gets away. You look at the screen, waiting, because no one deserves to live in fear, but then the screen turns black, the music plays, and the credits roll. I watch it happening now, see our future like a spectator who looks on from the safety of her sofa. I see Igor's unconscious form in the ER and the bullet the doctor extracted, the bullet the bodyguard had taken for Alex. I see Alex on that bed, no longer breathing, his blue eyes no longer alert. I see myself, my mom, Joanne, my friends, and everyone else Besov will use to get to us. Because he won't stop. Not unless I stop him.

Without another thought, I aim at his feet and pull the trigger.

Stopping, he shoots a surprised look at me from over his shoulder. A moment of silence follows as the smell of gunpowder fills my nostrils. Alex moves in my peripheral vision. I don't know if he's telling me to back down or calm down, but I don't do either as Besov's laugh tears through the air.

I pull the trigger again. The ice around his feet cracks. His laugh dies. The sound drifts away with the snow.

Crack.

He stiffens, his eyes widening.

It's too late.

The frozen layer gives. It breaks. His weight pulls him down.

A beat passes. And another. My heart slams against my ribs, each thud painful. Another second ticks into nothingness, but Besov doesn't surface.

The ice that cracked is now in my veins.

I killed someone. I didn't shoot him, but I pulled the trigger. And I'm not sorry. I'm not sure what shocks me most. That I did it or that I don't feel remorse.

"Katerina!"

I look toward the sound of that voice. Alex is making his way through the snow, using his hands for purchase on the steep part.

Just as he reaches me, my legs buckle. The gun drops from my hand as I go down.

He falls onto his knees next to me, grabbing my face between his hands. "Katerina, look at me. Look at me, my love. Stay with me. Stay with me, damn you. I'll get you out of here."

I fight to comply, but the screen is fading, the credits already rolling.

"It's a happy ending," I whisper as he holds me to his chest.

He smiles down at me, looking at me as if it's the last time he'll see me. He seems like he wants to argue, but he doesn't. Instead, he brushes a hand over my forehead and says in the saddest voice I've ever heard, "Yes." He seals it with a tender kiss. "It is."

Yes.

It was.

38

ALEX

*T*he room of the private clinic in St. Petersburg is basked in the dusk of day. The ceiling light is set on dim so as not to disturb Katerina. Her face is pale on the pillow, the same color as the white linen.

Placing a hand over hers where it lies on top of the covers, I study her like I've done for the past four hours. Her eyes move behind her lids as in a deep sleep, and her breath tickles the fine, almost invisible hair on her skin as she exhales.

Those are signs of life, as are her vitals that beep on the monitor next to her bed. Still, I feel a compulsion to watch her, a need to reassure myself. I almost got her killed. It can never happen again. The mere thought sends my mind into a tailspin and makes my insides clench into a tight ball.

Igor enters with a paper cup that he hands to me. "How is she?"

"Stable." At least, that's what the surgeon said. I won't relax until she opens her eyes and tells me herself.

His rugged face softens as he looks at her. "I guess we have something in common now. Both of us took a bullet for you."

He says it jokingly, trying to lighten the heavy atmosphere, but my jaw clenches involuntarily. As I've just told myself, *it can never happen again*. I'll make damn sure of it. Ivan Besov is no longer a threat. Stefanov is no longer around to hold a sword over my head. And since no one will dare rat me out to the authorities, I'm a free man. After the message I delivered by blowing up Vladimir's house, nobody will fuck with me.

"Any news on Besov?" I say his name with disdain.

The way Igor's upper lip curls tells me he feels the same about that fucker. "The body will probably wash up in the summer when the ice melts."

I take a sip of the hospital coffee, needing the caffeine to keep alert. I haven't slept in two days.

"Why don't you go catch a few hours of sleep?" I tell Igor. He's been on his feet for as long as I have. "The staff prepared a room for us. Leonid can take over."

Rubbing his eyes, he gives me a grateful nod. "I'll be back in four hours."

"Take six." He's no good to me half asleep on his feet.

Downing what's left of the lukewarm coffee, I crumple the cup in a fist and dump it in the trash can.

"Do you need anything?" Igor asks on his way to the door. "Dinner?"

"The nurse already offered."

He leaves with a nod.

I turn my attention back to Katerina. She's lucky. The bullet hit her in the fleshy part of her shoulder, and no vital organs were damaged. The surgeon said she'll be up in a couple of days and back to normal in a few weeks. That may be so, but she'll always carry a scar—a reminder of how close I came to losing her. I haven't stopped beating myself up about the accident, even though we had little chance of surviving any other way. If I'd allowed Besov to drive us to his destination, overpowering him in my injured state with no weapon would've been suicide on my behalf and murder on Katerina's. Rage consumes me just thinking about it.

Her eyelashes flutter. A soft moan escapes her lips.

I lean closer. "Katyusha? I'm here, my love."

She opens her eyes. Those gorgeous honey-tinted pools are hazy until she blinks them into focus. Her voice is raspy. "Where am I?"

I pick up a glass of water from the nightstand and bring the straw to her lips. "In a private clinic in St. Petersburg." Supporting her neck, I help her take a sip. "More?"

She licks away a drop. "I'm good."

A wave of tenderness rushes through me. "How are you feeling?"

Her smile is faint. "High on morphine, I guess."

"Good." I don't want her to suffer from pain.

"Did you find the body?"

I grind my teeth at the memory of her bleeding out in the snow on the banks of the frozen river. "No. It'll wash up in the summer."

Her pupils dilate even as her eyes grow large. "What then?"

"Then nothing," I say, stressing the *nothing*.

Biting her lip, she gives me a pained look. "I killed him."

I squeeze her hand in mine. "You defended our lives." My unspoken message is clear. I don't consider her a murderer. I won't allow her to carry that burden. "Understand?"

The frown pleating her forehead doesn't smooth out. "What I mean is I don't feel bad about what I did." She searches my face. "What does that make me, Alex?"

"Human," I say without hesitation.

Which also means she'll have post-traumatic stress from the events. Nightmares. Guilt trips. Anxiety attacks, maybe. No matter. I've already secured the best psychiatrist in New York City.

"Thank you," she whispers, relaxing slightly as she accepts the absolution I offer.

The heaviness of the situation sinks into my chest. I've made her a part of my world by falling in love with her. I've dragged her into the filth, and there's no going back. Not now. Not ever. She's been mine and I've been hers from the moment I laid my eyes on her.

Cupping my cheek, she says in a soft voice, "We'll

get through this together. We'll get through everything together." Her gaze is imploring. "Okay?"

Gratitude brushes away the darkness, igniting a spark of excitement for the future we're about to embark on together. "Thank you."

"For what?" she asks, letting her hand drop back to the bed as if holding up her arm takes too much effort.

"For knowing who I am and loving me regardless."

"I do. I love you, Alex," she says with a gentle light in her eyes, giving me the confirmation I crave.

A smile starts in my chest and works its way to my lips. It feels good, this smile that comes from inside. Normally, it's the other way around. Normally, a smile is nothing but a nonverbal form of communication that my mind dictates in suitable circumstances. But this one comes from the heart. I haven't smiled like this since my parents' deaths. It's been so long I've forgotten how a man is supposed to smile.

"What?" she asks, her lips curving in a similar fashion.

Brushing her hair away from her forehead, I take in her beautiful face. "Here we are, in St. Petersburg, only not under the circumstances we imagined."

"No," she agrees. "It didn't exactly turn out the way I expected. Did you call my mom?"

"Not yet. I wanted you to wake up first." I figure it's her call to make.

"Good." She relaxes visibly. "I don't want her to worry. I'm thinking…"

"Thinking what, kiska?"

"That she doesn't need to know everything."

I nod. "I respect your wish."

She searches my face. "When can we go home? I mean, to New York?"

"As soon as you're back to normal."

Her expression turns hopeful. "Do you mean that?"

Another bout of guilt tightens my chest. "Yes. Nothing prevents me from running my business from New York, the way I'd been doing when we met. We'll have to come back here every once in a while, but I promise you it will be under much more pleasant circumstances, and I'll make sure it doesn't interfere with your job."

Exhaling a breath, she says, "I can live with that."

I lift her hand to my lips and kiss every finger while I weigh my words. This is hard for me to say, because I'm going to ask something of her I don't deserve. "Katerina," I start, my tone serious. "About bringing you here…"

"I forgive you," she says before I can continue.

I stare at her, processing the gift she offers. There's only one way I can repay her. Solemnly, I promise, "I'll never make you sad again."

She grins. "I'll hold you to that."

"One more thing."

She raises an eyebrow, waiting.

The extreme lack of romanticism in our surroundings isn't lost on me, yet it feels right. Our relationship started in a hospital, so it seems fitting that I pop the big question in one. "Katyusha, my love, will you wear my ring?"

"You mean become Mrs. Volkova?"

Fuck, that has the perfect sound to it. My voice is hoarse. "Yes."

Her answer mirrors mine. "Yes."

I never expected my life to ever turn right again, but here in this room, in this city that held so much misery for me, it's as perfect as it can get.

Just as well.

Because regardless of her answer, I was never going to let her go.

They say little changes in the so-called sleeping neighborhoods of St. Petersburg. People are much the same. We have an inborn resistance against change. I'm no different. I will never be a good man. Cruelty and kindness will always live side by side in me. But whereas my enemies will always encounter my darkness, Katerina sparks the light I thought I'd long since lost. That's what I intend to hold on to, to the good memories and the new ones I'm making with the woman I love.

My Katyusha.

"*K*iska," Alex says, pulling my attention from the gravestones. Interlocking our fingers, he lifts our hands and points in the distance. "There it is."

The diamond ring on my finger sparkles in the sunlight, the stone seeming to catch and lock the bright rays inside. It's a princess cut surrounded by rubies—timeless and perfect.

I follow the direction of his gaze. It's impossible to miss the angel with the broken wing who mourns on the steps of a tomb. Her concrete dress drags on the grass, the hem damp from the sprinklers.

Silence falls between us as we make our way over. As I read the names engraved in the marble, I hold on to Alex's hand, offering my husband as much comfort as I can.

Viktor Volkov.

Anastasia Volkova.

The Russian Orthodox graveyard in St. Petersburg is beautiful. The grass is a bright green, and colorful iris and canna lilies grow around the trees. The perfume of honeysuckle is sweet in the air. The summer day is pleasantly warm. With the birdsongs and the buzzing of bees surrounding us, it's peaceful. It's a good resting place.

Not so long ago, when the graveyard was covered in a white layer of snow and I was recovering from a bullet wound in a private clinic, Alex found the old grave keeper near the gate, frozen to death. It's just as well. He wasn't going to stop until he'd made everyone pay for their part in putting our lives in danger.

Ivan Besov's body washed up on the shore of the river when the ice melted, just like Alex had predicted. The police opened an investigation when it became known that Stefanov had placed a price on the assassin's head, but it was closed due to a lack of evidence. The explosion at Stefanov's house was declared an accident due to a gas leak. I can only assume Alex's influence played a role in the speedy resolution of both cases.

Lena was fired. Alex made sure everyone knew she'd poisoned Dania, but he left out the finer details of the conspiracy. With that stain on her reputation, the only work she could find was doing laundry in a prison. For such an eternal snob, washing the sheets of the *lower class* she despises must've been her worst nightmare come true. A few weeks later, she fell down the stairs and broke her neck. The witnesses said she slipped because the floor was wet, but I suspect Mikhail had a hand in her untimely death. At least I hope it was Mikhail. I can't entirely rule out my husband's hand in this—a thought that should keep me up at night but strangely doesn't.

As for Dania, her father arranged a marriage to an old oligarch, a man who keeps her under his thumb. Eventually, she may still take over his business, but for now, she must deal with her father working closely with Alex, the man she's come to despise.

"Ready to go?" Alex asks.

When I turn my face, he's studying me with those piercing blue eyes, like I catch him doing so often. "Are *you?*"

"Yes," he says.

The word carries quietly on the breeze. It's soft, tranquil. The undertone of torment that was present when Alex told me about how his parents died is no longer audible in his voice. There's still sadness, but underneath the sorrow lies a tone of acceptance.

I study him back with the same intensity. The lines around his eyes are tight with awareness. He's eternally vigilant, but there are also times when he lets down his guard completely. Such as in bed.

"What?" he asks gently, a smile plucking at his lips as he brushes a wisp of hair from my cheek with his thumb.

"You're ridiculously handsome." And I'm giddily happy.

He chuckles. "You must be the only one who thinks that."

He's wrong. He's not handsome in a conventional way, true, but I'm not referring only to the strong features of his face and to the muscles bulging under his clothes. I'm talking about what's inside, about the man I've gotten to know. He's dangerous. Lethal. But he's also trustworthy and protective. He's a good husband, not only supporting my career as a registered nurse, but also encouraging me to complete my Doctor of Nursing Practice degree. He accepts my friends, and he loves my mom as if she were his own.

He searches my eyes. "Sometimes," he says softly, "I have to touch you to be sure you're real." He accompanies the words with action, gripping my hand tightly in both of his palms.

What happened to me has left a mark on him. I'm long since over the trauma of getting shot, both physically and emotionally, but he's still waking up in the middle of the night, sweating with nightmares.

Going on tiptoes, I kiss his lips. "I'm here."

The blue of his eyes darkens, the fierce intensity of his attention solely focused on me. "Yes, and you're not going anywhere."

"Nowhere," I agree. "Not without you."

He relaxes at the promise, the worry lines on his face smoothing out and the hard set of his jaw softening.

"Come," he says, tugging on my hand and turning toward the car where Yuri waits.

Not far behind Yuri, an entourage of guards is stationed. Their formal black jackets conceal guns and knives. More weapons are hidden under the floor-boards of their cars. Alex never lets me go anywhere without at least six bodyguards, but I've grown used to them. Igor now reports to me. Well, sort of. He's the head of my personal detail, but he still answers to my husband.

"I'm glad you brought me here," I say as Alex grips my elbow to steady me when my heel gets stuck in the thick carpet of grass.

"I'm glad you came with me," he replies.

As if I would've missed this.

I understand now why he commissioned the statue in his garden in New York City. It's a replica of his parents' gravestone.

At the bottom of the slope, he stops to inspect my sandal. Going down on his haunches, he grasps my ankle in his large hand, his fingers overlapping around the circumference, and wipes away the mud and tuft of grass stuck to my heel. I grip his shoulder for balance, waiting patiently while he takes care of me. I've learned that he needs this. He needs to provide, protect, and comfort. In turn, he lets me do the same for him.

Staring down at his dark head, his thick hair shining in the sun, I ask, "Do you still miss them a lot?"

He glances up at me. "Yes." A second passes before he straightens. "But that's the past, and we're the present. You're my family now." His voice lowers, the timbre dark and heated as he brushes his knuckles over my stomach. "And soon, we'll have a bigger one."

A flush of heat creeps over my cheeks. I know the guards are watching. "It may take time," I warn. I've only been off the pill for a month.

Lowering his head, he holds my gaze with unmistakable intent as he breathes the words over my lips. "I have time. Lots of it if I get to practice every day."

That makes me laugh. "You just want to impress me like on the first night, making me believe you're virile for your ripe age."

His eyes crinkle in the corners. He purses his lips, trying hard to hold back his smile. My heart soars.

Gripping my wrist, he yanks me against him, making our bodies collide. "Are you teasing me, Mrs. Volkova?"

The sudden move makes me gasp. The moment my lips part, he steals inside, swallowing my sounds and sweeping the depth of my mouth with his tongue. My knees grow weak. I cling to his arms, feeling the muscles flex under my palms as he splays his broad hands over my back and presses me impossibly close, close enough to arch my back and let me feel the hardness that grows against my stomach.

A graveyard is hardly an appropriate place. The men discreetly facing forward and pretending not to see make it even less appropriate, but I couldn't extract myself from his embrace if I tried. He renders me helpless. Flames burst over my skin, burning through my body to my core.

He clasps my ass, jerking me tighter against him. The men in their black suits and the black cars fade away. Where we are doesn't matter any longer. The feeling of summer that rides on the air grows into a bubble that isolates us in happiness. In euphoria.

My phone rings.

Alex groans.

Flustered, I pull away and say breathlessly, "Not here."

"You're right," he says in a gruff voice. "You should get that." He spears his fingers through his hair and messes it up in that way I love so much. "You make me forget where I am." His lips tilt in one corner. "You have that effect on me. Always have, since the first night."

Tearing my gaze away from his, I dig in my bag for my phone and look at the screen. "It's my mom."

"Take your time." He fishes his own phone from his pocket and wakes up the screen, already scrolling to his messages. Turning sideways to give me an illusion of privacy, he says, "Say hi to Laura for me."

I take a steadying breath before I press the phone against my ear. "Hi, Mom."

"Katie! You sound out of breath. Did I catch you at a bad time?"

I glance at Alex's imposing back. "Um, no. I've just been walking."

"How's the honeymoon?"

"Great. Alex has taken me to see all the popular tourist attractions we missed on our first visit. He's taking me somewhere a little less crowded tonight. How about you? How's your vacation?"

"Fabulous. William and I decided to give the nudist beach a try."

"I thought you were in Croatia?"

"We are, honey. We found a place here where I can work on a full-body tan."

Despite her enthusiasm, I can't help the nagging worry at the back of my mind. "How's married life treating you?" Carefully, I add, "Not feeling too claustrophobic yet?"

"Oh, no. William is going hiking in the mountains with a guide tomorrow. That gives me a couple of days to myself on the beach. Afterward, we'll meet up at that fancy hotel I told you about."

"That sounds wonderful." I'm glad they found the formula that works for them.

"How's Alex?"

"He's good. He says hi."

"Give him a kiss from me." Her voice turns rushed. "Oh, gosh. Look at the time. I've got to go, honey. We're going out for dinner. I'll call you again in a couple of days."

When I put my phone away, Alex asks, "Is she happy?"

"Ecstatic."

"I'm glad to hear that." He grins. "I've been to more weddings with you in the last six months than in my whole life."

I smile up at him. "Are you complaining?"

He takes my hand and continues on the path we set out on before we got sidetracked. "Not about ours. How are Jo and Ricky doing?"

"They just got back from Brazil. They want to invite us for dinner when we're home."

"Only if Ricky cooks." He makes a face. "Jo could do with some lessons."

I swat his arm. "That's not nice."

He adopts a serious expression. "But true."

"Okay, fine. I'll admit her moussaka was a bit on the burned side."

We arrive at the car. Yuri gets the door with a stoic expression. Alex makes sure I'm comfortable in the back and gets in beside me. Taking my hand in his lap, he points out the sites on our drive back home. Whenever we're together, he always needs to touch me, but I'm not complaining about that. I love his obsession with me. I need it as much as he needs to take care of me.

"Hungry?" he asks when we're back in our bedroom.

"Starving. It must be all the fresh air."

He nods with approval. "Good. I already asked Tima to prepare a spread."

On cue, there's a knock on the door. Alex opens it to let Tima enter with a trolley set with dishes. One by one, Tima lifts the silver lids to reveal every imaginable Russian starter and bite-sized food.

"Enjoy," Tima says with a grin, offering me a wink on his way out.

"I thought we'd just nibble on a selection," Alex says when Tima has left. "The dishes are all served cold, so you have time for a shower if you like."

My stomach heats at the nuance of his tone. "Sure. I could do with one."

As I walk to the bathroom, I'm aware of him following. His steps are quiet, like those of a lithe, feline predator, but I know he's there. His presence is too big to ignore, his male energy too overwhelming for me not to be conscious of how it lurks in the room, close on my heel. The hair on my arms raises with awareness.

Before I can reach for the zipper at the back of my dress, he catches the puller. He drags it down slowly, letting his fingertips brush over my spine as the sound of undressing reverberates with the rasp of the zipper. When the dress falls open from the top to the small of my back, he brushes the sleeves over my shoulders. The cotton tumbles to my feet, draping around my ankles.

Next, he works on the clasp of my bra, unhooking it with fluid efficiency. I stand quietly as he hooks a finger into the elastic of the matching thong. Instead of dragging it down my hips, he gives a sharp tug. A tearing sound cuts through the space, the lace digging into my skin for a second before cool air washes over my skin. The brusqueness of the act is in sharp contrast to the gentle way he got rid of the rest of my clothing, and that brief show of urgency makes liquid heat gather between my legs.

Clasping my waist, he turns me to face him and slowly goes down on his haunches, dragging his big, warm palms over my arms, my thighs, and finally, my calves. I swallow as I hold his gaze, taking in the dark, hungry intent in those magnificent blue pools.

Tenderly, he removes one sandal and then the next. When I stand completely naked in front of him, he straightens. Cupping one of my breasts, he rubs a thumb along the undercurve. My nipples harden instantly. I want him so much I'm aching. His hand is big enough that half of his palm covers my ribs. He holds me like this for a moment, simply caressing the underside of my breast as he stares into my eyes. He likes to read my reactions when he touches me. He likes to learn how to make me scream.

Seeming to have had his fill of my eyes, he drops his gaze to my lips. His eyes cut a slow path over me, pausing on my breasts. I grip his shoulders for purchase when he lowers his head, aiming for a nipple. The moment he closes his lips around the hard tip, a moan escapes my mouth. His tongue is hot, his teeth wicked. He knows how to make me come undone by doing nothing but caressing my breasts, but tonight, he doesn't make me beg. He goes lower, kissing his way down my body until he's crouching in front of me again.

I gasp when he hooks my leg over his shoulder. I already know where this is going. Still, I'm unprepared for the onslaught of pleasure that slams into me as he goes straight for his prize. He licks and nips, and in a matter of seconds, I come. My legs are like jelly in the aftermath of that quick and intense release, but he doesn't give me a reprieve. He strips with lightning speed, baring his hard male body and sizable arousal.

We don't make it to the shower. He catches my face between his hands and kisses me like he needs my air to breathe. I taste myself on his lips, the evidence of how badly I want him. When I fist a hand around the velvet flesh of his cock, he grips my hair in a ponytail and pushes me to my knees. I reciprocate, taking him into my mouth and licking the crest until his breathing speeds up and he pumps his hips as I suck him in deeper.

Like always, I swallow every drop when he comes, owning his release just like he owns mine. Coming like this takes the edge off, but it doesn't slow him down. If anything, it makes him greedier for me. Hauling me to my feet, he swings me into his arms and carries me into the shower. He holds on to me with one hand, splaying his fingers over my waist as he opens the tap with the other. While the water heats up, he kisses me, making sure to shelter me from the cold mist of the drops with his body.

When the spray is warm, he takes me underneath it, entering me with one thrust and then pausing to let me adapt. The heat that burns me up inside is different, greater than the pleasure of earlier. It's the kind of ecstasy that steals my mind. It robs me of my senses and makes me forget everything else.

After a few beats, he starts moving slowly, working

himself deeper. My moans spur him on. My whimpers make him punch his hips harder, but it's when I scrape my nails over his shoulders that he plunges inside and owns me. The tiles are cool against my back. Every thrust moves my body up the smooth surface. The ridges of the tiles' corners grate my skin, but I'm barely cognizant of the discomfort. As long as he's driving me toward an unbearable peak, every other sensation is mere background noise.

He palms a breast and tweaks my nipple. The sensation ignites more sparks in my core. He stops kissing me to look into my eyes. Drops cling to his dark lashes, glistening like diamonds against the backdrop of his blue irises. The color is arresting, but it's the fierceness of the possession sparking in their depths that I focus on. It's the all-consuming love reflecting back to me that holds my attention as he slips a hand between our bodies and finds my clit. He rubs the pad of his thumb in the way that always brings me to my knees, and when my legs buckle, he pivots his hips and comes just as I break and my inner muscles lock around him.

To say I see stars is a cliché, but that's what he does to me. The pleasure ripping through me is like an explosion of meteorites blasting through the atmosphere. When I close my eyes, the white-hot pinpoints of the stars as they burn out in the sky are like the static noise on a television screen. But that's not what causes the height of my euphoria. What drives me to that point is the bond between us. It's always present, no matter what we do, but I feel it strongest like this, naked in his arms, vulnerable and exposed. This is when both our bodies and our souls are bared.

Pressing his forehead against mine, he says with a tremulous breath, "Katyusha."

The endearment washes over me, filling me with warmth.

He kisses my lips, catching the bottom one with his teeth. "You make me crazy. *Sumashedshim*."

"*Sumashedshim*," I agree.

His voice is gruff. "Say you want me."

"*Vsegda*." Constantly, always, eternally, forever.

A glint of satisfaction lights up his eyes when he pulls away to look at me. "Your Russian lessons are paying off."

Lethargic, I lean against him, letting him carry my weight. "Mm."

"Come on," he says, his voice tender. "Let me take care of you."

After he's washed my body and my hair, he wraps me up in a fluffy towel and pats me dry before taking me to bed. He serves me dinner there, feeding me small bites and petting my hair as if I were the kiska—the kitten—he calls me.

When I'm sated, he pours us each a glass of wine. After a few sips, he lets me nap. It's close to midnight when he wakes me with a kiss on my shoulder.

"Katyusha." His deep voice penetrates my sleep. "Wake up, my love."

Blinking, I rub my eyes. "Is it morning already?"

"No," he says with a quirk of his lips. "It's almost midnight. Come."

He helps me from the bed and holds my robe open for me. When I'm protected against the cooler air of the night, he takes my hand and leads me to the rooftop terrace.

Folding his arms around me from behind, he rests his chin on the crown of my head.

"Look," he says.

I take in the vista. The colorful domes of the baroque-style buildings shine in the copper light of the sunset. Like a ball of gold, the sun hangs on the horizon. Above it, the sky is a fragile, delicate white, like the veil of a bride.

"A white night," I say in awe.

He kisses the top of my head. "A midnight day."

Turning in his embrace, I look up at the sharp angles of his face.

He chuckles. "The view is over there."

"No." I cup his cheek. "What I want to see is right here, in front of me."

"Yes," he says softly. "So it is. You. It's always been you."

When he lowers his head, I offer my lips, letting him kiss me under the midnight sun.

Alex and Kate's journey ends here. Thank you for following their epic love story!

To be notified about our upcoming books, sign up for our newsletters at www.annazaires.com and www.charmainepauls.com. All of our titles are available in print and audio as well.

Craving more edgy, suspenseful romance? Check out *Tormentor Mine* by Anna Zaires and *Diamonds in the Dust* by Charmaine Pauls. And don't miss our action-packed enemies-to-lovers collaboration, *Darker Than Love!*

Turn the page to read excerpts from *Tormentor Mine* and *Diamonds in the Dust,* and to learn more about our books. And don't miss the first sneak peek into ***Terrible***

Beauty, the new dark romance by Anna Zaires featuring Alina, Nikolai's sister from the *Molotov Obsession* duet.

EXCERPT FROM TORMENTOR MINE
BY ANNA ZAIRES

He came to me in the night, a cruel, darkly handsome stranger from the most dangerous corners of Russia. He tormented me and destroyed me, ripping apart my world in his quest for vengeance.

Now he's back, but he's no longer after my secrets.

The man who stars in my nightmares wants me.

"Are you going to kill me?"

She's trying—and failing—to keep her voice steady. Still, I admire her attempt at composure. I approached her in public to make her feel safer, but she's too smart to fall for that. If they've told her anything about my background, she must realize I can snap her neck faster than she can scream for help.

"No," I answer, leaning closer as a louder song comes on. "I'm not going to kill you."

"Then what do you want from me?"

She's shaking in my hold, and something about that both intrigues and disturbs me. I don't want her to be afraid of me, but at the same time, I like having her at my mercy. Her fear calls to the predator within me, turning my desire for her into something darker.

She's captured prey, soft and sweet and mine to devour.

Bending my head, I bury my nose in her fragrant hair and murmur into her ear, "Meet me at the Starbucks near your house at noon tomorrow, and we'll talk there. I'll tell you whatever you want to know."

I pull back, and she stares at me, her eyes huge in her pale face. I know what she's thinking, so I lean in again, dipping my head so my mouth is next to her ear.

"If you contact the FBI, they'll try to hide you from me. Just like they tried to hide your husband and the others on my list. They'll uproot you, take you away from your parents and your career, and it will all be for nothing. I'll find you, no matter where you go, Sara... no matter what they do to keep you from me." My lips brush against the rim of her ear, and I feel her breath hitch. "Alternatively, they might want to use you as bait. If that's the case—if they set a trap for me—I'll know, and our next meeting won't be over coffee."

She shudders, and I drag in a deep breath, inhaling her delicate scent one last time before releasing her.

Stepping back, I melt into the crowd and message Anton to get the crew into positions.

I have to make sure she gets home safe and sound, unmolested by anyone but me.

⁓

Order your copy of *Tormentor Mine* today at www.annazaires.com!

Men like us, we *see* things.
We *do* things, things that make us unfeeling.

That's the price of power and money, of living *la belle vie* and running the French mafia. Then she came along like a pretty wildflower pushing through the cracks on a dirty pavement—fragile yet resilient, a breath of beauty among the filth. She was supposed to be just another job, a nameless person I was to pluck from her life and hand to my brother, nothing but a pawn in the gamble of our diamond business.

There's a psychological label for men like us.
We lack empathy and guilt.
We do *things* to have what we want, things that make flowers wilt.

When I doze off, the rats soon discover I'm a harmless target and nip at the exposed flesh of my wrists and even at my legs through my tights. I swat and kick at them, but they're becoming fearless, even taking their chances when I'm awake. The broken skin burns at first, but after a while the cold numbs everything, so much so I don't feel the bite of pain as their sharp teeth gnaw at my flesh. The best way of warding them off is moving, but they follow and try to climb up my legs when they can't bite through my boots.

By the time the sun comes up, I'm exhausted and cold to my core. It's as if the damp has infiltrated my bones. I can't stand on my feet anymore. I think the rats may kill me before I starve. I'm not sure which is the most merciful. My stockings are torn and the expensive clothes ruined, dirty from the damp and black mold on the walls. It stinks worse than my apartment building down here.

Leaning against the wall, I kick at a rat that climbs onto the toe of my boot. The slosh of the water is quieter. It's low tide. There's something else, too, like the fall of a hammer. It comes closer. No, it's the fall of footsteps. My heart starts thundering in my chest when they descend the steps. I brace myself, praying for rescue, but the door swings open on Maxime's face.

He's wearing a pale suit with a pink tie, and his face is clean-shaven. When he opens the gate and enters my prison, a whiff of winter reaches my nostrils. It's clean and fresh, a stark contrast to my dirt and exhaustion, like a magnifying glass on his cruelty. He's cold and monstrous.

He's not my savior.

I back away, but he grips my hair with one hand, and carefully pulls off the tape with the other. It hurts. The skin on my lips stretches and cracks. I drag my tongue over them and taste blood.

Something inside me snaps. My vision turns blurry.

He turns me around to undo the cuffs. The moment my hands are free, I jump at him. I claw and hit, screaming like a mad person. I must be mad, because what I should be doing is escaping. I kick. I punch him in the gut. He only stands there and takes it, my blows doing no damage. After the next fist I jam into his stomach, I shove him and run.

I'm not even on the first step before he grabs hold of my ankle. I go down, stopping my fall with my hands. The heels of my palms burn as the skin comes off, but I kick with all my might. I dig my fingers into the stone, my nails breaking as he drags me back into my cell.

"No!"

He flips me onto my back and covers my mouth with his hand. My lips are pulled back, my jaw wide. I bite down until the pressure of his hand becomes so severe, I think my skull may crack.

"Are you done?" he asks through thin lips.

I shake my head, but we both know I am. The fight goes out of me, my energy spent.

"If you scream," he says, "I'll leave. I can do this for days until you're ready to listen."

When I go still, he removes his hand. "That's better."

I lie on my back on the damp stones, the wetness seeping through my coat and dress, through my very skin and into my heart. He's crouching next to me, studying me with one arm braced on his knee. His frame is big and powerful. The shadow he casts over me swallows me whole. Somehow, it seems darker and colder than the winter night I spent in my cell.

"I want you to listen to me, Zoe."

My gaze homes in on his face, on the non-symmetrical lines of his features and the bump on the bridge of his nose.

"When I take you home," he continues in his musical accent, "you have a choice."

My hope lifts a fraction. "To South Africa?"

"To France."

The words are a punch. I don't know how many more punches I can take. I force the question from numb lips. "What choice?"

"It can be like yesterday, like the day we spent, or it can be like this." He motions around the space. "What you decide is entirely up to you, but you should know that each choice comes with a price."

I hold my breath, waiting for him to carry on.

"If I take you to my family in France, this is what awaits you. You'll be locked up, a prisoner. The men will take turns with you, starting with my brother, and he's not a kind man. He'll keep you alive, but you'll wish you were dead. The only way I can protect you is to lay claim to you." His gaze pierces mine. "Do you understand what I'm saying?"

My body is shaking uncontrollably, my mind refusing to give meaning to the words.

"Do you understand, Zoe?"

I shake my head.

"You're going to have to become my mistress." The flames in his eyes burn glacially. "You're going to have to let me fuck you, convincingly and often."

Order your copy of *Diamonds in the Dust* today at www.charmainepauls.com!

MORE FROM ANNA ZAIRES AND CHARMAINE PAULS

If you enjoyed *Midnight Days*, check out the following titles from Anna and Charmaine!

Other Collaborations by Anna & Charmaine:

- ***Darker Than Love*** – Yan and Mina's action-packed enemies-to-lovers romance

Dark & Contemporary Romance by Anna Zaires:

- ***The Molotov Obsession Duet*** – Nikolai and Chloe's addictive, all-consuming love story
- ***The Twist Me Trilogy*** – Nora & Julian's dark, twisted love story
- ***The Capture Me Trilogy*** – Lucas & Yulia's breathtaking enemies-to-lovers romance
- ***The Tormentor Mine Series*** – Peter & Sara's intense captive romance

- *Wall Street Titan* – a sizzling contemporary romcom featuring a billionaire and a cat lady

Dark & Contemporary Romance by Charmaine Pauls:

- *Beauty in the Broken* – a dark forced-marriage romance about revenge and salvation
- *The Diamonds are Forever Trilogy* – a dark romance featuring a hot French mafia kingpin
- *The Beauty in the Stolen Trilogy* – romantic suspense set in South Africa's criminal underworld
- *The Loan Shark Duet* – a dark mafia romance with a *Beauty and The Beast* theme
- *The Age Between Us Duet* – an older-woman/younger-man romance that will melt your e-reader
- *Catch Me Twice* — a heartbreaking second-chance romance about betrayal and redemption

Sci-Fi Romance by Anna Zaires:

- *The Mia & Korum Trilogy* – an epic sci-fi romance with the ultimate alpha male
- *The Krinar Captive* – Emily & Zaron's

captive romance, set just before the Krinar Invasion

- *The Krinar Exposé* – Anna's scorching hot collaboration with Hettie Ivers, featuring Amy & Vair—and their sex club games
- *The Krinar World stories* – sci-fi romance stories by other authors, set in the Krinar world

Sci-Fi & Paranormal Romance by Charmaine Pauls:

- *The Krinar Experiment* – alpha alien kidnapping at its hottest, set in Anna Zaires's Krinar world
- *The Krinar's Informant* – an alpha alien captive romance, set in Anna Zaires's Krinar world
- *7 Forbidden Arts Series* – a dark, forced-mates paranormal romance

Laugh-Out-Loud Romantic Comedy by Misha Bell, the geeky, raunchy pen name by Anna Zaires and her hubby, Dima Zales

- *Hard Code* – a workplace romcom about a quirky coder tasked with quality testing sex toys, and her mysterious Russian boss, who steps in to help out
- *Hard Ware* – a hilarious slow-burn romance

featuring a sex toy company CEO, a hot, mysterious stranger, and star-crossed puppy love

- *Hard Byte* – a fake date romcom about a prime-number-obsessed Anglophile who makes a deal with the Devil, her boss, to save her dream project
- *Royally Tricked* – a raunchy royal romance featuring a daredevil prince and a germaphobic, movie-obsessed magician

Sci-fi and Fantasy Collaborations by Anna Zaires and her hubby, Dima Zales:

- *The Girl Who Sees* – the thrilling tale of Sasha Urban, a stage illusionist who discovers unexpected secret powers
- *The Bailey Spade Series* – the mind-bending saga of a girl who can explore dreams and steal memories
- *Mind Dimensions* – the action-packed urban fantasy adventures of Darren, who can stop time and read minds
- *Upgrade* – the mind-blowing technothriller featuring venture capitalist Mike Cohen, whose Brainocyte technology will forever change the world
- *The Last Humans* – the futuristic sci-fi/dystopian story of Theo, who lives in a world where nothing is as it seems

- *The Sorcery Code* – the epic fantasy adventures of sorcerer Blaise and his creation, the beautiful and powerful Gala

NOTE: *Terrible Beauty* is the new dark romance by
Anna Zaires featuring Alina, Nikolai's sister from the
Molotov Obsession duet. Sign up for Anna's newsletter to
learn more!

Cool lips brush my throbbing forehead, bringing with
them a faint aroma of pine, ocean, and leather. "Shh…
It's okay. You're okay. I just gave you something to ease
your headache and make this easier."

The male voice is deep and dark, strangely familiar.
The words are spoken in Russian. My fuzzy mind
struggles to focus. Why Russian? I'm in America, aren't
I? How do I know this voice? This scent?

I try to pry open my heavy lids, but they refuse to
budge. Same goes for my hand when I attempt to lift it.

Everything feels impossibly heavy, like my very bones are made of metal, my flesh of concrete. My head lolls to one side, my neck muscles unable to support its weight. It's as if I were a newborn. I try to speak, but an incoherent noise escapes my throat, blending with a distant roar that my ears can now discern.

Maybe I am a newborn. That would explain why I'm so ridiculously helpless and can't make sense of anything.

"Here, lie down." Strong hands guide me onto some soft, flat surface. Well, most of me. My head ends up on something elevated and hard, yet comfortable. Not a pillow, too hard for that, but not a stone either. There isn't much give in the object, but there is some. Also, it's oddly warm.

The object shifts slightly, and from the foggy recesses of my mind, the answer to the mystery emerges. *A lap.* My head is lying on someone's lap. A male someone, judging by the steely, thickly muscled thighs underneath my aching skull.

My pulse accelerates. Even with my thoughts sluggish and tangled, I know this isn't normal for me. I don't do laps or men. At least I haven't thus far in all of my twenty-five years.

Twenty-five. I latch on to that sliver of knowledge. I'm twenty-five, not a newborn. Encouraged, I sift through more of the tangled threads, seeking an answer as to what's happening, but it eludes me, the recollections coming slowly, if at all.

Darkness. Fire. A nightmare demon coming to claim me.

Is that a memory or something I saw in a movie?

A needle biting deep into my neck. Unwelcome lassitude spreading through my body.

That part feels real. My mind might not be functioning, but my body knows the truth. It senses the threat. My heart rate intensifies as adrenaline saturates my veins. Yes. Yes, that's it. I can do it. With strength born of growing terror, I force open my leaden lids and look up into a pair of eyes darker than the night surrounding us. Eyes set in a cruelly handsome face that haunts my dreams... and my nightmares.

"Don't fight it, Alinyonok," Alexei Leonov murmurs. His dark voice holds both a promise and a threat as he gently threads his fingers through my hair, massaging away the throbbing tension in my skull. "You'll only make it harder on yourself."

The edges of his calluses catch on the tangles in my long hair, and he pulls his fingers out, only to curve his palm around my jaw. He has big hands, dangerous hands. Hands that have killed dozens today alone. The recollection roils my stomach even as some knot of tension deep inside me unravels. For ten long years, I've dreaded this moment, and finally, it's here.

He's here.

He's come for me.

"Don't cry," my husband-to-be says softly, brushing away the wetness on my face with the rough edge of his thumb. "It won't help. You know that."

Yes, I do. Nothing and no one can help me now. I

recognize that distant roar. It's the sound of a plane engine. We're in the air.

I close my eyes and let the hazy darkness take me.

Sign up for Anna's newsletter at www.annazaires.com to be the first to find out more about *Terrible Beauty*!

ABOUT THE AUTHORS

Anna Zaires is a *New York Times, USA Today,* and #1 international bestselling author of sci-fi romance and contemporary dark erotic romance. She fell in love with books at the age of five, when her grandmother taught her to read. Since then, she has always lived partially in a fantasy world where the only limits were those of her imagination. Currently residing in Florida, Anna is happily married to Dima Zales (a science fiction and fantasy author) and closely collaborates with him on all their works. To learn more, please visit www.annazaires.com.

Charmaine Pauls was born in Bloemfontein, South Africa. She obtained a degree in Communication at the University of Potchestroom, and followed a diverse career path in journalism, public relations, advertising, communications, photography, graphic design, and brand marketing. Her writing has always been an integral part of her professions.

When she is not writing, she likes to travel, read, and rescue cats. Charmaine currently lives in Montpellier with her husband and children. Their household is a linguistic mélange of Afrikaans, English, French and Spanish. To learn more, please visit www.charmainepauls.com.

Printed in Great Britain
by Amazon

74816951R00285